Award-winning author **Jennifer Faye** pens fun, heart-warming, contemporary romances, filled with rugged cowboys, sexy billionaires and enchanting royalty. Internationally published, with books translated into nine languages, she is a two-times winner of the *RT Book Reviews* Reviewers' Choice Award. She has also won the CataRomance Reviewers' Choice Award, been named a TOP PICK author, and has been nominated for numerous other awards.

**Michelle Major** grew up in Ohio but dreamed of living in the mountains. Soon after graduating with a degree in journalism, she pointed her car west and settled in Colorado. Her life and house are filled with one great husband, two beautiful kids, a few furry pets and several well-behaved reptiles. She's grateful to have found her passion writing stories with happy endings. Michelle loves to hear from her readers at michellemajor.com

# THE ITALIAN'S UNEXPECTED HEIR

JENNIFER FAYE

# THE LAST MAN SHE EXPECTED

MICHELLE MAJOR

MILLS & BOON

First Published in Great Britain 2020
by Mills & Boon, an imprint of HarperCollinsPublishers,
1 London Bridge Street, London, SE1 9GF

*The Italian's Unexpected Heir* © 2020 Jennifer F. Stroka
*The Last Man She Expected* © 2020 Michelle Major

ISBN: 978-0-263-27895-8

0920

MIX
Paper from
responsible sources

FSC

# THE ITALIAN'S UNEXPECTED HEIR

JENNIFER FAYE

# PROLOGUE

*It took almost losing everything...*
*to make peace with a troubling past*
*and embrace a loving future*

*Paris, France, July*

"CONGRATULATIONS! I KNEW you could do it."

Enzo Bartolini turned to the beautiful woman standing next to him. The excitement in her voice and the sparkle in her eyes let him know she was more excited about this evening's crowning achievement than he was. And that was the exact opposite of how things should be.

He was supposed to be the excited one—the one who felt as though he was on top of the world. This win was something he'd dreamed of for years. And now that it was here—now that he was holding the plaque with his name on it—the victory felt hollow.

The exhilaration he'd envisioned for this auspicious moment eluded him. The feeling of accomplishment— of finally being worthy of his father's praise—was not to be. Shadows of the past smothered the brightness of the moment.

Still, Enzo forced a bittersweet smile to his face. In

truth, he hadn't truly won anything—at least nothing he felt worthy of claiming.

He'd encouraged his father for years to start entering his wine in competitions. Enzo knew the worldwide recognition would increase the demand for the wine and in turn raise its value. But his father had been stubborn, as usual. He'd said it was enough for him that he got to work the land each day and make a sizable profit. He didn't need awards or recognition, too.

However, Enzo needed it. He needed something to fill the huge gaping emptiness inside his chest. It had once been filled by the constant love of his parents, but they had been ripped from his life. In the time it took his parents to drive to the city for what? Groceries? Supplies for the vineyard? Whatever it was they'd set out to do that day, it had led to a horrific accident and forever changed the lives of their son and two daughters.

When Enzo had insisted on seeing the accident photos, his stomach retched. Perhaps he shouldn't have insisted. Perhaps he should have just taken the word of the police. But he'd been in shock, unable to process a life without his very dynamic parents in it. He'd demanded proof.

And then he'd been shown the photos. He'd only needed to see the one—the photo of a tangled-up piece of metal. It hadn't even resembled a car any longer. There was no chance his parents could have survived. None at all. Thinking there couldn't be anything else to compare to that devastation, he'd been wrong.

Enzo pushed aside those troubling thoughts. Tonight was all about the win. At last, there was once again something good in his life. So then why didn't it feel good? Why wasn't he on top of the world?

He reached to undo his black bow tie as well as loosen

the top button of his white dress shirt, when Sylvie said, "Don't. Not yet. I need a picture of you first."

His hand hesitated in midair before he lowered it to his side.

Over the past several months, Sylvie DeLuca had become a good friend. She had the brightest smile—like the one she was flashing him now. And she was a good listener—though he usually didn't have much to say. However, tonight, beneath the Parisian moonlight, he noticed her incredible beauty. How exactly had he missed it all this time?

"This is it!" Sylvie tugged on his arm. "We can take the photo here. It'll look amazing."

He stopped and glanced around. The Eiffel Tower was all lit up against the dark sky. So clichéd. And yet so utterly stunning.

"Stand right there." Sylvie pulled her phone from her sparkly black purse. "Turn to me."

And then he realized she was going to take his picture—all alone. Just like he was in life. The thought stole the smile from his face. He didn't want to be alone—at least for tonight.

Tonight he wanted Sylvie to be next to him. After all, she'd dropped everything to come with him on this trip. And he knew it hadn't been easy for her as a wedding planner to get her work done ahead of time and then show someone else what needed to be accomplished in her absence. Luckily for him, a wedding had been canceled, otherwise Sylvie wouldn't have been able to accompany him.

But she was here and she was captivating. It wasn't just him who noticed but everyone at the awards ceremony. Her black gown with the sparkly, strapless, fitted bodice was tapered at her tiny waist, and a plain, gauzy white material touched her hips and flowed to her ankles. And then the most delicate black heels showed off her painted toes.

She went from being a businesswoman in her smart tailored suits to a stunning siren who could turn all of the males' heads—his most especially. And it was making him quite uncomfortable. He wasn't sure what to say or do around her.

Because what he wanted to do now was pull her into his arms and kiss those very sexy, very tempting lips. But he resisted—just barely. They were friends. Nothing more. Even if she did look like some sort of goddess in that dress and that makeup that highlighted her alluring eyes, her high cheekbones and kissable lips. Wow!

She signaled for him to move to his right. "A little more. Perfect." She held up her phone to snap a picture.

"Oh, no." In the glow of her smile, he felt his dismal mood begin to lift. "You have to come over here and have your picture taken, too."

Sylvie shook her head. "Not me. I didn't do anything special tonight. You're the man of the hour."

"But without you, I might not have entered." It was true. She'd nudged him into submitting his wine to the prestigious contest.

Was that a blush? He looked harder but it was too dark to be sure. Maybe it was just that he was starting to know her well enough to know his words would cause her cheeks to pinken.

Tonight hadn't been some small, local contest. This had been an international event with worldwide recognition. He honestly hadn't thought their small winery had any chance of winning against the big establishments. But Sylvie had insisted he would never know unless he entered. And so he'd decided he had nothing to lose and entered.

She snapped a picture. The flash lit up, blinding him for a moment.

"That's not fair," he said. "I want a picture, too."

"I'll send you a copy."

"No. That won't do. I want one of us together, so I'll have it to remember this night." It wasn't until the words were out of his mouth that he realized how they might sound. Or maybe he was just being paranoid because he was having this very intense, undeniable attraction to her. His sister's friend—*his* friend.

He knew following this attraction through to its logical conclusion would be a mistake. Sylvie wasn't a one-night-stand kind of woman. She was a let's-get-to-know-each-other-fall-in-love-and-get-married type of woman. And that was the exact wrong type for him at this point in his life.

He stopped his rambling thoughts. What had gotten into him? He never allowed his thoughts to go in this direction with Sylvie. So why tonight? Was it being in Paris together? Was it one too many toasts to his winning success?

He latched on to the last thought and clung to it like it was a life preserver and he was a man adrift in a big, stormy sea. Or did he have it all wrong and Sylvie *was* his life preserver?

The next thing he knew, she was standing next to him. It was only natural to put his arm around her—for the picture, of course. But then she leaned into him, sending his heart racing.

*Just ignore it. You've got this.*

"Smile," he said—at least, he thought he said it. It was so hard to tell because he couldn't hear his thoughts over the echo of his heartbeat.

He snapped the picture. There. It was done.

But when he went to move his arm, she said, "No. Don't. Take one more."

There was a little voice in his head that said he should get while the getting was good, but that thought was drowned out by the thumping of his heart. It was just a picture. And she was just a friend.

He once more held the camera out in front of them. "Okay. Are you ready?"

When she didn't respond, he turned to look at her. It was the same moment that she turned her head to look at him. And with those stiletto heels, she was closer to his height.

When he thought back upon this moment, it would be the defining moment. This was when he should have turned away instead of staring deeply into her warm brown eyes that were so expressive. And right now they were saying that she wanted more from him than their platonic friendship. And so help him, so did he. So much more.

Her heart pitter-pattered.

Her breathing was soft and shallow.

Sylvie felt as though she was having an out-of-body experience. Maybe that was what she needed to tell herself in that moment to give her the courage to reach out to Enzo. Her hand cupped his freshly shaved cheek.

If she didn't do this now and quickly, she knew she would lose her courage. And though she'd been thinking about this for the longest time, if she didn't act now, she would never fulfill her wish. And the one thing she'd learned in her short life is that you had to grasp the happy moments because they were fleeting and few.

This was her happy moment. Enzo was the person who made her happy. And right now she felt so many intense emotions, she wasn't able to put a name to all the jumbled feelings zinging through her body.

But nothing was going to stop her from doing this one thing. She lifted up on her tiptoes. Even though her heels were high, they weren't enough for Sylvie to come face-to-face with him.

And then he was there, directly in front of her. And his mouth was just a breath away from her. An urge—or was it an impulse?—so strong, so swift, came over her. She was helpless to resist.

Not thinking through the consequences of her actions, she leaned forward, closing the distance. She pressed her lips to his. There was a distinct and swift intake of air on his part.

She'd surprised him? Really? She may be a virgin but that didn't mean she was totally naive. She'd seen the way he'd been looking at her tonight when he didn't think she was paying attention.

Her body trembled with nerves as her lips moved over his unmoving mouth.

*No. Please. This can't end like this.*

Inside, her heart was starting to crack. It had taken every bit of nerve to work up to this moment. She knew if she didn't make the first move, he never would.

And just when she thought he wasn't as into her as she'd thought, he reached out to her. His arm wrapped around her waist, pulling her to him. She followed his lead, letting her hands come to rest on his shoulders—his muscled shoulders gained from long hours of toiling the soil at the vineyard.

His lips moved over hers at a dizzying pace. Her heart beat so fast she thought it was going to pound its way out of her chest. She'd been kissed before but nothing like this. Those had been inexperienced schoolboys who'd only pretended they knew what they were doing, but Enzo, he knew exactly what he was doing. And she wanted him to show her more, much more.

Enzo pulled back. His breathing was ragged. He pressed his forehead to hers. "Sylvie, I... I—"

"Don't say it." She knew he was going to apologize for kissing her and it would ruin this moment—this very precious moment.

"But I shouldn't have let things get out of hand—"

"What if I wanted things to get out of hand?" Her gaze searched his. "I kissed you. Enzo, I've wanted to kiss you for the longest time. Tonight I finally worked up the courage."

Wow! Where had that come from? She never talked this boldly to men. Maybe that was why she didn't have a steady boyfriend—why she was still a virgin. In the past, she could blame her limited experience with men on caring for her ailing mother. But now it was all on her—what did or didn't happen was totally up to her.

She was tired of standing on the sidelines, watching her life rush past her. It was time to do what she wanted, instead of just dreaming about those things. It was time she took charge of her life.

And right now she wanted Enzo.

She trusted him more than anyone else in the world. These past few months they'd spent almost every day together. She knew him and he knew her. He was kind. He was thoughtful. And he had a big heart where his family was concerned.

And then there was his looks. Mmm...tall, dark and sexy didn't even begin to describe him. His dark eyes were mysterious and held a host of secrets that she longed to unravel. And his thick brown hair made her hands tingle with the impulse to comb her fingertips through it. And his mouth, well, she'd already proven it was most desirable.

For a moment Enzo didn't respond. His eyes registered his surprise at her forwardness. Part of her was proud of herself for speaking up. The other part of her was scared that he would let her down with a painful thump to her heart.

His gaze searched hers. "Sylvie, I'm in no position to start something serious. I—"

She placed a fingertip to those kissable lips. "I'm not asking you for anything permanent. I'm just asking you for the here and now. Let tomorrow take care of itself."

Hesitation showed in his eyes. "I don't want to hurt you."

The fact he cared that much meant a lot to her. And it was enough. Throughout the trials and tribulations of her life, she'd learned to be cautious with her heart.

She sent him a reassuring smile. "You won't hurt me. You've always been so sweet and kind."

Silence greeted her very honest words. All of this openness had her heart racing. What was she going to do if this all blew up in her face? After all, she was no temptress. She was not experienced in the ways of men. For all she knew, she could be making an utter fool of herself.

"Do you want to continue this back at the hotel?" His deep voice was thick and rich like the tiramisu dessert they'd indulged in at the dinner before the awards ceremony.

When her gaze met his, she saw desire burning in his eyes. Her insecurities were temporarily subdued. Her insides melted. Her core quivered with its own desire.

She didn't trust herself to speak. Instead, she lifted up on her tiptoes once more and pressed her lips to his. She deepened the kiss, opening her mouth to him, showing him that she didn't want this most exciting, most romantic night to end. In fact, this was just the beginning.

And then she pulled back. She laced her fingers with his and then started walking in the direction of their hotel. His thumb moved over the back of her hand. His roughened skin from working with his hands all day made his touch feel a little different, a little more exciting. Everything about Enzo was exciting.

The quick walk passed in silence. And then they came to a stop in front of the first hotel room they came to. It happened to be hers. Her heart raced as anticipation pumped through her veins. At last, she was going to find out what all her friends were talking about when they mentioned their boyfriends and got that dreamy look in their eyes. Not that Enzo was her boyfriend. She wasn't sure what to call him because *friend* didn't begin to cover their increasingly complex relationship.

She turned to him and asked, "You haven't changed your mind, have you?"

Both of his dark brows rose high on his forehead. Had she said something wrong? Doubts circled in her mind. Her head lowered. His silence increased her rising anxiety. She worried her bottom lip. She'd done this all wrong—

He placed a finger beneath her chin and lifted until their gazes met. "Why would you think I've changed my mind? You're the most beautiful, most amazing woman I've ever met. I just can't believe you want me, too."

"I do." Her voice was so soft that she wasn't sure she'd actually vocalized the words, but there was a look of acknowledgment on his face.

How could he not know all this time that she'd wanted him? She thought it was written all over her face every time she looked at him. It must be obvious she was utterly and totally inexperienced. She couldn't help but wonder why he'd want to make love to her when she didn't know what she was doing. She thought of asking him, but her mouth was dry and her mind was having trouble communicating with her mouth.

But luckily this time, she didn't have to do anything because it was Enzo who leaned down and pressed his lips to hers. His kiss, though gentle enough, was full of desire. It whipped up her pulse and stirred her own embers of desire.

Tonight she would become a woman in every sense of the word. And her friends would no longer be able to hold anything over her head. Tonight she would find out all about lovemaking with the most amazing man in the world.

# CHAPTER ONE

*Tuscany, six weeks later*

HE HAD A SECRET.

A secret he'd shoved to the far recesses of his mind.

A secret he'd held on to for too long.

Enzo paced back and forth across the spacious balcony. A frown pulled at his face as a stress headache settled in his forehead and wrapped around his head, tightening like a vise.

He'd known for many years that one of the Bartolini siblings wasn't a true Bartolini by blood. His chest tightened just like it did every time he replayed the tumultuous events in his mind. The reason he'd never said anything—never admitted the painful truth—was that he thought he was the illegitimate sibling.

He raked his fingers through his hair as he blew out a breath. He'd totally made a mess of things. And after everything that had happened with his mother's journal and the reading of his parents' will, he still hadn't gotten his act together.

His mistakes continued to mount. Even though it had been weeks since the Paris trip, Enzo was still kicking himself for letting things get out of control with Sylvie.

And rightly so. Sylvie had been a virgin. *A virgin.* The word echoed in his mind.

She should have saved that special moment for someone whom she loved. The evening should have included flowers and champagne as well as a bunch of other romantic platitudes.

Guilt settled on his shoulders like a big soggy cloak. Instead, the evening had been all about him and the vineyard. It should have been about her and how special she is. How had he missed all of this? He'd searched his memory, trying to recall if she'd told him that she was a virgin. But he was certain she hadn't mentioned it.

And yet, their night of passion had happened and now he could barely face her. He felt like she was expecting something from him. And yet, he didn't have anything to offer her. His life was a mess.

And to top it off, tomorrow was his birthday.

Nothing about this week felt festive. And that was fine by him. He wasn't in any mood to celebrate his birthday or anything else.

Enzo stood on the balcony of his family's grand estate, which had recently been remodeled into a boutique hotel. It was hard to believe that it had been less than a year since his parents stood in this very place. Now they were gone and with them went his illusion of the family he'd been a part of.

Since their deaths, the changes were falling like dominoes, one right after the next. Nothing was like it had been. Everyone was making life-changing decisions. And now it was his turn.

It should have been the biggest decision of his life. And yet, it felt predestined. The decision should have taken time—lots of time. It would have been surprising to make a momentous decision like this so quickly. However, this decision had been made for him before he even knew there was a question.

One evening was all it'd taken to change everything. That wasn't much time at all in the grand scheme of things. However, he'd drug his heels about making it official.

And now, with his decision at last vocalized, the Monday-morning sun rose in the sky just as it had always done. It was oblivious to the monumental changes going on in Enzo's life. And so he went about life just as he had been doing. He'd already been out in the fields inspecting the vines. It wouldn't be long now and they'd be able to harvest the grapes.

His first season in sole charge of the vineyard and it was going to prove to be their biggest and best year. His father would have loved to see all their hard work come to fruition. If only that horrific car accident hadn't stolen both of Enzo's parents away.

If his parents were still here, Enzo's family wouldn't have been blown apart by a deep, dark secret that his parents had been harboring for many years. It was a secret Enzo had thought he knew the answer to. But when DNA results revealed his youngest sister, Gia, was not a Bartolini by blood but rather a result of their mother's affair, he'd been utterly floored.

He'd seen the way the news had stunned Gia and ripped her heart apart. But he couldn't have been prouder of her when she pulled herself together and went in search of her biological father. Not everyone could do such a thing. He wasn't sure he could have done what she did...

"Enzo, I have the mail." Sylvie, the estate's wedding planner, stepped onto the balcony.

He didn't turn around. "I don't want to look at it now. Just toss it in the office." Then, realizing he'd forgotten

his manners—manners his mother had instilled in him—
he said, "Thank you."

Sylvie stepped up next to him. "You might want to see
these two things."

Her words stirred his curiosity. "Why's that?"

"They're from your sisters."

A smile tugged at his lips. Through it all, they'd still remembered his birthday. When Sylvie held out two pieces
of mail, he readily accepted them.

The first was a postcard. It was from the island of Lapri.
The front of it had a picture of a dog licking gelato with
the beach in the background. Okay, so a postcard wasn't
exactly a birthday card, but it was the thought that counts.
He flipped it over, already knowing it was from Gia.

*Having a great time. The villa is almost remodeled.*
*I'll have to find another house to work on. G*

That was it? His gaze searched the card again. No
birthday wishes. No *I miss you*. No *I'm coming back*.
Not even a *Love, Gia*. Just a little note and an imper-
sonal, unfeeling *G*.

His good mood deflated like a balloon stuck with a
sharp needle. A big *whoosh* and his mood was back to its
prior melancholy state of being.

Enzo blew out a deep sigh. This confirmed that their
close-knit family was forever fractured. Nothing would
ever be as it had been. If only he hadn't held on to that
secret—the one he wasn't supposed to know anything
about—maybe then things wouldn't be so different.

"Aren't you going to open the other one?" Sylvie's voice
drew him from his thoughts. "It looks official. It has a crest
on it and everything."

Enzo lifted the cream-colored envelope and saw the

purple seal on the back. It was from his other sister Bianca. He noticed that the envelope was weighty, like there might be a card inside. A little smile played at the corners of his mouth. Bianca was always good at remembering his birthday.

He recalled the one time she'd planned a surprise for him. It was a birthday party in the garden. The only problem was she'd only invited her friends—her girlfriends. And most of them had crushes on him. Bianca had a good laugh, but he'd never been so glad for a party to end.

He slipped his finger under the flap—

"Stop!"

He hesitated and turned to Sylvie. "What?"

She wore a look of horror, as though he was about to destroy something sacred. "You can't just rip that open."

"Why not?" It was an envelope. Sure, it was of much finer quality, but still, it was an envelope. "If I don't open it, how will I know what's inside?"

"Wait. Don't move. I'll be right back." She rushed back inside the villa.

He thought about going ahead and opening it, but he didn't want to upset Sylvie. She was going to be upset enough when he told her his news. There was no need to make this day any worse. He just didn't know why Sylvie was making such a big fuss over an envelope.

A minute later she returned, holding up a silver letter opener. "Here you go."

He took the letter opener that was older than he was and handed down from his grandparents to his parents and now to him. The metal tip slipped easily through the fold and he yanked. The paper tore in a straight line. Nice and neat, just like Sylvie wanted.

He withdrew the card. As his gaze took in the words, he

realized it wasn't a birthday card but rather an invitation. Neither sister had remembered his birthday.

"What is it?" Excitement rang out in Sylvie's voice.

He didn't want to discuss it. Instead, he wordlessly handed the invite to her.

She took it and began to read. Oohs and ahs accompanied each line she read. "This is amazing. You must be so excited to be invited to your sister's wedding. Can you believe you'll be related to a real-life prince?"

Enzo cleared his throat. "I don't care who marries my sister as long as he makes her happy." By the raised brows on Sylvie's face, he realized his voice had been gruffer than he'd intended. "I'm sure Prince Leo will make her happy. She certainly seemed excited enough when she moved to Patazonia."

"Oh, she was." Sylvie wore a dreamy smile.

He didn't want to talk about his sister, especially not the new life she'd been thrust into by their parents' unreasonable will, which had pushed all three siblings to compete against each other for ownership of this estate. Maybe if it hadn't been for the unusual will and ridiculous requirement, his family would still be together—

He halted his thoughts. That wasn't the truth. It was his fault. He should have tried harder to protect his sisters—to keep them all together.

*You're the big brother. You have to watch out for your sisters. Keep them safe.*

His father's words echoed in his mind. How many times over the years had his father told him that? Too many times to count. And now when it was urgent for him to do just that, he'd failed them.

Not only had he failed his sisters but he was also about to disappoint Sylvie. And just like his sisters, she wouldn't see this news coming.

* * *

What was going on?

As Sylvie continued to study the distinct frown on Enzo's face, the more confused she became. He'd been acting strange ever since he got home from the wine competition—which he'd won. But instead of being excited, he'd been moody and quiet. And worst of all, he'd pulled away from her.

Whereas they'd started off as friends, joking and laughing with each other, they now acted like mere acquaintances. Gone was the warm, easy companionship.

When he'd invited her to Paris, she'd thought it was the start of something serious between them. Boy had she been wrong. So very wrong.

Within a couple weeks of returning from Paris, everything looked dismal. Not only had Enzo put up a wall between them, but with his decision to close the boutique hotel, the wedding business was dwindling. People had been drawn in with the package deal. Now with just a wedding venue and no lodgings, well, the competition was drawing away business.

Maybe if she hadn't acted spontaneously in Paris—if she hadn't forced their relationship to the next level—she'd be able to convince Enzo to reopen the hotel. But with the mood he was in these days, that wasn't going to happen.

If it wasn't for that one unforgettable night, things would be different. Heat rushed to her cheeks when she recalled the night he'd won the prestigious competition. It had been a very special night for her, too. Perhaps they'd celebrated a little too much and then one thing led to another until she'd wound up in his arms all night long. She'd let herself believe he cared for her—like she cared for him.

But then they'd returned to Tuscany. It was like their

passion had all been a steamy, stirring dream, but a dream nonetheless. And though that had been weeks ago, she was still trying to figure out what had happened.

They just needed to address the elephant in the room. The air needed clearing because she had important business to discuss with him. And this time she wouldn't let him come up with an excuse to walk away—like he'd done so many times before.

"Enzo—" she waited until she had his full attention and then she continued "—we need to discuss the future of the wedding business. I have some ideas to go over with you."

This was it. This was further than she'd gotten in the past. She straightened her shoulders and met his gaze, letting him know she meant business. Would he stay this time and hear her out? Or would he make an excuse again?

When he started for the door, he said, "Maybe later. I need to get back to work."

In the past she'd let him escape. Maybe she should have spoken up before now. Maybe she shouldn't have let things drag on to this point. But it was so hard when the first time you make love and you think it was great—special even— and the guy thinks otherwise.

At first, she'd cried into her pillow at night. But time had helped soothe her wounded heart—or was it her pride? Perhaps a little of both. Either way, she wasn't going to be ignored. No one deserved that, not after what they'd shared.

She rushed over to the doorway before he could escape inside. When she stepped in front of him, his widened gaze settled on her.

"Sylvie, this isn't the time." His tone was gruff. "I have things to do."

She settled her hands on her hips. "Not before we talk."

He sighed. A moment of tense silence passed before he said, "Okay. What do you want to talk about?"

"You."

This got his attention. His gaze connected with hers, sending a jolt of awareness zinging through her body, but she refused to acknowledge it. Not now. Not like this.

"What about me?" His tone was cool and distant.

"I want to know why you've been acting different since we slept together—like we're strangers."

For a moment there was some sort of emotion in his eyes, but in a blink it was shuttered behind a wall of indifference. "I don't know what you mean."

Her back teeth ground together. He wasn't going to do this to her. During the years of caring for her mother, she'd learned to be a fighter—fighting to keep a roof over their heads, fighting to have her mother admitted to a new clinical trial, fighting to make their lives as normal as possible. Through it all, she'd learned how to speak up and not back down.

Frustration bubbled up within her. "Don't do this. Talk to me. I don't understand what went wrong. I… I thought we both wanted that night. Didn't we?"

He continued to stare at her. If he thought she was going to turn away, he had another think coming. She was the best starer in her primary school.

Then he let out a breath. His shoulders lowered just a bit, as though what had been holding him up had escaped in that breath. "I don't know what you want from me."

"How about the truth? Why have you been avoiding me?"

The silence returned. It dragged on so long that she was pretty certain he was never going to answer her—never going to tell her what she'd done wrong.

"Why didn't you tell me?" There was a note of accusation in his tone.

"Tell you?" She had no idea what he was talking about. "Tell you what?"

"That you were…you know."

"No, I don't know. Tell me."

His mouth pressed closed as his dark brows drew together into a formidable line. "Tell me that you were a virgin."

Her mouth opened to reply but no words would form as her mind raced with a million thoughts at once. Instead, she stood there with her mouth gaping open.

He was mad because she didn't make a big deal out of her virginity? Seriously? How in the world could he be mad about that? Realizing that her mouth was still gaping open, she promptly closed it.

Enzo continued to stare at her like he really expected her to answer him. She didn't know what sort of answer he expected. Or why she had to explain herself.

"I… I didn't know my virginity needed to be stated before we made love. Would it really have made a difference?"

"Of course it would have." He raked his fingers through his thick, dark hair, sending the short strands scattering. When his gaze met hers this time, there was an intensity there that she'd never seen before. "How could you think otherwise?"

"Because I wasn't thinking about it when we were standing in front of the Eiffel Tower. All I was thinking about was you." Intense heat rushed to her face upon realizing that she'd said too much.

"Didn't you think I deserved to know?"

"No." Was that selfish of her? She didn't think so. It's not like any of this really affected him or their time together. There was something else going on here—something he wasn't telling her.

Then he sighed. The lines on his handsome face smoothed. He turned away from her. He moved to the balustrade and then rested his forearms on the rail.

"I'm sorry," he said. Though with him turned away from her, she had to strain to hear his words. "I shouldn't have said that. I just have a lot on my mind."

She wanted to ask if he was also sorry that they'd slept together, but she held back the words—but barely. At least they were getting somewhere. Now, if she could just keep him talking.

"Is it your sisters?" She'd known ever since she'd come to live and work at the Bartolini estate that his parents' sudden deaths had caused not just a ripple through his life but a tsunami of pain that had shaken each Bartolini sibling to the very core.

"Yes. No. Not really." There was anguish in his voice. Whatever was bothering him went deep, very deep.

She moved to stand next to him at the rail. The scene of the rolling hills of the vineyard was stunning and usually captivated her attention, but right now she was fully focused on Enzo.

Sylvie placed a hand on his arm. "You know you can talk to me about anything?"

He turned his head to look at her and then turned away. "Not about this."

She stifled a sigh. Had they really come full circle? "Is this about Paris?"

"Yes. And no."

She normally considered herself a patient person. After all, to be a good wedding planner, you needed to remain calm at all times, even when the bride was having an utter meltdown and blaming the whole world. Right now Sylvie would give anything to be dealing with a nervous bride and not a stubborn Enzo.

Sylvie straightened her shoulders. She wasn't backing off. "You need to tell me what's on your mind because this guessing game isn't working for me. If you're mad about me being a virgin—"

"No. It's not that. And I wasn't mad that you were a virgin. I was mad that I didn't know." He turned to her. Pain evident in his eyes. "If I had known, I would have…" He paused. "I would have backed away."

"Why? Do you have a thing against virgins?"

"No. Of course not." He shook his head. "But you should have shared that moment with someone special—someone you love."

"Oh." This time she was the one who glanced away. Heat licked at her cheeks.

# CHAPTER TWO

HE WAS MUCKING up this conversation. Royally.

And worst of all, he was hurting Sylvie.

Enzo inwardly groaned. She had a heart of gold and deserved someone better than him. She should have a man who had it all together. Someone who could look at her like she'd hung the stars.

That was why he'd been keeping his distance. He'd suspected before they flew to Paris that she might have some feelings for him, but other times he was certain he was just reading more into their friendship than was there.

And then she'd kissed him in front of the Eiffel Tower. Was it awful of him to admit that he hadn't seen it coming? Not at all.

Of course, that might have been because he'd just had one of the most important conversations of his life. There had been an offer to buy Barto Vineyard as well as the entire estate.

Now, of course, this hadn't been the first offer for the estate. Over the years, his father had had plenty of inquiries. All of which his father had immediately dismissed. To his father, this place—this land—it was in his soul. He needed it as much as he needed his next breath.

However, Enzo now saw the estate in a much different view. This may be where his family had started, but it was also where that family had splintered apart. The secrets that were kept within the stone walls of the villa all these years were like poison, killing the family that he'd once known.

Now one sister lived in Patazonia and was renouncing her Italian citizenship in order to become a princess. And his other sister had left the mainland to live on a Mediterranean island—far from home. It was though his sisters couldn't wait to get as far away from this place as they could. And maybe they were right.

Maybe it was time for him to move on—time for him to forge a new life somewhere far from Tuscany and all the memories tied up in this place.

And that was why he hadn't immediately dismissed the offer to buy the estate. But he hadn't accepted the offer, either. He'd needed time to think it over. And that was what he'd been doing ever since they'd returned from Paris. Thinking. And thinking. And thinking some more.

And at last, he'd come to a decision.

Not an easy decision. Not that he'd expect something this big, this profound, to be made easily. But now that he solely owned the estate by default—as both of his sisters had found their happiness elsewhere—the decision was solely his to make.

And now it was time to share the news with Sylvie.

He glanced over at her, knowing how this was going to crush her. His chest tightened. "Sylvie, there's something I need to tell you."

The color leeched from her face. "What is it?"

She was so pale now that he was worried about her. "Do you feel all right?"

"The news. What is it?"

He hesitated. "Maybe we should sit down."

"No. I'm fine right here. What is it you wanted to tell me?"

He drew in a deep breath and then let it out. It didn't

matter how long he put this off; it wasn't going to get easier for either of them. It was best just to get it over with as quickly as possible. "I've agreed to sell the estate."

If it was possible for her face to grow paler, it most definitely had. Even her normally glossy pink lips were devoid of gloss this morning and had lost their color.

"You did what?" Her voice faded with each word.

And then she swayed.

He moved, his arms wrapping around her. Instinctively, he pulled her to him. "I've got you."

She pressed her hands to his chest. "I'm fine. Let me go."

He guided her over to one of the chairs at a table on the terrace. "Can I get you anything?"

She shook her head. "Stop fussing. I'm fine."

"No, you're not. You almost passed out over there. Are you sick?"

Again, she shook her head. "I'm not sick. I keep telling you, I'm fine."

"People that are fine don't pass out."

"I didn't pass out."

"Okay, then you almost passed out. I'm not letting this go until you tell me what's going on. Is it the news?"

She shrugged. "I didn't eat breakfast this morning and I went for a run."

"On an empty stomach?" No wonder she'd almost passed out.

She shrugged once more. "When?"

"What?"

"When is the estate being sold?"

"I don't know. I just made the call this morning. We have to work out the details. Nothing has been fully decided."

She didn't say anything to that. She got to her feet and quietly walked away, leaving him feeling worse than he had before.

He thought she would yell at him—blame him for ruining her business. Anything would have been better than the silent treatment. Though he supposed he deserved it because ever since Paris he'd been quiet, too—trying to figure out the right thing to do for his family and for himself.

But was it the right thing for Sylvie?

His proclamation had stunned her.

The next morning Sylvie sat behind her desk in the guesthouse. She didn't feel as though she'd accomplished a thing that morning. At least nothing that was on her to-do list.

She'd spent most of yesterday in this little cottage on the estate. And she intended to do the same today. She told herself it was because she had a lot of work to do, but the real reason was that she was avoiding Enzo.

The cottage was quiet and out of the way. It was used in part for wedding services, from choosing a gown, to dress fittings, to choosing decorations and everything else. Princess Bianca—well, she wasn't officially a princess until Christmas—had invested most of the income from the weddings back into the business, building it up. Now the business was amazing. And Sylvie felt as though she had a dream job, but like with all dreams, it was coming to an end.

Her stomach felt as though it was on the high seas, swaying this way and that. As such, her appetite was non-existent.

All the while her mind was on Enzo. How could he sell the estate? This was the same place he'd competed with his sisters over in order to claim ownership. And now he just suddenly changed his mind? She didn't understand.

It also meant she would once again be homeless. Tears rushed to her eyes but she blinked them away.

She never used to be emotional. She couldn't afford

to be when she'd had to care for her mother. She'd had to be the strong one. Her mother had needed her to lean on.

She'd been calm and collected when, after her mother's death, the bank had repossessed the small house she'd grown up in. With only part-time work so she could care for her mother, she hadn't been able to keep up with the mortgage payments.

For a time, she'd been on her own with nothing more than what she could carry. It had been horrible but not as bad as losing her mother and knowing that she was all alone in this world, after having lost her father in a horrific accident when she was just a baby.

But Enzo's circumstances were different than hers. He had not only a home but also a family to rely on. Whether he was willing to acknowledge it or not, this estate was his destiny. The Barto Vineyard was as much a part of him as the blood flowing through his veins. But how did she get him to see this?

There was a knock at the door. Before she could get up, she heard the door creak open.

"Sylvie?" It was Enzo. "Sylvie, are you in here?"

"In the office."

Her empty stomach shivered with nerves. What did he want to talk about now? She didn't know what to say to change his mind about the sale.

Enzo stepped into the office. His tall stature and broad shoulders seemed to fill the room, making the office feel much smaller than it truly was. He looked around the room, never letting his gaze rest on her. His intent on taking in everything in the office made it seem like he'd never been in here before, but the truth was he'd been in the office countless times.

When the silence turned uncomfortable, Sylvie asked, "Was there something you needed?"

He hitched his thumbs in the corners of his jean pockets and ducked his head. "I wanted to say I was sorry for how I handled things yesterday."

"You mean springing it on me that I've lost not only my home but also my business, too?"

He kept his gaze down toward the floor as he nodded. "Don't worry. I plan to help you out."

"Help me out?" She didn't like the sound of that. She wasn't a charity case. She'd already had to accept the help of others after her mother passed on. That had been so hard to do. She wasn't going to do that again. She had worked hard to put away some savings. It would tide her over until she came up with another job.

He nodded and then his gaze met hers. "You just have to tell me where you want to settle and I'll make sure you have a place to live. If you want, I can set you up with your own wedding business."

Her mouth gaped. Realizing she must look like a guppy, she pressed her lips together as she attempted to gather her scattered thoughts.

"Why?" When he sent her a puzzled look, she elaborated on her thought. "Why would you do something like that? It's so...so generous."

He rubbed the back of his neck. "Because it's my fault you're losing your place to live and work. It seems like the only right thing to do."

She seized upon that last part of his explanation. "The right thing to do? So you're doing this out of some sense of obligation?"

"Well, yes."

That was what she figured. He was a man driven by his sense of duty and obligation. She didn't want to be one of his obligations. "That won't be necessary. You don't owe me anything—"

"Of course I do—"

"No, you don't." She stood so he didn't have quite such a height advantage over her. "I'm not part of your family. There's no reason for you to feel obligated where I'm concerned. I…" She almost mentioned that she took care of not only herself but also her mother, but decided against bringing it up. There was a lot she still hadn't shared with him because she hadn't wanted to scare him off with all her heavy baggage. "I can take care of myself."

A frown settled on his handsome face. "Of course you can. I didn't mean to imply otherwise. But I just feel bad about you moving here all the way from Patazonia and already the business is shutting down. That's not fair."

"Life isn't fair. I learned that a long time ago."

Like when her mother struggled with three jobs to keep a roof over their heads when Sylvie was young. Her mother had been a seamstress, one of the best in the land, but when business had dropped off because people started buying clothes over the internet, her mother picked up cleaning jobs to help balance the budget.

"Sylvie, what are you talking about?"

She shook her head. "It's nothing." He eyed her as though trying to read the truth in her eyes. Worried he'd see too much, she glanced away. It was time to change the subject away from her. She lifted her gaze once more. "Are you sure this is what you want to do?"

"What? Help you? Of course I am."

She shook her head. "No. I mean sell this place."

This time it was his turn to glance away. "I'm certain."

"But just months ago you were determined to beat both of your sisters and win ownership of the villa, the vineyard—the entire estate. How can you change your mind so quickly?"

His brows gathered in a firm line and when his gaze landed on her, it was dark and stormy. "Because this isn't the place it used to be. It's broken and tarnished. It's best for me and my sisters to put it in our rearview mirrors and keep moving forward."

Ouch! She had no idea he was harboring such hostilities regarding his childhood home. But something told her selling the estate wouldn't resolve the turmoil going on inside him. It went far deeper than grapevines and a place to lay his head at night.

"But what will you do?" she asked. "Where will you go?"

"I don't know. Maybe back to Paris. I have a standing invitation to go work at a prestigious vineyard there."

"But it won't be your vineyard." She'd seen the pride he took in the grapes at the Barto Vineyard. Even though it was an enormous vineyard with many employees, Enzo made sure to take part in all facets of the operation. "It won't have your family name on the wine."

His dark gaze was unreadable in that moment. "Maybe that's for the best. After everything that happened here this year, it is best to close the door on all of this."

It was then that Sylvie realized how big of a challenge she'd set for herself in changing his mind about remaining here. But she wasn't a quitter. She was a fighter. It was one of the last things her mother told her.

*Never give up on life. Keep fighting for what's most important.*

And right now Enzo's heritage was at stake as well as her business. She was as certain as she was standing here that he would regret parting with this land as much as she would regret not fighting to keep her home and occupation.

"I have to go," he said. "We'll talk more about this later."

Sylvie tried to think of a reason for him to stay. She glanced down at her desktop and her gaze landed on her calendar. "Wait." When he paused at the doorway and turned back to her, she said, "We need to talk about the sale. I need to know what weddings to work on relocating to a new venue."

He frowned. "I don't know. Nothing is official. The buyer is flying in two weeks from now to take a tour of the grounds."

"He's buying a place he's never seen?" Who did such a thing?

"He's been here for a wedding. And he's enjoyed the wine for many years. He says he's getting older now and is ready to settle down."

"How is running a vineyard settling down?"

Enzo shrugged. He worked from sunrise until sunset and always had more than he could get done in one day. "Not my problem."

"Can we go over my calendar?" she asked.

Enzo checked his wristwatch. "Not now. I have to meet up with Vito. We're having problems locating a replacement part for one of our tanks. Maybe later."

He already had one foot out the door when she thought of how she could gain more of his time. "How about dinner?"

He paused once more. "I can't eat until late."

"No problem. It'll give me a chance to throw something together." She wasn't sure what it would be but suddenly her appetite was starting to come back.

"Okay. If you're sure."

"I'm positive."

When he was gone, Sylvie worked to finish up the last of her urgent admin. The rest could wait until later. Right now she had something important on her mind—saving the estate. She had two weeks to convince Enzo that this was where he was meant to be. But how could she do it?

# CHAPTER THREE

INSTEAD OF THINGS getting better, they were getting worse.

And it wasn't just the broken equipment in the winery.

Enzo had been grouchy with Sylvie and he hadn't meant to be. In fact, that was the very opposite of how he meant to act around her. Until that unforgettable night in Paris, she had been one of his closest friends.

Even though he had been busy doing everything he could to market his wine to new stores and foreign vendors, he always made time for her. Sylvie's smile was contagious and lightened his darkest days. Meeting up with her had always been the highlight of his day. Then he'd gone and mucked everything up.

Why hadn't he just been a gentleman and walked away after she'd kissed him? Because he couldn't. The magnetic pull between them had been something he'd never felt before.

And that night in Paris, wow. That night had been amazing. He still thought of it when he was alone in bed and sleep was evading him, as it did often these days.

The question was how did he get things back on track with Sylvie? He missed their friendship, but every time he was around her, words didn't come out the way he meant them to. And now when she looked at him, he felt even guiltier not only for the night in Paris but also for now taking her home and job. If only she'd let him help her get resettled somewhere else, he would feel better. In fact, he intended to talk to her about it tonight at the dinner she'd insisted on preparing.

He checked the time. It was almost eight. How did it get to be so late? He knew he better head up to the guesthouse before she thought he'd forgotten about dinner. The last thing he needed was to make things even worse between them. They were bad enough already.

And so he set off for the guesthouse where Sylvie was now living and working. He could fix things. He wouldn't give up until she listened to reason.

As he neared the guesthouse, his thoughts turned to its prior resident. His youngest sister, Gia, had stayed here after their parents had died. Only she hadn't stayed here long. It seemed to him that she couldn't get away from the estate fast enough, first to find her biological father, who turned out to be a total and utter jerk, and then finally to move permanently to the island of Lapri with some guy she barely knew. But who was he to judge?

He'd believed everything his parents had told them without question. And when he'd overheard something that conflicted with his illusion of the perfect family, he dismissed it as a figment of his imagination. He'd failed his sisters. And he'd failed himself.

Enzo stepped up to the door of the guesthouse and rapped his knuckles on the heavy wood. When a few moments passed and Sylvie hadn't answered, he knocked louder. Still nothing. He moved to the side of the door and peered inside the window. It was dark in the front room. He figured she was in the kitchen at the back of the little house and hadn't heard him.

He walked to the back door and knocked. Still, there was no answer. What was up with that? He searched his memory and was certain she'd invited him to dinner tonight. He backed up and noticed there were no lights on back here, either. Was it possible he'd gotten his wires crossed? Had she meant the main house?

Not wanting her to know just how distracted he was these days, his pride refused to allow him to text her. He'd just walk up to the main house and pretend that was where he'd intended to go all along.

However, when he reached the back of the villa, it was dark inside, too. How could that be? Maybe he really had misconstrued what she'd told him.

Through the window in the door, he noticed the soft glow of the small light over the big farmhouse sink—his mother had always left on a light for his father when he'd worked late in the fields. As Enzo grasped the brass doorknob of the kitchen door, he gave himself a mental jerk. He tried not to think about his parents. Every time he did, his mood went south. That wouldn't be fair to Sylvie, who had gone out of her way to make him dinner. At least he thought she had.

He pushed the door open and stepped inside. He moved to the kitchen and flipped on the lights. The kitchen was spiffed up and as he inhaled, he definitely detected some basil and tomato sauce. He had a feeling he was on to something.

As it was a bit chilly outside that evening, he was certain Sylvie wasn't planning a terrace dinner. Perhaps she'd decided to utilize the dining room in order to use the long table to spread out her paperwork that she wanted to go over with him.

He started in that direction. However, when the doorway to the dining room came into sight, he noticed the door was almost closed while a flicker of soft light shone through the crack. Sylvie had planned a candlelight dinner for him?

As soon as the thought came to him, he dismissed it. He'd ruined any chance of anything romantic between them. Not that he was interested in starting a relationship. In fact, that was the last thing he wanted.

His personal life was a disaster. He might have won full ownership of the Bartolini estate but he'd lost what made it special—his family. In truth, he hadn't even won control of it. He'd won out of default. His sisters didn't want the place. They'd rather move far away and start over. Not that he could blame them after the way their lives had imploded upon finding their mother's journal.

But he wasn't going to think about that now. Right now he needed to make sure Sylvie hadn't gotten the wrong idea about tonight's dinner.

He pushed the door open. There was a single candle lit in the vast room. He squinted into the darkness. "Sylvie?"

The lights flicked on, momentarily blinding him.

"Surprise!" It wasn't just Sylvie's voice but a whole host of voices.

When his sight adjusted, he glanced around. Crowded into the dining room were all the workers from the vineyard as well as friends and neighbors. And then his gaze rested on Sylvie.

His jaw muscles tightened. He didn't want to celebrate his birthday. Not at all.

But everyone looked at him with a big smile on their faces and expectation in their eyes. He was certain they all had better things to do with their time, but they'd taken time out of their lives to come here to celebrate his birthday. They didn't know that this year of all years he didn't have the heart to celebrate.

Still, he forced a smile to his face. Many of these people had worked for his family for decades. He owed them more than a fake smile, but it was the most he could do at this particular moment.

And then he was swallowed up in the moment. People were shaking his hand, clapping him on the back and wishing him a happy birthday.

What they didn't know and what he didn't tell them was that they would never come together like this again. And the vineyard workers would be losing their jobs in the near future, when the new owner took over.

Until this point, Enzo had refused to let himself acknowledge this very obvious—very painful fact. He knew if he was to consider it, he might very well back away from the offer. And then what? He remained here?

He didn't want to think about the past and wonder what else their parents had lied to them about. He wanted to do what his sisters had done and turn his back on this place.

Of all the people here this evening, he noticed that his sisters weren't among the guests. Not that he would expect them to drop everything in their very busy lives and travel here for his thirty-second birthday. But they'd never not remembered to give him a card. No matter where they were in their lives or in the world, they always remembered each other's birthdays. Until now.

"Great party, huh?"

Enzo glanced to his right. "Yeah."

Next to him stood his right-hand man, Vito. He had also been his father's second-in-command. His father and Vito had grown up together. But looking at Vito now, the only thing betraying his true age was his silver hair and mustache. Other than that, the man didn't look old enough to have grown children, nor did he act as though his first grandchild was on the way. He was a man with an abundance of energy and a smile for most anyone.

"It's too bad your parents aren't here to share this with you," Vito said. "They'd love it."

Enzo didn't want to discuss them. He had too many mixed emotions where they were concerned.

"Did you get something to eat?" Enzo asked.

"I was headed that way. I just wanted to wish you a happy birthday." He extended his hand. They shook before sharing a quick one-armed hug. And then Vito moved toward the food.

The fact Sylvie went to so much trouble for him should have touched him—touched him deeply. And it did. But there was also another feeling nagging at him. Guilt. A huge case of it.

Why had she gone to such trouble for him? He didn't deserve it. He had let his frustrations show around her and that wasn't good. He could do better where Sylvie was concerned. He would do better.

There were meats and cheeses. A fruit platter took up a large portion of the table. Pasta was heaped in a large bowl with oil, olives, fresh diced tomatoes and herbs. There was enough food here to feed a small army. And as good as it all looked and smelled, he didn't have an appetite.

"Where's your plate?" Sylvie asked once the crowd thinned out around him.

"I…uh…didn't have a chance to get anything." He hoped she'd drop the subject, but he knew her well enough to know she'd push until he ate something.

"Then let's get you something." She reached for a plate and handed it to him. "Fill it up before the food is all gone."

If he had to eat, she did, too. "Where's your food?"

"I haven't had a chance to get some, either. So why don't we get some together?" She smiled at him. How was it possible that someone's smile could be so bright it warmed a spot in his chest?

He grabbed a plate for Sylvie and handed it to her. "Lead the way."

And so she did, helping him fill his plate until there was absolutely no room left. "How am I supposed to eat all of this?"

"You've worked hard all day. And those are all your favorites. I'm sure you'll find a way."

It was then that he stared down at the plate. She was right. These were all his favorites. "You did this, didn't you?"

She shrugged as she added some fresh fruit to her plate. "I just remembered. And I might have texted Bianca."

He smiled—his first smile of the day. "I'm not so sure how I feel about you and my sister being such good friends."

"Are you afraid I'll learn all of your secrets?"

Her innocent words struck far too close to home. "I don't know what you're talking about."

The smile slipped from her face. "Doesn't everyone have things they are holding back?"

He didn't want to have this conversation. Not at all. "Let's sit down and eat."

As they made their way to a couple of empty chairs, he rolled around her words in his mind. Was she referring to his family's secrets? Because he was certain she didn't know his secret. Or was she referring to her own?

Once they were seated, his curiosity was piqued. "Are you saying you're a woman of mystery?"

She arched a brow. "Would you like that?"

He pursed his lips together. There were still so many things about Sylvie that he didn't know. And he couldn't help but think he wanted to know everything about her. But now that he'd decided to sell the estate, she would be leaving here. Maybe not today. Maybe not tomorrow. But soon. Too soon.

It was best to let the subject drop. "What I'd like is to enjoy this food because there's this great big cake with my name on it."

Sylvie smiled. "You saw that?"

"How could I miss it? It's huge and in the center of the table. How did you get the bakery to make it so quickly? Or did you have this party planned for a long time?"

"Actually, I didn't realize it was your birthday until yesterday when I saw a notation on my day planner. There wasn't any time to order a cake so I made it—"

"You baked me a birthday cake?"

She shrugged. "Kind of."

"I don't understand. You baked it or you didn't?"

"It's a box cake. Actually, it's four boxes. I wanted to make sure there was enough for everyone."

"Box or not, you're the first person aside from my mother to ever bake me a cake." The gesture touched him more profoundly than it should have. He leaned over to her. He was so tempted to reach out and turn her head toward him so he could press his lips to hers. The thought was so very, very tempting.

But not wanting to ruin this moment, he pressed a kiss to her cheek instead. "Thank you, for all of this."

Color filled her cheeks. "You're welcome."

And then before she could eat her food, she was called away to the kitchen. He wanted to go after her—to offer his help with whatever it might be. But he knew he couldn't push this thing between them—this second chance at a friendship.

"She's certainly something, isn't she?"

Enzo glanced up to find Vito standing there, smiling. "Excuse me?"

"Sylvie, she did all of this for you. You're one lucky man to have her in your life."

"She's not in my life." The statement came out with more force than he'd meant.

Vito's bushy brows rose high on his forehead. "Really? I thought you two were a couple."

Enzo gave a firm shake of his head. He cleared his throat. "We're just friends." Not wanting to continue this discussion, he said, "Excuse me. I need to go check on something."

As Enzo walked away, he couldn't stop thinking about what Vito had said. There was still a part of him that wished Vito was right. But he had absolutely nothing to offer her.

His life was in turmoil. He wasn't even sure where he was going to live once the estate was sold. And then there was the fact he didn't deserve to have Sylvie in his life. He didn't want to fail her like he'd failed his sisters.

# CHAPTER FOUR

THERE WAS A PEP to his step.

This was going to be a good day.

Enzo had slept well for the first time in forever. He tried to tell himself it was exhaustion that had let him slumber. But he wasn't that good of a liar. He knew it was the engaging party last night. And Sylvie.

She was such a remarkable woman. He had no idea she'd been planning a surprise party. And she'd made sure to invite everyone who worked at the vineyard as well as the neighbors. It had been so thoughtful—so sweet.

Some man was going to be very fortunate to marry her. She would make a loving wife. Not to mention a wonderful mother. The vision of her holding a baby in her arms filled his mind. The baby would be a little girl and she'd be the spitting image of her mother. A smile tugged at the corners of his mouth.

Then the image morphed as he envisioned Sylvie laughing at something. A man moved next to her, placing an arm around her waist and pulling her gently to his side. She melted into him. The love in her eyes—

Enzo's thoughts screeched to a halt. The smile that had been playing on his lips turned to a distinctive frown. Not that he had any claim over Sylvie. They may have shared a night—a special night—but it was over. And he wanted her to be happy. He just didn't want to think about her being happy with someone else.

"Enzo, are you out here?" Sylvie's voice was carried on the morning breeze.

It was though his thoughts of her had drawn her to him. Of course, that was silly. Things like that didn't happen.

"I'm over here." He took a sip of his quickly cooling coffee and then he turned to her.

"Good morning." She sent him a smile.

Was it just him or did she look a bit on the pale side? It was probably the party last night. It had been hugely successful, but it had to have been a lot for her to set up so quickly. And then it had run late into the evening.

He suddenly felt bad for not ending the party sooner. But after he'd eaten the delicious food and amazing cake Sylvie had baked, which he didn't believe could have come out of a box, he'd had a renewed energy. He'd made his way around the room talking with everyone who took time out of their busy lives to show up.

And gifts. There were gifts for him. A smile tugged at his lips, knowing people cared that much. There were books, wine from competitors, which were gag gifts, a wall hanging and more. It had been an amazing night. And it was all thanks to Sylvie. Sweet, sweet Sylvie.

He moved toward her and pulled out a chair from the table. "Here. Have a seat." When surprise registered in her eyes, he added, "You must be tired after all you did yesterday."

She hesitated then she sat. "Just a little tired. Although, I have to admit I was asleep last night as soon as my head hit the pillow."

"I bet. You really went above and beyond." And then he realized to his horror that he'd been so caught off guard last night that he hadn't thanked her. At least, he couldn't remember doing it. He sat next to her. "Thank you so much for the party. No one has ever thrown me a surprise party."

A smile lit up her face. "You're welcome. But it wasn't just me. Everyone chipped in and helped."

"But it was your idea and that cake, it was so good. I wanted to have some for breakfast but I couldn't find where you hid it."

"I… I didn't hide it." The smile slipped from her face. "I'm sorry. It's all gone."

"I'm not surprised. It was delicious."

"I can bake you another one."

"Are you kidding?" When he saw the serious look on her face, he said, "I don't want you to go to all of that trouble."

"I would."

"I know you would. And I really appreciate it—appreciate you." Now, what had he gone and added that last part for? It sounded too intimate. Too much like they were involved. Or maybe he was overthinking things. "Let me get you some coffee—"

"No." When he turned to her, certain he hadn't heard her right, she said, "I… I'll get some later."

"Later? Since when don't you drink coffee as soon as you wake up?"

She shrugged. "I think I've been drinking too much of it. My stomach has been bothering me. So I'm taking a break."

"Maybe you're getting sick."

She shook her head. "I feel fine otherwise."

His gaze searched hers. What was going on with her? Maybe she'd overdone it yesterday. Or maybe it was stress over the pending sale of the estate.

*Buzz. Buzz.*

His phone vibrated in his pocket. He didn't want to be

interrupted now. He wanted to make sure nothing serious was going on with Sylvie. But when he checked his caller ID, he couldn't not answer it.

"Happy birthday," Bianca said.

Gia echoed her words.

"You're both on here?"

"Yes," Bianca said. "We feel awful about missing your birthday."

"It's okay." It wasn't, but his pride refused to let him make a big deal of this. "No big deal—"

"Yes, it is," Gia said. "We didn't mean to miss your big day."

"But we have something special planned for you." A giddiness filled Bianca's voice.

That didn't sound good. His sisters and surprises could be a dangerous combination. "You don't have to do anything special. I'm fine."

"Of course we do. Mamma would expect us to do something," Gia said.

Silence filled the phone line. He knew that everyone was thinking of their parents and missing them. But at least his sisters had the strength to move on. He had to do that now, too—get away from all of the memories.

Still, he knew his sisters would keep going on about making a big deal out of his birthday unless he gave them a reason not to. "In fact, Sylvie—" he lifted his gaze, finding that she'd left the veranda, probably to give him some privacy "—planned a big surprise party."

Both of his sisters gushed at once and then they started pummeling him with questions about who was there and what had happened during the party. But it was the last question that he stumbled on. Was he involved with Sylvie?

The word *no* rushed to the back of his mouth, but then

it stuck there. Why was he hesitating? They weren't involved. Not since Paris.

"Enzo, are you still there?" Bianca asked.

"He just doesn't want us to know what we've suspected all along—he's totally into Sylvie." Gia's voice was gleeful.

"Stop." His voice came out gruffer than he'd intended. He didn't need his sisters ganging up on him right now—and certainly not about Sylvie.

"Woah!" Gia said. "Did we hit a nerve?"

"Gia," Bianca said, "I think we better leave it alone."

He knew he needed a distraction. And boy, did he have a huge distraction. He'd been putting off telling his sisters that he was selling the estate. He wasn't sure how they would take the news. The last thing in the world he wanted to do was cause them more pain. Still, they had moved on with their lives. Would the sale be an issue for them? Regardless, he needed to tell them now—before things progressed with the sale.

Enzo swallowed hard. "There's something I need to tell you both."

"I know," Bianca said, "you're getting married."

Gia gasped.

"What? No." He shook his head. "Where do you two come up with this stuff?"

"Well," Gia said, "you are getting older—"

"Gia," Bianca said, "it was a rhetorical question."

"Oh."

He smiled and shook his head. Maybe not everything had changed. His sisters were still acting like the fun, loving sisters he remembered back before the car accident upended all their lives in ways they never could have imagined.

"Okay, you two. I'm not getting married." The smile

faded from his face. "But I do have something very serious to tell you."

An ominous silence fell over them.

"Are…are you sick?" Gia asked.

"Not that serious," he said. This was going all sorts of wrong. He just needed to say it and get it over with. "I'm selling the estate."

"What?" came the collective response.

He gave them a moment to get past the initial shock. He cleared his throat. "When I was in Paris, I was made an offer I can't turn down."

"But you competed against us in order to win the estate," Gia said.

"We thought you wanted it," Bianca said. "What about the vineyard?"

"What about our family home?" Gia's voice held disbelief.

He hadn't been sure how they would take the news, but he didn't think he'd have to defend himself. "Seeing as both of you have moved away—far away—I didn't think you'd care what happened to the estate."

"We care," Gia said.

Another strained silence filled the line.

"But we care about you more," Bianca said.

"Bianca?" Gia said. "You surely can't want to part with our childhood home."

"What I want and for that matter what you want, doesn't matter. We picked our futures. It's time to let our brother do what's right for him."

He should say something, anything, but he wasn't sure what that should be. He loved his sisters and he didn't want to do anything to upset them. Would they understand that he just couldn't stay here? He couldn't have a daily reminder of his failures in life.

"I'm sorry," Gia said. "Bianca's right. You were always there for us. We'll support whatever decision you make. But are you really sure you want to do this?"

This time there was no hesitation. "I'm sure."

"But where will you go?"

"What will you do?"

His sisters peppered him with questions and though he had work to do, he indulged them. After all, they were taking this news really well. And if answering all their questions—questions that didn't pertain to Sylvie—made them feel better, he could do that for them.

By the time he hung up the phone, an entire hour had passed. Before he headed to the vineyard, he wanted to say something to Sylvie. He found her in the kitchen, finishing a glass of fresh-squeezed *spremuta* and a roll with butter and jam. He was relieved to see the color in her cheeks and that she had an appetite.

"Sorry about that," he said. "It was my sisters."

"No problem. I just wanted to give you some space." She placed her plate and juice glass in the sink. "And now I have to finalize some details for a wedding this weekend."

"Ah, sure. I need to get to work, too."

"I'll talk to you later."

With that, she was gone and he was left alone with his thoughts. His sisters said they were okay with the sale, but he had to wonder if that was the truth. And Sylvie was being so nice to him—too nice. What was up with that?

## CHAPTER FIVE

So what had his sisters said?

Sylvie was dying to know if he'd told them about the sale of the estate, but she resisted questioning him because it wasn't her business. But that didn't keep her from wondering if they thought it was as big a mistake as she did. Would they be her allies?

Well, obviously not. Because there was no way she was going to wedge herself between the siblings—even if Bianca was a friend, a good friend. No, this was a battle she was going to have to wage on her own.

And it didn't help that Enzo kept doing one thing after another to surprise her—like at the party last night. In the beginning, he hadn't been overly enthused by it. In fact, she wasn't even sure if he'd stay for it. But as time went by, he started to eat the food, talk to the guests, and by the end of the evening he was laughing and smiling. Who'd have imagined?

So the first part of her plan was a success; now she just had to keep going. She had to keep finding ways to remind Enzo what was important about this place. And so far she had no plan of action for today. Worst of all, the day was almost over.

They'd just finished dinner, which they'd shared since they were the only two staying at the estate. They'd agreed that in order to make it fair, one would cook and the other would clean up—though they both always seemed to share cleanup duty.

Tonight Sylvie was washing the pans, and Enzo was drying, when the front door chimed. They both turned to each other with a puzzled look on their faces.

Sylvie was the first to speak. "I'm not expecting anyone."

"Neither am I." Enzo set aside the pan and towel.

As he headed for the door, Sylvie dried off her hands. They didn't get a lot of visitors at the estate now that the hotel was closed. Curiosity got the best of her and she turned for the front door.

She rushed to catch up with Enzo. But with his long legs and swift strides, she didn't have a chance to catch him before he reached the door. So she hung back. After all, this wasn't her home—not really. And soon she'd have to move—whether she wanted to or not.

She stood in the hallway as Enzo swung the door open. What—ahem, or should she say who—stood there was surprising, to say the least. A clown.

Like a real clown with curly, fire engine-red hair that poked out in all directions and a little black boiler hat on top. In his hand was a fistful of red ribbons leading to at least two dozen helium balloons. His face was painted white with his eyes outlined in black. And red paint had his mouth painted into a permanent smile.

When Sylvie realized her mouth was gaping she pushed her lips together, but they immediately bowed up into a smile as laughter bubbled up inside her. What in the world?

The clown wore a red jumper of sorts with a big lace collar.

Before Enzo could speak, because obviously he was having problems making sense of what he was seeing, the clown broke out into a rendition of the birthday song topped off with a little dance. Sylvie couldn't hold back her amusement. This was just too much.

Apparently, her laughter came out louder than she'd hoped because Enzo turned to her and frowned. His grumpy scowl just made her laugh that much harder. Whoever did this had definitely caught him off guard. And then she realized who would have done this. His sisters.

Sylvie reached for her phone in her pocket and started recording. The clown danced around, sang and then bowed at the end.

Enzo didn't say a word. The clown looked at him expectantly. Enzo stood as though he'd turned to stone. He really needed to lighten up.

Hoping to defuse the situation, Sylvie rushed forward to stand next to Enzo. She applauded the clown, who handed over the balloons to Enzo.

"Wait," the clown said, "there's one more thing."

The clown rushed back to his car. Yes, it was a little clown car with a black top hat, different-colored spots all over it and a big red nose on the hood. It was quite… She couldn't find the right word, so she settled for *unusual*. Sylvie wasn't even sure how the man fit in the car.

"Did you do this?" Enzo's voice rumbled with unhappiness.

"Oh, no." She held up her hands as she shook her head. But the smile just wouldn't fade from her face. This was priceless. "I had absolutely nothing to do with it. I'm innocent. I swear."

As soon as he absorbed what she'd told him, she saw the flicker of light go on in his eyes. "My sisters. They did this."

"That would be my guess."

His scowl darkened. "Wait until I see them again."

"You'll what?" She knew it was an empty threat. He loved his sisters dearly.

She'd always longed to be a part of a bigger family. She wanted at least a sister. Someone to style hair with and paint their nails. It would have been amazing to have someone to grow up with—to share the good and the bad.

Instead, it was just her and her mother. Thank goodness they had good friends and neighbors. But it wasn't quite the same as having brothers and sisters of her own—not to mention a father. A pang of sorrow settled in her chest.

And now, after observing Enzo and his sisters, she couldn't help but envy their closeness, the way they teased each other and the way they pulled together. It was special. And sometimes she wondered if Enzo realized just how special a relationship he had with his sisters. Sylvie would give anything to have just a little part of that family camaraderie.

Before Enzo could answer, the clown returned with a white box. "This is for you. I hope you have a happy birthday."

"It's not my birthday," Enzo said grumpily.

The clown's forehead scrunched up. He shrugged, turned and walked away.

Enzo closed the door. "When my sisters said they had something special planned, I had no idea they'd go this far."

Sylvie lightly elbowed him. "Lighten up. They just wanted to make you smile. Not scowl like you're doing now."

"I'm not scowling." His brows were still drawn together as his lips pressed into a firm line.

"Really?" She arched a brow at him as she smiled.

"I'm not." He attempted a smile but it didn't work out. The disgruntled look on his face only succeeded in sending her into another fit of giggles. Immediately, his frown returned.

It took her a moment or two to gather herself. "So what's in the box?"

He glanced down at the white box in his hand as though he'd totally forgotten. He let go of all the balloons when he went to open the box. Both of their heads lifted as the balloons sailed up and up in the two-story foyer.

"Great." Enzo frowned at them. "Now, how am I supposed to get those down?"

"You aren't. They'll come down in time." She studied him as he stared up at the balloons. "You did get helium balloons as a kid, didn't you?"

He shook his head. "No balloons. Just a nice dinner, cake and a couple of presents."

Sylvie couldn't believe she had something over on him. Her mother had planned themed birthday parties with balloons and hats and whatever else she could think of. Enzo might have had the big, loving family that she'd always wanted, but her mother had doted on her and given her other special memories that she hadn't thought of in a very long time.

"What?" Enzo was studying her.

"Um, nothing. I was just remembering my birthdays from when I was a kid."

"What were they like?"

She shrugged. "My mother would invite all of the local kids and she'd always have a theme. One year it was jungle animals. She would have games and little prizes. Nothing that cost much but just enough to make the kids feel special."

"Those sound like some good memories."

"They are. And thank you for helping me to remember." But she didn't want to dwell on the past and all that she'd lost since then. "So what's in the box?"

She moved over next to him as he lifted the lid. They both peered inside to find a beautiful cake. The background was white frosting but the decorations were deep purple flowers, hunter green leaves and a gold vine winding its way around the cake as though it was some sort of wreath.

She couldn't help but think of the vineyard when she looked at the cake. Sylvia wondered if his sisters had picked the decorations out intentionally. Of course, there weren't any grapes or barrels, but the color scheme with the purple flowers and green leaves on a vine certainly resembled the vineyard. She couldn't help but wonder if Bianca and Gia were sending their brother a message. Were they gently urging him to keep the estate?

Sylvie's gaze moved to Enzo. His scowl had softened. In fact, there was a small smile pulling at the corners of his lips. He liked the cake? And the reminder of the vineyard that he was selling?

She glanced back at the cake and then realized she'd missed the rest of the decoration. In the center of the cake in purple frosting was scrolled out *To The Best Brother*.

"Aww…" Sylvie smiled. "That's so sweet."

"But so not true." He closed the box.

"Of course it is."

He shook his head. "If it was, I wouldn't have let them down when they needed me most."

He walked away before she could respond. Not that she knew what to say to that. Enzo was being harder on himself than he should be. Sure, he was selling the estate, but that didn't make him a bad brother. She had to help him see this if she had any hope of him changing his mind about selling the estate.

\* \* \*

Why was everyone making such a fuss?

Enzo placed the cake box on the kitchen counter. His sisters knew he didn't like a fuss being made over his birthday. A card was fine. It was discreet but meaningful. What his sisters had done was big, loud and embarrassing. They did it because they felt guilty over forgetting his birthday.

Honestly, he couldn't blame them. They had new, exciting lives now. He would, too. As soon as he concluded the sale of the estate. Which meant he had to talk to Sylvie about the weddings she had scheduled. They'd either have to hold off the sale or, preferably, move the events to another location. He'd even pick up the tab for moving them elsewhere.

"Do you mind if I cut the cake?" Sylvie's voice interrupted his thoughts.

His gaze moved from her to the cake and back again. "You want to eat it?"

Her fine brows drew together. "That is the purpose of cake, isn't it?"

"Uh, yes. Go ahead." He was flustered and not making sense.

The truth was that he was dreading their upcoming conversation. He knew how much the wedding business meant to Sylvie. That was why he'd let her continue the business after he'd shut down the hotel. But now he had a potential buyer and he couldn't put the conversation off any longer.

Maybe talking over cake would make what he said easier to take. Oh, who was he kidding? This wasn't going to be easy.

He thought after he told her he was selling the estate that she would have been angry with him, but instead, she'd thrown him a birthday party. What was up with that?

Maybe it was shock. Maybe the reality wasn't sinking in. Or maybe she'd misunderstood him and thought he said he was thinking about selling.

This evening he had to make sure she understood this sale was a certainty. And they needed to figure out dates for winding up the wedding business. He was pretty certain from what the buyer had said that he wouldn't be inclined to open up any part of the estate for strangers to come in, either to tour the winery or to host a wedding.

And for that, Enzo felt awful. He didn't want to hurt Sylvie. She'd been nothing but kind to him. But he would make this up to her. He wasn't sure how yet, but he'd figure out a way.

"I thought we'd eat dessert outside. It's such a lovely and warm evening." Sylvie held a plate with a slice of chocolate cake out to him.

He accepted her offer and followed her to the veranda. It was one of his favorite parts of the house. The veranda was spacious and yet it wasn't too big. It overlooked the vines and that normally made him smile. There was just something about the fresh earth, the abundant vines and the promise of a bountiful harvest that made him happy.

But right now his attention was fully focused on Sylvie. She moved toward the balustrade and then turned back to him. With the setting sun splashing brilliant oranges, pinks and purples across the sky, it was like she'd just stepped into a painting. And he was totally captivated by her beauty, both inside and out.

For a moment he imagined what it might be like if they'd carried on their fling after returning from Paris. Would they have romantic evenings like this followed by passionate, sleepless nights?

Or would their hot flame have burnt out by now? If so,

where would that have left them? He definitely didn't think they'd be standing here sharing cake.

He told himself he was right to end things when he did. But looking at Sylvie now with her hair down over her shoulders and a light breeze combing through her silky hair, he didn't feel right. He felt like he'd made the biggest mistake of his life.

"Aren't you going to sit down?" Her voice jarred him from his thoughts.

"No. I have to check a new valve we installed at the winery earlier today. And if I sit down now, I might not move again."

"I understand. I have days like that."

They turned back to the beautiful scenery. They ate their cake in silence. The cake was so delicate that it practically melted on his tongue. The mascarpone frosting was whipped to perfection. And the berry filling gave the cake a pop of flavor. He might have preferred skipping the singing clown but his sisters had outdone themselves with this cake.

All too soon the cake was gone. And the moment he'd been dreading had arrived. How did he say this to her without ruining this easiness that they'd regained? Maybe that was it. Maybe he should let her know how much all of this meant to him.

"I should get moving," she said. "I need to go over my to-do list for the wedding this weekend." She took his empty plate from him, stacking it with her own and then turned toward the house.

"Wait," he said, still trying to figure out how to word this.

She turned back to him with curiosity showing in her eyes. "What do you need?"

"I need to talk to you." He rubbed his damp palms

down over his jeans. "I mean, I wanted to apologize to you about Paris."

"We've been over this. I really don't want to talk about it."

"I know. I'm sorry. What I was trying to tell you in my own jumbled way is that I don't want it to ruin our friendship."

"It hasn't." She sent him a reassuring smile. "You and I, we'll always be friends."

He stepped toward her. His gaze met hers. "Do you really mean that?"

"I do." There had been no hesitation in her words.

"Thank you."

"For what?"

"Giving me a second chance."

She had no idea how much her words meant to him. It wasn't until that moment that he realized just how important their relationship was to him. She meant more to him than he was willing to admit, even to himself.

His gaze dipped to her lips. There was a tiny dab of frosting on her bottom lip. He longed to lean forward and lick it off her berry-red lips. The urge swelled within him.

The truth was that he couldn't forget about their steamy encounter in Paris. It haunted his dreams at night. Teasing and taunting him.

During the day he thought he'd finally gotten a handle on things. But standing here so close to Sylvie, he realized that he'd only been fooling himself. She had gotten into his blood and he had no idea how to undo the spell she had over him.

When he lifted his gaze upward, he noticed the twinkle of interest in her eyes. Desire stirred in his gut. In that moment he started to question his judgment. Maybe just a little kiss wouldn't be so bad. After all, she didn't seem to reject the idea. In fact, the look in her beautiful brown eyes was one of interest. She was interested in him?

Was it possible she didn't regret their night together like he'd been imagining? Had he jumped to all the wrong conclusions?

He halted his rambling thoughts. He stepped back and raked his fingers through his hair. He couldn't believe he'd almost talked himself into kissing her.

"Sorry about that," he said. "I need to get going."

Before she could say anything, he strode away. He didn't trust himself to stay there in the last lingering rays of the sun with the most beautiful woman he'd ever known.

It wasn't until he was almost to the vineyard that he realized he hadn't done what he'd set out to do. He hadn't talked to her about winding down the wedding business. And now he was hesitant to go near her again. She had to know that he'd almost kissed her.

His feet kept moving. Their talk could wait for another day—a day when he had his head screwed on straight.

Sylvie was off-limits to him. It was the way it had to be. He refused to hurt her again when he couldn't commit to a relationship—not when he let down the people closest to him.

# CHAPTER SIX

HAD THAT REALLY HAPPENED?

Had Enzo almost kissed her?

Saturday morning Sylvie was still thinking about that moment on the veranda a few nights ago. In fact, it'd taken up a lot of her thoughts. Perhaps too many because she'd had to rush to put the finishing touches on this wedding. A wedding that was about to take place in the garden.

And yet, when she was supposed to be checking last-minute things off on her to-do list, she was thinking about the way Enzo had stared into her eyes—the desire that had flashed in them. And then there was the way his look had sent her heart racing.

At times his gaze could be so intent that it was like he could see straight through her—like he could see what made her tick. All this time she'd been fooling herself into thinking she had kept her attraction to him under wraps—that there was no way he knew just how much she wished he would pull her into his arms and kiss her. But then what?

This is where things got really muddled. In her daydreams and for that matter, in her nighttime dreams, she never got past the arms wrapped around each other and the lips pressing to each other. She supposed it was because she couldn't imagine what normally came next—a loving and committed relationship.

The truth was relationships didn't last. She'd learned that lesson over and over again in her life. It was best to just keep things light and simple.

Because putting her tattered heart on the line wasn't something she was willing to do. The thought of letting herself feel deeply for Enzo and then losing him—she gave herself a mental shake. It wasn't going to happen. She wouldn't let it.

The only reason she had planned the surprise party was to remind Enzo of what he had here at the estate—what he would lose if he were to sell it. The party, the cake and all the other arrangements she'd seen to... Well, those had nothing to do with her feelings for him because...because she had those all under control.

So how did she explain what had happened in Paris? It was that city—the city of love. It had cast some sort of spell over her—over them. But once they'd returned to Tuscany, they were both able to see what a mistake they'd made. There was nothing between them—nothing more than a casual friendship.

Okay, maybe that wasn't quite true. Maybe it was more like a close friendship—at least that was the way things used to be. Enzo used to confide in her and she had done the same with him. But ever since that one night, there had been an awkwardness between them—much like a wall. One that each of them had taken some comfort in hiding behind. But now it was getting in her way. Now she needed to knock it down, if she was going to convince him not to sell the estate.

*Ring. Ring.*

It was the house phone. The only thing it was used for these days was business. Personal calls went to their cell phones. Sylvie checked the time on her fitness tracker. There was less than an hour now until the wedding ceremony. Surely, this wasn't bad news regarding the wedding.

The phone rang again.

Her gaze quickly skimmed down over her checklist. No. Everything was done and the caterer had already set up finger food in the dining room. There was nothing to worry about.

And yet, as she picked up the phone, she couldn't help but wonder if this phone call would somehow help or hinder her efforts to keep her home and a job at which she was quite skilled.

"Hello. This is the Barto Vineyard. How may I help you?"

"Hello. My name is Jameson Asaro and I'm with *Tuscany Views* magazine. We're interested in doing a big spread about your vineyard and the prestigious award your winery won in Paris."

"Oh. Wow." Her mind was racing. This could be the help she needed to sway Enzo's decision about keeping or selling the estate. "That would be wonderful."

"Can I take that as confirmation that you'd like us to visit the estate to do our research for the article?"

"Um, can you hold on for a moment?"

"Sure."

She pushed a button on the phone, putting it on hold while she fished her cell phone out of her pocket. She quick-dialed Enzo. The phone rang and rang before going to voice mail.

She knew if Enzo was out in the fields that there were many places with no reception. Of all the days for him to be out of reach. Frustration balled up in her stomach. This was so important.

She moved the landline receiver back to her ear. "I'm

sorry about that. I was just trying to reach someone at the vineyard. Could we get back to you—?"

"I don't think you understand the urgency of this. We just had a last-minute cancellation and we need a big story. Something we can cover right away."

"Oh. I… I…uh…" What was she supposed to say? She tried to imagine Enzo's response. Would he welcome the coverage? It was really special. This online and print magazine stretched throughout Italy and beyond its borders. It was quite a coup.

"I need a decision now." The man's voice was firm.

Her palms grew damp. The last thing she wanted to do was to make the wrong decision and have Enzo upset with her. As it was, they were just starting to find an easiness with each other after Paris. If she were to make the wrong choice here and they went back to acting like strangers again, she'd never convince him that selling the estate was a big mistake—a huge mistake.

But what if she were to pass on the publicity, would Enzo get upset? In fact, she'd been so busy worrying about what he'd do if she were to accept the offer that she hadn't stopped to think about it in reverse. Turning down the offer could be a mistake, too. Either way it was a gamble.

Her stomach knotted knowing the man on the other end of the phone was expecting her to make a decision now— right now. And if she picked the wrong one, it could mean losing her ability to reason with Enzo.

She worried her bottom lip. All her attention was focused on whether she should or shouldn't. Should or shouldn't. The words revolved around in her mind at a dizzying pace—

"Hello," the man said, "are you still there?"

The moment of truth had arrived. "Um, yes, I am."

"And are you willing to do the article?"

"Yes." The word popped out of her mouth and then she realized it was too late to take it back. Her fate had been sealed. She just didn't know how any of this was going to work out. And dealing with the unknown was something she didn't do well. She liked plans and certainties.

"Very good. We'll arrive Thursday."

"As in this coming Thursday? Less than a week from now?"

"Yes, ma'am. Is that a problem?"

A problem? Not that she could think of, but Enzo might have a differing opinion. "No, it's not."

"Good. We'll need a tour of the vineyard. We're going to need photos."

"Photos?" She hadn't considered what all would be involved with this.

"Yes, we'll need photos to go along with the write-up."

"Of course." She would normally have anticipated this if her thoughts weren't being pulled in so many different directions.

Thankfully, the estate was in tip-top shape. So pictures shouldn't be a big deal. Right? Surely, Enzo would be happy about this interest in the vineyard, wouldn't he?

She assured herself that she had nothing to worry about. After concluding the phone call, she wrote Enzo a note and left it in what was now his office. And then she set off to change into her dress for the wedding. It was almost time for the bride and groom to say *I do*.

What was wrong with him?

Every time Enzo was in Sylvie's vicinity, he was nearly kissing her or thinking about kissing her. And that just wasn't right. He was the one taking away not only her job but also her home.

And there was another thing. He kept delaying talking to her about the final date for the last wedding at the estate. No matter how much he dreaded doing it, the talk had to take place. In fact, he'd put it off too long as it was.

After a long day in the fields, he had one more thing he needed to do. He wanted to test these new oak barrels for leakage and then he would head to the little guesthouse on the property where Sylvie lived. He was certain she wouldn't want to see him, not after the way he'd handled himself earlier that week—or rather how he'd been out of control, letting his desire dictate his actions. That was why he'd been up extra early every morning and returned late each evening.

"Something on your mind?" Vito asked.

"No. Why?"

Vito nodded toward the hose. "Because you're spilling water all over the floor."

"What?" Enzo glanced down to see that the barrel was full and the excess water was forming a puddle on the floor. He rushed to turn off the water. When the hose was drained, he turned to an amused Vito. "Aren't you supposed to be on holiday with your family?"

"I just stopped on my way out of town to check on things and see if you need anything."

Enzo grabbed a rag to clean up his mess. This accident was minor but it was indicative of why he didn't belong here any longer. He was forever distracted. Where once his work had been all-encompassing and fulfilling, now his mind was on other things. "Thanks, but I don't need a thing. Have a good trip."

Vito didn't say a word for a moment. He just stared thoughtfully at him.

Enzo grew uncomfortable beneath his friend's stare. "Whatever it is, just say it."

"I'm wondering what's on your mind." Vito's expression turned serious. "Or should I say *who*?"

Enzo shook his head. "No one is on my mind." *Liar.* "I just have a lot to do before the estate sale goes through."

For a moment a strained silence filled the air. Enzo knew Vito didn't agree with his decision to sell the estate. They'd already had a heated disagreement. Enzo was hoping Vito would accept the inevitable, even if he didn't agree with him. Enzo was certain the new owner would keep him on to manage the place, as they'd already discussed it.

"Seems like Sylvie is trying to sway you into changing your mind about the sale," Vito said as he propped himself up against the worktable.

Enzo moved around the barrel, searching for any leaks. So far it looked good. "She's wasting her time. It's practically a done deal."

"You didn't sign the papers, did you?" There was concern in Vito's voice.

"No. But I will as soon as we work out the final terms."

"So there's still time for you to change your mind?"

"It's not going to happen." If this was anyone but his father's best friend, he would have told Vito to buzz off already. But Vito was a part of the family. He was like his uncle and no matter how much he stepped on Enzo's nerves, he just couldn't tell him to get lost.

"Did you ever consider raising your family here? Maybe with Sylvie."

That was it. He wasn't getting away with that—favorite uncle or not. Enzo straightened to his full height. But when he turned, he found Vito had already made a hasty exit. No one could ever accuse Vito of not being a wise man because right about now Enzo was about to unload all of his pent-up frustration when—

"Enzo?" It was Sylvie's voice. "Enzo, are you in here?"

"Back here," he called out. It was only after he'd spoken that he realized the mistake he'd made. He was in no frame of mind to deal with her. He was certain she'd want to talk about that almost-kiss and want to analyze its meaning.

Her footsteps approached and he braced himself for her anger or accusations. He just needed to get it over quickly and then he'd tell her that he needed her final date for the wedding business. Quick. Simple.

He gave himself a mental shake. Nothing was simple when it came to Sylvie. It was more like complicated and confusing. But Vito had been right. She was doing everything in her power to sway his decision about the sale. It wasn't going to work. But that didn't keep him from wondering what she'd try next.

"Oh, there you are." She joined him at the worktable.

"What did you need?"

"Did you happen to see the note I left you in the office?"

He shook his head. "I haven't been in the house since this morning. I always make plans to stay far away on wedding days."

"I don't blame you." It was the first time she'd said something like that.

"You make it sound like you don't like the weddings."

She shrugged. "I just know they get loud and congested. And if you don't have to be there, it's best to find a nice quiet corner of the estate. I know that's what I'd do if I could."

He wasn't sure what she was trying to tell him. And he wasn't in the mood to figure it out. But since she was here and before he forgot, he said, "Sylvie, we have to talk about the wedding business."

When her gaze met his, there was a sadness in her eyes. The look tore at his gut. It felt like no matter what decision he made it was going to be the wrong answer for someone.

But Sylvie was smart and talented. She would land on her feet. And it wasn't like he was planning to kick her to the curb. He would pay for her moving costs and her housing until she was able to get settled. He'd even help her find another job, not that he knew anything about weddings. Still, he would do what he could with job references and utilizing all of his contacts.

"What about it?" she asked in a softer voice than normal.

He sighed. This was so much harder than he'd imagined. "We need to set a final close date for the business." When she didn't say anything but instead stood there looking at him like he was the enemy, he said, "I'm sorry things worked out like this."

He didn't know what he expected—for her to yell at him or to stomp off. But she did neither of those things. She started naming off weddings from memory. They were weddings that stretched well into the next year. He knew canceling them would create a lot of drama for not only Sylvie but also the couples and their families. The guilt mounted.

"When you told me the estate was to be sold," Sylvie said, "I started working out a plan. I spoke with a stellar wedding planner in Florence. She was willing to take on some of my clients. And the ones she couldn't fit into her schedule, I plan to handle myself but with a different venue. I just have one final wedding here at the estate."

"You did all of this already?"

She looked at him like, *well, of course.* "I couldn't afford to wait around and hope something would change. We're talking about the biggest day in someone's life. I couldn't ruin it and so I've been spending most of my time making alternative plans."

"I bet it didn't go well."

She glanced away and shook her head. "There were a lot of upset people."

"I'm sorry, Sylvie. I never meant to put you in such an awful position." Once again he hadn't been able to spare the feelings of someone he cared about. If only he'd thought of all the ramifications of selling the estate; maybe he could have made this easier on Sylvie. He wasn't sure how and it really didn't matter now. The damage was done. "What did you come here to tell me?"

She wrung her hands together. "There was an important phone call this morning, while you were out in the fields. I tried to reach you."

His gut twisted up in a knot of worry. "Was it my sisters? Did something happen to one of them?"

"No." She shook her head. "Sorry. I didn't mean to worry you. It's nothing like that."

He blew out a pent-up breath. "Then what was this important call?"

"It was about your big win in Paris." She sent him a smile that didn't quite reach her eyes. "Word is out and *Tuscany Views* magazine wants your story."

"My story?" He shook his head. "I don't have a story. You told them to go away, didn't you?" When she didn't immediately answer, a feeling of dread came over him. "Sylvie, what did you do?"

"All they want is to speak with you and take some photos."

"Impossible."

"Why? You deserve this. You work hard around this vineyard."

"Because..." His mind raced for a reason the interview and article were a bad idea, aside from the fact that he didn't feel he was deserving. "Because this place isn't set up for photos."

"What? Of course it is. It's always kept up for vineyard tours and wine-tasting parties."

"Not anymore. I've started taking things down and packing up the place for the new owner."

It was then that she glanced around at the bare walls. She moved to the doorway of the large wine-tasting room. There was nothing left on the walls or shelves. The room was bare except for the furniture because he had yet to find someone willing to buy it.

All the vineyard's rich history was now boxed up and put in storage. He didn't know what to do with it all. He was going to talk to his sisters about the wall hangings and plaques as well as the photos. It was a lot to go through.

"It shouldn't take long to put it all back up," Sylvie said with a hopeful note in her voice.

"When is this reporter supposed to be here?"

"Thursday."

"As in five days from now?"

Sylvie nodded. "See. Plenty of time."

At last, he had his out without hurting her feelings. "Not enough time with just one person to do it all and look after the vineyard."

"One person?" Her fine brows drew together. "But what about Vito and the others?"

"Vito is off on holiday. So are a couple of other guys. They needed a break before harvest. And the other guys are busy clearing a new field to be planted for next season. The new owner wants to expand the vineyard."

"Oh. Okay." Sylvie paused as she processed this information. "We can still do this. I'll help you."

He shook his head. "I don't think so. It's not your job."

"But I told them you'd do it and I didn't get their number so I can't call them back."

"It's a magazine. I'm sure you can call the office and they'll put you through to the reporter."

"I didn't catch their name."

He frowned at her. He had a feeling no matter what he said she'd counter it with an answer. He knew where she was going with this. She was hoping this interview and media coverage would change his mind about selling the estate. It wouldn't.

But she was so intent on him doing this that he felt as though he owed it to her after he'd ended her wedding business. "Okay."

Her eyes widened. "Okay, what?"

"We'll do it."

"You'll do the interview and let them tour the estate?"

He didn't want to; he really didn't. Selling this estate wasn't easy for him, and reminding himself of everything he was about to turn his back on wouldn't help matters. But all the good memories were interlaced with all the bad memories—things he wanted to forget.

Still, when Sylvie looked at him with hope in her eyes, how could he turn her down? Right now he felt if she asked him for the stars and the moon, he'd climb the tallest ladder and gather them for her.

But he also remembered what Vito said about Sylvie doing anything she could to change his mind about selling the estate. He couldn't allow her to get her hopes up that he would reverse his decision and then have her crushed once more.

He cleared his throat. "Sylvie, I'll do the interview and tour, but you need to realize that I'm not going to change my mind about selling the estate. It's going to be sold."

Emotion flashed in her eyes, but in a blink it was gone before he could make it out. "I understand. Thank you for agreeing to do this. It'll make a really nice memory for you and your sisters."

He didn't know about that. Still, he kept putting one foot in front of the other as he marched toward the estate sale. He'd made the decision to turn his back on this place and it had seemed right at the time. So then why was he starting to get the feeling it was the worst decision he'd ever made?

# CHAPTER SEVEN

WOULD THIS WORK?

Sylvie hoped so.

But how had Enzo figured out what she was up to?
Sylvie thought she was being so stealthy, and all along he
knew she was trying to sway his decision about selling the
estate. So much for her secretiveness.

But maybe this was better. He knew where she stood on
the sale. Why keep it a secret? If someone vocalized their
opposition to the sale, perhaps he'd rethink his decision.
Not that her opinion was that important to him or anything.
Still, he might listen to her, if she could do it the right way.

It wasn't until he mentioned he had been packing things
that she realized there were photos and mementos missing
from the main house. Now she knew where they'd gone.
Enzo was slowly and steadily removing signs of the Bartolini family from the estate—like some sort of human
eraser. She had to wonder if by removing the physical
things if it would remove whatever memories were attached to them. Was it really that easy to turn your back
on the past?

It was midmorning by the time Sylvie made it to the
winery. She'd intended to be there much earlier, but she'd
gotten caught up finding a new venue for an upcoming

wedding. It broke her heart to turn away business, but Enzo wasn't giving her much option.

When she stepped into the winery, she found Enzo making notes on his digital tablet. "Sorry I'm late. I had some work that needed doing."

"If you don't have time for this we could cancel—"

"No." She shook her head. "I can manage everything." She glanced around at the bare walls. They were like canvases just waiting to be adorned with color. "I like it here."

"You do?"

She nodded. "I don't know why. Maybe because it's so different from the main house. Whereas the house is cozy and warm, this room is huge—" she gazed up at the two-story ceilings "—and it has an industrial feel with the metallic tanks. I don't know. I just like it."

Enzo glanced around as if trying to see it the way she did. "I spent a lot of time down here as a kid. This was the best room to hide in when playing hide-and-seek with my sisters. They were afraid of the big tanks so they didn't venture in here much."

She smiled as she imagined Enzo as a small child. "So what you're saying is that you cheated."

"I did not. I won fair and square. They could have come in here, if they'd wanted."

"Uh-huh." She continued to smile as she shook her head. "And your father didn't mind you playing in here."

"He minded. But he didn't know everything that went on."

"So you were sneaky, too?"

His dark brows drew together. "Hey. I don't think I like the picture you're painting of me as a child."

"Just calling it like I see it." She laughed at his look of outrage.

"I definitely don't want you talking to the reporter." He

turned, setting the tablet on the worktable. He retrieved a utility knife and moved off to the side of the table where there was a stack of cardboard boxes. He sliced open the tape on the top of one.

"I could give them a more balanced story," she said, enjoying this bit of banter. It'd been far too long since they'd had this much fun together. This day was definitely looking up. "With what I'm learning about you, they could do an exposé about the real man behind the image."

His brows drew together. "What image?"

"Oh, I don't know. The handsome winemaker with an award-winning touch."

His frown lines smoothed as a smile lifted the corners of his mouth. "I wouldn't give up your wedding work. Journalism definitely isn't your calling."

"What? I liked that tag line. Maybe this is better—Sexy Winemaker Wins Big."

"First, who is this sexy person? And second, it wasn't that big."

"And who's being modest now?"

He didn't answer her as he lined up the framed prints on the table. "These are the photos we had hung in here for the tours that give a brief tutorial of the winemaking process."

She moved next to him. She gazed down at the photos that she'd seen numerous times in the past, but this time she saw them differently. Instead of telling the story of how grapes were turned into wine, she saw the story of Enzo's past.

In the first photo was a picture of a woman picking grapes. She was smiling brightly while holding a cluster of grapes. Sylvie didn't need to be told; it was clear it was his mother. Carla Bartolini had been a beautiful woman, just like her daughters.

Sylvie made her way down the table, looking at each

photo. Enzo quietly followed her. She wanted to ask him what he was thinking but she didn't want to disturb the moment.

She paused in front of the photo of a man in this very room. Though she'd never met Aldo Bartolini, she knew without a doubt it was Enzo's father. The resemblance was that great.

There were other photos of Enzo and his sisters when they were young. In one framed photo, the entire family was standing in front of four large holding tanks. "You all look so happy."

"Looks can be deceiving," he muttered.

"Really?" Her gaze moved from him to the photo and back to him again. "Are you saying you and your family weren't happy in this photo?"

"I'm saying I don't know." He moved next to her and stared at the photo. "I thought we were happy. But now I know all those happy moments were covering up big secrets. I don't know what was real and what was just for show."

"Maybe you don't need to figure it out. Maybe you just need to accept the memories the way they are in your mind. I'm sure your parents would want that for you."

"But how can they be so happy when they were keeping something so explosive from us?"

"Perhaps it's because they'd made peace with their decision. They had to believe they were doing the right thing for their family. And then they let it go because otherwise it would have destroyed the family you knew. Just like you need to let go of the anger at them and the guilt you've heaped on yourself before it destroys you."

He shook his head. "I don't know if I can do that. You don't understand."

Sylvie turned to him. "Why are you so willing to just reject the happiness you felt? It was a real and genuine emotion. You should be embracing it instead of rejecting it."

"Is that what you're doing? Embracing the good memories of your mother?"

"I'm trying."

"But you're still blaming yourself for not being there for her as much as you feel you should have been."

She nodded.

"Then how is that so different from what I'm doing?"

She glanced away. She supposed that in a way, it wasn't. Maybe they both had some letting-go to do. Maybe it was what they both needed to do before either of them could be truly happy.

And then she remembered something she'd forgotten in her grief. It was a conversation with her mother near the end. Sylvie had been apologizing for having to leave for work when her mother had told her she understood. And she was proud of her. She said that Sylvie was the best daughter she could have ever hoped for. And that soon she would be reunited with Sylvie's father, and both of them would be watching over her, smiling down upon her. She urged Sylvie to find a love like that for herself—a love that would last all of eternity.

Sylvie's gaze moved to Enzo. What would her mother make of him? Would she tell Sylvie to cut her losses and leave the estate? She had so many questions. In this moment she missed her mother with such a fierce intensity.

"Sylvie, are you okay?" The concern in Enzo's voice drew her from her thoughts.

She glanced at him. "What?"

"You're crying."

"I am?" She ran her fingers over her cheeks. They were damp. "I'm sorry. I was just remembering a conversation with my mother."

"It must have been serious."

"It was one of the times when I had to leave her to go to work and she told me she understood. She said she was proud of me. I can't believe I'd forgotten that." She left out the part about finding true love. She didn't want Enzo reading anything into it. Her gaze met his. "Thank you."

"For what? Making you cry?"

"No." She smiled. "For giving me back a memory—an important memory."

"You're welcome, though I don't think I did anything."

"Sometimes it's just having someone to listen. And you were that someone today."

He smiled at her. "Let's put these prints back on the wall."

"Sounds like a plan." They set to work side by side.

Enzo honestly didn't think he'd said much of anything important.

But Sylvie seemed to think differently.

For the next few days they worked together as a team cleaning, sorting and arranging. Sylvie had been extra nice to him. If he had sparked a memory in her mind, he was happy he'd been able to do that for her.

Trying to remember the past wasn't his problem. He clearly recalled his past with his parents and the illusion of a happy family. The problem was he also remembered the carnage and agony after both of his parents died.

That stupid journal had compounded matters. Why had his mother kept it? If they hadn't read it, no one would have been the wiser. Well, that wasn't true. He knew the secret. At least some of it. And the guilt for keeping that information to himself was something that dogged his steps throughout the estate.

They'd hung the prints in the tank room. And then

they'd moved to the main house, putting family photos back on the walls—some of his immediate family and others of their ancestors in black-and-white photos. By the time they had the villa fully decorated, Monday was over and they were exhausted.

Come Tuesday morning, they put back all the decorations in the barrel and tank room in the winery. There was only one room left. The wine-tasting room was part museum and part tasting space for visitors. It had taken Enzo days to take everything down and pack it away.

He glanced around at the bare, expansive walls that used to hold a collage of vineyard history. "I don't know if we're going to get this all done."

"Sure we are." Sylvie's gaze followed his before returning to him. She sent him a reassuring smile. "We just have to hurry. We'll put everything back where it came from. It will save us the time of having to figure out where things should go."

He didn't see where that would save much time. But there was no time to argue. So while he moved the squared black display stands with glass tops back into position, Sylvie opened one storage box after the next, unwrapping awards, novelties and plaques with descriptions of each item. Enzo wasn't sure why he'd packed absolutely everything but every time he went to part with something, he found a reason not to do so. His sisters might want it. The item might be valuable. Vito might want some of it. There was always an excuse close at hand.

"I have some photos on my phone that might help us put the smaller things back where they were." Sylvie pulled out her phone and placed it on the table.

Curiosity had him walking over and taking a look. There were a number of photos, not only of the wine-tasting room but also of the main house and the surrounding grounds. "Are you an amateur photographer?"

"Hardly. I just love this place and I wanted to be able to remember it. You don't mind, do you?"

"No. Not at all."

"I bet the young, ambitious you in these photos would have never imagined this day would come."

As Enzo gazed at the old family photos, he heard his father's voice in his mind: *Life never goes the way you plan. It's finding your way through life's detours that's worth the effort.*

Enzo realized this was his detour in life. He just had no idea where it was going to lead him. First, he had to wind things up here at the estate and it was proving to be more complicated than he'd ever imagined.

"Enzo?" Sylvie was giving him a strange look. "Everything okay?"

"Um, yeah. Fine. Let's get these things where they belong."

And so they worked for a while in silence. He couldn't believe she'd talked him into putting all of this stuff back. What was it about Sylvie that he was willing to do things he wouldn't do otherwise?

"What do you think?" Sylvie's gaze moved around the room. "Think we'll get it done today?"

"Today? Do you have something you want to do tomorrow?"

She smiled and nodded. He knew that smile. She looked that way when she had a plan he wasn't going to like, not like at all.

He pressed his hands to his waist. "Sylvie, what do you have in mind?"

"I thought we could head into Florence. I was thinking some flower arrangements and candles and maybe a wreath or two…or three would brighten up this place. The photos are a nice touch but the decor needs softening a bit."

He rubbed the back of his neck. "Don't set your heart on it."

She turned a serious gaze on him. "I'm not giving up on this. I'll go to Florence alone if I must."

Her words brought forth another memory. Enzo recalled his father standing in this very room saying to him, *Never give up on those you love.*

And another of his father's sayings: *Forgiveness is one of the greatest things you can give yourself and others.*

It was almost like his father knew this day was coming and in his cryptic way, he was guiding his son. But Enzo just couldn't brush aside what his parents' secret had done to his sisters. It wasn't right. Maybe his father should have taken some of his own advice.

"Enzo—" Sylvie's voice put a halt to his thoughts "—if you don't want to go, you can just say so. You don't have to scowl at me."

He was scowling? He hadn't realized his thoughts had transformed onto his face. With concerted effort, he smoothed the frown lines. "Sorry. It wasn't you. I just had a memory."

"Of your parents?"

He nodded. "It was of my father. He used to share with me these little bits of wisdom."

"Like what?"

Enzo told her what he could remember. As he was talking about his parents, he started to see them in a new light. They were more than a married couple running this estate with nary a hiccup. When you scratched beneath the surface, they were flawed individuals. But when you went even deeper, they were loving parents.

"Maybe you should reconsider selling the estate," she said.

He shook his head.

"But you have good memories. Maybe not all of them are happy—"

"Sylvie, stop!" He paused as though reining in his frustration. "It's too late."

"But you haven't signed any papers yet—"

"I gave my word."

"That's not the same as signing a sales agreement."

"For me it is." And with that he walked away.

Sylvie let go of the subject—for now. Instead, she focused on the work. Sooner or later she was going to have to admit defeat. Just not today.

# CHAPTER EIGHT

THEY WORKED WELL TOGETHER, complementing each other's skills. He did the heavy lifting. She did the final touches.

After Enzo placed the last print on the wall, he glanced around the room. His gaze settled on Sylvie as she arranged some mementos in one of the lighted glass cases. The winery looked as it had before. No. Sylvie's little adjustment here and there had made it look picture perfect.

It was late in the evening when Enzo said, "That's it for tonight."

He noticed that Sylvie didn't argue.

He led the way to the exit. He paused by the door and flipped off the lights in the winery. He knew he wouldn't sleep that night, not with all the thoughts darting about his mind. Still, it was no reason to keep Sylvie from getting some rest.

Darkness fell over the building as they stepped outside. He typed the code into the security pad before turning back to Sylvie. In the moonlight she looked like an enchantress. And it'd be so easy to forget all the reasons he shouldn't hold her close and kiss her like he'd wanted to the other day.

Instead, he started to walk. To head to the main house, he would need to walk straight ahead but instead he turned down the path to the left and continued moving toward the guesthouse. In silence they walked in the moonlight. His thoughts were filled with memories of another night when he'd been along with Sylvie. It had been an evening they'd thrown caution to the wind. It was a night they wouldn't repeat.

All too soon they were standing outside Sylvie's door. He turned to her. "Thank you for all your help today."

"You're welcome. But I think it should be me thanking you since this photo shoot was my idea."

"I know I wasn't thrilled with the idea in the beginning. And I'm sorry."

"And now?"

"Now..." His thoughts swept back over the day and all that had happened. "I think it was a good idea. The perfect way to say goodbye—to this place." He was quick to add the last bit because no matter what, he wasn't ready to say goodbye to her.

Having Sylvie walk out of his life would be harder than saying goodbye to his childhood home. But he supposed he deserved it, after sitting on his family's explosive secret all those years.

"Enzo, what is it?" Sylvie's voice was soft.

He shook his head. "Nothing."

She opened the door. "Come in."

"It's too late. And with us heading into the city tomorrow, you'll want to get some rest."

"Are you sure?"

He nodded. "I'll be fine."

In the moonlight he could make out the outline of her face but he couldn't read her eyes. He'd be willing to guess that there was a look of disbelief in them. But that was okay. This was all his problem, not hers.

When she stepped inside, she flipped on the lights. He'd

just turned to walk away when they were plunged back into darkness.

"What in the world?" The sound of the light switch being flipped on and off filled the air.

Enzo immediately spun around. "Let me see."

The only problem was that it was pitch-dark inside the house and when he went to step through the doorway, he bumped into Sylvie. He immediately reached out to steady her. He pulled her to him, perhaps with more urgency than was necessary because all of a sudden her body was pressed against his.

In that moment he hesitated. He didn't want to let her go and she didn't seem interested in going anywhere. The thought of kissing her came rushing back to the forefront of his mind. And here in the dark, who would know?

They would know. He would know. He didn't deserve Sylvie. She was the most kindhearted—the most generous—the most caring woman he'd ever known. And she deserved someone better than him. She deserved someone who faced challenges no matter how great and protected the people they loved. That wasn't him.

The thought doused the burning embers within him. He swallowed hard. "I…uh…should see what the problem is."

It was with great reluctance that he moved past her. She was quiet. If she knew of the torment going on within him, she didn't say a word.

Having memorized his way through most of the buildings on the estate over the years, he made his way to the kitchen. He felt around the wall for the light switch. He flicked it on and there was once again light.

He turned back to Sylvie, who was still in the shadows. "Looks like you have a burnt-out light. Which is strange because there should be two bulbs in that light fixture."

"Well, there are." There was some hesitancy in her

voice. "The one bulb burnt out the other day, but I didn't get around to changing it."

"I see. No problem. I'll have it fixed for you in no time."

"But you don't have to bother tonight. You must be tired."

"I doubt I'll sleep tonight." The words had slipped past his lips before he realized he was saying too much. Sylvie would want to know why he wasn't sleeping, and he wasn't up for revealing his past. The day of looking at old photos and taking a stroll down memory lane had been more than enough for him. And most of all, he just didn't want to disappoint Sylvie. She thought he was a nice guy, a good guy, and he wanted to remain that in her eyes.

And so he set to work, locating the items he would need. He knew someone else could tend to this in the morning, but he wanted to take care of Sylvie, just as she was trying to care for him by showing him what he would be giving up by selling the estate. Perhaps the gestures were not on the same scale, but he was doing what was needed in the moment.

A few minutes later he had the bulbs replaced. It was time to make his exit before he lost his head once again. But when he looked around, he didn't see Sylvie anywhere.

"Sylvie, everything is done." When there was no response, he said, "Sylvie?"

"Back here."

He walked to the back of the house, where the living room had been moved to make space for the wedding business in the front rooms. He found Sylvie seated on the couch.

She patted the cushion next to her. "Come have a seat."

He checked his wristwatch. "I... I don't think so." The truth was he didn't trust himself being that close to her. "It's really late."

"But you said you wouldn't sleep tonight."

That was true. He hadn't meant to tell her but it was too late to walk it back now. "I'll be fine."

"I've made you something to help you sleep." When he still didn't move—still didn't trust his judgment in this exhausted state—she said, "Come."

There was a firmness to her voice—the same sort of tone his mother would use when she meant business. It was amazing the things his mother could get people to do without raising her voice. Sylvie had that same poise and command. Someday she'd make a good mother. Of that he was certain.

And so he took a seat next to her, leaving a respectable distance between them. He couldn't help but feel this was a mistake, but he remained seated.

Sylvie held out a red mug. "Here. Drink this."

When he reached for it, their fingers brushed. A rush of anticipation electrified his body and it had absolutely nothing to do with the drink. His gaze met hers. He felt himself once more slipping under her spell. Enzo glanced away before it was too late. He stared down at the white frothy drink, knowing that any chance he'd had at getting some sleep was now officially gone.

He swallowed hard. "What is it?"

"It's some warmed milk that my mother would make for me whenever I was worked up from a nightmare or the night before a big test." She took a sip from her own cup.

He lifted the mug. The first thing that struck him was its soft fragrance. He wasn't sure about drinking it. He eyed up Sylvie as she took another healthy sip. Not wanting to hurt her feelings, because he was quite certain at this late hour she really didn't feel like going to all this bother, he took a small sip.

He swallowed. "This isn't warmed milk. Well, it's not just milk."

She smiled and nodded. "It has some honey, vanilla and a touch of lavender. Plus a few other things. Do you like it?"

"I…ah…" His lips pursed together as he considered the answer. He didn't hate it, but he didn't love it, either. "It's so unique. I don't think I've ever had anything like it before."

"Just keep sipping it. Trust me, it'll help relax you." She frowned at him. "You can't relax when you're perched on the edge of the couch as though you're ready to spring out the door at any moment. Sit back and relax."

This most definitely wasn't a good idea, but he was already sitting in her living room at this late hour; why not just lean back? It wasn't like she was going to throw herself into his arms. Was she? The thought definitely appealed to him.

Every muscle in his body was tense as he slid back over the cushion. And even when he was fully on the couch, he couldn't lean back. He sat fully upright, staying on guard, not letting down his defenses because he knew how easy it was to forget about circumstances when Sylvie was in his vicinity.

"Do you think there's anything that will change your mind about selling the place?"

It was the first time she'd come straight out and asked him the question. The answer that rushed to the back of his throat was one she didn't want to hear. He shifted his gaze to the contents of the mug. It might not be his favorite drink but it was better than having to speak and see the disappointment in Sylvie's eyes.

He held the mug to his lips and drank; all the while he could feel Sylvie's gaze upon him. Why couldn't she just give this up? But he knew she was waiting for an answer. The woman definitely had a lot of tenacity.

He lowered the mug. "No. I'm not going to change my mind."

"Is there anything I can say or do—?"

"No, Sylvie. This is what has to be done." The debate of keeping the estate or letting go of the ghosts of the past churned within him. "You just don't understand."

"I would, if you told me." Her voice was soft but not forceful.

The secret he'd been holding in all these years came rushing forward, teetering on the edge of his tongue. He hadn't told anyone because he was ashamed. But maybe if he wanted to let go of the ghosts, he needed to be up-front with her. If he could trust anyone, it was Sylvie.

Not giving himself time to back out of this confession, he turned to her. In her eyes he saw caring and sympathy. He wasn't worthy of either. That undid his final bit of hesitation.

"Sylvie, I know this place means a lot to you, but to me, it is filled with ghosts of the past. Lies and secrets that I just can't live with anymore. I need to move on—to start over."

"But wasn't all of that dealt with when Bianca found your mother's journal?"

"No." That single-syllable word hung in the nighttime air with all its possible implications.

He raked his fingers through his hair. Why did she keep pushing? She wasn't going to like what she uncovered. He wasn't the upstanding guy that she thought he was.

Sylvie scooted closer on the couch. She reached out, placing her hand on his thigh. It was all he could do not to jump back. Her touch was gentle and warm as she attempted to put him at ease. But didn't she realize what he'd been trying to tell her? He didn't deserve her kindness and understanding.

He jumped to his feet. He placed his mug on the end table. "I have to go."

"Enzo, wait." She rushed over to him. "I'm sorry. I pushed and I shouldn't have done that. Please forgive me."

Frustration and guilt churned in his gut. "Stop!"

Confusion clouded her eyes. "I'm sorry. I keep saying the wrong things."

"No. Stop apologizing. You haven't done anything wrong. I have. I don't deserve your sympathy. If you knew…"

The words hung there. The sentence went unfinished because he just couldn't bring himself to finish it—to ruin the illusion she had of him.

"We won't speak of it anymore." She reached for his hand and gave it a gentle tug. "Let's sit back down. You didn't finish your milk."

While his body followed her, his mind said he was making yet another mistake. He should head for the door. And yet, he kept taking one step after the other until he was seated on the couch next to her again.

Sylvie reached for her mug and then took a sip. "You should finish drinking yours before it goes cold. It's not as good then."

He reached for his abandoned mug. The sooner he finished it, the sooner he could leave and be alone with his thoughts.

"If you don't want to head into the city tomorrow," Sylvie said, "I can go alone."

He'd given his word and he intended to keep it. "I'll be ready to go first thing in the morning."

"But you'll be tired—"

"So will you." He wanted her to quit being so nice to him because it just made him feel worse.

But if he were to tell her the truth—tell her the deep, dark secret that he'd been keeping for years, then she'd realize she didn't have to work so hard to be nice to him. In fact, she'd probably be anxious to leave the estate and start over somewhere else—just like his sisters had done after the journal had revealed the fractures in their perfect family.

"If you ever want to talk," she said, "I mean really talk, I'm a good listener."

"Sylvie, stop." He didn't look at her. He knew if he did, he'd never get the words out. "You don't understand what's going on."

"I will," she said ever so softly, "if you tell me."

"I knew."

The words popped out before he could stop them. It was the first time he'd made a vocal admission.

Sylvie's fine brows drew together. "Knew what?"

He'd told her this much, he might as well get this over with and let the pieces fall as they may. "I knew my parents' secret—that one of us was illegitimate."

"You mean from reading the journal?"

He shook his head as he stared blindly down at the milky mixture that remained in his mug. "I knew years before my sisters read the journal."

"Oh…" Her breathy response was more of a wow response.

"As you know, I'm the oldest. And when we were kids, I got to stay up a little later than my sisters. It was only a half hour but to me it was a big deal—something Bianca and Gia didn't get to do. During that time, I would read in bed." In his mind's eye, he could see that night so clearly that it was as though he were still there. "I can't remember which book I was reading but it was one of those that you keep telling yourself you'll put down and go to sleep after one more page."

Sylvie didn't say a word. She didn't move. She just sat there taking in everything he was saying. And he knew in the end she would look at him with disappointment and think he was a coward. Rightly so.

He drew in an uneven breath. "I knew it was late. Really late. And I heard some yelling. I was surprised because my mother always made a point of not raising her voice. She said yelling wasn't necessary to get your point across. And then I heard a door slam."

He wished he'd stayed in bed—that he'd gone to sleep when he was supposed to instead of shining a flashlight on his book and reading under the covers, because then he wouldn't have overheard something that impacted so many choices he'd made in his life.

"I was supposed to have been asleep hours ago, but when I heard the shouting and the door slam, I thought something was wrong. In bare feet, I ran down the hall toward my parents' room. I didn't have to put my ear against the door because they were talking loud enough to be heard through the closed door."

He paused as he gathered his thoughts. Part of him wanted to stop here—to shove away the memory that had been troubling him most of his life—but the other part of him needed to say this—to put it out into the universe.

He drew in a deep breath, trying to calm his insides. And then, ever so slowly, he blew out the breath. "I heard my mother say she needed to tell us that my father wasn't the biological father of us all. Some of the words were muffled with her sobs. But then my mother said she'd messed up by having that affair and how guilty she felt." Enzo paused, struggling to keep his emotions in check.

"My father told her she couldn't tell us—that we were too young to understand. And then she mentioned me and how I wasn't a little boy any longer. But my father said it wasn't fair to tell me a secret that I couldn't tell my sisters."

Sylvie reached out, placing her hand on his arm. It was a quiet gesture—a caring touch. And it gave him the strength to finish.

"I'm not sure how long I stood there, trying to make sense of what I'd just heard. My mother had an affair. And at the time, I was certain I was the illegitimate child. Why else would she have mentioned my name?"

"It must have been such a shock."

He nodded. "My mind was reeling. I wasn't a Bartolini. I didn't belong."

"Did you approach your parents?"

He shook his head. "I went to bed that night and eventually I fell asleep. In the morning my parents acted totally normal. And being a kid, I was able to convince myself that it was just a dream. But deep inside I knew it was so much more than a dream."

"And so all of these years you've been dealing with that on your own? Without being able to talk to anyone?"

"But it isn't about me. It's about my sisters. I was too ashamed—too worried about my own feelings—to speak up. But I should have said something. I should have done something."

"You were just a kid. That's a lot to handle."

He raked his fingers through his hair once more. Frustration over his inaction and anger at his lack of courage twisted his gut up in a knot. "I can't hide behind that excuse. I had a chance to speak up when my sisters found that journal. And yet, I kept the awful secret to myself. I didn't think of how it would eat at them—the not knowing."

Sylvie's hand slid down his arm until her fingers

brushed over his palm. The sensation sent a sizzling sense of awareness zinging up his arm. Her fingers slipped between his as she squeezed his hand.

"I know your sisters wouldn't blame you for being shocked when the secret came out. It had been years and you'd convinced yourself that it was a dream."

"But I should have said something. I was ashamed that I wasn't a Bartolini. I was scared they wouldn't look at me as their big brother. I didn't want our relationship to change. I thought if I sat on the information that I'd have a little longer until the DNA results revealed the inevitable—I wasn't a biological Bartolini."

"You'd just lost your parents—you were afraid of losing your sisters."

"That's not good enough." He pulled away from her and stood. His gaze drifted to the floor. "If I was a good brother—if I'd have protected my sisters the way my father had always told me to do—I would have spoken up."

Sylvie placed her fingers beneath his chin and lifted until their gazes met. "Maybe you should have spoken up sooner, but what you would have told them would have been misinformation. You are a Bartolini by blood. Perhaps it would have been worse for your sisters believing one thing, only to find out it wasn't the truth."

"But if I'd have had the courage to speak up all those years ago, my parents could have talked to us. They could have explained their actions. Now we're left with guessing at their motives."

"And this is why you're selling the estate? You don't feel that you deserve it?"

He shrugged. "My sisters both moved away and started over. It's time I do the same thing."

"Have you told your sisters all of this?"

He shook his head. "I can't." His sisters were all the family he had in this world. "I can't risk losing them."

"Do you really think that will happen? Because I don't. I know your sisters love you as much as you love them. And nothing will break you apart."

In her gaze he saw truth and compassion, but it wasn't enough to change his mind. "I... I can't do it."

"If you don't, I don't think you'll ever find that fresh start you're seeking, no matter how far you move from here."

He wanted to argue with her. He wanted to tell her that she was wrong. But he didn't. Sylvie was a smart woman, but the risk of revealing his secret to his sisters was too great. They'd already lost so much—been through so much. And he didn't want them to look at him like— like he'd let them down.

"You won't say anything, right?" he asked.

"You know you can trust me. It's not my secret to tell. But for your own sake, you need to tell them."

"I... I have to go."

"Stay." She approached him. "We don't have to talk."

The thought of spending the night getting lost in her sweet, addictive kisses was so very tempting. Every fiber of his body longed to reach out to her and draw her close. But he knew if he did that, he'd never let her go.

And that wouldn't be fair to Sylvie—sweet Sylvie, who believed in true love, happily-ever-afters and the good-ness in people. But he could be none of those things to her.

His gaze automatically moved to her lips. Why did it seem like such a natural thing to kiss her good-night? Per-haps it was the same reason he'd entrusted her with his most deeply held secret.

But he just couldn't complicate matters even further. Not after he'd just told her the reason they shouldn't be together. He wasn't a person she could count on because he let down the people he loved.

He raised his gaze to meet hers. "I'll see you in the morning."

Disappointment—or was that pain?—showed in her eyes. In a blink it was hidden behind a blank stare. She didn't say anything as he turned and walked away.

With each step he felt as though he was doing the wrong thing. Sylvie might be the best thing that ever happened to him, but he wasn't the best for her.

# CHAPTER NINE

THE DAY COULDN'T have been more beautiful.

The sun was bright. The blue skies were clear. And the air was warm.

But the mood in the car was anything but bright and cheery. The shadows under Enzo's eyes said that he hadn't gotten much sleep, if any. She'd at least drifted off for a few hours but her stomach wasn't feeling the best. She wrote it off as motion sickness. It would soon pass.

After a quiet car ride, they arrived in Florence. Without much sleep, espresso was very tempting. When Enzo repeatedly offered to get her some, her stomach still wasn't up for it.

On her phone, Sylvie did a search of stores in Florence. "There are a lot of shops we can check for decorations."

"Sounds like a plan."

She started reading off the directions. When she looked up, she noticed he'd turned in the opposite direction. "The shops are the other way."

"This is just a little detour."

"But we have to get back to the vineyard and finish setting up."

"Relax. We have time. And you did say you've never taken time to look around the city."

It was true. Since she'd moved from Patazonia, she

hadn't spent much time in Florence. Sadly, the few times she'd visited this beautiful and historically rich city, she'd been here to do wedding business and so still hadn't seen much. She'd dreamed of one day taking the time to visit some of the city's sights, but there was always a meeting to attend, a need to rush back to the estate and never enough time to just relax and be a tourist.

The fact he was taking a detour this morning was something she'd wanted for a long time. So why was she fighting it? Why didn't she just let go of her worries and enjoy the day—wherever it led them?

Enzo parked the car. Sylvie stepped out and lifted her face to the morning sun. It warmed her skin and energized her. This was going to be a good day after all. This tour of Florence with Enzo as her guide would be priceless.

"Where are we going to start?" Excitement pumped through her veins.

"This way." He gestured over his shoulder. "I hope you wore your walking shoes."

"I did." She never imagined she would be touring Florence, but she'd dressed to do some serious shopping and that involved a lot of walking.

The people of Florence shared friendly smiles and greetings. They made Sylvie feel as though she fit right in. Enzo started off by telling her that he wasn't a professional tour guide so he wouldn't be able to answer all her questions about the city, but he would do his best. She had no doubt that he was the perfect person to show her the sights.

"Unless you want to take a professionally guided tour," he said. "I'm not sure what time slots are available. Whatever it is, we can make it work. I don't want you to miss out on anything."

Sylvie placed a hand on his forearm. "Stop. I would like you to do the tour, if you're still willing."

He nodded.

They set off, side by side. There was just something about seeing the city through his eyes that appealed to her. And with Enzo's mood improving, the company was the best part of all.

"Our first stop is the Ponte Vecchio Bridge or Old Bridge," Enzo said. "It's one of the oldest bridges in Europe. And it still has houses built on it, though most of them are now shops."

"I can't even imagine living on a bridge." She marveled at the idea.

"There are some great views from there."

They started across the crowded bridge. There was an energy flowing through the crowd as they laughed and talked amongst themselves as well as conversed with the vendors, most of whom were jewelers. She was immediately drawn in by the showcases. She told herself that she was only going to browse. She didn't have any extra money to splurge on any of the dazzling baubles for sale—not when she was about to lose her home and job. But looking didn't cost anything.

She was in awe at some of the remarkable pieces. But there was a necklace of silver and gemstones designed to look like a cluster of purple grapes with green leaves all wired together. It was remarkable. And she loved it. Then she looked at the price. It was too much for her budget. She gave it a lingering glance then, with a resigned sigh, she moved on.

She didn't say anything to Enzo about the necklace, but when he was drawn in by a wristwatch, she backtracked to take a second look at the necklace. She didn't want to explain to Enzo why she couldn't buy it. She didn't want to make him feel guilty over the events at the estate. After all, it was just a necklace—a stunning, handcrafted necklace—but a necklace all the same.

As they continued across the bridge, Sylvie pushed thoughts of the necklace to the back of her mind. It wouldn't change things to dwell on something she couldn't have. However, the memories made today were priceless. She loved everything about her time in Florence—including her tour guide. As soon as the thought came to her, she dismissed it. Where had it come from? She was just letting the excitement of the day and their newfound easiness with each other get to her.

She paused by the bridge's outlook to take in the beautiful view of the river and the surrounding city.

"Wait here," Enzo said. "I'll be right back."

He disappeared into the crowd. She wasn't sure where he was going, most likely tracking down some espresso. A yawn tugged open her mouth. She refused to give in to her tiredness. Today she would take in all the sights. Tonight she could sleep. But right now she didn't intend to miss a thing. Or at least whatever they had time to see.

Enzo returned. "Turn around."

"What?"

"Turn around." When she frowned at him, trying to figure out what he was holding behind his back, he said, "Trust me."

With a bit of trepidation, she did as he asked. He reached around her, placing something on her neck, but he moved so fast that she couldn't get a good look at what was in his hand. For a moment she thought it was the necklace she'd liked so much, but she dismissed the notion. He wouldn't know about it, as she hadn't mentioned it.

But as she reached for the pendant, Enzo said, "Hold still. I'm having a hard time with this catch." When she stopped moving, he said, "I've almost got it... There we go."

Sylvie moved her long hair, letting the chain rest against her neck. And then she lifted the pendant, finding the stunning mixture of gemstones and wire art. "How did you know?"

When she turned a smile to him, he returned the gesture. "I was hoping for that reaction."

"What reaction?"

"Your smile. It brightens the whole world—at least my entire world."

His words caused her heart to pitter-patter faster. "Thank you so much." She fingered the pendant. "I love it. But you shouldn't have done it. I'll pay you back—"

"No, you won't. That was a gift from me to you."

"But—"

"No buts, just enjoy it. It looks good on you."

They moved on, stopping to visit the bust of goldsmith/sculptor Benvenuto Cellini, where lovers from near and far had visited and affixed hundreds of locks to the fence surrounding the statue. Legend had it if they threw the key in the Arno River, their love would be eternal.

Sylvie wondered about having a love like that—a love like her parents'. She didn't believe it happened for everyone. It wouldn't happen to her, but the thought of having a love that endured time, trials and tribulations was very tempting indeed.

From the bridge, they visited Piazza della Signoria, Florence's town center with its remarkable open-air sculpture gallery with its stunning works of art. There was so much to take in that it couldn't all be done in a day, but they kept moving.

Sylvie snapped photo after photo on her phone. She didn't want to forget a single moment. At the Galleria dell'Accademia, she marveled at all the statues and paintings. However, the sculpture of David by Michelangelo made her pause and admire the level of skill involved. Sylvie never considered herself a fan of Renaissance, but she was starting to change her mind.

With a lull in the crowd, she paused to consider how someone could carve stone with such detail. It was truly amazing. It would definitely take a lot of talent and strength as well as imagination. She wondered if people doubted Michelangelo's talents in the beginning. Did his parents encourage him to do something more traditional with his life—like blacksmithing? Or did they encourage him to follow his dreams?

She thought of her loving mother, who'd always wanted the best for Sylvie. She'd thought Sylvie had talent designing wedding dresses but believed it took more than talent to make it in this sometimes challenging world they lived in. And so her mother had encouraged her to find a more traditional career. Sylvie had heeded her mother's cautious words, but she couldn't help but wonder what would have happened if she'd been brave and followed her dreams.

Sylvie turned to Enzo. "Thank you for bringing me here. I will never forget this day."

"There's something I've been meaning to say to you and for one reason or another, I've kept putting it off." His sincere gaze met hers. He drew in a visible breath. "I'm sorry for how I acted after Paris. It wasn't right. I tried to blame you and it was so wrong. The truth is the night meant more to me than I was willing to admit. I made every excuse possible to avoid dealing with those feelings. Thank you for not giving up on me and giving me time to get my head screwed on straight."

His words touched her heart, making it flutter in her

chest. She wasn't quite sure what he was trying to tell her. A part of her wanted to delve deeper into this subject, but the other part of her didn't want to ruin this moment. As hard as it was for her, she believed it was best for both of them to accept what he was willing to give and not push for more. But that didn't mean she didn't owe him an apology, as well.

"I'm sorry, too." She glanced back at the famous statue as emotions churned within her. "I was freaked out, too, after Paris. I never expected things to go in that direction. And then I thought you were mad at me, which made everything worse." She chanced a glance in his direction. "I don't normally act so bold."

A smile played at the corner of his lips. "I like that bold side of you."

"You do?"

He nodded. "Bold looks good on you."

She smiled, too. His gaze caught and held hers. Her heart pounded in her chest. It was so loud it echoed in her ears. How was it possible this man could have such a powerful draw over her?

"About last night—"

"We were both exhausted," she said. "There's nothing more that needs said about it."

His gaze searched hers. "You don't think less of me?"

"No. I think you're a very caring brother and friend."

And then his gaze noticeably lowered to her lips. Was he going to kiss her right here in front of all these people? She didn't care who watched. All she cared about was being in his arms once more.

Her heart thumped harder and faster with each passing moment. The background faded away. In that moment it was just the two of them—

Someone bumped into Sylvie. She landed against Enzo's

muscular chest. Jarred from the magical spell that had been spun over them, Sylvie jumped back. They both turned to find a teenage boy.

"Sorry." The boy's face was flushed.

"Be careful," Enzo warned. "You could have hurt someone."

The boy nodded and moved on, submerged into the crowd.

Enzo turned to her. "Are you all right?"

She nodded as her heart slowed. The stolen moment was over before it'd even begun.

"Come on," Enzo said, "we need to keep moving. I don't want you to miss visiting the shops before they close."

He took her hand in his and moved onward, working their way to the exit. Her hand felt good within his grasp. She refused to define what it meant. A label on this thing happening between them would ruin the moment. It was best just to live in the moment and not analyze it.

# CHAPTER TEN

HER FINGERS BRUSHED over the pendant.

A warmth swirled in her chest.

She told herself not to read too much into the friendly gesture. Enzo didn't want attachments—in fact, he was doing his best to minimize his commitments in life with the sale of the estate. She'd do well to remember that. Her hand lowered to her side.

They'd made their way through a number of stores. In a secondhand shop, she found some crystal vases. And then in a florist shop, she found some dried flowers that were stunning. There were vivid reds and deep purples as well as ivory flowers. In addition, she picked out some fresh arrangements. Considering the magazine people would be there the following day, the flowers would just be blooming when she got them home.

She turned to Enzo, who was standing by the door as though anxious to move on. While the sales clerk packed her purchases, Sylvie approached Enzo. He looked totally bored out of his mind.

She held out a fresh bouquet of deep purple and white blooms. "What do you think?"

He shrugged. "They're fine."

Not the ringing endorsement she'd been hoping for, but she supposed it'd have to do. "Do you like the other things

I picked out?" When he nodded, she asked, "Do you even know what colors I picked?"

"Pink?"

She sighed. For a man who spent most of his time dealing with grapes and vines, his interest certainly didn't extend to flora and fauna. "No. Reds and purples."

"Oh. Yeah."

"Don't worry, we're almost done." And that was when her gaze skimmed past him to the notice just over his shoulder. It was an ad for an apartment.

She initially dismissed it. But as she turned to walk away, she realized Enzo hadn't given her any real reason to believe he was going to change his mind about keeping the estate. If she didn't take this situation seriously, she'd end up homeless again. Having gone through that situation once, she wasn't about to let it happen again—especially when she was in a position to prevent it.

She turned back and read the write-up again, paying attention to the details. One bedroom. Pets allowed. The thought of coming home to a dog or cat appealed to her. Her gaze latched on to the rent. It was affordable. Very affordable.

When she realized the apartment was right above the florist, she knew she couldn't leave here until she saw it. The posting said to inquire at the desk and that was exactly what she intended to do.

"I'll be back," she said to Enzo.

"Where are you going?"

"To see an apartment." That was unless it was already taken. She hoped not because it fit in her tight budget. She had a decent amount in savings, but she really hated to rely on it to live. So modesty was the course of action until she secured a job. The next item on her to-do list.

"An apartment? What apartment?"

She didn't stop to answer him. She was a lady on a mission. But she could hear his footsteps behind her. She came to a stop at the checkout counter. The young man who'd been waiting on her was gone, so he likely had stepped into the back.

Enzo leaned close to her. "Why are you interested in an apartment?"

"Why do you think?"

"Well, I know what you do with an apartment, but what I don't understand is why you would want one here. I thought you'd return to Patazonia."

She shook her head. "I don't have any reason to return. My mother was my only family and now that she's gone, I'm on my own. I like it here and I've made some contacts here in Florence. I'm hoping to be able to find a job here."

Enzo grew noticeably quiet. Did he feel bad that she had to search for a new home? It didn't stop her from talking to the young man, who said the apartment was vacant. The sales clerk handed over the key and told them to head upstairs to have a look.

And that was exactly what they did. The apartment wasn't anything fancy, not at all. It was older and could use a fresh coat of paint, but it was clean and with a little work it could be cozy enough.

"You know the kitchen faucet is going to need replaced," Enzo pointed out.

"I'll mention it to the landlord."

"And the bedroom door sticks."

She didn't say anything as Enzo continued to point out the apartment's faults, but all she could see was its possibilities. She needed this to work out. She needed a plan—a way to move forward.

There was a ledge above the kitchen sink where the morning sun would come in. There were small shelves on the walls of the living room where she could place the framed photo of her mother and a picture of her favorite spot by the stream on the Bartolini estate. Little by little she could put her personal stamp on the place, making it feel homey like...like the home she already had in Enzo's guesthouse.

Thoughts of leaving the estate made her sad. She couldn't believe how quickly she'd felt so comfortable there. Maybe it was the country setting or maybe it was her handsome host. Her gaze moved to Enzo as he examined the closet. She was going to miss him—sharing meals with him, morning coffee out on the veranda and their talks.

Tears rushed to her eyes. She blinked them away. She was not a crier, but ever since she'd learned she was losing her home and business, her emotions had been harder to conceal.

"Are you ready to go?" Enzo asked.

She gave the tiny apartment one more look, still not ready to commit to this new future. She nodded her head. "Let's go home."

With the flowers collected and stowed in the car, Enzo drove them back to the vineyard while Sylvie stared out the window at the beautiful scenery. But it wasn't the tall Cypress trees lining the road or the rolling hills that captured her attention; it was the war raging within her between sticking out her plan to convince Enzo to change his mind about the estate or cutting her losses and moving to Florence now. The sooner she got there, the sooner she'd accept the reality of her situation—she had no future with Enzo.

She focused her thoughts on what was awaiting her in Florence. The location of the apartment was superb as it was in the heart of the city. And best of all, it was furnished. Old furniture, but it appeared to be well taken care of. All the money she'd save with the low rent and not having to buy furniture would help stretch her savings until she landed a job.

But she also realized she'd been the one responsible for inviting the magazine to the estate. She had to stay and see this through until the end. And then she would move on—no matter how hard it would be for her.

# CHAPTER ELEVEN

THE BIG DAY had arrived.

Praises and compliments were bandied about.

But all Enzo could think about was the small apartment in Florence—where Sylvie was considering living. It was so much smaller than the house on this estate. And it needed a lot of work.

He knew those were all excuses. The truth of the matter was he didn't want her moving there. He didn't want her to be so far away.

And yet, he couldn't ask her to stay here. Because soon, he would no longer own the estate. So what did that leave him? To ask her to move to France with him? Impossible. That would mean strings and commitments, things he was just now untangling himself from with the sale of the estate.

"This is great." The reporter, Jameson Asaro, seemed more interested in smiling at Sylvie than exploring the estate. "I think we have all we need of the villa and vineyard."

"Are you sure?" Sylvie asked.

"You've been an excellent guide." Jameson smiled once more at Sylvie. "I've really enjoyed your company."

Color rose in Sylvie's cheeks. "Thank you."

Unhappy with this conversation, Enzo cleared his throat

as he made a point of checking the time on his wristwatch. It was definitely time to move this interview along.

"You know, Enzo's father built all of this," Sylvie said. "Isn't that right, Enzo?"

He knew she was trying to get him to talk. He didn't like this guy or the way he flirted with Sylvie. Still, Sylvie was looking at him expectantly. "Um, yes. That's right. He inherited the land from my grandfather, but until that point, it was just wide-open space." He pressed his hands to his trim waist. "This was all my father's hard work."

The reporter made a note on his digital tablet. "But you have worked on the grapes, right?"

"Yes. I've been instrumental in blending the grapes."

"How did you do that if you were living and working in France?"

"I started the work before I moved to France. And though my father and his crew did the day-to-day maintenance, I came home periodically to oversee things."

"So you and your father must have worked closely together."

Enzo paused, recalling his time with his father. In the beginning his father wouldn't listen to Enzo's ideas. But as the years went by and Enzo gained more experience, his father would actually seek out his advice. It had been the greatest feeling in the world. "We did."

The reporter made a notation in his notes. "Then why move to France? Why not work here with your father?"

"My father believed in everyone learning to be independent."

"So you were planning to return?"

He didn't like the direction of these questions. He never should have agreed to the interview. He didn't want to dissect his life with his father. He didn't want to acknowledge that he'd headed off on his own to learn as much as he could in order to return to the Barto Vineyard and make it bigger and better. And to one day have his father hand over the reins—trusting Enzo with what his father had created and worked his whole life to make thrive.

"Yes." Enzo's voice rumbled with emotion. He slammed the door on those memories. He swallowed hard. "We should get going." He turned for the door. "I've arranged to give you a horseback tour of the estate. It's the only true way to see the place." He paused and turned back to them. "Do you ride?"

The reporter's questions were opening doors to Enzo's past.

But would they be enough to change the course of the future?

Sylvie's breath caught as she waited to see how this would play out. Luckily, both men were agreeable to a horseback ride. She let out the pent-up breath.

In the next breath it struck her that Enzo had planned the horseback tour on his own, without even consulting her. If he didn't care about the estate and was so anxious to get rid of it, would he have gone to the bother? Would he have gone along with any of this?

She didn't think so. As they all got saddled up, she was smiling broadly. Enzo might not be willing to admit it, but he was attached to the estate. Talking about selling it and doing it were two totally different things. When it finally came down to putting pen to paper, she didn't think he could do it.

Once the reporter and photographer were seated on two of the most mellow horses in the stable, Sylvie mounted Duchess at the same time Enzo climbed on Emperor. Off they went. Enzo took the lead and she was curious where he would lead them. It didn't take her long to figure out he was leading them to her favorite spot, next to the stream.

"You own all of this land?" the reporter asked.

"Yes." Enzo didn't expound upon the answer.

Sylvie had taken up the rear, sandwiching their two visitors in between so no one got lost, because there was a lot of land out here in which to wander off in the wrong direction.

"It's very picturesque." Sylvie admired the passing scenery. "I love to come out here when I have time just to take in the quiet beauty and unwind."

"How long have you worked here?" Jameson asked.

"I just started working here this year." And yet, it seemed so much longer. "I immediately fell in love with the estate." And she was pretty crazy about its owner, but she kept that part to herself.

It seemed like she'd been keeping more and more to herself these days. In the beginning of all this, she and Enzo could talk about most anything. It was like they had an immediate rapport—

*Whinny!*

The next thing she knew Duchess came to an abrupt stop. Before she could think to react, the horse reared up. Sylvie clung tight to the reins and tightened her legs. But gravity was too much for her. She thought she heard Enzo call out her name.

She went airborne.

A scream tore from her lungs.

And then she landed on the hard ground with a thud. The air whooshed from her lungs. And as her head hit the ground, blackness engulfed her, swallowing her whole.

She just had to be all right.

That was all Enzo could think when he saw Sylvie motionless on the ground. And that was what he thought when she came to and insisted that she was all right. She was more worried about the horse, who'd been spooked, than herself. Against his wishes, she'd gotten to her feet.

It was all he could do to convince her that they were going to the A&E. When he'd pointed out that she'd blacked out momentarily, she'd grudgingly conceded but insisted that no ambulance was necessary. And so he drove her. She was so stubborn.

And now, as they waited in a hospital cubicle, Sylvie grew restless. He couldn't blame her. This place was boring but necessary.

"This is silly to wait around here," Sylvie said. "There's nothing wrong with me."

"That bump on your head would indicate otherwise."

She sighed as though giving up the fight. Because there was no way she was getting out of the hospital until the doctor cleared her.

A few minutes of silence passed between them. In that time Enzo's mind went to a dark place as he thought about how close he'd come to losing her. The thought of his world without Sylvie in it—well, he couldn't imagine it. Never seeing her bright, sunny smile again or being able to pick up his phone and hear her soft voice and infectious giggle. He halted his troubling thoughts. Thankfully, none of that had happened.

"I'm sorry."

The words were so soft—so faint—that he wasn't sure he heard her correctly. "Sorry?" When she nodded, he asked, "For what?"

"For ruining your interview with the magazine. I can't even imagine what they must think."

He wanted to tell her that he didn't care what they thought. The only important thing was her well-being.

But he stopped himself. He told himself that he didn't want to hurt her feelings since she'd arranged for the magazine coverage and worked so hard to make the estate look picture-perfect. He ignored the part about how his admission might convey how much she'd come to mean to him—as a friend, that is.

"Everything is going to work out fine," he said with a conviction he was lacking because he knew they'd soon be parting ways and—and he'd miss their conversations.

"Ms. DeLuca?" A doctor they hadn't seen before stepped into the cubicle.

"Yes." There was a slight tremor in her voice.

Enzo couldn't help but wonder if she was worried about having to spend the night in the hospital. Before he could reassure her that everything would be all right, the doctor turned to Enzo. The words froze in Enzo's throat.

"I'm Dr. Costa." The older man wearing a white coat held out his hand. "And you would be?"

"Enzo." Suddenly, he felt nervous. What was the doctor going to say? Was there something wrong with Sylvie and that was why a new doctor was here? As the doctor's eyes prompted Enzo for more information, Enzo found his voice once more. "I'm, uh, Sylvie's friend."

The doctor nodded in understanding. "If you could go to the waiting area, I'd like to speak to Ms. DeLuca."

"I'd like him to stay," Sylvie said. "He's never going to believe I'm okay until he hears it from you."

The doctor's bushy white brows drew together behind his silver-framed glasses. "Okay, then."

Would the doctor have asked him to leave the room if nothing was wrong? Enzo didn't think so. And he wanted to be there for Sylvie to lean on if the news wasn't good.

The doctor focused on Sylvie. "You've had quite a fall

and you have a slight concussion. Your other tests came out fine. Are you having any cramping?"

Sylvie's eyes showed her confusion. "No."

"Any spotting?"

"Spotting?" Her voice wavered. When the doctor nodded, she said, "No."

"That's good." The doctor smiled at her. "Now, if your friend will step outside, I'll just check and make sure everything is all right with the baby."

The breath hitched in Enzo's throat.

*Baby? What baby?*

Surely, the doctor was confused. Enzo turned his attention to Sylvie. All the color had leached from her face. Judging by her wide-eyed gaze and her slack jaw, she was as surprised by this diagnosis as he was.

"Just move to the waiting area," the doctor prompted as a nurse rushed in. "We won't be long."

Enzo turned his stunned gaze to Sylvie. He didn't want to walk away. He had questions. Lots of questions.

He opened his mouth to say something but his voice failed him.

How had this happened?

That was a foolish question. He recalled very vividly how this had happened. Every last sizzling detail.

The doctor cleared his throat, startling Enzo into action. On wooden legs, he walked away. But not far. Not far at all.

She was pregnant.

It wasn't as big of a shock as Sylvie had expected.

Maybe because way down deep in her subconscious, she'd suspected it. She just hadn't allowed herself to admit it. After all, what were the chances that the first time you make love that you would turn up pregnant?

She didn't think the odds were very high. Leave it to

her to be the one in a million. But it explained her symptoms, from her tender breasts, to her upset stomach, to her heightened emotions. And if she were to finally slow down enough to consult her day planner, she'd likely notice that her cycle was late. Inwardly, she groaned. This was the worst timing—the absolute worst.

When the doctor finished his thorough exam, he said, "Everything appears good. But considering the severity of your fall, I'd like to do a transvaginal ultrasound." He went on to explain the procedure to her.

"I'll be able to see the baby?" she asked. Hope and excitement swelled within her chest.

The doctor nodded. "And we should be able to hear its heartbeat." The doctor typed some notes into the computer that was mounted on a cart. "Was that the father who was just in here?"

"Yes." There was no hesitation in her answer because Enzo was the only man in her life, if you could stretch the meaning of being in someone's life.

"Would you like to have him in here for the ultrasound?" When she nodded, the doctor said, "As soon as you're all set up, someone will go get him. The technician should be in shortly."

And then the doctor left her alone. It was quite loud in her head as one thought preceded another. Quite often they were in contradiction of each other. But in the end, they all boiled down to: What was she going to do now?

## CHAPTER TWELVE

IT WAS A black screen.

And then some gray lines washed over the monitor.

Enzo squinted, trying to make out the image of a baby—of his son or daughter. That thought momentarily caused the breath to become trapped in his lungs. How was it that he was going to become a father when he hadn't even gotten his own life straightened out?

The technician wearing pink scrubs, with her dark hair pulled up in a messy bun, made some adjustments, clearing up the picture. She pointed to the screen. "There's your baby."

Sylvie gasped. And then she sniffled and swiped at her cheeks. "Can you tell if it's a boy or girl?"

"It's too early. That will happen in your second trimester."

Sylvie turned to Enzo with a teary smile. "It's so small. I… I hope I didn't hurt him or her in the fall."

Enzo wanted to reassure her that everything would be all right, but he couldn't make her that promise. Instead, he reached out and took her cold hand in his. He rubbed his thumb over the back of her hand.

"Would you like to hear the heartbeat?" the technician asked.

"Oh, yes. Please." The excitement rang out in Sylvie's voice.

A new sense of guilt settled over Enzo. After the way his own family had crashed and burned, he was scared to be responsible for a baby. What if he messed up?

Sylvie squeezed his hand, drawing him back to the present. A rapid *swoosh-swoosh* filled the air.

"That's your baby's heartbeat," the technician said. "A baby's heart beats more rapidly than an adult's."

For the moment Enzo halted his rambling thoughts and focused on his son or daughter's heartbeat. The *swoosh-swoosh* drove home the reality of this situation.

He and Sylvie were having a baby.

This shouldn't be happening. The timing was all wrong. The situation was wrong. And his being a father was all sorts of wrong.

*Pregnant. Baby.*

The words echoed in Enzo's mind during the ride home. It had been a particularly quiet ride as he tried to come to terms with the events of the day. He wasn't the only quiet one. Sylvie had barely said a word since they got in the car. Was she as stunned as he was? Or had she known all along? Was that why she'd been so excited to hear the baby's heartbeat?

He hadn't needed to ask Sylvie if the baby was his. The fact she'd been a virgin until their night in Paris was enough to answer his question. Things had gotten out of control that night. Obviously, mistakes had been made. Big mistakes.

And now he had no idea what to do.

He opened the door of the guesthouse. She walked past him because she refused to let him carry her—even though he'd tried to do just that. She insisted when the doctor said she was to rest for a couple of days that it didn't mean she couldn't walk. She was so stubborn.

Once inside, she refused to go to bed and instead settled on the couch. He sat with her. He rubbed his palms over his jeans. Unable to get comfortable, he jumped to his feet. He started to pace.

He had questions, lots of questions. But he didn't know if now was the right time to ask them. In fact, it probably wasn't the time. He kept his mouth shut and his feet moving over the hardwood floor.

"Ask me," she said.

He stopped and turned to her. "What?"

"You want to ask me about the baby, so go ahead. And yes, the baby is yours."

"How long have you known?" His gaze searched hers as though he could tell if she was lying or not.

"I didn't. I swear. I just found out when you did."

He raked his fingers through his hair. "This… It changes everything."

She glanced down, smoothing out a nonexistent wrinkle in her blouse. "I don't want it to sway your decision."

"What decision?" Was she referring to their relationship? Or had she already skipped ahead to marriage and living happily ever after? Because that had never crossed his mind. Well, not really. Maybe once or twice. But that was it.

Frown lines etched her eyes. "I don't want you to keep the estate out of a sense of obligation."

He didn't say anything. Once more he started to pace. He had a lot to think over before they continued this discussion. There was so much to consider.

"Enzo, I'm sorry."

He stopped. His gaze sought out hers. "Sorry for what?"

"For further complicating your life."

He believed her. He really did. But he didn't blame her. He blamed himself. And right now he couldn't give her the words of reassurance she wanted to hear. He needed time to think.

"We'll talk tomorrow," he said, glancing away. "It's getting late. Do you want anything to eat?"

She shook her head. "I'm fine."

He'd gotten them some takeaway at the hospital while they waited for the test results to come back. It'd taken a while because he insisted the doctors check her thoroughly. He had to be certain she and the baby were all right.

Sylvie stood as though to head for the door. "I'll just let you out."

He shook his head. "I'm not going anywhere."

"What?"

His gaze met hers. "I'm sleeping right here on the couch."

"But...but it's too small for you."

He crossed his arms, refusing to budge. "It'll be just fine. And I want to be close by in case you need anything. After all, you have a concussion."

"A slight one."

"But one all the same."

She opened her mouth as though to argue but then she closed her mouth and walked away. Apparently, she wasn't up for a fight she wasn't going to win.

He resumed pacing and thinking. There wasn't a tired bone in his body. He was totally wound up. He was going to be a father. They were going to be parents. Sylvie was the mother of his baby. The image of her holding a baby filled his chest with a warm, fuzzy sensation.

Sylvie returned, interrupting his daydream. She placed a blanket and pillow on the couch. "You'll need these."

"Thank you. But I'm the one who should be waiting on you."

"I'm fine." Her hand moved to her abdomen. "We're fine. I promise."

She turned and walked away. He wanted to go after her. He wanted to pull her into his arms and hold her close, reassure himself that she was truly fine. But he didn't move. He didn't have the right to touch her—even if she was carrying his baby.

His feet resumed their motion. His gaze moved about the room, coming to rest on a mannequin in the corner of the room. The light from the lamp caught the beads and sequins, making them glitter. It was new to the room. He was drawn to it.

He moved around the armchair that was blocking his full view. And then he realized it was a wedding dress. At first, he assumed it was just part of the wedding business, but a closer inspection revealed that the dress was in the process of being sewn.

What was it doing here? The business bought dresses, not created them. And if this dress was a part of the business, it would be in the front rooms, in the space dedicated to the business, not back here in Sylvie's private rooms.

What in the world? Was Sylvie making her own wedding dress? But why? To marry whom? Him? The breath hitched in his throat. That couldn't happen.

But there was a baby to consider—their baby. Still, didn't Sylvie understand he wouldn't make a good husband? He'd end up hurting her without meaning to.

# CHAPTER THIRTEEN

THE NIGHT HAD been restless.

And the morning wasn't much better as Sylvie hurt everywhere, including a few spots she hadn't known existed. But she refused to let that get her down. The fact the baby was safe was the balm she needed to get up and get moving.

*The baby.*

Those two life-altering words kept playing over and over in her mind. She knew she should be shocked and scared, and she was, but there was also a sense of awe.

She placed a hand to her still-flat abdomen. It was so hard to believe there was a little baby in there. But it was true. She'd seen it with her own eyes. And Enzo had witnessed it, too.

*Enzo.*

What was he thinking? Last night he'd looked like the earth had moved out from under his feet. She had no idea what mood he'd be in today.

Knowing there was no point delaying the inevitable, she took a quick shower and dressed. When she stepped out of the bedroom, she was surprised to find Enzo rushing around her small kitchen. He didn't seem to notice her. And so she took in the moment. He looked very busy with whatever he was cooking. From the mess of dirty dishes on the table and counter, she'd hazard a guess that cooking wasn't something he'd mastered.

Not wanting to be caught staring, she moved on. In the small living room, she reached for her digital tablet. She wanted to see the teaser the magazine had planned to post online prior to the release of the magazine.

After all, that was the reason she'd been on horseback. She just hoped it was a glowing article. Perhaps it'd help Enzo's mood. Maybe he'd see possibilities for the future that he'd been unwilling to accept before.

But when she pulled up the online magazine, the first thing to come up on the screen was a horrific photo of a fire—a wildfire. Her gaze caught the headlines: "Burning Inferno."

She went on to read that the fire was a ways away from the Bartolini estate. They weren't sure yet how it'd started, but so far there was zero containment. Sylvie's heart ached for all the destruction and the danger to humans and wildlife. It was an utter nightmare. Hopefully, they'd get it under control quickly.

Under the circumstances, she assumed the article about the vineyard would be sidelined for now, but that didn't keep her from scrolling down over the page.

Near the bottom of the webpage, she spotted a photo of herself and Enzo. What in the world was she doing in the photo? It wasn't anything they'd posed for as she'd made sure to stay out of the camera's range. But there they were among the vines, staring into each other's eyes. The picture made it appear as though they were lovers and that just wasn't the case—not since Paris.

She couldn't even recall this moment, and if Enzo was staring lovingly into her eyes, she'd think she would remember it. All she could figure was that it was a fleeting moment made to appear as something more. Beneath the photo was a headline that caught and held her attention: "Italian Billionaire Off the Market?"

She gasped.

"Sylvie, what's the matter?" Enzo's voice came from behind her. "Is it the baby?"

The next thing she knew Enzo was standing next to her. She pressed the tablet to her chest as she shook her head. What was the point of hiding it from him? He was bound to find out soon enough. With great reluctance, she handed him her tablet with the write-up about them as a couple.

Between news of the wildfire and then the sensationalized headline, her stomach churned. She moved to the couch and sat before her legs gave out. Things were spinning out of control faster than she could deal with them.

When Enzo turned to her, she couldn't read the emotions in his tired, bloodshot eyes. She swallowed hard, insisting her stomach calm itself. Not that it would listen to her.

"I'm sorry." Her voice cracked with emotion. "I… I had no idea they were in this to make sensationalized headlines. If I'd known, I never would have agreed to the visit." Her gaze fell to her hands. "I thought I was helping."

Enzo sat beside her. "This isn't your fault. This is totally on that reporter's shoulders."

"You're not mad at me?"

"About the interview and this write-up? No."

She noticed how he singled out the article, but he hadn't said anything about the baby. She couldn't stand the unknown. She needed to know where they stood. "And the baby? Are you mad at me?"

"Did you intentionally get pregnant?" His gaze searched hers, as though seeking out the truth.

"No. I wouldn't do such a thing."

"Then there's no reason to be mad at you. But I am mad

at myself for letting things get out of control and putting us both in this difficult position."

She reached out to him, touching his arm. "You can't take on all of the blame. I started everything by kissing you."

Pain and regret were evident in his eyes as he pulled away from her touch. "But I shouldn't have acted on it. This is all my fault—"

"Stop." Her voice was firm. "We aren't going to play the blame game. What's done is done. We just have to figure out how to move forward."

Enzo sighed as he rubbed the back of his neck. "You're right. Why don't we start with breakfast?"

"Not yet. We haven't finished talking."

"Just tell me what you want me to do."

"I don't expect anything from you."

"Except not to sell the estate." Enzo frowned. "What I don't get is why you care so much if I keep this place or not."

"Because there's something about this estate…an ease… a hominess…that draws me in. It's so easy to imagine all the happy memories within the walls of the main house. It's something a lot of people strive for all of their lives. But you have it all, right here."

"What I have is a house of lies. Looking back, I can't tell what was true and what was just a well-crafted lie by my parents. This house is where I let down my sisters. It is my biggest failure."

She paused, considering her next words. "After my mother died, I lost our house. I was so far behind in the payments that it was only the bank's goodwill that let my mother stay there until the end. But after that I was out the door. I was homeless. I never knew where I was going to sleep. But thanks to some amazing friends, I only spent a night or two without a roof over my head."

"You never told me that before."

She glanced down at her clasped hands. "I've never told anyone. It's not something I'm proud of."

That made him stop short. His gaze met hers. "You have nothing to be ashamed of. In fact, everything you did for your mother took incredible strength and love. It didn't end the way you wanted but you did a remarkable thing."

Heat rushed to her cheeks. He made it sound like she did something other people in her position wouldn't have done. She didn't think that was the case.

"Thank you but I just did what I had to do."

The wedding was over.

The guests were gone.

And the villa had been put back to rights.

Late Saturday afternoon, Sylvie was exhausted. Even though it had been an intimate morning wedding with just family and close friends, there had still been an abundance of details to see to. It was a bittersweet moment for her as the wedding had been a smashing success, but it was also the last wedding she'd ever hold on the Bartolini estate.

With this mix of emotions churning within her, she felt restless. She needed some fresh air. A stroll would give her a chance to sort out all she needed to do once she moved to Florence. Because come the morning, whether she wanted to or not, it was time to move on—without Enzo.

He'd be there for the baby, of that she didn't doubt, but he wouldn't be there for her, not like the close friend he'd come to be over this past year. And maybe that was for the best. Because if she truly let a man into her life, she needed him to be there out of love, not obligation.

With her trusty bag slung over her shoulder, Sylvie

made her way to the stable. The earthy scents of the hay and horses, which may be a turnoff to some, grounded her. She craved that sense of peace today.

One of her passions she'd gained since moving to the estate was horseback riding. As a child she'd always dreamed of having her own horse, but living in the city made owning a horse an expensive challenge—money her mother didn't have.

She moved to Duchess's stall. Immediately, the horse moved to greet her. If a horse could smile, Duchess would be doing so now as she nuzzled Sylvie's hand, urging her to fuss over the horse.

Whenever Sylvie went riding, it was always Duchess she selected. The mare was gentle and patient. In fact, this was the horse Sylvie had learned to ride on when she'd first arrived in Tuscany. But sadly, they wouldn't be able to take one last ride together.

"I'm sorry, girl." Sylvie ran her hand down over the mare's neck. "We can't go riding because I'm having a baby."

Duchess was the second to hear her news. The words felt so strange as they crossed her lips. She was still getting used to this new reality.

The horse studied her with those big golden-brown eyes. And then Duchess whinnied as though to say she understood.

"I'm going to miss you."

With a heavy heart, Sylvie walked away. Duchess put up a fuss, banging on her stall. She didn't want to be left behind. The horse's displeasure tugged on Sylvie's heart.

Today the stables didn't give her the comfort she'd been craving. Still feeling restless, Sylvie continued walking. With no particular destination in mind, she kept putting one foot in front of the other.

The sun was sinking toward the horizon when Sylvie came to a stop at her favorite spot on the estate. The small stream snaked its way along the edge of the estate. And in the background was a beautiful view of the rolling hills.

With autumn not far off, evenings arrived earlier and earlier. Sylvie wasn't ready to let go of this summer—this magical and amazing season. Who'd have thought she'd have an opportunity to visit Paris? The City of Love had been on her bucket list as well as visiting the Eiffel Tower and now she'd done both—and not alone.

She'd swear that city cast a spell over its visitors—she was convinced of it. Otherwise, how else could she explain her being so bold with Enzo—starting something that spun totally and deliciously out of control?

Now that they were back in Tuscany, she could see things clearer. It was abundantly obvious to her that they didn't belong together. Where he wanted to wipe away the past—pretend it didn't exist, she wanted to cling to it so as not to make the same mistakes. Where he acted hastily, such as deciding to sell the estate, she liked to mull things over and make a plan. Whereas he was stubborn and refused to admit when he'd made a mistake, she accepted her mistakes while trying to do better.

She grabbed the blanket from her bag and smoothed it out in front of a large rock. It was there that she sank down and leaned back. For a moment she took in the beauty of the scenery from the slow-moving stream to the lingering sunshine peeking through the branches of trees on the other side of the stream to the blue sky with the puffy white clouds. She wished she could draw landscapes because this was a sight that should be replicated and shared.

She withdrew her sketch pad from her bag along with her set of drawing pencils. She flipped open her sketch pad and stared down at the wedding dress she was designing. Drawing was something she'd started to do as a child. She'd loved to draw and color princess dresses, big and puffy. Some had fairy wings. And others were more sci-fi.

But as she grew older, her drawings grew more refined and a lot more realistic. Still favoring a fairy-tale dress over the more everyday dresses, she morphed to wedding dresses. In her mind it seemed to be a natural move for her. At first, her drawings had been of dresses that already existed. The detail work of a wedding dress took a lot of studying and a lot of discarded pages. But eventually she started working on dresses of her own design. At first, they had basic lines and decorative traits. But eventually, she learned to trust her imagination and her skills.

Once she had some original drawings, she used the skills her mother gave to her. Her mother was a seamstress—one of the best in all of Patazonia. Her mother would even give her some helpful hints, but while her mother realized her daughter's real talent, she tried to talk her into more traditional work such as being a seamstress. Her mother didn't believe a nobody like Sylvie would ever make it designing her own fashions, no matter how pretty they were.

She knew her mother had the best of intentions. Sylvie agreed with her. Who would want to buy her fashions? But that didn't keep Sylvie from spending her free time doing the one thing she'd been doing since she was a little girl—back in the days when she thought anything was possible—designing wedding dresses. Though these days it was rare when she had time to devote to her hobby. Today was one of those rare days.

And knowing there wasn't much time before the shadows would grow long and she'd need to head back, she started moving her pencil over the heavy white paper. In no time she was caught up in what she was doing.

A line here. A button there. A plunging neckline. Erase. Erase. A not so plunging neckline. A layer of lace over the bodice. A fitted waistline with a sash of satin. This was definitely one of her favorite dresses by far. And maybe that was why it was taking her the longest to complete. She wanted everything to be perfect—

"Sylvie?"

Her heart lurched straight into her throat. She jumped. Her pencil skidded across the page. As her heart pounded, she turned to find Enzo alighting from his black stallion, Emperor.

"Sylvie, is everything all right?" Enzo approached her. "You look like you just saw a ghost."

It took her a moment to regain the use of her voice. "I'm fine. I was just so caught up in…" She hesitated. She hadn't shared this part of her life with him. "In thought."

"Sorry. I didn't mean to scare you." He sent her a guilty smile.

It was so hard to stay upset with him when he looked at her that way. "It's okay. What did you need?"

"I heard you were at the stables and then you just disappeared. I… I wanted to check on you. And I knew Emperor would enjoy a ride. But I can leave if you want me to."

"No." The word was out of her mouth before she had a chance to decide if their spending alone time was a good idea or not.

After all, there wasn't another soul around. It was once again just the two of them. Why did that conjure up all the wrong thoughts?

# CHAPTER FOURTEEN

NOTHING ROMANTIC WAS going to happen.

Enzo already made it quite clear he wasn't interested.

Sylvie moved to the side of the blanket. Enzo joined her. He glanced over at her sketch pad. She'd forgotten all about its still being open. Her initial instinct was to close it, but it would seem rude and she wouldn't do that to Enzo.

As Enzo studied her sketch, she studied him. She wondered if their baby would be a boy or girl. She liked the idea of having a little boy—the spitting image of his father. Her heart filled with love.

And Enzo's dark brown eyes were unforgettable. Would the baby inherit his father's penetrating gaze? Or would they inherit her nothing-special lighter brown eyes? Would their son or daughter be tall like their father? Short like her? Or fall somewhere in between? She had so many questions.

Sylvie wondered if Enzo was curious about their child. They might not have worked as a couple but that didn't mean she didn't want him in their child's life.

In fact, after not knowing her father at all, Sylvie was quite anxious for Enzo to be an active part of their child's life, which was another reason she wished he'd change his mind about selling the estate. She'd heard him say in the past that if he didn't live here that he'd probably move back to France. And that was so far away that he'd only see their child once in a while. Not nearly enough for a close relationship.

"Sylvie?" Enzo waved his hand in front of her face. When she blinked and focused on him, he asked, "Did you hear anything I just said?"

"Umm…" Heat rushed to her cheeks. "Sorry. I guess I zoned out. That wedding this morning might have had a small guest list but there were a lot of little details and I'm more tired than I thought."

"Then we should get you back to the house. The doctor said you should take it easy for a few days."

"It has been a few days and I'm fine." When he frowned at her, she said, "Besides, these are the last lingering days of summer and I want to enjoy them before they're gone."

"There's always next year."

"But things will be so different then."

"You mean the baby?"

"Partly." She glanced away. "It's complicated."

He glanced back at her sketch pad. "I didn't know you were artistic."

"I… I'm not. This is just a sketch. It's no big deal."

"It's a huge deal. Call it what you want but that's a definite piece of art. Wow! You're talented."

Heat rushed back to her cheeks. She wasn't used to people complimenting her sketches. "Thank you."

"May I have a closer look?"

She handed over her sketchbook. She wasn't sure why he was making such a big deal of it. She didn't think her sketches were that good and maybe that was why she couldn't finish this dress. In her mind the dress was magnificent, but when she attempted to transfer that image to paper it didn't come out quite the way she imagined.

Enzo held up her sketch and really studied it for a moment. "Do you have more of these?"

She nodded.

"May I look at those, too?"

She nodded once more. She never knew just how exposed she would feel by sharing her sketches with someone. It was like they were looking at a piece of her soul. It was all bare and open for their inspection. And if they didn't like it—if Enzo didn't like what he saw—it would hurt. It would hurt a lot.

He turned page after page. Some were close-ups of the bodice with all the lacework or beading. Others were full dress sketches. She drew what she thought she'd need in order to take the drawing and turn it into a full-fledged dress.

"This is so impressive."

"It's not that good."

His gaze momentarily lifted, meeting hers. "Yes, it is." Then he glanced back at the sketch pad. "Why do you plan weddings instead of designing dresses?"

She shook her head, dismissing such a ridiculous notion. In her mind she heard the echo of her mother's voice: *No matter how good you are, you're still a nobody.*

"It's just a hobby."

He was quiet for a moment as he turned the page. He lifted the sketch pad closer to his face, inspecting each minute line and swirl. "Wait. Is this why you have a wedding dress in your living room?"

"It is. But it's not finished."

"Is it the first one you've sewn?" When she shook her head, he asked, "May I see the other one?"

"I no longer have them."

"Them?" He sounded surprised. "You made more than one?"

"I did."

"What happened to them?"

"I sold them." She lowered her gaze to the striped pattern on the blanket. She could feel him staring at her expectantly.

This part of herself she didn't share with others. Part of the reason she didn't talk about it was the associated pain with that trying time in her life, and the other was the sadness with having to part with her very first wedding dress.

"I get the feeling you didn't do it voluntarily."

She shook her head. What would it hurt to tell him? After all, she'd been privy to much of the drama after his parents' sudden deaths. "I had to sell them in order to pay my mother's medical bills."

"Oh. I'm sorry to push."

"It's okay. I don't talk about it much but it's not a secret." She said this much; she might as well tell him the rest. "When my mother was sick, I worked at a wedding boutique. They sold dresses and accessories as well as planned the weddings." She paused as the painful memories came flooding back.

"And that's how you got the job of working with Bianca?"

"Yes. I worked my way up in the business, but I never learned who recommended me to the royal palace."

"I can see why they did. You're very organized and great with people."

"I try. It's not always easy."

"But your true talent is here." He pointed to her sketch pad. "You put so much of yourself into those dresses. It must have been horrible to part with them."

"It was, but I'd do it again to help someone I love. I can create a new dress, but it's people who are irreplaceable." And if her mother was here right now, she'd be able to show her that you don't have to settle. Sylvie was making a name for herself in the wedding world.

"I'm sorry," he said. "I didn't mean to upset you."

"It's not your fault." She blinked. "I'm fine. I was just thinking about my mother. I feel like I let her down."

"I'm sure you didn't. You have a heart of gold and I'd be willing to bet this entire estate that you did everything you could for her and she knew it, too."

Sylvie glanced down and picked a piece of lint from her jeans. "I just feel bad that when she was so sick, I couldn't be with her all of the time. I had to continue working in order to pay the bills and keep a roof over our heads."

"That couldn't have been easy, feeling like you were being torn in two directions."

"I made sure to have the neighbors stop in and check on her. When the time came, I set up a schedule so there'd always be someone with her."

Enzo reached out and placed his hand over hers. He gave it a squeeze. "You know we have something in common."

She didn't move her hand, taking comfort in the warmth of his touch. She turned her head, finding he was much closer than she'd thought. "What's that?"

"I feel as though I failed my sisters. After our parents died, I was supposed to protect them—make it easier for them. And yet, I did the exact opposite."

"Have you talked to them? Told them your secret?"

He glanced away. "I can't. They'll never understand."

"Give them a chance. They might surprise you."

His gaze met hers. "Why do you care?"

Her heart beat faster. She wondered if he suspected that she had feelings for him. Heat crept up her neck, warming her cheeks. "I don't think you'll ever be able to forgive yourself and make peace with the past without being honest with your sisters."

"Maybe. Maybe not. But telling them is too big of a gamble. I couldn't take it if they never spoke to me again."

Sylvie reached out and gave his hand a quick squeeze. "They love you. That won't change."

"But I could have done more…"

"You did your best. And that's all anyone can do."

When he gazed at her, his eyes were filled with agony. His pain was so palpable that it sliced into her heart. No wonder he'd decided to sell the estate. He was trying to get away from the pain.

And in that moment all she wanted to do was to comfort him. Without thinking of how her actions could complicate their already messy relationship, she leaned to the side. And there he was. His lips were so close to hers.

He didn't move. She didn't even think he was breathing at this point. The breath hitched in her own throat. She tilted her chin upward and pressed her lips to his.

There was no room in the moment for things to move slowly because the air between them was charged with emotion—deep, raw emotion. And that came through in their kiss. His lips moved over hers with a need she'd never experienced before. And she was there for him, meeting his kiss with a need of her own. She had missed him. Even though they'd coexisted on the same estate, they'd never been farther apart. Until now.

She reached a hand out to him, wrapping her fingers around the back of his neck and then letting her fingers comb up through his thick, dark hair. She shouldn't be doing this. She'd promised herself that whatever they'd shared was over. It was best to keep things simple, but they were not simple right now. Not at all.

In this moment things were hot and getting hotter. And

all thoughts of reason had totally escaped her. She was caught up in comforting Enzo and perhaps herself, too. Because as much as she tried to tell herself that she would be all right if the estate was sold, the thought of losing her home again was dredging up excruciating memories of the past when she didn't have a home.

But here in the fading sun with Enzo kissing her, the pain of the past and the worry of the future didn't matter so much. All that mattered in this moment were he and she.

As their kiss intensified, she felt as though she were floating above the ground. She leaned back against the blanket, drawing him with her. He followed her until her back was pressed upon the blanket. He leaned over her, giving her his full attention—oh, what attention.

A whinny followed by the pounding of hooves caused Enzo to pull away with a frustrated groan. He stared over her shoulder, in the direction of Emperor.

"Is something wrong?" she asked.

"Doesn't appear to be. Emperor must be growing bored." Enzo sat back and held out a hand to help her up. When she was fully upright, he said, "Sylvie, I've decided not to sell the estate. I tried to phone the buyer, but I wasn't able to reach him. I'll tell him when he arrives tomorrow."

Sylvie shook her head. "Don't do it."

"What's that supposed to mean? Aren't you the one who's been waging a campaign to convince me to call off the sale?"

"Would you have changed you mind about selling the estate if there wasn't a baby?"

Enzo averted his gaze and remained silent.

That was all the answer she needed. As hard as she'd tried to remind him what this estate meant to him—to his family—she'd failed. And now there was only one thing for her to do.

"You should sell the estate." Speaking these words was like an out-of-body experience for her. "It's what you intended to do all along. I don't want you to keep it and later blame me or the baby because you feel trapped here."

Enzo was silent for a moment as though absorbing her words. "And if I do sell the place, where will you go?"

"I'm moving to Florence. I'm taking that apartment above the florist."

"But, Sylvie, you can't. This is your home."

She shook her head. "Not any longer. With today being my last wedding and the buyer showing up tomorrow, I don't see a reason for me to put off moving to the city and starting my search for a new job."

Two deep lines formed between Enzo's brows. In his eyes, she could see the wheels of his mind spinning. She didn't know what he was thinking, but whatever it was wouldn't change her mind about leaving.

He visibly swallowed. "Don't go."

"What?" Surely, she hadn't heard him correctly.

"Don't leave. Not yet."

"You want me to stay here and watch you make the biggest mistake of your life?" She shook her head. "I can't do that. My leaving now while things are still amicable between us is what's best for everyone."

His darkened gaze narrowed on her. "I'm glad you've figured out what's best for everyone because I sure haven't." And with that, Enzo stood and, without another word, he strode over to Emperor. With the pounding of hooves, he rode away.

Tears stung her eyes. In truth, she couldn't bear to see the estate sold. For the first time since her mother died, Sylvie truly felt at home. And it was with a very heavy heart that she would leave here.

But she'd reinvented herself after her mother passed on

and she would do it again. Her gaze moved to the sketch pad on the blanket. She would find a job as a seamstress. It was steady, reliable work. She definitely preferred a job in the background instead of dealing with nervous brides and anxious mothers.

She sighed. It was for the best. Her baby was counting on her to provide a steady, loving home—not one full of drama. Love was fleeting. Hadn't she been taught that lesson over and over?

Her mother and father had a fleeting love. Her mother used to say that it burned so bright, so hot, that it'd burned itself out. Theirs had been a love-at-first-sight scenario. They were engaged in a month and married within six months of meeting. Her mother had been pregnant with Sylvie a month later. Everything in their relationship was rush-rush. Looking back now, Sylvie supposed that was just her mother's nature, always rushing here and there until cancer struck her down and trapped her in bed. Sylvie shoved aside the painful image.

Her parents' love had been short, but her mother swore that it was one of those loves that was so all-encompassing that she would never love anyone else the way she'd loved Sylvie's father. Sylvie never understood what her mother had meant, but she was starting to get an idea because that night she'd spent with Enzo, from dinner at the awards ceremony, to visiting the Eiffel Tower, to strolling through Paris, to winding up in his arms that night, had been like a love affair in fast-forward motion. It all went by so fast and now all she had were the memories.

No. That wasn't exactly true. She had their baby.

And unlike her father, who died in a work-related accident just short of her parents' first anniversary—Enzo was healthy and would go on to live a long life. She had to believe it.

She couldn't help but think of how her mother had gotten sick just as Sylvie had finished school—just when she'd made it through her turbulent teen years. She and her mother had just found solid ground when her mother had received her diagnosis.

It was around that time when Sylvie had met a guy, not just any guy, but someone she thought she could get serious with, but as soon as her mother was diagnosed, he was gone. It was then that Sylvie had accepted that she could only count on herself. It was a hard-learned lesson and one she shouldn't forget.

And that was why she needed to end things here with Enzo. No more kisses. No more physical contact of any sort because where they were concerned one thing just naturally led to another and that wasn't helping either of them.

No more excuses. No more delays. It was time she left once and for all.

# CHAPTER FIFTEEN

SYLVIE WAS GONE.

It was for the best.

No matter how many times Enzo told himself that it didn't feel like it was for the best. Still, it wasn't like he couldn't drive to visit her whenever he wanted. After all, when the estate was sold, he'd be moving, too. But now with news of the baby, he was rethinking his plans to move to France. That was a lot farther from Sylvie and the baby than he wanted to be.

But the problem was that she'd moved before they'd had time to sort out the future and make arrangements concerning the baby. He'd wanted to stop her from leaving, but what did he have to offer her? His life was in disarray. He didn't even know where he'd be sleeping next month.

After weather delays, the buyer, Mr. Renezo, had arrived a day late and had enjoyed everything about the estate—that was before the winds and wildfire took a distinctive turn. The fire was creeping toward the Bartolini estate—Enzo's home. Firefighting efforts were hampered by wind gusts that jumped fire lines.

In the wine-tasting room, Enzo had just sat down with Mr. Renezo and their attorneys to sign the sale papers. Enzo hadn't eaten that day. His stomach was bothering him. He blamed it on his nagging headache. All of Sylvie's reasons for him not to sell kept nagging at him.

Though the wildfire troubled Mr. Renezo, he was still willing to buy the estate so long as the fire didn't touch the property. That was a big *if* and they both knew it. But since the man had taken time from his busy schedule to fly in, they were ironing out the details.

The problem was that Mr. Renezo didn't want to keep the estate as it was. The man planned to destroy many of the buildings Enzo's father had built, including the little house where Sylvie had stayed. Even the main house wouldn't be recognizable when this man was done. Any memory of Enzo's family would be wiped away.

Part of Enzo realized when the sale was complete that it was Mr. Renezo's property to do with as he pleased, but the other part of him couldn't reconcile himself to the fact that his childhood home would no longer exist as he'd always known. When he'd started down this road, he'd never realized just how difficult it was going to become.

Needing a break from answering Mr. Renezo's questions, Enzo headed outside the winery. A hint of smoke hung in the air. There was no escaping it.

Another of his father's bits of wisdom came to him: *Change doesn't come easily but it's necessary.* Enzo just had to keep moving forward until the deal was complete. Everything would work out then. Wouldn't it?

Vito came rushing up to him. His tanned face was marred with deep worry lines. Enzo's heart sank down to his work boots. Had the fire reached the Bartolini property?

"How bad is it?" Enzo's words were rushed.

"It's bad. Do you have room for another family?" Vito asked. He'd returned early from his holiday when he heard about the fire.

Enzo raked his fingers through his hair. With evacuation orders up in the area, he'd been taking in displaced families. After all, he had an unoccupied hotel. He might as well put it to good use. The only problem was that it had filled up quickly.

"Put them in my room," he said. "I'll grab what I need and bunk down here with the rest of the crew." Vineyard workers who didn't have a family of their own was camping here, ready to do whatever was necessary.

Besides, now that Sylvie was gone, he spent as little time in the main house as possible. The estate was so empty, even with all these people staying here. Nothing was the same without Sylvie's bright smile and bubbly laugh.

With a resigned sigh Enzo turned toward the door. It was time to go back inside and sign the sales agreement—if the wildfire didn't incinerate the estate first.

Mr. Renezo looked up from the papers in front of him when Enzo entered the room. His silver hair was trimmed very short, revealing his lack of hair atop his head. From behind his silver frames his sharp gaze studied Enzo. "Everything all right?"

Enzo nodded. At least for the moment. "We should get the sales agreement signed."

"Just remember I've had my attorney write in a clause that if the wildfire destroys the property that this agreement is null and void, so if your rushing to sign is some sort of idea that you'll sign it and be off the hook if the worst happens, think again."

"The idea never crossed my mind. Let's do this." Enzo needed to get this over with, the sooner the better. Because the longer they took, the more the doubts about his actions circled overhead, weighing on him.

As he lifted the pen, he saw Sylvie's image in his mind.

She was frowning at him and shaking her head in disapproval. But she didn't understand. No one understood that this place represented his failures—the secret his parents kept—the secret he'd hid.

It was best to forget the past and just get on with the future. A fresh start that included a baby. Sylvie and his baby. He would do better by their child. There would be no secrets—secrets that shook the foundation of their family.

As they were about to sign the sales agreement, Vito rushed into the room. He didn't apologize for his presence. And by the distinct paleness of his face, it was clear that things had gotten worse.

He moved to Enzo's side. Vito leaned over and whispered, "We have to go. The fire is headed right for us."

In that moment Enzo wondered if this was his punishment for all the mistakes he'd been making with his sisters, with the estate—with Sylvie. Was the choice to stay or go being taken out of his hands? Was his past about to go up in smoke?

In the next breath he realized he wasn't a quitter. He refused to let the flames of fate take the decision of whether he should stay or go out of his hands.

He would stop the fire—he hoped. He would protect this land that had been left to him—that was so rich in memories. Some good. Some not so good.

And then he thought of Sylvie. She was always lurking at the edge of his thoughts. This estate is where he'd first met her. For whatever reason, she loved this place. And that was all the reason he needed to do whatever needed to be done.

# CHAPTER SIXTEEN

THIS COULDN'T BE HAPPENING.

Sylvie glanced out the window of the Bartolini estate. The whole villa had been closed up to protect its residents from the thickening smoke. Luckily for them, even though the fire was now threatening the edge of the Bartolini property, the estate was vast.

When Vito had called her to let her know that the wildfire had spread and was now heading for the estate, she'd stopped job searching and immediately returned. She had no idea what she could do to help. She just knew she had to be here for Enzo.

After already having a close call with the baby, she wouldn't take any chances by going out to the front lines where they were doing everything possible to stave off the fire. But that didn't mean she couldn't cook for all the dislocated people seeking shelter at the estate or the men and women fighting to save it.

"Do you have more bread?" Anna, Vito's wife, asked. "The sandwiches are going fast."

"I have some that just came out of the oven," Sylvie said. "I don't know if it's cool enough."

Anna placed her hand on one of the loaves. "It's cool enough. These guys are hungry."

"I'll slice it up." Sylvie grabbed a knife and set to work thinly slicing the bread. She wished there was more she could do than just stand around working the kitchen. "Have they said how it's going? Are their efforts holding off the fire?"

"They said so far so good but that could change with a gust of wind."

The thought of it sent a shiver of apprehension skittering down her spine.

And then she realized that Enzo shouldn't be facing this nightmare alone. Sure, she was there, but she wasn't family. He needed his sisters.

She wasn't sure how Enzo would feel about her interfering, but lately she had the feeling he wasn't thinking clearly. He was being driven by ghosts of the past. Maybe it was time he was surrounded by the people who loved him here and now—his sisters…and her—even if he didn't love her in return.

She pulled her phone from her pocket. She had Bianca's number but not Gia's. She was certain once Bianca heard the news that she'd call her sister.

Sylvie hurriedly pressed Dial before she had a chance to talk herself out of it. The phone rang once, twice, three times. Her heart started to sink. Bianca was very busy these days, between planning her Christmas wedding and assuming her new royal duties.

But then the call was picked up and Bianca's voice came on the line. "Sylvie, hi. What's going on?"

"Bianca, thank goodness. Have you talked to your brother recently?"

"No, why?" Concern rang out in Bianca's voice. "What's wrong?"

"It's the estate. There's a wildfire…its headed for the villa."

* * *

Everything had changed.

And now it was about to change once more.

The speed at which Enzo's life was evolving was dizzying. He paused and leaned upon the shovel he'd been using to help widen the cleared property line between his estate and the neighbors', where the wildfire was wreaking utter devastation. He grabbed a rag from his back pocket to run across his sweaty brow.

He gazed out over the vineyard as a light layer of smoke mingled with the sun's rays. The sunlight bounced off the droplets of dew, making them sparkle as though the long lines of grapevines were in fact strung with glittering jewels.

It wasn't so long ago that this place had been his dream. He'd gone off to make a name for himself so that when he returned, his father would take him on as a full partner—respecting his input. But that day had never come. It was snatched away from both of them when a delivery truck ran a stop sign.

In the end Enzo had won the vineyard by default. It certainly didn't feel like a win. It definitely felt more like a tremendous loss—the loss of his parents, the loss of his idyllic vision of them, the loss of his love for these rolling hills and lush vines where he and his sisters used to go exploring.

A sound caught his attention. He glanced over his shoulder. Caught up in his memories, for the briefest second he expected to see his sisters, Bianca and Gia, trekking their way toward him, laughing about something. When he'd ask what was so amusing, they'd shake their heads and say he wouldn't get it. But in reality, there was no one there. It was just a gust of hot, smoky wind rustling the leaves on the nearby vines.

Bianca had moved on. In just a few short months she would become the Princess of Patazonia. He hadn't been so sure about this love affair with a prince. In fact, he'd tried to keep them apart after Bianca returned from planning a royal wedding in Patazonia with a broken heart. But in the end, he saw that they truly belonged together.

And then there was his youngest sister, Gia. Her path to true love was not so simple. Not simple at all. To know that she'd been lied to all of her life by the people she was supposed to trust the most, their parents—it was unimaginable. And yet, through the darkest time in her life, she'd found love. Now both of his sisters were in committed relationships.

But not him—

"Enzo?"

He turned to find Vito standing there. He wasn't sure what to say to his manager, who was also the closest thing he had to a parent these days. He'd done what Vito had implored him not to do—sold the estate. Well, almost; pen had not been put to paper because of the wildfire.

Worry showed in Vito's eyes. "I wanted to let you know that the fire has really kicked up over the next hillside. They've thrown everything they've got at it. Perhaps it's time we pulled back."

"Did the firefighters tell us to move?" Enzo asked.

"Not yet. They said to be alert. They're trying to contain it before it gets this far."

"Good. Let's hope they succeed," Enzo said. "Tell our men, as always, it's totally their choice if they stay or go. I will understand if they need to go. But I'm staying until we're instructed otherwise." He paused and looked at his friend, dirt and sweat smeared on his aging face. "You should go, too."

Vito shook his head. "If you're staying, I am, too."

"I don't think that's a good idea." He pointed to the dark cloud in the distance. "You can see the fire isn't far off."

"I'm not leaving you out here alone."

"Have I told you lately how stubborn you are?" Then Enzo's gaze met Vito's. His voice softened. "Thank you for always being there."

"I'm not the only one who cares about you. I've seen the way Sylvie looks at you. It's the way my Anna looks at me."

He shook his head. "It's never going to work out." Not the romantic way. Even if the thought tempted him, he knew he'd ruined his chances with her. "She's gone."

"But it doesn't mean she can't come back. If you were to talk to her—tell her how you feel."

"Vito, now isn't the time."

His old friend nodded. "Just don't give up, on the estate or on Sylvie."

"I can't think about any of that now." Enzo turned back to the nightmare unfolding before him.

"I hope they're able to stop the fire before it reaches us."

"Me, too." Enzo didn't know why it should mean anything to him. After all, he was about to walk away from it. But he couldn't dismiss all the memories lurking all over the grounds. From birthday dinners that his mother had planned to his father teaching Enzo when he wasn't much more than a toddler about the soil and grapes.

For so long he hadn't wanted to relive those moments—the real moments that weren't tainted by lies. But Sylvie had slowly pulled back his blinders, seeing what had always been there in front of him. Family, happiness, anger, love and history. Theirs hadn't been a perfect family like he'd wanted to believe, but through it all, he'd felt loved.

"You know, for a man who doesn't care about the vineyard, you are fighting awfully hard to save it." And with that said, Vito walked off to check on the other men.

Enzo wanted to dismiss Vito's words, but as he got back to work, Vito's words haunted him. Why was he out here giving it his all? Why hadn't he paused for just two seconds to sign the sales agreement instead of springing out of the chair and rushing out the door as though the flames were licking at his heels?

How did Vito see through Enzo? It was like the older man was telling him what he was afraid to admit to himself. In that moment Enzo finally acknowledged what his heart had known all along—he loved this estate with all its happy and sad memories because when they came together, it made for a life of loving and caring. And he loved Sylvie—even if he'd fought it for months because he was scared of letting himself become vulnerable once more and being hurt by someone else he cared about. And he loved the baby—even though he knew he was going to make mistakes along the way and not always have the answers.

Still, he wanted a second chance to make the estate a loving home for their baby—a second chance to show Sylvie just how much she meant to him. But was it too late for all of that?

# CHAPTER SEVENTEEN

WHERE WAS ENZO?

Was he safe from the fire?

Sylvie sent up a prayer for his safety, as well as all the others out on the front lines. She'd just finished cleaning up after the midday food rush. In just a few minutes it'd be time to start preparing dinner.

She couldn't help but feel she wasn't doing enough. Her hand moved to her midsection; she had precious cargo on board that she had to make her priority. No one knew about the baby yet but Enzo. It wasn't that she didn't want to tell people—she did. She was so excited about the baby, but there was a part of her waiting until she'd worked out things with Enzo before she spread the joyous news.

As she stood on the veranda, her favorite spot in the villa, she noticed the smoke in the distance was practically gone. She squinted. Was that right? Was the fire diminishing? Hope swelled in her chest. For the past three days that was what she and everyone else at the Bartolini estate had been praying for. Had their prayers finally been answered?

But they weren't the only ones praying. Bianca and Gia were, too. Both sisters had dropped everything and flown in immediately following Sylvie's call. All three of them, along with Vito's wife, had been working side by side in the kitchen, making sure everyone was fed and as comfortable as was possible under the circumstances.

"Did you hear the news?" Bianca rushed out onto the veranda, all smiles.

"News?" Sylvie hadn't heard anything. As soon as the kitchen was squared away, she'd slipped out here for a little quiet time.

"The best news." Gia stepped up beside her sister.

They may only be half-sisters according to biology, but their facial features were similar, from the set of their eyes to their pert noses and full lips. And their relationship was so close that they could finish each other's sentences.

The news of Gia's conception had undoubtedly been devastating, but it appeared the sisters had recovered and were closer than ever. Now, if only Enzo would come around, maybe he wouldn't be in such a rush to put all of this behind him.

Anxious to know the news, Sylvie said, "Well, don't just smile at me, tell me what's happening. Is it the fire? Is it out?"

"Not out," Bianca said, the smile slipping from her face.

"But contained," Gia added.

"And the vineyard, was it spared?"

The sisters' expressions creased with worry lines.

"We haven't heard from any of the men," Bianca said. "But they should be back soon."

"And the evacuation order has been lifted so everyone is packing to head back home," Gia said. "Except for us. We've talked it over and we're sticking around for a while."

"I'm sure Enzo will appreciate it." Sylvie's thoughts turned to Enzo, wondering if she should leave before he returned. "I know he's missed both of you."

Bianca glanced down at her clasped hands. "Yeah, we really messed up forgetting his birthday."

"It won't happen again," Gia said emphatically. "We added it to our calendars on our phones."

"No matter where we are, we'll always remember," Bianca said.

Sylvie nodded in understanding. "Well, now that everything is under control and you two are sticking around, I should go pack."

"You're leaving?" both sisters asked in unison.

Sylvie lowered her gaze and nodded. "I need to get back to Florence."

"Stay," the sisters said at once.

To be a part of this family would be like a dream come true, and it had nothing to do with their vast wealth or Bianca's becoming a real-life princess or Gia's living on a romantic island in the Mediterranean or the way Enzo cared for his sisters like some mother hen. No, it had everything to do with the love that abounded among the three siblings, keeping them together through their parents' deaths, through a strange codicil to their will and through the discovery of an earthshattering secret. To be a part of a love that strong is something most people could only dream of.

Gia moved to Sylvie's side and put her arm around her. "What's wrong?"

"What?" Sylvie had been so deep in her thoughts that she hadn't realized her distress had shown on her face.

"You're crying." Bianca's eyes displayed concern.

Sylvie pressed her fingertips to her cheeks, feeling the dampness. She swiped away the tears. These pregnancy hormones had her crying at the drop of a hat. "It's nothing."

"Enzo might believe that line, but we don't." Bianca crossed her arms as though letting her know she meant business. "Talk to us. Is it our brother? Has he upset you?"

Maybe she should tell them. After all, they were the

baby's aunts. The urge to confess swelled within her until it was a loud roar in her ears.

"I'm pregnant with Enzo's baby." The words just came tumbling out.

Both women's mouths opened and for a moment no words came. They looked at each other. And then their attention returned to Sylvie.

After a moment Bianca pressed her lips together as though she was gathering her thoughts. "Does Enzo know?"

Sylvie nodded. "It was a shock for both of us."

"And what did he say?"

"Not a lot at first. Then he said he was calling off the sale of the estate. I told him not to. The baby wasn't reason enough to change his mind—to remain someplace he doesn't want to be. I don't want him blaming me or the baby for his having to stay here."

"He wouldn't do that," Bianca said.

"I never believed that he wanted to leave here," Gia said. "When we were kids all he talked about was one day running the vineyard just like Papá."

"Do you love our brother?" Bianca asked.

Without hesitation, Sylvie said, "Yes."

They talked for a little more about the baby and Enzo. Both Bianca and Gia encouraged her to give Enzo some more time. They were certain once he got over the shock that things would look different for both of them.

"I can't stay here and hope he'll fall in love with me." Sylvie took a step toward the doorway. "I have to go make a life for the baby and myself."

Concern filled Bianca's gaze. "Isn't there anything we can say to get you to stay? I'm sure Enzo will want to see you and thank you for all you did."

Sylvie shook her head. "It's best I go."

And with that, she walked away, feeling as though she were leaving a part of her behind—her heart. But Enzo had made his decision. When Vito had called to let her know the wildfire was threatening the estate, he'd told her that Enzo was meeting with the buyer to sign the sales agreement. Nothing had changed Enzo's mind about staying here—not her and not the baby.

# CHAPTER EIGHTEEN

LEAVING THIS TIME was harder than the first time.

Sylvie packed her few things in her bag. She couldn't help feeling things with Enzo were going to get more complicated before they figured out a way to peacefully co-parent. She didn't even know what that would be like if he were to move to France, but for their child's sake, they'd figure it out.

It was then that she realized she was folding and re-folding the same shirt because there was a part of her that was hoping to see Enzo before she left. Though another part insisted it would be easier on everyone if she quietly slipped away. His sisters would be here for him. With that thought in mind, she hurriedly placed the rest of her clothes in the bag and zipped it.

*Knock-knock.*

Sylvie figured it was Bianca or Gia, who were once more going to try and convince her to stay. "Come in." At that point she realized she'd forgot her sunglasses on top of the chest of drawers. She turned to retrieve them, confident that at last she had gathered all of her things. She turned back around, surprised to find Enzo standing just inside the doorway. "Enzo, you're back."

He nodded. It was then she noticed the dark streaks of soot on his face, his scattered hair and his disheveled clothes. "My sisters told me you were getting ready to leave. Weren't you even going to stick around and say hello before you left?"

Her gaze searched his. What was he trying to say? Was he disappointed she was trying to avoid him? Or was that just wishful thinking on her part?

"I… I didn't want to get in the way." She glanced down at her bag, opening the side pocket to place her sunglasses inside. "I'm sure you have a lot of catching up to do with your sisters."

"Do you even want to know how the estate faired?"

Immediately, her gaze rose to meet his. "Of course. Were you able to save it all?"

He shook his head. There was a torrent of emotions in his eyes but she wasn't able to distinguish one from the other. He reached up and rubbed the back of his neck. "We lost some vines."

"I'm sorry." She truly was sorry. "Hopefully, they can be replanted."

He nodded. "It'll take time but it's doable."

"I'm sure the new owner will be relieved." She lifted her bag and swung the strap over her shoulder. It was time to make a quick exit while she still had her emotions in check.

"Sylvie, there isn't going to be a new owner."

"There isn't? But I thought the papers had been signed."

"I got called away before we signed the papers. You might say the whole deal went up in flames." A half smile pulled at his lips.

Her heart was pounding. What did this mean? She refused to jump to conclusions. She wasn't going to get her hopes up just to have them dashed. After all, there was a baby counting on her to get this right.

"You could stay on, here at the estate," he said.

She shook her head. "I need to return to Florence and continue searching for a new job."

"And the baby?"

"I would never keep you away from him or her. Florence isn't that far away. I'm sure we can work out a visitation schedule."

"You won't reconsider staying here?"

She gave a firm shake of her head. "I have to start a new life for myself and the baby. It's better this way."

If she were to stay here, she didn't think she'd ever be able to get over Enzo. He'd always be around. They'd be bumping into each other at every turn. And a one-way love—it just wasn't enough for her.

Even though her parents' love had burned bright and quickly, it was something genuine—something so strong that her mother held on to the memories of that love until her last breath. If Sylvie was going to risk her heart to another, she wanted a strong, passionate love like theirs had been.

"I... I understand." Though the tone of his voice seemed to say the opposite. "I'll take care of the rent—"

"No, Enzo. I told you I'll take care of myself."

"But that's my baby you're carrying."

"It's mine, too, and I'll make sure we're taken care of."

He turned to her and frowned. "Why are you being so stubborn?"

Her mouth gaped. It took her a moment to gather herself, but that didn't stop her from glaring at him. "I'm not."

"All I'm trying to do is my part as far as the baby is concerned, but you won't let me. If you think I'm not going to support my own child and not be there as much as possible, you're very wrong."

"I would never stop you from being there for our child. I... I just need to do this transition on my own." She needed to prove to herself that she could do this because being a single mother scared her. She remembered how hard her mother had worked to provide for her, and she worried that she wouldn't be able to give her son or daughter as good a life as her mother had given her.

"But that's the thing. You don't have to do it alone—you don't have to do any of this alone. Marry me."

*What had he said?*

Her gaze searched his to see if it was some sort of joke. But the look on Enzo's face said he was perfectly serious. He wanted to marry her.

She needed to hear that he loved her as much as she loved him. She wouldn't accept anything less. Then she would make a home with him—have a family with him.

"Why?" she asked.

"Why what? Why get married?" When she nodded, he visibly swallowed. He wasn't comfortable with this conversation. That was her first warning. He cleared his throat. "We're having a baby. Isn't that reason enough?"

No, it wasn't reason enough. Not even close to it. There was so much more to a marriage than children. And if their union wasn't founded in love, how were they ever to make it through the storms life threw their way? Their marriage would get blown off course and flounder.

He approached her. His gaze beseeched hers. "Sylvie, marry me."

With strength she didn't know she possessed, she said, "No."

Before her pregnancy hormones realized what she'd just done and sent her into a fit of tears, she stepped around him. With her head held high, she headed for the door. Inside, her facade was starting to melt. It was a good thing she'd already arranged for a ride into the city because if she stayed here any longer, she might change her mind. And that wouldn't be good for any of them—including the baby.

*Goodbye.*

She didn't say the word. She didn't trust her voice as there was a giant lump in her throat. Instead, she blinked back the tears and kept walking.

# CHAPTER NINETEEN

*No.*

One single syllable. Two tiny letters.

Combined, they had the power to deeply pierce his scarred heart.

Enzo stumbled as he made his way to the kitchen. He walked blindly as all his resources were focused on reviewing exactly what had gone wrong with their conversation. It shouldn't have gone so far off the tracks. He'd gone over it word for word while out in the fields. He'd been certain Sylvie would see that marrying him was the best option. She loved the estate and had been happy here. At least, that was what he'd thought. If she would have agreed to marry him, they'd have lived happily ever after right here in this very house.

But when he'd rushed back to the villa to share news that the fire had been defeated, all those well-planned, well-chosen words had gone straight out of his head. At first, he'd been caught up in the beautiful sight of her. It was in that moment he realized just how much he'd missed her. He'd missed talking to her, listening to the lilt of her voice and her laughter, it was contagious.

But today had been different. She'd been different. He'd noticed the stubborn jut of her chin and the pain in her eyes. He should have realized it wasn't going to be so easy to rectify the past. But he'd been so wound up, so ready to profess his well-planned words.

Yet, when he opened his mouth those words he'd planned…well, they'd gotten all jumbled up somewhere between his brain and his tongue. And maybe he had rushed things a bit with that proposal. But she was being stubborn and he'd grown more nervous with each passing moment.

He knew she loved the estate—enough to wage a campaign to stop him from selling it. So the only reason he could come up with for her to turn him down was that she didn't love him. Maybe she cared about him as a friend, but she couldn't see him as anything more than that—

"Enzo, what's wrong?"

He didn't have to lift his head to recognize that voice. It was Bianca. When his gaze rose, he found not one but both sisters staring at him with worry reflected in their eyes.

"Where's Sylvie?" Gia asked.

"She left." His voice sounded hollow as he slumped down in a kitchen chair.

"Left?" Bianca said. "I thought you were going to talk to her."

He lowered his gaze to the tabletop. "I did."

"And she still left?" Gia pulled out a chair across the table from him.

"She did."

Bianca sat next to him. "Why didn't you stop her?"

His gaze jerked up to meet hers. Frustration bunched up in his gut. "Don't you think I tried? I even told her we should get married."

Bianca and Gia turned to each other. They didn't say a word, but they were communicating nonetheless. He hated when they did this and left him out. He had no idea what they were thinking—no, that wasn't true. He knew what they thought. He screwed this all up. And he couldn't disagree.

His chair scraped over the slate floor tiles.

"Don't go." Bianca stood, as if to follow him.

He shook his head. "I don't need you to tell me that I've made a mess of everything—starting when we were kids."

"When we were kids?" Bianca sent him a puzzled look.

"What are you talking about?" Gia moved to Bianca's side.

He hadn't meant to bring up the past. He'd just been so worked up and the words had come tumbling out. It was a mistake. But how was he going to take it back now that his sisters were laser focused on him?

And then he heard the echo of Sylvie's voice urging him to open up about the past. She'd told him to be honest with his sisters about everything and trust that they'd make it through another revelation.

But the thought of revealing the secret he'd been keeping more than half his life was daunting. His gut knotted up. What if they never spoke to him again?

"Enzo, talk to us." Bianca's voice drew him from his internal debate.

"You better sit down for this," he said in a resigned tone.

His sisters exchanged worried glances as they took a seat. And then he told them about that long-ago night when he'd overheard his parents' argument about their mother's affair. It was a memory he hoped he'd never have to revisit after today.

Silence greeted his confession. And it stretched out into an uncomfortable void.

Enzo shifted in his seat. "I'm really sorry. I've messed up big-time."

Bianca's fine brows drew together. "You really thought they were talking about you?"

He nodded.

"Is this why you've been acting so strange?" Gia asked. "Why you look like you've been carrying around the weight of the world?"

He shrugged and then nodded. "I'd put that memory out of my mind. I'd convinced myself it was just a horrible dream. And when you want to believe something enough, it's pretty easy to do." He paused and drew in a deep breath. He had one more admission to make. "And then when the journal was found, the memory came back. I… I should have said something then. But I was…afraid."

Another awkward silence filled the air. What were they thinking? Would they understand? Or would they remain angry with him?

*Knock-knock.*

Enzo inwardly groaned. Now wasn't the time for interruptions. He needed to work this out with his sisters—sisters who were being unusually quiet. It wasn't a good sign.

Bianca jumped up. "I think it's Mr. Caruso."

"What's the family attorney doing here?" Enzo asked. And then a thought came to him. "Does this have to do with the sale of the estate?"

"I don't know," Bianca said. "He called earlier and asked if he could drop by."

"Do you think it's something bad?" Gia asked as they all moved toward the front door.

No one answered her question. Enzo hoped Gia was wrong. They'd already had enough bad stuff to last a lifetime.

Bianca swung the door open and greeted Mr. Caruso. His face was pale and drawn as though he had a matter of great importance weighing on his mind.

After they ushered him into Enzo's office because the

living room was still a bit disheveled from their guests, Enzo turned to the older man. "What's wrong?"

"I don't know quite how this happened." Mr. Caruso started to pace. "It really shouldn't have happened. In all my years as an attorney, I've never seen something like this." The man's words were rushed.

"Sit down." Gia guided him over to a chair. As she stood behind the chair as the man took a seat, she raised her brows at her siblings. She then moved to a nearby chair to sit down.

Mr. Caruso clutched his leather satchel with both arms. "I'm so sorry. I had to replace my assistant a while back and it took a few candidates until I found one that was a good fit. I don't know if it happened then or what—"

"It's okay." Enzo sat behind what had been their father's desk. "Just tell us the problem and we'll go from there."

Mr. Caruso searched through his satchel and pulled out a legal-size envelope. He held it up. "This was supposed to have been with your parents' will. Somehow it got misplaced."

"What is it?" Enzo hesitantly asked, wondering if it was yet another bombshell.

Gia frowned. "We're not sure we want to learn any more family secrets."

"I agree," Bianca chimed in. "It's been a roller-coaster year. Maybe you should just keep whatever that is."

Mr. Caruso looked perplexed. "I… I can't do that." He stood and held out the envelope to no one in particular. "Who should I give it to?"

Neither Enzo nor his sisters reached for it.

Mr. Caruso placed the envelope on the edge of the desk. "I'll just leave it here until one of you feels like reading it. Again, I'm so sorry about this."

Not one of the three of them spoke. They sat there staring at the envelope as though at any moment it was going to explode. Dread consumed Enzo. Hadn't they already been through enough?

"I'll see myself out." Mr. Caruso made a hasty departure.

Enzo wasn't sure how long they just sat there staring at the envelope wondering what bit of dynamite it contained. Would reading it once again blow apart their worlds?

Gia sat forward. "This is ridiculous. We can't pretend we don't know it exists. And we can't spend the next year or so wondering what it says."

Enzo cleared his throat. "I agree." He turned his attention to Bianca. "If we're going to do this, it needs to be unanimous. What do you say?"

Bianca hesitated before she nodded in agreement. Gia did the same.

Enzo reached for the envelope. Across the front, each of their names were printed in their father's handwriting. Enzo's gut twisted into a knot.

*Here we go again.*

He stuck his finger beneath the flap and yanked, opening the envelope. His heart pounded in his chest as he recalled the nightmare that had unfolded after they read their mother's journal.

*Please don't let this be like that.*

Enzo withdrew two sheets of paper with his father's handwriting. His instinct was to skim through the letter and make sure there was nothing that was going to upset his sisters, but he knew that wasn't fair to them. Hadn't he already learned the price of keeping secrets?

Enzo cleared his throat and began reading aloud.

*"Enzo, Bianca and Gia, I apologize for what you have gone through with the contest to win the es-*

*tate. Your mother told me not to do it, but I didn't want any of you to make a life-altering mistake like your mother and I have done. By fighting for the villa you've each had a chance to figure out what the place means to you. I know that each of you loves the estate, perhaps for different reasons, and that's okay. But without the contest it would be easy for each of you to forget its meaning. Just as your mother and I became so complacent in our marriage that for a moment we forgot what it meant to both of us. I can tell you all that your mother is the love of my life. And I believe she feels the same for me. We experienced troubles in our time. I would say it was my fault, though she would vehemently disagree. I had become so absorbed in growing the vineyard that I forgot about the importance of family. My fatherly advice to each of you is not to forget your family is your priority. Their love, safety and happiness must come first. Always. If you're reading this letter, it means your mother and I are no longer with you. But never doubt we're looking down upon each of you, cheering you on and loving you all. And hoping that each of you finds the one great love in your life like your mother and I have done. I hope by now the three of you have found your way back to being family once more. That was our final parting gift—by pulling you apart, the three of you would come back together closer than ever. We love you. We always will.*

*Papá and Mamma."*

When Enzo finished reading the letter, stunned silence filled the room. His sisters swiped at their damp eyes. Enzo blinked repeatedly.

It took Enzo time to absorb what he'd read. His parents may have made mistakes but how could he hold that against them when he'd been making one mistake after the next?

And then he remembered something else his father had told him: *Family means not giving up. No matter what.*

"I may not agree with Papá's methods," Bianca said, breaking the silence, "but he's right. I feel closer to both of you than I have since we were kids."

"I agree," Gia said.

Enzo wasn't sure he'd heard them correctly. "You mean you aren't mad at me for not speaking up about the secret?"

His breath caught in his chest as he waited for their collective answer. He knew he didn't deserve a pass. If it had been reversed and they'd kept him in the dark, he'd have been very upset. But it didn't keep him from hoping for forgiveness.

"You should have told us," Gia said.

"You should have trusted us." Bianca looked more hurt than angry.

"But it's over now. And you have to let this go," Gia said, "before you're so busy looking over your shoulder at the past that you miss your future."

"She's right," Bianca said. "Sylvie told us everything."

His eyes widened. "Sylvie told you about the baby?"

Bianca nodded. "She did. She said she was going to sit on the news until you two figured things out, but she just couldn't hold it in any longer."

"Sylvie should be here with you—with us." Gia's pointed stare was directed right at him. "If you don't go get her, I will."

"But the estate—"

"Will be fine while you're gone," Bianca jumped in. "We'll take care of things here."

"And if you want," Gia said, "I can start renovations to turn this place back into the home we once knew it to be."

The thought appealed to him. Maybe that was why he'd felt such a disconnect with the estate—his home no longer felt like a home but rather the hotel it'd become. "You would do that?"

Gia smiled and nodded. "I'd love to."

Love for his sisters lifted the corners of his mouth. "I don't know how to thank you."

Gia's gaze met his. "Easy. Go get your family."

Enzo made his way to his room to shower and pack. He was off to the city. But how was he supposed to prove to Sylvie that he'd always be there for her and the baby?

Then he realized he couldn't just expect Sylvie to change her plans once more; he knew he was the one who would have to make the concession this time. And a plan started to take shape.

# CHAPTER TWENTY

SHE MISSED HIS smile and the warmth of his deep laugh.

She missed the estate with its picturesque rolling hills and the horses.

She missed all of it.

Sylvie stuffed the sad thoughts to the back of her mind. That was her past. This was her future. It had been a week since she'd turned down Enzo's marriage proposal.

But was it a proposal? Not really. Traditionally, it would involve popping the question and he hadn't asked her anything. Enzo's mention of marriage was more akin to suggesting a restaurant for dinner.

A marriage proposal should be filled with emotion. Love should be mentioned—in fact, it should take center stage. It didn't have to be delivered on bended knee. A ring would be nice but not a requirement. However, for her the love part was nonnegotiable.

*Knock-knock.*

Sylvie turned from where she was washing her lunch dishes. She didn't have to answer the door to know who was on the other side of it. The delivery guy from the florist downstairs.

Every day that week, Enzo had sent her flowers with little messages.

The first had said *I'm sorry.*

The next had said *I want to make things up to you.*
Each new bouquet came with a note:

*I'm working on a surprise.*
*Please give me another chance.*
*It won't be much longer.*

And finally...

*I miss you.*

She had to admit it was like getting pieces of a love let-ter. She grew anxious to know what today's message would be. She realized that a true love letter should say he loved her and so far that hadn't been the case.

She moved to the door and opened it. There stood Vin-cenzo, who worked downstairs in the flower shop. He was the owner's grandson, who was planning to one day take over the family business.

He smiled. "These are for you."

She accepted the red rosebuds. She paused to sniff them. They made her smile. Red roses meant love. Was Enzo working up to tell her he loved her?

She turned and paused, trying to figure out where to put them. "You do know I'm starting to run out of room."

"I think the guy has it really bad for you. Maybe you should give him another chance."

She had to admit the flowers were wearing down her resolve, but she had to wonder when Enzo was going to make his plea in person. "I just might do that."

She was anxious for Vincenzo to go. She wanted to read the attached card in private, even though Vincenzo was the one who had written it and attached it to the bouquet.

Vincenzo hesitated as though he wanted to say more, then he wished her a good day and moved on.

Sylvie closed the door before rushing over to the small kitchen table. She placed the vase on the counter and then reached for the envelope. With each bouquet and note, she felt her excitement rise. What would he say today?

She opened the little envelope and pulled out the card.

*The surprise is ready. Below is the address and time. Please come.*

Frustration balled up in her stomach. She didn't want to wait. What exactly did he have planned? With Enzo it could be anything. But she'd never been so excited for anything in her life.

She placed her hand over her tiny baby bump. "We're going to see your daddy today, little one. I don't know how it'll work out, but I promise, no matter what, we're both going to love you with all of our hearts."

He wasn't sure this was going to work.

He wasn't even sure she would show up.

Enzo straightened his tie for the fourth or fifth time. Maybe he should have invited her to dinner in person. But he'd hoped to capture her attention with the notes. But did it work? Would she show up?

He'd been working nonstop on this surprise since he'd arrive in Florence a week ago. Gia had phoned a few times to ask his input on the renovations at the villa. They were growing closer once more. It sounded like she already had a line on some workers to launch the project. With the villa safely in his sister's hands, he could focus on his own work.

He'd paid double-time to have a crew work round the

clock on his surprise for Sylvie. It wasn't complete, but it was far enough along that she would get the idea.

He moved to the table in the middle of the room with the white tablecloth and two red taper candles. He'd already lit them. Maybe that was a mistake. What if she was late? The candles would melt down and not look nice. But he'd wanted to have the mood set for when she arrived—if she arrived.

"Mr. Bartolini—" the head of a string quartet approached him with a violin in hand "—would you like us to begin playing?"

"Not yet. You can start just as soon as—" What did he call her? His girlfriend? The mother of his baby? "—as soon as my guest arrives."

*If she shows up…*

He had caterers in the back keeping food warm to serve an elegant, hopefully long dinner. He'd tried to pull out all of the stops tonight, but to be honest, he'd never planned an evening like this so he wasn't sure if he was missing anything or not.

He started to pace. He yanked at his buttoned collar. It felt too tight. He wasn't sure about any of this, including his suit. Maybe he should—

*Tinkle. Tinkle.*

The bell above the front door alerted him that someone had arrived.

*Please let it be Sylvie.*

He turned and in the dimmed light, he made out her very familiar petite form. Boy, had he missed her. He'd missed everything about her. But tonight wasn't about him; it was about her. And showing her that he was the right man for her.

She'd checked the address three times.

It was a storefront. And it didn't look occupied. Though

the soft glow of light shone through the white curtains over the windows.

Certain she had the right place, Sylvie opened the door. A little bell rang out her arrival. She stepped inside. The overhead lights were dimmed and a violin started playing. What in the world...?

Her gaze moved to the single table in the middle of the room. There were two table settings and candles. In the center of the table was a bud vase with a single long-stem red rose. Her heart swooned. Had Enzo set all of this up for her? And where was he?

It was then that he stepped out of the shadows and approached her. He smiled but it didn't quite reach his eyes. Was he as nervous as she was?

"Thank you for coming," he said.

"Enzo, what is all of this?"

"This is my new store, Barto Wines."

"You're opening a wine store?"

He nodded. "It's something that I'd been planning to mention to my father when he had his accident. I abandoned the idea while trying to navigate the aftermath of my parents' deaths. But now seemed to be the right time to move to Florence—"

"You're moving here?" That was something she hadn't expected. Not at all. "But why not France, like you'd talked about?"

He peered deep into her eyes, making her heart beat faster. "I have an apartment upstairs. No matter what you or the baby need, I will be here. Day or night."

"But...but you can't do that. What about your life? Your dreams?"

"That's what I'm trying to tell you. My dreams revolve around you." He stepped closer. "I'm sorry for how I handled things. It took my sisters and my parents to point out the mistakes I've been making. I've talked to my sisters about the past, like you suggested."

Hope swelled in her chest. "How did it go?"

"It wasn't easy, but just like you predicted, they forgave me."

"I'm so happy to hear that."

"And now it's time I apologize to you, for being such a fool." He stared deep into her eyes, making her heart pound. "I've made one mistake after the next and I probably don't deserve a second chance, but I've learned my lesson and I promise I'm going to be honest with you and support you, no matter what. And I'll always be there for our little one."

He was saying all the right words. Perhaps she should say something, too, but she didn't want to interrupt him, not when she had the feeling he was about to tell her something very important.

"Sylvie, I love you." Her heart swooned as he continued. "I think I've loved you since you arrived in Tuscany. How could I not with your glowing smile and infectious laugh? You light up my days like no one else has ever done. And without you in my life, it's all shades of gray."

She stared into his eyes, making sure she hadn't just imagined the words he'd spoken. But his eyes showed his love. "I love you, too."

He let out a visible breath. "I was hoping you'd say that. You don't know how worried I was that I'd screwed up everything."

"You didn't screw anything up. Things are working out just like I always imagined they would."

He leaned toward her just as she lifted up on her tiptoes and pressed her lips to his. Tears of joy dampened her eyes. Right now she was a trembling ball of excitement. Her dream was coming true. And then much too soon, Enzo pulled back.

"Hold that thought. I have one more surprise." He pulled a small remote from his pocket. With the press of a button, a dazzling array white lights in a star pattern moved across the ceiling and walls. He held out a hand to her. "Would you dance with me?"

She nodded, afraid words would fail her. She placed her hand in his and he pulled her close. Her heart was pounding so hard in her ears that she couldn't hear the music. She followed Enzo's lead as they made their way around the floor.

This was what her mother had always meant about finding that one great love in your life. Sylvie never could have guessed it would feel this good. She was head over heels in love.

When the music stopped, Enzo dropped to one knee just like in a movie. "Sylvie, I haven't always said the right thing or done the right thing, but I hope you'll be able to see past my mistakes and know that I love you with all of my heart." He reached in his jacket pocket and held a diamond ring out to her. "Will you do me the greatest honor of being my partner in life?"

Tears of joy clouded her eyes. She blinked because she didn't want to miss any of this. "Yes. Yes, I'll marry you."

He slipped the ring on her trembling finger and then he straightened. He smiled at her as she swiped away her happy tears. "How did I get to be so lucky?"

"I'm the lucky one to have you in my life."

"But where will we live? Your apartment? Or mine?"

He smiled. "Wherever you want, but I do know of this villa and vineyard that would be perfect for a growing family."

"Really?" She felt so very blessed in that moment and hoped her mother was looking down over her, seeing her get her happily-ever-after.

He nodded. And then he leaned forward, pressing his lips to hers.

# EPILOGUE

*Kingdom of Patazonia, December 20*

THIS WAS IT.

The big day had arrived.

Bianca Bartolini's stomach shivered with nerves. She stood in the preparation room in the Grand Cathedral of Patazonia surrounded by the family she'd been born into and those she chose to call family. And as much as she wished her parents were here, she knew they were watching down over her. Of that, she was certain.

She'd stood in this very room before. It had been in her position as a wedding planner. She'd been nervous back then, too, but for a totally different reason.

Today she was the bride. *The bride.* A big smile pulled at her lips. The thought of being Leo's wife excited her beyond belief. It was the responsibilities that went with the position that made her nervous, though she tried to hide it from everyone. Her self-doubts were still there, lurking in the background. She was about to become a princess. The thought stole her breath away.

Most of all, she was grateful that her rapidly expanding family was with her. She smiled as her gaze moved around the room. She'd be lost without their unfailing love and support.

"Love looks good on you." Gia smiled.

"I'm truly happy." Bianca's gaze landed on her younger sister, who was glowing with happiness. "And I have a feeling it won't be long until we're at your wedding."

Gia's face filled with color as she glanced away.

"Gia, what aren't you telling me? Are you already engaged?"

The color in her face deepened. "Not exactly."

"What's that supposed to mean?"

Gia hesitated as though she was trying to figure out how to answer her. Just as Bianca was about to prompt her sister, Gia said, "We've talked about getting married."

"And?"

"That's as far as it got. I've been busy working on remodeling houses and he's been busy with his new algorithm."

Bianca reached out and squeezed her sister's hand. "He's good for you. I see how you light up around him. Don't put off the important things in life." Her thoughts strayed to her parents and how life could be so unexpected.

The smile fell from Gia's face. "You aren't the only one thinking of Mamma and Papá today." She swiped at her eyes. "But I think they're here. I can see Papá when Enzo smiles. And I see Mamma in your eyes."

"And I see both of them in you. The patience you have is so like Papá. And your talent for making everything look perfect is just like Mamma."

"What have we missed?" Enzo stepped up to them with his new bride.

Enzo and Sylvie had had a small ceremony at the villa as soon as Gia had completed the renovations. Instead of being here at Bianca's wedding, they should be off on their much-deserved honeymoon. But they'd delayed their departure until after the New Year. They both agreed that there was nowhere else in the world they'd want to be right now.

Sylvie had officially given up her wedding planner business. With Enzo's encouragement she was following her dreams and designing wedding dresses full-time. In fact, Bianca was wearing a Sylvie Original.

Bianca made sure to tell everyone that Sylvie was a rising star. Orders were already pouring in after seeing a few of Sylvie's designs. Just wait until the world saw Bianca's royal wedding gown.

"You just missed our little sister getting worked up," Bianca lightly teased her brother.

"I was not," Gia said as if by instinct. "Okay. Maybe a little. It's just that our little family is growing. And Mamma and Papá aren't here to see it."

"They're here," Enzo said. "They're definitely here."

With that, the door opened and the royal wedding planner stepped into the room. "Everyone out. Except you—" she pointed to Bianca "—and you." She pointed to Enzo, who was to walk her down the aisle. "The ceremony is about to begin."

Bianca hugged Gia and then she hugged Sylvie.

"Oh!" Sylvie paused.

"Is something wrong?" Enzo was by her side instantly.

Sylvie smiled. "Nothing is wrong. Everything is right. That was just our little football player in there, letting me know he's awake."

"It's a boy?" Bianca and Gia asked simultaneously.

"Oops." She glanced at her husband. "I thought you told them."

He shook his head. "I didn't get a chance with all of the wedding stuff."

Bianca rushed forward. First, she hugged her brother

and then Sylvie. "Congratulations. I have a feeling this coming year is going to be absolutely amazing."

"I agree," Gia said.

The room cleared as the procession music began to play. This past year had been full of highs and lows but through it all, she and her siblings had stuck together. Bianca's heart was full of love. It was only going to get better from here.

And now it was time for her to go marry her very own Prince Charming. She placed her hand on the crook of her brother's arm. She couldn't help but think of her father when she looked at Enzo. They were so similar in looks and mannerisms. Her heart swelled with love.

The two large wooden doors swung open and Bianca stepped into her future. When her gaze connected with Leo's, her heart fluttered in her chest. Her insecurities faded away. All she felt now was love. Love for her new country, love for her family and most of all love for the prince of her heart.

\* \* \* \* \*

# THE LAST MAN
# SHE EXPECTED

## MICHELLE MAJOR

For Annie—you are one of the best friends
I have and the best moms I know.
Love ya, lady.

## Chapter One

As a cool September breeze tickled the hair at the nape of her neck, Mara Reed drew in a deep breath and tried to steady her nerves. There was no reason for the bead of sweat rolling between her shoulders, but it tracked its way down her spine with little regard for the mild fall weather.

Colorful balloons bobbed on strings tied to the front-porch rail of the two-story brick house as she and her daughter approached. The sound of voices drifted toward her from around back—happy laughter and children shouting in pleasure. She could imagine the group of family and friends gathered, an involuntary shudder snaking down her spine in response.

Sometimes forcing a smile and putting on her best social face was a real pain in the—

"Mommy, what's wrong?" Evie's feathery brows drew together under the frames of her glasses as she squeezed Mara's hand. Her brown eyes, tinged with worry, looked impossibly large behind the lenses. "We're late for Anna's party. Do you wanna not go?"

Mara smiled down at her five-year-old daughter, ignoring the slight ache in her cheeks. "Of course we're going to the party. We're here, and it's going to be so much fun. There will be cake and ice cream and Josh said they have a bounce house."

"I don't want to mess up my new dress," Evie said, her hand slipping from Mara's.

"The dress will be fine," Mara assured her daughter. "You look beautiful, sweetie. Let's go in. Anna will be waiting for you."

"She has lots of friends here." Evie bit down on her lower lip as she studied the front door, and Mara hated the uncertainty she could feel radiating from her daughter. Hated how familiar it felt. She refused to believe that she'd somehow transferred her own nerves to her precious girl.

"But only *one* best friend," Mara reminded the girl, "and that's you."

Evie gave a small nod then flashed a gap-tooth grin and headed up the stairs in her sparkly ballet slippers and poufy-skirted party dress.

Smoothing a hand over the peplum blouse she'd

chosen for the afternoon, Mara followed, her smile set firmly in place. She hated this reaction in herself, the uneasy mix of anxiety and dread she had in social situations.

No one would guess it, of course. In the past year she'd become a master at hiding her feelings, stuffing them down and locking them away until she barely had to acknowledge them herself. Only sometimes she could still feel their slippery tendrils tugging at her resolve.

She'd moved to the picturesque town of Starlight, Washington, nestled at the base of the Cascade Mountains east of Seattle, a year ago and had immediately started working at the coffee shop her aunt owned in town. Her nerves didn't plague her at Main Street Perk. During her shifts making coffee and serving food to the shop's loyal client base, she could ignore—if not forget—the way her life had so spectacularly imploded.

She wasn't the divorced single mother who'd failed at almost everything. The coffee shop patrons didn't care that she was a wreck on the inside or couldn't make small talk to save her life. She provided the caffeine and pastries they needed to get through the day, and that was enough at Perk.

Outside of work, she struggled with the affable camaraderie inherent in small town life. She had to remind herself she'd chosen Starlight for Evie, so that her daughter could have as close to an ideal childhood as Mara could provide on her own. The divorce had been brutal, and Mara knew she'd never truly release the guilt over her inability to give her daughter the gift of being raised by parents who loved each other.

Her love for Evie would have to be enough.

They entered the house, and Evie called out a shy greeting to her best friend, Anna. The precocious birthday girl, with wide blue eyes and a brilliant smile, ran forward and reached out a hand that Evie grabbed with so much enthusiasm it made Mara's heart clench.

Josh Johnson, Anna's dad, waved from across the kitchen as Anna led Evie out onto the patio behind the house. As a child, Mara had been like Anna, bold and fearless, ruling the school lunchroom and playground like it was her own little kingdom.

Oh, how times had changed. She was doing her best to make this town her home but feared she'd never regain the self-assurance she'd had before her life fell apart. If only she could whip up confidence as quickly as she could manage a complicated drink order.

Josh excused himself from the group of women surrounding him and moved toward Mara. "They won't bite, you know," he admonished gently when he got to her side, inclining his head toward the quartet of hipster-stylish young moms.

"I'd feel better if I could just make them a cappuccino and call it a day." Mara crossed her arms over her chest. "They're nice to you."

"They feel sorry for me." Josh ran a hand through his shaggy brown hair. "I hate that."

Mara didn't know Josh's ex-wife Jenn, but she still harbored an intense hatred for the woman. She'd walked out on Josh and Anna shortly before Mara moved to town. Anna had been undergoing chemotherapy to battle her leukemia diagnosis. According to Josh, the girl's mom left the day of her final treatment. Mara had been through enough in her life to manage empathy for almost any person, but she couldn't imagine anything so heartless as deserting a sick child.

"You don't need pity from anyone." Mara waved a hand toward the French doors open to the backyard. "You're rocking the Mr. Mom detail. Look at those decorations. It's a princess paradise out there."

"Two-day shipping and a call to the rental company for the unicorn bounce house," Josh answered. "Easy enough."

"Give yourself a break, buddy, and take a compliment. I don't hand them out like candy."

Josh sighed. "Good point. Besides, this party is the only thing I've done right in a long time." He nudged her shoulder. "I'm glad you're here. Both you and Evie. At the party and in Starlight."

"Me, too." Mara smiled, ignoring the sidelong glances she could feel from the moms huddled near the island. She knew parents at the elementary school liked to speculate on her relationship with Josh. Evie's first day at the local preschool last September had coincided with Anna's return after chemo. Although the two girls were opposites in personality, they'd formed an immediate bond. Evie didn't care about Anna's shorn head or the stigma of cancer the way some of the kids had. Mara's quiet, reserved daughter was simply happy to have a friend.

Mara liked Josh right away and appreciated how hard he worked to take care of Anna and reduce the fallout from his ex-wife leaving him. Despite what certain people wanted to believe, their friendship was strictly platonic. He was handsome enough, with dark hair, boyish features and an easy, open smile despite everything he'd been through.

She valued the gift of having a friend who understood the struggles unique to single parenting, but there wasn't a single spark of attraction between them. Even if she'd been ready to date after her divorce, she had a brotherly affection for Josh that suited them both.

She returned the nudge, the closest either of them came to a friendly hug. "Let's head outside and you can bask in the rosy glow of all those pink balloons."

"I'm going to talk to some of the parents from the girls' soccer team," Josh said. He'd volunteered to coach the newly formed team for the fall season, which made him a hero on several different levels. "Want to come with me?"

Mara made a face. "I think I might stick a fork in my eye instead."

"They're nice," Josh said with a laugh.

"It's a fact universally agreed upon," she answered, rolling her eyes, "that soccer moms aren't 'nice,' even when the team is in kindergarten. I'm sure that goes double for the dads."

"You need to branch out more. Make friends."

"I made a friend in town," Mara countered. "And she has a friend who I also like. That's two new friends, which means I'm full up at this point. Go be the good coach. I'm going to check on Evie in the bounce house."

She skirted around several small groups of parents, forcing herself to smile at a few people she recognized from the coffee shop. It would be easy to join in a conversation and probably the right thing to do. The whole reason she'd chosen Starlight was for the community. It felt like a place where Mara and Evie could thrive. Mara had come to town last year for her cousin's wedding and had quickly decided to make the town her permanent—or at least permanent-for-now—home.

It still amazed her that Aunt Nanci had been so willing to take them in. Nanci Morgan and her sister, Mara's mother Nina, had been estranged for years. Mara's parents hadn't bothered to show up to Nanci's daughter's wedding. But Mara had been happy to attend her cousin Renee's celebration, grateful for a weekend escape from the disappointment that infused every conversation with her mom and dad since she moved in with them after her divorce.

Everything about Starlight called to her, from the quaint downtown to the mountains rising up from the valley floor, as if they cocooned the town in a massive embrace. She'd wanted a place to start over but shedding the anger and bitterness of having her heart broken, stomped on and her life upended in a divorce so brutal that some days she still felt the pain like a physical blow, was no easy task.

Starlight welcomed her, but she couldn't quite bring herself to accept the invitation, always waiting for the proverbial rug to be pulled out from under her.

She couldn't say how much of Evie's reticence was inherent in her personality and how much was a result of the emotional trauma of watching her parents rip each other apart. Mara had tried to hide it, to speak only kind words about Paul or not to say anything, but she knew she was a terrible actor. Her daughter was insightful in the way introverted children could be, observant and wise beyond her years.

Anna helped with Evie's shyness, and the two girls seemed to be connected by some invisible tether of friendship.

Mara moved closer to the bounce house, squinting to see through the mesh webbing on the side. A half-dozen kids, most of whom appeared to be of kindergarten age, jumped on the inflated floor of the structure, launching themselves up with shrieks of laughter. There was one dad in the mix, using his weight to send the kids flying. The side of her mouth tipped into a true grin. Even she was unable to resist the pure joy and excitement that the children exuded.

All but one kid.

Mara gasped as she realized Evie stood in the corner of the bounce house, her arms out to either side, grasping at the sides as if to hold herself steady. Every few seconds the floor would undulate, taking Evie to her knees until she could manage to straighten to her feet again.

Sit down, Mara wanted to call as she hurried toward the front of the inflatable structure. Her daughter would do better if her center of gravity stayed low. Evie sometimes suffered from motion sickness, and Mara could imagine the girl's potential embarrassment if the party ended with her tossing her cookies all over the birthday girl.

Anna was jumping with the rest of the kids, unaware of Evie's distress. The dad didn't seem to notice either. Mara pushed past the two moms supervising the entrance.

"No shoes," the one told her as Mara began to climb into the structure.

"Right." Mara kicked off her ballet flats and climbed into the bounce house, losing her balance as she tried to stand. She dropped then rolled against the side of the house, wondering how the hell a bunch of little kids could cause so much movement.

She started to shout at them to stop jumping but shut her mouth when her gaze caught on Evie's. Her daughter gave a tiny shake of her head, letting Mara know she didn't want the attention. Mara nodded and flashed what she hoped passed for a reassuring smile. How many times had she offered Evie that same false hope in the past year?

"Hold on, girl," she muttered under her breath as she managed to scramble to her feet. The rest of the partygoers hadn't noticed her, so she stuck close to the edge, taking slow steps and trailing her open palm against the side of the structure to keep her balance.

"I feel sick," Evie said as Mara reached her.

"Let's get you out of here and into the fresh air," Mara said, smoothing away a wisp of hair that had come loose from Evie's braids and now stuck to her damp forehead. "Want me to carry you?"

Evie shook her head. "I can walk."

"That's my brave girl." Mara made her voice calm and soothing as she smoothed a hand over Evie's dark hair. Although the temperature outside was perfect for an early September weekend, it felt at least ten degrees warmer inside the structure. The air smelled of a mix of sweat, feet and chemicals. No wonder Evie's stomach was upset. Why were bounce houses so popular anyway?

"Evie, what's wrong?" Anna called as they made their way toward the entrance.

"I just need her for a second." Mara smiled and gave a thumbs up to the birthday girl. "She'll be right outside."

Anna nodded before returning to jumping, and Evie sent Mara a look of such gratitude it made tears prick the backs of her eyes.

A birthday party was supposed to be fun, not an event to make her daughter feel even more of an outsider.

Why couldn't anything be easy these days?

As they got closer to the opening, Evie lost her balance and face-planted on the floor, sending her glasses flying.

Mara's stomach pitched. "It's okay, honey." She bent and plucked up the frames before they got wedged in the side of the house. As she turned back, a pair of wide shoulders blocked her view of her daughter for a moment. Then the man who'd been jumping with the kids hauled Evie up, her poufy pink skirt flouncing around her, and helped her out of the structure.

Mara couldn't decide whether to be grateful for the help or nervous Evie would freak out at the attention.

As long as she didn't puke, Mara thought as she

lost her balance again. She tumbled forward to the edge of the entrance, and the corner of the flap that covered the opening snagged on her shirt because that's how the day was going. Why not flash half the party on her way out the door? Then a warm, slightly calloused hand touched her bare back before she could yank the fabric into place again.

Righting herself, she turned to thank whoever had rescued her daughter only to come face-to-face with the man who'd helped ruin her life.

"You," she whispered, her throat going dry. Rage roared through her.

Her ex-husband's pit bull of a divorce attorney offered a friendly smile, clearly not recognizing her. "It's kind of crazy in here, right?"

Crazy pretty much summed up what Mara was feeling at the moment. Crazy angry. Crazy bitter. Crazy with the need for revenge.

The one thing that didn't feel crazy was moving forward, crowding Parker Johnson and whispering, "I hate you," before trying to elbow her way past him.

Confusion marred his movie-star handsome features as he reached for her. "Wait. I don't even know you."

She yanked her arm away, throwing him off-balance in the process. He stumbled a step and then he was gone, falling through the opening to the bounce house and landing with a thud on the hard ground.

\* \* \*

"Your friend is crazy," Parker Johnson muttered, hissing as his brother pressed a bag of frozen peas to the knot on the back of his head.

"She's not," Josh insisted tightly. "Hold the peas, Parker."

His hand replaced Josh's, and he tried not to wince. "You should have seen the look in her eyes when she said she hated me. If she'd had a dull knife in her hand, she probably would have gutted me."

"You were her husband's divorce attorney," Josh said, as if that explained everything.

"I've been a lot of peoples' divorce attorney."

"And you've never been practically knocked unconscious? I'm shocked."

Parker narrowed his eyes and ignored the truth of the statement. "Funny."

Josh moved toward the window of the small laundry room that held the extra freezer where he'd found the peas, and pulled the curtain aside enough to see out. "We need to sing Happy Birthday and cut the cake. This party needs a distraction. I don't want Anna's celebration to be a total bust."

"Go," Parker told him. "I'm fine."

Josh turned with a sigh. "Are you sure you don't need a trip to the ER? It looked like you popped your head pretty hard. You might have a concussion."

"I don't have a concussion. I have a dull headache,

but at this point my pride is what hurts the most. She caught me off guard."

"Mara's great, but the divorce was really tough on her. She lost everything. Starlight is a good place to start over, but she's had trouble letting go of her anger."

Parker swallowed down the lump of guilt that tried to lodge itself in his throat. He hadn't become one of the top attorneys in Seattle by allowing himself to feel bad for the work he did. If he took someone on as a client, their marriage was already way off the rails. Yes, he was cutthroat. Of course his tactics bordered on ruthless. Those things made him the best.

There was no room in his life for entertaining another person's bruised feelings. When a marriage went south, weakness only led to more heartache. He'd learned that lesson from his parents and he figured he knew way more about losing everything than Mara Reed ever would.

"Take care of Anna and the party," he told Josh. "I'm sure you'll love reliving the moment I was felled by a woman."

"A woman who probably weighs fifty pounds less than you," Josh clarified with a small smile. Josh and Parker shared the same build, big and broad, although that's where their physical similarities ended. They had polar-opposite personalities, as well. Frankly, Parker was stunned at how natural the role of dad came to his little brother. "Mara is tiny."

"That should make the story even better." Parker had noticed Mara the moment she climbed into the bounce house, chiding himself for admiring the figure of one of the moms at his niece's nauseatingly pink sixth birthday party. He'd registered her enthusiasm for getting into the structure but realized the venture wasn't for fun as she'd awkwardly moved toward a kid cowering in the corner.

Parker had been happy for an excuse to stop bouncing with the kids. When the girl had fallen, he'd helped her out, just in the nick of time based on the unnatural shade of green coloring her face.

Next he'd placed a steadying hand on the woman when she'd stumbled. In his mind it had been an innocuous touch, so her reaction had shocked him. The woman hadn't stuck around after he'd fallen, had climbed out, then lifted her daughter into her arms and disappeared amidst the crowd of partygoers that surrounded him, most of whom he'd known since childhood.

His wannabe mortal enemy had been a stranger, or so he'd thought until Josh explained that her ex-husband was Paul Reed. Parker hadn't particularly liked the man he'd represented in divorce court three separate times, but friendship was by no means a requisite of his job. In fact, he tried to keep his professional and personal lives separate. Since he usually worked seven days a week, he had very little personal life to speak of.

The sound of a throat clearing several minutes after Josh returned to the party had him glancing toward the laundry room door.

"Come to finish me off?" he asked as Mara Reed walked into the room.

She sniffed. "How's your head?"

He removed the bag of peas, tossing them to the top of the dryer. "I've taken harder hits."

"Not that I meant for you to fall, but I can't say you didn't deserve it," she told him, crossing her arms over her chest.

He raised a brow. "That's an interesting way to apologize."

She gave a humorless laugh. "I'm not here to say sorry."

Parker felt his mouth drop open. "You practically pushed me out of the bounce house."

"Not quite. You grabbed for me and I evaded you with my catlike reflexes. Is it my problem that you're clumsy?"

He had to admire her moxie. The moment had happened so fast, but he was pretty sure she'd given him a tiny shove when he stumbled. Not that he'd throw her under the bus by telling anyone. "If you didn't seek me out to apologize, why are you here?"

"You took everything from me," she said instead of answering, her husky voice laced with bitterness.

"Your anger is misdirected," Parker said, shifting under the weight of her stony glare. "I'm not your ex-husband." He'd represented hundreds of clients over the years, but this was the first time he'd actually been confronted outside the courtroom. He didn't like the way Mara Reed made him feel, as if he'd been the one to cause the destruction of her marriage.

"No," she agreed, her hazel eyes giving him a slow once-over. Despite her obvious dislike of him and the obstinate set of her heart-shaped jaw, there was no denying Mara's beauty. She had dark hair with a few hints of burnished gold highlighting it and pale, luminous skin that would have inspired the finest Renaissance painter.

She was taller than average, something he'd always appreciated in a woman given that he stood well over six feet. She'd fit perfectly with him, a thought that almost made him laugh for its absurdity. He couldn't imagine any scenario which would make Mara want to be close to him.

"You made it possible for him to destroy me," she said, her voice oddly devoid of emotion. He wanted to deny it, but the truth was he couldn't remember the details of her case, especially since she'd been Paul Reed's much younger third wife. He'd already been twice down that road with his client. It was a mental trick he employed, not allowing himself to see the opponent as a person. Mara Reed had been a name to him, an entity he'd set out to take down like he was a remote-control drone zeroing in on a target.

"It wasn't personal."

She flinched, and he wanted to take back the words. They were simple enough as part of his job, but he imagined they felt like salt dumped into an open wound to Mara. Despite his now pounding headache, he didn't mean to hurt her. He understood what he did for a living and had come to terms with the man he'd become as a result, even if he didn't always like himself because of it.

"It was to me," she whispered and walked away.

## Chapter Two

"Thanks for holding down the fort," Josh said as he entered the kitchen later that night. "How's your head?"

Parker gingerly touched two fingers to the small goose egg on the back of his head. "It's fine."

Josh grabbed a beer from the refrigerator, popped the top and then took a long pull. "It meant a lot to Anna to have you here."

"I should have been around for her treatments. If I'd known—"

"I had it under control," Josh said without emotion despite the pain etched across his features. For a second Parker barely recognized his kind, gentle, teddy bear of a brother.

"Your daughter had cancer and your wife left you." Parker shook his head as he reached for the final length of pink streamers hanging across the breakfast nook. "Hell, Josh, I'm good at what I do. At least I could have helped with the divorce."

"I didn't need help, and I told you I don't want to talk about Jenn. It's fine."

"Then do you want to talk about where you went tonight?" After the guests left the party and Anna was tucked in for bed, Parker had been ready to head back to Seattle when his brother asked him to stay at the house so he could run a quick errand.

"Not really."

"Is it a woman?" Parker had a feeling the explanation wouldn't be so clear-cut, but he had to ask. "If not Mara then—"

"There's no woman," Josh insisted, placing his beer on the counter. "Definitely not Mara." Josh grimaced. "That would be like dating my sister."

"We don't have a sister," Parker felt the need to point out. He couldn't imagine how his brother—or any man—wouldn't be attracted to Mara.

"You know what I mean. Tonight was business."

"What kind of construction emergency happens at eight on a Saturday night?"

Josh stared at him a long moment and then said, "I bought the Dennison Lumber Mill."

The breath whooshed out of Parker's lungs like he'd been punched in the gut. "How? Why?"

"It was right after Anna finished chemo. Jenn had left and I was overwhelmed. I felt like I didn't have control over anything and I wanted—"

"To saddle yourself with an abandoned building?" Parker scrubbed a hand over his face. "The building that was the bane of Dad's existence. When I think about all the frustration that place caused him and the ways he took out his anger on us…" He stalked to the edge of the kitchen, swallowing down the bile rising in his throat.

His father's long tenure as mayor of Starlight had been marred by one huge failure. Mac Johnson had tried to prevent the lumber mill from closing, and the fact he hadn't been able to plagued him and triggered his temper on many occasions. Almost a hundred local jobs had been lost when the mill owners pulled out, a hit a small town like Starlight couldn't afford. Parker hated everything about the mill and what it represented in his childhood. How could Josh tie himself to that building?

"I wanted to succeed where he failed," Josh said into the silence that stretched between them. "I needed something—a project, a goal—something to make me feel like I had control."

Parker schooled his features and turned to face his brother. He wouldn't show how much the thought of that place got to him. "Has it worked?"

"I can barely step onto the property without wanting to puke. I'd planned to turn it into a multiuse

space. Adaptive reuse is all the rage in historic pres-
ervation these days. But I'm so behind schedule and
now…" Josh let out a humorless laugh.

"Tell me."

He watched as his younger brother's fingers tightened on the edge of the counter. They were only
fourteen months apart, but Parker had always taken
care of Josh, or at least he'd tried to when they were
younger. That had mainly consisted of keeping them
both out of reach of their mercurial father, who'd
been beloved by the community but feared and hated
within his own home.

Parker still wondered what would have happened
if his mom had found the courage to leave Mac when
he and Josh were boys. But there was no changing
the past. Lillian Johnson had done the best she could,
he supposed. Yes, she'd stayed with an abusive husband but had attempted to prevent Parker and Josh
from becoming targets. She'd hidden her bruises and
kept a smile on her face, but both boys had known
how difficult Mac made life for their mother.

Josh, a quiet boy who never developed the subtle skill of staying out of his father's crosshairs, had
been particularly sensitive to the violence. Parker
had made it his mission to protect his brother, although it hadn't always worked and more often than
not, Parker would end up comforting Josh in their
darkened bedroom after one of Mac's violent tirades.
After a sudden heart attack killed Mac during Park-

er's senior year of high school, all bets were off. Parker left Starlight and the difficult memories behind, hoping his brother would do the same.

But Josh had stayed, working on construction crews in the area and eventually getting his general contractor's license. He'd met Jenn at a local bar and they'd gotten married in Vegas after a whirlwind romance. Parker hadn't even known about the wedding until months later.

Despite their distance, Josh had seemed happy, which made Parker happy. He hadn't pushed for a closer relationship with his brother or his young niece. They had their own lives, he told himself. Up until a few months ago, he believed that dinner once a year and a few texts back and forth were enough.

Not anymore.

"I'm going to default on the loan if the project doesn't open on time," his brother said, his eyes drifting closed as if saying the words caused him pain. "There's a second mortgage on the house, and I'm behind on those payments, too, so…"

Parker muttered a curse. "What do you need? How much?"

"I'm not a stupid kid." Josh shook his head. He'd always been quiet, sweet and stubborn as hell. "I don't need you to bail me out."

"I know you're not a kid." Parker forced himself to take a slow breath. He could hear the thread of agitation in his brother's voice. "Despite the struggles,

you've made a great life for yourself. I don't know
how you made it through Anna's treatments on your
own. To take on a project like the mill at the same
time is amazing. But if you need help—"

"I'm not taking your money."

"It doesn't have to be money." Although writing a check would be easy, Parker knew it wouldn't
solve the deeper problems of their past. Returning
to Starlight reminded him of all the things he'd done
wrong in his life, and top on that list was leaving his
younger brother. "You're not alone in this. You never
have to feel like you're alone."

Josh pressed his fingers to either side of his head.
"I can't fail. Dad always expected me to fail."

"He's been gone for years," Parker murmured,
even though he understood the way memories could
hold a person hostage. Physical injuries healed
quickly enough, but they'd never discussed the lingering emotional scars each of them harbored as a
result of growing up with an abusive parent.

Josh had always seemed so much like their
mother, and Lillian flourished after her husband's
death. She became a totally different person, no longer the broken, scared woman he'd known growing
up. Mac's death had been a release of sorts. Un-
shackled from her horrendous marriage, she'd reinvented herself.

She'd gone back to college, and now worked as
a nurse at a pediatrician's office two hours away in

Spokane. She had a large group of friends and had dated the same man, a retired postal worker, for the past few years. She rarely came to Seattle and didn't ask Parker to visit her. She seemed to expect nothing from him, never pressuring him to settle down the way some mothers did.

It was almost as if she'd blocked that whole period of their lives from her memory, and Parker thought Josh had done the same thing. Parker was the son who'd taken after their father, both in looks and temperament. He hated his resemblance to Mac more than anything and tried to ignore it, which was part of the reason he kept his distance from Starlight. Locals loved to walk down memory lane with him, never realizing the way they remembered his dad was categorically opposite of the man Parker had known.

"I think you need to talk to Mom, too," Parker told his brother.

"She helped enough when Anna got sick. She took time off work to stay with us during the worst of the recovery and stocked the freezer with meals."

"If you asked for more help—"

"I can't do that to her." Josh forced a smile. "Or to you."

"I'm offering." He understood Josh's desire not to revisit the past or relive the details of the abuse that had almost broken them. Of course Josh had never really had it all together. Parker didn't either, even though it might look that way to an outsider. How could either of them ever be truly stable and steady given the way they'd grown up? Too much had been broken to ever be fully fixed.

"I won't take no for an answer," Parker continued. "We're going to make your plan a reality." He had no idea how but knew for certain he'd find a way. He had to, given what the mill had meant to them as children. If they didn't make it work, it felt like somehow their father still controlled them. He wouldn't give that hateful man the power to ruin his brother's life from beyond the grave.

"I won't take your money," Josh repeated.

"Put me to work."

Josh laughed. "Not a lot of need for a divorce attorney on a construction site."

"You know what I mean. It will be like the old days. You and me side by side." Parker and Josh had gotten summer jobs working for a local construction crew in high school. It had been one of the best summers Parker could remember, with a reason to leave the house early each morning and then working all day. The physical labor gave him an outlet for his pent-up frustration and the feeling of helplessness that pervaded their home.

"What are you talking about? You can't just put your life on hold."

"I'll make it work." Parker's mind raced with the logistics. His calendar was full at the office. Divorce was good business. But if his secretary could switch client meetings and appointments around so they were clustered once a week, he could drive into Seattle for a marathon day at the office and then manage most everything else remotely. He was at the point where he had to turn away new clients because he hadn't wanted to hire an associate. Parker liked being a one-man show. He'd spent much of his life having no control and wasn't willing to share it with anyone.

"I've been feeling kind of burned out lately," he told his brother, which was both true and not. "This will give me a chance to reevaluate. Plus, there's this new guy…he graduated from my alma mater in the spring. He submitted his résumé months ago and now pesters me every week about a job…maybe it's time I give the kid a chance."

"If you're serious…" Josh gave him a grateful smile, and the hope in his brother's eyes made Parker's throat tighten. It reminded him of all the late-night promises he'd made to Josh when they were kids—how Parker was going to take care of things and give them a better life than the one they were living. He couldn't help feeling like he'd failed his brother back then.

As heartless as it sounded, it had been a stroke of luck for their father to die. Parker hadn't had anything to do with it. While he was grateful to be rid of the violent man, the heart attack had robbed Parker of his mission to save Josh. Now was his chance to atone.

"When are you scheduled to open?"

"Three weeks from yesterday."

"How far behind are you?"

"Close to a month," Josh admitted quietly. "A couple of the tenants have pulled out. I lost my flagship restaurant. Nanci Morgan from Main Street Perk has agreed to open a second location for the coffee shop in the space, but it's not enough. I have a meeting at the bank tomorrow to talk about an extension."

Parker nodded, keeping his features neutral. He wasn't sure if he could actually pull this off, but he'd never let his brother know that. "I'll go with you. Finn will understand." One of his best friends from high school, Finn Samuelson, had recently moved back to Starlight to take over running his family's bank, First Trust. He trusted Finn to help.

Josh blew out a long breath. "We can do this."

"You bought the Dennison Mill." Parker remained unsure how to process the information.

Neither of them spoke for several moments, and Parker couldn't help but wonder if his brother was reliving all the ways they kept their father's violence a secret from the community.

"How do you stay here?" Parker asked suddenly.

Josh blinked, as if not understanding the question. "It's home."

"Don't the memories get to you? Everywhere I go in town it feels like he's a part of it."

"I'm making my own memories, ones that don't involve him. Ones that aren't tied up in my failed marriage or with Anna being sick. I have to keep trying."

Parker blew out a breath, leveled by his brother's inherent optimism. "I admire you, Josh."

"Give me a break. I'm on the verge of losing everything. You're the big success."

"You won't lose," Parker promised. He might not know much about adaptive reuse and he hadn't built anything in years, but he'd figure it out.

Josh gave him the goofy thumbs-up Parker remembered from their childhood. "Not with you on my side."

Parker opened his mouth to argue then snapped it shut again. He hoped he was worthy of his brother's confidence. It was difficult to admit, even to himself, the guilt he still harbored over his failure to protect his younger brother when they were kids. Now he had a chance to finally make up for that, and he wouldn't let either of them down again.

"It must have been worse than you described."

Mara looked up from the dough she'd been rolling in her aunt's kitchen, Evie tucked in her bed upstairs. She wiped the back of her hand across her forehead. "I couldn't sleep," she told Aunt Nanci, who stood yawning in the doorway, wearing her favorite red flannel pajamas. "I'm sorry if I woke you."

"It's almost two in the morning," Nanci said, her voice gentle.

Mara glanced from the clock hanging on the far wall to the six trays of sweet rolls lined up on the counter. "Yeah."

"Did you actually push Paul's attorney or did he trip? You seemed upset so I didn't want to ask earlier. You know I wouldn't blame you if you'd helped him out of the bounce house. It must have been a shock to face him."

Mara bit down on her lower lip then sighed. "He tripped, but I wasn't sorry he fell. What kind of parenting role model does that make me?" Guilt twisted her stomach, both from the example she'd given her daughter and for causing such a commotion at Anna's birthday party. Yes, there were a lot of things she'd do differently in that moment. "People are going to talk and make it a bigger deal. If you want me to take off a couple of days until the gossip dies down, I understand."

Nanci let out a small laugh. "Are you kidding? I imagine people will be flocking into the shop to get a look at you. You know how this town loves fresh gossip. Although I doubt any of the regulars will be surprised. Most of them are half terrified of you on a good day."

An uncomfortable sensation flitted along the back

of Mara's neck, and she picked up the final tray of rolls, turning to place them in the preheated oven. She was aware of her reputation, but that didn't mean she liked it.

"I'm not scary."

"Right." Nanci laughed again then drew closer to the wire racks the held rows of cooling pastries. "Lucky for both of us, you're an artist with coffee and bake better than anyone I've ever met. The Sunday-morning crowd will be thrilled at the extra cinnamon rolls. Usually we run out by nine."

"I'm *not* scary," Mara repeated with more force than was probably necessary. "I don't want to scare people."

"Intimidate is a better word," Nanci told her. "Although I suppose Parker now has reason to watch his back."

"I'm done with Parker Johnson," Mara said. "According to Josh, he was only here for Anna's party. I'll be able to avoid him if he comes for another visit."

"You might be the only woman in the world who'd want to avoid that fine specimen of a man. His father was quite the looker back in the day, and Parker is the spitting image of Mac with those piercing eyes and that chiseled jaw. Heck, he might be better looking than his dad was and that's saying something."

Mara absolutely did not want to think about how handsome Parker was or the way it had felt to have his warm hand touching her back. "It's difficult to imagine he grew up here."

"Why?"

Mara shrugged, wiping her hands on a white dish-towel. "I can't see him as a child. It would seem more fitting that he sprang fully formed as the ruthless shark I know him to be."

"I understand your divorce was awful, but we both know Parker was doing his job for your ex-husband."

"Don't defend him," Mara said through gritted teeth. "He helped Paul take everything that mattered from me. My ex-husband made me out to be…crazy and unstable. He ruined my professional reputation just to be spiteful." She threw up her hands. "He got to move on with his mistress and I had to start over."

"I'm on your side," Nanci said, coming forward to offer a quick hug.

The gesture made Mara's heart pinch, like it was suddenly too large to fit into her chest. Nanci had hired Mara at the coffee shop before she'd even moved to town and had been willing to work around Evie's schedule, first at day care and now kinder-garten. Mara still had no idea what made the aunt she'd barely known growing up take Mara and Evie under her wing, but she was eternally grateful for the chance.

She hadn't planned on staying in Starlight when she'd arrived for her cousin's wedding, but the town had offered her a way to rebuild her life and leave the past behind in Seattle. Now that it was home, she'd do whatever she could to make a future here for her daughter.

"I actually have something I want to talk to you about." Nanci pinched off a corner of one roll and popped it into her mouth. Her eyes drifted shut, and she moaned in pleasure. "It's so darn good," she murmured. "How do you manage not to eat any of what you bake?"

Mara felt a blush rise to her cheeks at how happy the compliment made her. "Sugar isn't my thing. You know that."

"I still don't understand it."

Mara simply shrugged, unable to explain it herself. She'd only started baking after her separation. When Paul had first moved out of the house they'd shared, she hadn't been able to sleep. Every noise or creak had set her on edge. She'd spent way too many nights watching reruns of baking competitions on the food channel.

The process had intrigued her—the mix of chemistry and magic involved with baking. She'd taken Evie to the grocery and bought all the ingredients she'd need to replicate what she saw on television, her mind whirring with inspiration. Having something to think about besides her imploding marriage had been a blessing. Her first couple of creations were inedible, rock-solid cupcakes, and cookies that resembled Frisbees.

Somehow those failures spurred her on to work harder. She made her first successful batch of cookies the day Paul fired her from the luxury hotel management company he owned, where she'd worked as an interior designer since graduating from college. She brought the treats to Evie's day care and the women there had gone crazy for the cookies. A trivial win, but at that moment it meant the world to Mara.

Nanci hadn't known about the baking when Mara moved to Starlight, and it still wasn't part of her job description, but her aunt was happy to have her in the kitchen at home or at the shop whenever the mood hit. "What did you want to talk about?" Mara asked.

"The reason I woke up is because Renee called." Nanci wrapped the rest of the sweet roll in wax paper. "There have been some complications with the baby, and the doctor is putting her on bed rest for the final few weeks of her pregnancy."

"Why didn't you say something right away?" Mara wrapped her arms around her aunt, sighing when the older woman sagged against her. Renee and her husband, Brett, had moved to Texas right after the wedding because Brett was in the army and stationed in the Lone Star State.

"I'm trying not to overreact," Nanci said, pulling back. "They're going to need me to be calm. She phoned from the hospital. She's okay but the doctors are keeping her for a few days to monitor the baby's vitals. Brett leaves for a week of training tomorrow, so I've already booked my flight."

"Of course you have," Mara agreed. "What can I do to help? I'll watch the house and the cats. If you need me to pick up extra shifts at Perk, I'll find a way to manage Evie's schedule."

Nanci placed a hand on Mara's arm. "You're sweet. I'd appreciate your help at the shop, but I also need you to step in and take over plans for the second location. Josh needs more help than he's letting on at this point. Not just with the coffee shop but in the overall design. He needs you."

"I can't." Mara swallowed back the nerves that surfaced at the mention of planning and design. "I walked away from that kind of work. I'm a barista now."

Nanci arched a brow and Mara was reminded that her sweet, maternal aunt had also been a single mom who ran a successful business. "Don't pretend you aren't overqualified for what you do around here. I understand your ex-husband screwed you over in the divorce and tried to annihilate your career in the process. You've taken more than your share of blows. But he didn't wipe out your talent, Mara. I've owned Perk for ten years, and I love it. Starlight is my home and now it's yours, as well. I'm starting to think I bit off more than I can chew agreeing to open a second location in Josh's new space. He might be over his head, too. I was there on Friday, and I don't know how that boy expects to open next month with all the work still to do." She shook her head. "I guess I could back out at this point."

"No." The word escaped Mara's lips with more force than she expected. "Josh will be able to pull it off."

"I hope so," Nanci said after a moment. "You can make sure he does."

Mara nodded despite her doubts. She didn't understand the exact reasons he'd invested so much in repurposing the mill but knew it meant a lot to him. Josh was a friend and she wouldn't let him down. "I'll do whatever it takes," she agreed.

## Chapter Three

Mara dropped Evie at school on Monday morning then drove out to the old lumber mill Josh planned to convert into retail and restaurant space. He'd only shared bits and pieces of his overall strategy, but what she knew of the concept was strong.

She'd studied adaptive reuse in college but hadn't ever used the concepts in real life. Her ex-husband developed sleek and modern hotels, and she'd adjusted her preference for more traditional styles to his desire for a minimalist look in each of his new properties. From the start, she'd modified most everything to Paul's wishes, she realized now. What a fool she'd been. She'd fallen hard and fast for the charming and twice-divorced executive who was almost two decades older than her, foolishly believing him when he told her he was attracted to her intelligence and drive and not because of his unrealistic obsession with youth.

Things had been good at the start, and she'd truly loved the man she'd married after only two months of dating. In retrospect, Mara could see she'd become a textbook case of a woman trying to work out her emotional issues with a distant father by falling for the same type of man. Her father was a researcher, prominent in his field and far more dedicated to his job than he had been in being a husband or father. He and Paul had so much in common it was almost scary when she looked at it now. Her gut churned with shame over how gullible she'd been. The turning point was when she'd gotten pregnant with Evie a year into their marriage.

The pregnancy might not have been planned, but as soon as Mara knew she was carrying a baby, she was thrilled. Her ex-husband, not so much. She shook her head, unwilling to let herself relive how Paul had eventually cut both Mara and their daughter out of his life.

She climbed out of her Toyota SUV, one of the few possessions she'd taken with her after the divorce, and walked toward the building. It was suspiciously quiet for a construction site, and she wondered why there wasn't a crew already at work. If the project was as behind as Nanci made it out to be, they needed to get things moving. Now she wished she'd asked more questions about Josh's business instead of simply swapping parenting advice. Maybe she wasn't as good of a friend as she thought.

There were three main structures, the largest building two stories with a covered porch on the front side. Each building was painted a rusty crimson color and the signage identifying the Dennison Lumber Co. had been fashioned from old redwood boards and looked original to the site.

Turning in a slow circle, she took in the property through the lens of design. Butterflies danced across her stomach at the unrealized potential. She could imagine a courtyard between the largest building and the other two, picnic tables and planters with colorful flowers situated around the space.

Then she shook her head, remembering this didn't belong to her. She'd left her job at Paul's company—been fired actually—after being trashed in the press. It had been reported that her ineptitude in design delayed the opening of the most recent hotel they'd built. Her rational side knew she'd done nothing wrong. Her husband and his executive team had been looking for a scapegoat for a project that went over budget due to issues unrelated to her work. But her confidence had taken a hit, and she'd lost her professional network along with every one of her friends during the divorce.

Mara had learned an important lesson about reaching too high for her dreams. Her mom seemed to relish reminding her of the old saying that she was *no better than she should be*, the bit of sugarcoated snark making Mara question whether the success she'd had working with Paul had been a result of their relationship as opposed to her talent.

Her parents' marriage was traditional, with her father as the breadwinner and leader of the household while her mom took care of his needs in between tennis dates and luncheons. She'd never understood Mara's desire for a career. Mara was fairly certain her mom put the blame for Mara's divorce squarely on her shoulders because she hadn't been devoted enough to Paul. Now she was here as a favor to her aunt. She trusted Josh could figure out whatever issues he was having on his own and open the project on schedule.

"Hello?" she called as she walked through the main entrance.

"In here," a man answered from a room to one side of the main space, although it didn't sound like Josh. She moved toward the doorway, trying not to be disappointed at the obvious lack of progress. The interior of the building was airy, with a vaulted ceiling covered in reclaimed wood planks. A few dividing walls had been framed along either side of what would be a wide hallway, and she could see at least the start of electrical wiring. But it certainly didn't look like the microretail-and-restaurant center she expected.

"Is Josh around?" she asked as she entered the makeshift office. The small room held an antique desk, a folding table covered with plans and papers and one empty bookshelf.

Her heart dropped to her toes as Parker turned in the leather chair to face her. "He drove out to pick up a load of framing materials." To his credit, his features remained neutral. If he was as shocked to see her as she was to find him here, he didn't let on.

Mara had no such ability for a poker face. "What are you doing?" she demanded, not bothering to keep the thread of hostility from her tone.

He ran a hand through his dark blond hair, lighter and more expensively cut than his brother's. Mara tried—and mostly failed—not to notice the way the muscles of his arm bunched at the movement. Parker wore a faded gray University of Puget Sound T-shirt and jeans, and she forced herself to remember him in his tailored suit and the sanctimonious expression he'd worn as he regurgitated the lies her husband had told about her in divorce court.

One thick brow rose as his ice-blue eyes pinned her in place. "Right now, it feels like I'm bailing water out of the hull of the Titanic." He shrugged. "I don't suppose you brought an extra bucket with you?"

She shook her head and tried to process his words.

"But *why* are you in Starlight? Josh said you were going back to Seattle."

"My plans changed," he answered simply.

Placing her hands on her hips, she stared, waiting for him to elaborate. "You don't belong here," she said when the invisible strand of tension crackling between them overwhelmed her. She couldn't seem to keep her mouth shut around this man.

"You have no idea," he agreed, far too readily in her opinion. He looked away, out the small window toward the front of the property. "Josh needs my help, and I'm not going to abandon him ag—" He stood abruptly, and Mara took an automatic step back.

What did he mean by abandoning Josh? She could have sworn he'd been about to add *again* to that sentence. She knew Josh had grown up in Starlight and his dad had been the mayor for years. Nothing he'd shared about his childhood gave her the impression that he was close to anyone in his family, but he didn't say much. Their friendship was based on a connection between single parents. Each of them helping the other navigate the rocky waters of handling everything on their own.

"I'm here until the project opens," Parker clarified. "Hopefully on schedule, but if you're the praying type, we're getting close to the point of needing a miracle."

"You're a divorce attorney," she told him as if he didn't realize it.

"We prefer the term *family law* and you can call it a sabbatical," he said with the phoniest smile she'd ever seen. A tingle of awareness zipped along her spine despite her animosity toward him. Apparently her body hadn't gotten the memo that Parker Johnson was pond scum. "I'm going to take a few weeks and then return to my practice renewed, refreshed and—"

"Ready to ruin more lives?"

His smile dimmed but didn't fade completely. Instead, his eyes crinkled at the corners like he appreciated her attitude, even though it was directed at him.

"Unfortunately, divorce often brings out the worst in decent people," he told her.

"My ex-husband certainly didn't handle the end of our marriage with any shred of decency," she said through clenched teeth.

"I'm not here to argue that point." Parker shoved his hands into his pockets, dropping his gaze to the floor. Something about his stance gave Mara the impression he didn't think much of Paul either. "I have a job, and it isn't to judge. I advocate on behalf of my client while helping them see beyond their own self-interests. Not everyone has an easy time with that."

"Especially when your client is a raging narcissist," Mara snapped then took a breath. Although she knew Parker had only been doing his job during her divorce, the memories were still painful. It wouldn't do her any good to relive them over and over. She held up a hand when Parker would have spoken. "I'm not sure Paul has ever been capable of seeing anything beyond his own wants and needs. Let's agree to put aside our past history," she offered.

"Gladly."

"Fine."

An awkward silence descended over the musty office as they tried not to make eye contact.

After a moment, Parker cleared his throat. "You were looking for Josh. Is there something I can do for you?"

She arched a brow.

"I mean, besides go jump in a lake or whatever's going through your mind at the moment."

As much as she wanted to, she couldn't help the smile that curved her lips at the way he'd read her thoughts. "My aunt sent me out," she explained. "Aunt Nanci flew to Texas today to be with my pregnant cousin, and I guess she was concerned about the progress of Josh's renovations. She's opening a second location of the coffee shop out here."

Parker nodded. "I hope your cousin and her baby are okay. Josh told me your aunt stepped in when the owner of the restaurant originally committed to the space backed out."

"Um…" Mara glanced over her shoulder. "Where was he planning on putting a restaurant? There's no kitchen. The coffee shop won't need one if we bring in pastries from the location downtown, but he'll eventually need something bigger to anchor the space."

"I noticed that, too." Parker gestured to the door. "Would you like a tour?"

No, her brain warned. Mara needed to put some distance between herself and the man who should be her sworn enemy.

"Sure," she murmured instead.

He gave a tight smile as they moved into the main area of the mill. "I'm surprised you don't know more about what's been going on here since you and Josh are friends."

"We're good friends," she agreed, following when he headed toward the far end of the building. "But most of our conversations revolve around the girls and school and kindergarten activities. It's amazing how much you can manage not to share about yourself when you have kids to talk about instead. Do you have kids, Parker?"

There was a slight stiffening of his shoulders, but he tossed an easy smile over his shoulder. "Nope. No wife or girlfriend either, if you were curious."

"I wasn't," she lied.

"This is the area where the restaurant was supposed to go." He pointed to an unfinished wall framed with two-by-six studs. "He has gas lines, electrical and plumbing run back there for the kitchen, but that's as far as it's gotten."

"Why?" she asked, more to herself than the man standing next to her.

Parker answered anyway. "This place holds a lot of memories for Josh, most of them unhappy. According to what he told me, he bought the mill almost impulsively. Clearly he had a plan because he has approval from the town council on his renovations, but I think it's been more complicated than he expected. He didn't realize he'd need to spend so much time out here."

Mara frowned. "What kind of memories?"

Suddenly Parker's expression shifted, and she saw a kind of vulnerability in his blue eyes that she hadn't expected. Emotion tumbled through her, and she forced herself to step away from him. She was here to make sure the coffee shop opened at Dennison Mill, nothing more.

"He hasn't talked to you about how things were growing up," Parker said softly.

"I know your dad died when Josh was sixteen and your mom moved to Spokane after he graduated high school. But I wasn't joking when I said most of our conversations revolve around the kids."

"Did he mention me?"

"Not really," Mara admitted with a wince.

Parker laughed without humor. "Figures. Our dad was a big deal around town back in the years when he was mayor. Everyone loved him, but he wasn't a kind man, especially to his family. It still surprises me that Josh stayed in Starlight, but he loves it here."

"It's a great town."

"I guess."

She drew in a breath, unable to resist asking, "When you say he wasn't a kind man, what does that mean?"

He turned to her fully and the stark pain in his gaze made her want to reach for him. Of course she wouldn't, even though she understood how difficult it must be to share these details with her. Maybe that's why her and Josh's friendship had been so easy. They had the girls so they didn't have to scratch beneath the surface and reveal any of their true scars to each other.

It was strange to be sharing this moment with Parker, but she knew it was important so she forced herself to nod and give him an encouraging half smile.

"He was abusive. Violent. Mean and petty." The words rolled off his tongue without emotion.

"I'm sorry."

"Don't be, although I'd appreciate if you didn't mention it to anyone. Josh and I don't often discuss the past or our dad, especially around Starlight." He gave a quiet chuckle. "I won't bore you with the details of why the lumber mill is significant, but it means more than anyone can understand for Josh to make this a success. With everything he dealt with as a child and what he's been through in the past year, he needs a win. I put my life and my practice on hold to be a part of it. We won't fail."

"I can help," she blurted then felt color flood her cheeks. She'd told herself she wouldn't get involved beyond what her aunt had asked her to do. And that was when she thought Josh was handling everything. Josh, her easygoing friend who was no threat to her emotions or tied to memories she didn't want to revisit. The idea of being near Parker with her conflicted reaction to him—could she even manage it?

"A coffee shop on this side of town will definitely bring in customers but what we need—"

"I mean I might be able to offer a few suggestions for the project as a whole. I have some background in architectural design." She wanted to take back the words as soon as they were out, but in her heart she still loved the process and potential of this kind of project. She also wanted to do something to help Josh. His friendship had made a huge difference in her life. Maybe she could dip her toe in the water without really getting involved. "If you show me the plans, I can possibly come up with some ideas of how to modify them so you get back on track sooner."

He inclined his head, scratching his chin with two fingers.

She should plug her ears. Mara hadn't dated since her divorce, which had to explain why such an innocuous sound was so sexy to her.

"Why?" Parker asked. "We can't pay you. Hell, he can't pay what he owes to most of the subcontractors at this point."

"Josh is my friend and the sooner this place opens, the better it will be for my aunt's shop. I want to help them both."

"And you don't have a problem with my involvement?"

The fine hairs at the back of her neck stood on end. "I wish you'd go away, but I can ignore you."

He flashed a grin. Darn the man and his handsome face. "We'll have to talk to Josh, but I'm sure he'll say yes."

"Right," Mara breathed, the significance of how she'd just put herself out there sinking in. Anxiety crawled along her spine. Her rational mind knew that losing her job and the ruin of her professional reputation had been a calculated move by her ex-husband, but she couldn't seem to shake the blow her confidence had taken. "I need to go now."

"Don't you want to see the plans?"

"Josh has my email. Send them over." She backed up a step. "I need to go," she repeated, starting to turn.

"Hey, Mara," Parker called when she was almost to the building's entrance.

She looked over her shoulder at him.

"I look forward to watching you try to ignore me," he said, all broad shoulders and cheeky grin.

Without hesitation, she gave him a one-fingered salute and walked out the door.

*Chapter Four*

Mara was in the zone on Wednesday morning when Sam Sheehan burst into the shop. Main Street Perk had been slammed all morning, and she was busy making coffee drinks. She focused her attention on tamping the ground coffee then pulling the perfect espresso shot. It was exactly what she needed after two nights of restless sleep with dreams that featured a handsome—if hated—divorce attorney.

Parker had emailed her the plans for the lumber mill renovation, while Josh had followed up with a call to say he had things under control but would still appreciate any insight she could offer. Based on the dichotomy between the plans and the actual progress in the space, her friend used the term *control* in its loosest sense.

She'd responded to both men with a generic answer about reviewing things and getting back to them. As enticing as the space was to the designer in her, she'd walked away from Parker having second, third and fourth thoughts about getting involved beyond helping with the coffee shop.

The thought of spending time with him accounted for a big part of it. The attraction simmering between them was like an itch under her skin that she couldn't seem to reach. The easiest way to avoid the desire to scratch it would be to stay far away from Parker. Plus, as lame as it made her feel, she liked the boundaries of her friendship with Josh.

From the bits of detail Parker had shared, the mill project held a lot of painful memories for both brothers, and it scared her to think of being a part of something that meant so much.

What if her ideas were horrible or messed things up beyond repair? What if she was the untalented hack her husband had claimed? His accusations and lies had pulled the rug from under her and she still couldn't manage to find her footing when it came to believing in her talent. It would be easier to stick to coffee. Ordering a new espresso machine and stocking a display case were straightforward. She could handle straightforward.

Sam, who owned an insurance company in town,

spoke to the midmorning crowd. "Ya'll wouldn't believe the mess. It's a disaster over there. The roof is basically rubble and the fire alarm set off the sprinkler system. They're saying the school will be closed at least for the rest of this week."

Mara paused in the act of finishing a flat white. She stepped from behind the coffee machine and placed the drink on the counter. "What school?" she called.

A small group of people had gathered in front of Sam, their faces a mix of shock and curiosity.

"Was anyone injured?" one of the women asked. "Teachers or children?"

Shivers of dread skittered along Mara's spine, and she pulled her phone from the back pocket of the jeans she wore. Two missed calls from the elementary school, three from Josh and a slew of unread texts.

"Sam!" she shouted even as she untied her apron, the din of conversation filling the coffee shop coming to an abrupt halt. "What happened at the school?"

"The gymnasium roof collapsed," he said, throwing up his hands as if she shouldn't be surprised. "Didn't you get a notification? They sent out an automated call to all the parents."

"I need to go," she called over her shoulder to Janet, the older woman working the counter along with Mara this morning. The customers in line cleared a path for her, and the understanding and sympathy in their gazes made her heartbeat even faster.

"Of course." Janet was already reaching for the phone on the back wall. "I'll call in Toby. Take the whole day, Mara. We'll be fine."

"No injuries reported," Sam said as she rushed by on her way out.

"Thank you." Was she speaking to Sam or uttering a prayer of gratitude?

Starlight Elementary was only about a mile from downtown, but the short drive seemed to take hours. She didn't bother to look at her phone again, too afraid of distracting herself when anxiety already had her stomach churning and her hands trembling. As the school came into view, she could see the lights of fire trucks, police vehicles and an ambulance. Students and adults gathered in clusters across the street from the one-story building.

She quickly pulled to the curb, turned off the SUV and jumped out, then ran in the opposite direction of parents and children heading away from the scene.

No injuries, she repeated to herself to calm the frantic emotions that welled her throat. Evie was fine. Mara just had to find her.

She wished she'd paid more attention to the email about the school's evacuation protocol. Suddenly someone shouted her name. Brynn Hale waved from the far end of the crowd.

"She's here, Mara," Brynn called with a wave of

her hand, and Mara tried not to burst into tears as she hurried forward. Keep it together for Evie, she told herself.

"Where?" Mara asked, her voice trembling slightly.

Brynn shifted to reveal Evie dressed in the polka-dot leggings and matching T-shirt she'd chosen that morning. Mara grabbed the girl and pulled her tight to her chest, breathing deeply as Evie hugged her.

"Mommy," Evie whispered. "You're here."

"Of course, sweetheart. I'm sorry it took me so long to reach you."

"It's okay, Mommy. Anna's uncle found me."

Mara blinked, and glanced up to see Parker and Anna watching her.

"Parker?"

He gave her a tiny half smile, and Anna popped out from his other side.

"Hi, Mara," Anna said. "The gym roof broke. It was really loud."

"I bet it was scary, honey," Mara said, giving Evie another squeeze, "but it's good you girls were together. I'm glad no one was hurt."

"We can't go to school the rest of the day," Evie said softly. Now that Mara knew her girl was safe, she turned her attention to the school. Her breath caught as she took in the destruction. Debris littered the school playground, and she could see where the gym roof had caved in on itself. She sent up a silent prayer no one had been hurt.

"We should do something fun." She smoothed a hand over Evie's braids. Right now, she wanted to take her daughter's mind off what had happened and how bad it could have been. She needed to distract them both. They'd figure out the rest once the officials assessed the damage. "We can have a picnic lunch out at Meadow Creek if you'd like."

"Can Anna come with us?"

"Of course."

"And her uncle?"

Mara blinked, unsure how to answer. "Give me a minute to work things out."

She straightened and turned first toward Brynn, who held the hand of her ten-year-old son, Tyler. "What exactly happened?"

The petite brunette shook her head, her big blue eyes wide with concern. "They haven't told us anything yet. Thank heavens no one was in the gym at the time of the collapse."

"I'd guess water damage," Parker offered from behind Mara. "I heard the principal say the art room was destroyed, as well."

Brynn made a face. "There's going to be a lot of work ahead of us."

"Us?" Mara asked.

"I'm PTO president this year," Brynn told her with a grimace. "I agreed to it before…" She bit down on her lip then shrugged. "Obviously we have no idea the extent of the damage. The school has insurance, but I can guarantee we'll need to do fund-raising to help cover some of the costs."

Mara nodded, amazed by the other woman's immediate focus on helping. She'd met Brynn through her friend Kaitlin Carmody and had the feeling they could be close even though Brynn had lived in Starlight her entire life and Mara was new to the community. Brynn was another single parent, widowed after a car crash killed her husband over the summer. She'd heard the gossip about Daniel Hale, that he'd been driving with his mistress and his car had gone off the cliff, the fiery crash taking both their lives. Mara's struggles paled in comparison to the tragedy Brynn and her son had faced.

"I'll help," Mara offered without hesitation, earning a smile from the other woman. She'd managed to keep herself closed off from most of the community for the better part of a year and now she couldn't seem to stop herself from volunteering where she saw a need.

"I appreciate it. I'm going to take Tyler home now, but I'll call Principal Watkins tonight and figure out the most urgent needs." Brynn glanced over Mara's shoulder. "Good to have you back in town, Parker. I'll see you both later."

"Thanks for the wardrobe help," he said, earning a small chuckle from Brynn before she led away her son.

Mara looked around to see the crowd quickly

dispersing as more parents were reunited with their kids. Keeping a hand on Evie's shoulder, she turned to Parker.

"Thanks for being here," she said stiffly, then frowned as she registered the too-small Starlight Elementary T-shirt stretched across his broad chest. "What's with the shirt?"

He tugged at the hem, which barely covered the waistband of his faded jeans. She hadn't noticed the ill-fitting piece of clothing earlier, her attention solely on Evie and assuring her daughter's safety. But now she couldn't seem to wrench her gaze away from the strip of hard abs revealed every time he shifted.

"I puked on him," Evie said before Parker could answer, fisting her fingers in the fabric of Mara's cotton pants.

"No big deal," Parker added with a gentle smile. "I sort of felt sick to my stomach in all the chaos, as well."

"Evie throws up a lot," Anna explained, wrinkling her nose. "She gets scared and pukes. She's good at making it to the bathroom." They all studied Parker's shirt. "Usually."

"I'm sorry." Mara's chest tightened at Evie's apology. The stress vomiting had started in the midst of the divorce. Their pediatrician had sent them to a therapist, who'd given Evie coping strategies to deal with the nausea. Mara also had a prescription for antinausea medicine, but sometimes accidents still happened. She knew her shy daughter hated attention on her, especially for her sick stomach, and wished she had a foolproof way to calm Evie's nerves. And her own, come to think of it.

"It's okay, sweetie," she said, cupping Evie's head against her leg. "Today was stressful and—"

"I was happy for an excuse to get some merch from my alma mater. Starlight Elementary Bobcats forever." Parker traced his fingers over the big cat emblem on the front of the shirt.

The urge to hug him blasted through Mara like a tornado. He looked ridiculous in the shirt but somehow even more irresistible. She wouldn't have expected this type of effortless kindness and hated to admit how much it warmed her cold heart.

"What's an almer otter?" Anna asked, and Evie giggled.

"It means I went to school here," he explained. "Brynn tracked down a shirt for me since mine…" He trailed off then quickly added, "Shirts are easy to replace, but not so much silly nieces." He ruffled Anna's hair, the gesture all the more endearing for how uncomfortable he looked making it. "I'm glad everyone is okay and…um…happy to have the afternoon to spend with you."

Mara suppressed a sigh at how sweet he was acting. Acting, she reminded herself. The real Parker was the one she'd seen in court, the one who'd dragged her name through the mud without batting an eye. At least that's what she wanted to believe. Seeing him outside the courtroom made it more difficult.

"Where's Josh?" Mara asked, needing a buffer between her and the unbidden attraction she felt for this man. "Maybe he'll want Anna with him this afternoon? It's been a chaotic morning."

"He's meeting with the county building department." Parker shrugged. "I called him to let him know everything's fine, but I'm the designated adult for Anna today."

"Uncle Parker let me have cookies for breakfast," Anna reported cheerily. "He doesn't know much."

"You said it would be okay with your dad." Parker narrowed his eyes at the precocious girl.

Mara couldn't help the chuckle that escaped her lips. "You really don't know much," she said, echoing Anna's assessment. The school's principal, Gary Watkins, hurried by with the fire chief, looking harried and stressed. "We should head out. They've got a lot of work to do to assess the damage, and we're not helping."

"I hope they fix it quick." Anna fell into step next to Evie.

"I don't," Evie muttered. "I hate gym class. Mommy, are Anna and her uncle coming to our picnic?"

"Can we, Parker?" Anna tossed a pleading smile

over her shoulder. "Otherwise, I might not have a healthy lunch."

"I could manage healthy," he protested even as he shot a questioning look toward Mara. "But we happen to be available."

"You've gone from big-shot attorney to blue-collar worker and backup childcare. Quite a step down for you, huh?" As soon as the petty words were out of her mouth, Mara cringed. Luckily, the girls seemed occupied in their own conversation, but that didn't excuse her rudeness. It would be easy to blame the outburst on the adrenaline of the past thirty minutes but she knew it had more to do with trying to keep her defenses up around Parker, even when it wasn't warranted.

To her surprise, he seemed unfazed by the criticism. "It's a change, but not a bad one. I don't think I realized I needed a break until Josh's predicament forced me to take one." He drew in a breath. "I may not know much about kids, but I like spending time with my niece."

"I'm sorry," Mara said. "I understand you're helping your family. It's kind of hard for me to wrap my mind around the idea that the guy I only met as Paul's jerk of an attorney has an actual heart."

"It's probably at least two sizes too small if that helps," he said with a wink.

Mara giggled then quickly clamped shut her mouth and bit down hard on the inside of her cheek.

She wasn't a woman who giggled and flirted, especially not with Parker, despite his newly uncovered redeeming qualities. She hadn't even considered dating since her divorce and this man absolutely wouldn't make a good candidate for a boyfriend, even if she wanted one. Which she didn't. Not even one teensy bit.

They'd come to where her car was parked, and she turned to Parker. "Meet at the picnic area by the Meadow Creek trailhead at noon."

He nodded. "It's a plan. What can we bring?"

"Drinks," she said and hoped he didn't notice she was looking at a spot just past his shoulder. Making eye contact was just a little too much for her senses to handle at the moment. Parker affected her on a lot of different levels.

"Got it," he said then took a step toward Anna.

"See you soon, Evie-Stevie," the girl said.

Evie grinned in response. "See you, Anna-Banana."

Mara unlocked the car and watched her daughter climb in the backseat. It was only ten thirty, so maybe she could squeeze in a cold shower before their picnic. She needed something to calm her overheated hormones. All her doubts about working on the Dennison Mill project came rushing in again. The last thing she needed was more time with Parker, so she did her best to ignore how much she was looking forward to this afternoon.

\* \* \*

A few minutes before noon, Parker pulled into the Meadow Creek parking lot. He hadn't been to the picnic area since he was a kid, when his mom would take Josh and him on weekend outings so as not to disturb their father.

Mac Johnson's beloved hobby had been making model airplanes, and his study had been dedicated to the activity. The bookshelves were lined with the completed models, arranged to Mac's exacting specifications. A table had been placed against one wall of the paneled office where he'd done most of the work. It wasn't until he was older that Parker questioned why his dad never included either son in the work, but Mac had little interest in his family unless it involved making an impression on his constituents in town. The office had been off-limits, and the one time he and Josh had gone in and accidently broken one of his precious models, there'd been hell to pay. The sound of a cracking belt and Josh's plaintive whimpers as he took the brunt of the abuse still made Parker's skin crawl. His father knew that watching Josh be punished was worse than any physical pain Parker might endure, which was part of the reason Josh was such a target.

It was still strange to think of the dichotomy between his dad's public persona and private personality. How could a man who was so generous in his career be such a bastard at home? Parker's two best friends, Finn Samuelson and Nick Dunlap, had an idea that things were rough in the Johnson household, but Parker had never shared the extent of the abuse. His dad's viciousness went way beyond knocking around his kids and wife, although they all lived with the everyday fear of getting backhanded. The emotional trauma hurt the most—the constant stream of subtle insults and criticisms meant to undermine and chip away at a person's self-esteem until there was nothing left.

Parker had always feared he took after his dad and worked to find constructive outlets for his emotions. He exercised like a madman to exhaust himself physically and always kept his relationships casual and fun, not wanting anything heavy to potentially trigger him. Becoming a divorce attorney served him on several levels. For one, he never wanted any person to feel stuck in a bad marriage the way his mother had. But he could also channel some of his latent bitterness in court, doing his best to make sure his clients got most, if not all, of their stipulations met.

Mara challenged what he understood to be certain in the world. He might not have liked her ex-husband, but he'd believed Paul Reed when he explained that Mara had been a shallow gold digger who wanted to use their child as a weapon for her own financial gain.

Parker understood how a person could distort the truth to serve their own purposes. Unfortunately, he was coming to realize his client had been doing all the manipulating. How many other people had he misjudged in his career? He didn't want to consider what it said about him that he'd been so willing to go after whoever sat on the opposite side of the courtroom, justified in his tactics based on what his mom had endured. Obviously, not every marriage went bad because of abuse, but for Parker divorce had been black and white...until he'd met Mara.

"Why are you sad, Uncle Parker?" Anna asked from the backseat.

His stomach pitched. He'd always prided himself on his stiff poker face, and now he was being called out on his emotions by a kid. If a few days in Starlight could affect him this intensely, what shape would he be in by the end of his stay?

"I'm fine, Banana. Just thinking about stuff." He gave himself a mental head shake and glanced in the rearview mirror. The girl stared solemnly at him, which was unlike his boisterous niece. "What's wrong?"

"Hickies," she answered, and his jaw dropped.

"Come again?"

"I got hickies." She held her hands to her neck, and it sounded like she was holding her breath. How had he not noticed one or more hickies when he'd picked her up at school?

His niece was a handful, but before this moment Parker had assumed that was a good thing. Her formidable confidence had allowed her to survive both cancer and her mother leaving with her spirit intact as far as he could tell. Now he realized just how far out of his element he was, stepping in when Josh couldn't reschedule his meeting. He had a vague awareness that kids matured faster these days but a kindergartner with hickies…

Suddenly Anna drew in a deep breath and gave an exaggerated swallow. "I think they're gone," she told him with a toothy grin.

He undid his seat belt and turned to study her unblemished neck as understanding dawned. "Hiccups," he said.

"I get them sometimes. I used to a lot more when I had chemo."

A lump formed at the back of his throat even as relief flooded through him. "You're a very brave girl, Anna."

She tilted her head to one side as she studied him. "That's what Daddy always says."

"Your daddy is a smart guy."

"I know." She placed her hand on the window and smiled again. "Evie's here." She unbuckled the seat belt, opened the car door and then climbed out of her booster seat.

Parker gripped his hands on the steering wheel, swallowing down his guilt at not being around to help Josh and Anna sooner. While he'd been wrapped up in the most superficial of first-world issues an hour away, his brother had been dealing with a divorce and a sick kid on his own.

Parker still couldn't believe his mom hadn't shared Josh's ordeal with him, even if Josh had asked her not to. As a member of the family, Parker had a right to know. At least that's what he wanted to tell himself. The truth was if he'd been a better brother, he would have been involved regardless of the circumstances of Josh's life. He wouldn't have walked away from his childhood and never turned back. If he'd been a better brother—

He startled at the knock on the car's window, turning to see Mara staring at him. She looked confused, which made sense since he was sitting in the parked car by himself, deep in thought. Bad thoughts. Thoughts that did him no good and made him want to turn the key in the ignition and drive as fast as he could away from Starlight and all the memories this town held.

Instead he opened the door and climbed out, running a hand through his hair as he glanced toward the path that led to the picnic area near a bend in the creek. Anna and Evie were climbing on an outcropping of boulders, engrossed in conversation. Both girls had been through difficulties in their young lives but neither seemed scarred by the sort of emotional trauma that had marked his childhood. Did that make him weak and cowardly?

"You okay?" Mara asked, taking a step away as she watched him.

"Yeah." He opened the back hatch of the Audi and pulled out the small cooler he'd packed. "We came here when I was a kid. I forgot how pretty it is this time of year."

Her features softened as she nodded. "Fall is my favorite season. The leaves changing and the cooler temperatures make it perfect. We've got a few weeks until the height of color hits. It's all so cozy."

Parker paused with his hand on the back of the SUV and glanced at the trees that edged the forest. The leaves fluttered in shades of gold and copper, bright against the green needles of the pines that made up much of the border. He liked that she'd taken the time to appreciate their surroundings and had pointed it out to him. Often in the city, Parker spent his days heads-down in cases or checking off his mile-long to-do list and forgot to notice the beauty of the world around him.

Plus, those few sentences were the most conventional Mara had offered in their few conversations, and he couldn't deny he wanted more. "I've grown partial to summer since I moved to Seattle," he offered, walking with her to the trailhead. "There's so much rain otherwise, and I like seeing the sun."

"That's another reason why this valley is nice." She adjusted the tote bag slung over her shoulder. "The weather is better than in the city."

"Drier," he agreed. "Let me take that." He reached for the straps, his fingers accidentally brushing the smooth skin on the back of Mara's arm. He'd noticed the same thing that day in the bounce house. Once again he wondered at the paradox of her prickly nature and her soft body. He liked the contrast.

He liked her, which was stupid. There were so many reasons a woman like Mara would be wrong for him. If only he cared about any of them at the moment.

## Chapter Five

Mara led the way toward the picnic tables situated under a canopy of Douglas firs not far from the creek's edge. Although the area was often crowded on the weekends, today they had the path to themselves.

The girls chattered happily behind her, but it was Parker who held her attention. When he hadn't emerged from his fancy SUV after Anna got out, she'd approached the driver's side to find him staring into space, his hands clenched around the leather steering wheel. The side window was tinted, but she hadn't been able to miss the pain marring his movie-star-handsome face.

Damn the man for being human. She hadn't doubted he had a pulse...but his heart was another story. It had been so easy to make him the bad guy along with her ex-husband, worse than her ex, even. She'd chosen Paul, or at least allowed herself to be chosen by him. If he was the driving force behind her life being ruined, what did that say about her ability to be in a successful relationship? Not much, which offered her little hope for the future.

It served her to believe that Paul's ruthless attorney had goaded him into smearing her character, destroying her career and making her doubt herself on every level. She knew that wasn't true. Her ex had wanted to bring her low and perhaps to punish her for deviating from the path he'd laid out for both of them.

But he was still the father of her child, although he hadn't seen Evie since last Christmas and rarely bothered to call and check on her. Mara couldn't help but blame herself for marrying someone with whom she was totally incompatible. If she'd done better, Evie would have a true family right now, the kind of white-picket-fence life Mara wanted for her. Instead, she was a single mom, overworked and sleep deprived, doing her best but always worried it wasn't enough. That she would never be enough.

She'd gotten through the sorrow and anger of the past two years by compartmentalizing her emotions. Things had become black and white for Mara. People were good or bad and she had no room for gray in her world. The shaded parts made her question, made her feel, made her want things she'd tamped down in her effort to get on with life.

Parker was the epitome of gray for Mara. She felt more comfortable with him in the black-and-white category. Somehow she knew this afternoon together wasn't going to help keep her feelings for him any clearer.

Drawing in a deep breath that she hoped would help loosen the knots in her stomach, Mara turned and smiled at the girls. "I hope you're both hungry." She added a wink for Anna. "We can use lunch to teach your uncle about the food groups. Wouldn't want him thinking Goldfish are a protein."

Both Evie and Anna giggled while Parker thunked the heel of his palm on his forehead. "Not even the extra-cheesy Goldfish?" he asked.

"Nope," Mara answered, trying to keep her lips from twitching.

One broad shoulder lifted and lowered. "I guess you learn something new every day. Girls, I need you to show me the way."

Yeah, Mara silently agreed. Like the fact that the man you thought was your sworn enemy might not be so bad after all.

It didn't matter, she reminded herself. Her attraction to Parker aside, Mara wasn't looking for a romantic relationship of any kind with any man. She barely had time to shower every day. Between her shifts at the coffee shop, taking care of Evie, helping Nanci with the shop's books and doing the baking she loved, Mara fell into bed exhausted every night, lucky to remember to wash her face and brush her teeth. Making an effort to attract a man didn't begin to appear on her list of priorities.

"I assume you like peanut butter and jelly," she told him to a round of cheers from the girls.

"From what I remember when I was a kid, I do." He placed the bag of food and the cooler on the wooden table side by side. "I have to admit it's been a while. If I'd known about the menu, I would have brought milk."

She reached into the bag. "I'm joking. It's PB&J for the girls and chicken salad for us."

"Is it strange to say I'm oddly disappointed?"

"You won't be after your first bite of my chicken salad." She glanced at him out of the corner of her eye. "Although there are plenty of stranger things about this picnic."

"Aunt Nanci says Mommy's chicken salad sells out every day at Perk," Evie announced, climbing on the bench seat on the opposite side of the picnic table. "All her stuff is super yummy."

"Then I can't wait to try it."

"She bakes better than Aunt Nanci, too," Evie continued, and Mara marveled at her shy daughter's suddenly chatty nature. Evie usually said as few words as possible to adults, especially men. It had taken her months to make eye contact with Josh, and he was one of the easiest going men Mara knew.

Quite the opposite to his brother.

"Daddy loves her muffins," Anna added, never one to be left out of a conversation.

Mara heard Parker's muffled snort and swatted him on the arm. "Your mind is in the gutter."

"More like on your muffins," he said with a chuckle.

"Blueberry's my favorite." Anna reached for a grape from the container Mara set on the table.

"Mine are chocolate chip," Evie offered.

Parker tapped a finger on his chin as if deep in thought. "I wonder which ones I'll like the best?"

"I'm not giving you any muffins," Mara muttered under her breath.

"You can buy them at the coffee shop," Evie said helpfully. "Mommy bakes on Tuesday, Thursday and Saturday or whenever she's in a grumpy mood."

"Good to know." Parker handed each of the girls a juice box.

"I bake when I'm happy too," Mara protested, feeling her brows draw down when Evie's gaze dropped to the table.

"You aren't happy very much," her daughter said and the quiet admonishment was like a dagger to Mara's heart. Her pulse thrummed in her throat. How did her daughter pick up on that? Mara did her best to be cheery with Evie. She read books and sang songs and played games. She smiled even when she wanted to cry, and apparently all of her "fake it 'til you make it" efforts at positivity had been for nothing.

Before she could form a coherent response, Parker made a show of taking the bag of chips from the tote, pretending to lose his grip and sending the bag flying in the air.

Evie and Anna squealed with delight as he hopped up onto the bench, continuing to bobble the chips before finally cradling the bag like it was a precious baby. "We don't want potato crumbs," he said, stroking the foil wrapper. "I'm not letting you go again."

Mara forced a smile as she distributed sandwiches, appreciating the distraction he'd provided while trying to overcome the sting of Evie's words.

She was happy. Happy-ish, anyway. Her mind whirred with ideas for how to put on a better face for her daughter. She'd make up silly dances while cooking dinner. She'd laugh harder at the stories Evie told about her adventures with Anna on the playground. She'd smile even when her cheeks ached with the effort of it.

She would not allow her daughter to see her unhappy.

"Soda or sparkling water?" Parker asked, his tone soft, like he understood how fragile she felt in this moment without needing to acknowledge it.

"Water," she answered, picking up the chip bag.

She opened it and peered inside. "I think you managed not to crush a single one."

"I have gentle hands."

Her stomach pitched at the low timbre of his voice, and she almost dumped the entire bag onto Anna's plate.

The girls were engaged in a weighty conversation about the best shade of magenta in the crayon box at school so didn't seem to notice. Evie had moved on from the happiness comment as if it had been nothing more than pointing out a gray hair or something equally as trivial.

Mara was the one left stuck in the emotional quagmire, one that couldn't be easily remedied by a box of hair dye.

"As long as we're clear that those hands aren't getting anywhere near my muffins," she told Parker, striving to keep the conversation light. She took a seat on the bench next to him, making sure to keep as much physical distance between them as she could manage.

He leaned in closer. "But I'd be so good at cradling them."

Her throat went dry and she realized she'd chosen the wrong tactic for casual conversation. Flirting with Parker was a terrible idea. "Who's excited for the soccer game this weekend?" she asked Evie and Anna.

"Me," Anna said around a bite of sandwich. "I'm

gonna score three goals. Daddy said I'll get a hat that does tricks."

"Three goals in hockey is called a hat trick," Parker explained.

Evie frowned. "But we play soccer. I don't know how to ice skate."

"People use the term for any sport when you score three goals in one game." Parker popped a grape in his mouth, not making a big deal over either girl misunderstanding the term or what it meant. Mara would have expected him to react differently—with impatience or patronizing them for their lack of sports lingo knowledge.

"I won't score," Evie said, placing the uneaten half of her sandwich on the plate.

"You have to have faith," Parker assured her.

"Evie's afraid of the ball," Anna told him matter-of-factly. "She hates soccer."

"She doesn't hate it," Mara said quickly, her heart sinking when Evie's rosebud lips thinned. "Do you hate it, sweetheart?"

"I'm bad at it," Evie mumbled. "The worst on the team."

"Daddy will put you next to me on the field," Anna said, patting her friend's shoulder. "I'll cover your position and mine."

"Josh coaches the soccer team?" Parker grabbed another handful of chips.

Mara nodded. "The parents asked him to step in

when the dad who was supposed to coach took a new job with a lot of travel."

"I bet you're not bad," he said to Evie. "Some athletes take longer to develop than others."

A wisp of a smile crossed Evie's face before she shook her head. "I'm bad," she repeated.

"We'll practice more," Mara offered immediately. "I'll order a goal for the backyard with two-day shipping. Maybe you'll be off school for the rest of the week and you can take a ton of shots."

"Maybe," Evie agreed but she didn't look convinced.

Mara took another bite of sandwich. She'd perfected her chicken-salad recipe shortly after moving to Starlight, and the coffee shop sold wrapped sandwiches in the deli case. They were one of the most popular items, but right now the food in her mouth seemed to have all the flavor of cardboard.

"I'm done, Mommy," Evie said after one last grape.

"Me, too," Anna announced. "Wanna fro rocks in the creek?"

Evie shrugged. "I'll watch you."

Anna beamed, as if Evie's attention was her due. The difference in personalities suited both girls. Despite having gone through months of cancer treatments, Anna remained confident and outgoing. Evie was happy to tag along in Anna's shadow, as much as Mara would have liked her daughter to realize how talented and special she was in her own right. But the dynamic suited the two of them so she didn't push for more.

"Please play in the clearing where I can see you," she told the girls. "And remember to stay a few feet back from the creek." Meadow Creek was little more than a babbling brook at this time of year, so she felt safe supervising the girls from the picnic area. "I'll be down as soon as I clean up from the picnic."

"I'll help," Parker offered, standing as the girls skipped away. "Unless you want me to go along?"

"They'll be fine for a few minutes. We have a clear view of them from here."

"They're so different," he said, lifting the soda can to his mouth. "But neither of them seems to care."

"Not one bit," Mara agreed, feeling her shoulders relax a bit. She might have messed up a lot of things in her life, but she knew in her heart that settling with her daughter in Starlight wasn't one of them. "We moved here right before the start of the preschool last year. Anna had just finished chemo treatments, so she was totally bald. She'd also lost a bit of weight and looked…well…"

"Sick?" Parker asked softly.

"Yeah. It was her second year at the preschool and should come as no surprise that she'd been the most popular girl in her class the previous year. But when the new year started, some of the kids were freaked out by the way she looked." She shook her head. "The teacher tried to make the cancer seem like a part of life, but you know how kids can be."

"Little jerks," he muttered.

"Some of them, although in my opinion the parents could have stepped in more to help lessen the stigma. It was rough on Anna." Mara turned to him. "Hasn't Josh told you any of this?"

A muscle ticked in his jaw, and he focused on collecting the empty drink containers. "I didn't know about Anna's cancer until I was here over the summer for a friend's funeral."

"Brynn's late husband?"

"Yeah. Daniel and I went to high school together. We were all friends."

"Brynn is a great person and so positive despite what she's been through. I admire her for that. I'm kind of jealous of her for that, as well. Based on what my daughter just said, I need to work on my attitude."

"I like your attitude," he told her. "You don't take crap from anyone."

Mara felt her cheeks heat at the compliment. If only it were true.

"How often do you come back to Starlight?" she asked but kept her gaze on the two girls playing near the water. Somehow it seemed less prying when she wasn't looking into his blue eyes.

"Never." He grimaced. "I'm not proud of it, but before now I didn't think my presence, or lack of a presence, mattered."

"You matter to Josh," she said, placing a hand on his arm. The muscles bunched under her fingers, and she pulled away like she'd accidentally touched a hot coal.

Arm's length. That was a safe distance.

"I'd do anything for him," Parker said, falling in step with her as she walked toward the edge of the creek. "And for Anna. I might not have been around, but they're my family. If I'd known they needed me…"

"You know now." She ran a hand through her hair, wishing she had a scrunchie to pull it back. "You're here. Give yourself a break, buddy. Until you know better, you can't do better."

"I guess."

"Trust me. I'm an expert at self-flagellation. It doesn't help anything."

"Although I have no problem with your attitude, I'm curious. Why you aren't happy?" he asked suddenly, and Mara's spine stiffened.

"I am."

"That's not what Evie said."

"I'm a single mom working to support my kid. She confuses unhappiness with exhaustion. Like I said, I'm going to work on it." Mara flashed her cheesiest grin. "Ignore the bags under my eyes and focus on my jubilant smile."

"Jubilant," he repeated, one corner of his mouth kicking up in a way that made her pulse quicken.

"That word suits you." He picked up a stone, rubbed it between two fingers and sent it skipping up the shallow creek.

The two girls clapped and squealed and begged him for more. Parker obliged then squatted down near the water's edge and chose two stones, handing one to each girl. He explained what made a skipping stone a good choice and the best arm motion for a successful throw.

Anna danced in circles as he spoke, seemingly unable to contain her enthusiasm. Evie, on the other hand, listened intently, her chubby fingers gripping the stone she held in the exact way Parker demonstrated.

He went first on the next toss, over exaggerating the flick of his wrist in order to make the action clear for his pint-size pupils. His stone skipped three times across the calm water before sinking under the surface.

Anna stepped forward and hurled her rock so far it landed on the opposite bank. "I'm strong," she said with a laugh, lifting her arm to display her tiny muscle.

"You are indeed," Parker agreed before switching his gaze to Evie. "Are you ready to try?"

Mara held her breath as her daughter nodded. It was silly, of course. The small act of skipping a stone meant nothing in the grand scheme of life. Mara hadn't mastered it the few times she'd tried.

She could see how badly Evie wanted to get it right. Her daughter bit down on her lip and scrunched up her face.

"Relax," Parker said quietly. "You've got this."

For a moment, Mara imagined he was speaking to her. Then Evie lifted her arm to the side, flicked her wrist and sent the stone soaring toward the creek. The dark rock skipped twice in quick succession, eliciting cheers from Anna and Parker.

"You did it, Ev," Anna shouted, hugging her friend. "You skipped."

Evie's smile was so bright and true, it made Mara's heart ache.

"Nice work, girl," Parker said, patting Evie on the back. "You're a natural."

Evie beamed even more if that was possible. Mara's heart thudded with joy in response. Talk about jubilant.

"Let's look for centipedes now," Anna said. "I bet there are some under the rocks."

"Okay," Evie agreed, and with a last glance at the water, she followed her friend away from the creek.

Parker watched them go then picked up another stone and held it out toward Mara. "Want a turn?"

She shook her head. "I'm happy." She pressed two fingers to her chest. "Right now, at this moment, I'm really happy. Thank you."

Parker's lips parted and his nostrils flared like

he couldn't quite catch his breath. Mara knew the feeling.

He moved closer, crowding her slightly, but she didn't back away. She felt rooted in place, like the pine trees surrounding them.

His glacier-colored gaze flicked to the girls then immediately back to her. Then he leaned in and kissed her, a featherlight brush of his mouth on hers. She felt the contact all the way to her toes and almost moaned in protest when he pulled back.

But she didn't protest, although her breath hitched again when he drew his thumb across the delicate skin below her eye. "You should feel happy more often. Jubilant, even."

She closed her eyes and forced herself to think of all the reasons why she couldn't let this man close to her. Her shattered life topped the list.

Fisting her hands at her sides, she remembered what had led to the current state of her life. Nothing tamped down desire like a healthy dose of festering bitterness.

"Do you remember my divorce?" she asked, opening her eyes to stare at him again.

It took a second, but she saw the moment when his defenses returned. The subtle shuttering of his gaze and his posture going rigid. "I do."

She nodded. "Then you know why I am the way I am." She touched the tips of her fingers to the place he'd just stroked, needing to wipe away her body's awareness of him.

"In order to get full custody of Evie, I had to agree to no child support payments from Paul. No alimony. No settlement. I walked away with my daughter, my clothes and a car." Her fingernails dug into the soft flesh of her palm, and she welcomed the stab of pain. "My ex-husband is worth millions and his lifestyle means he has the best of everything. I got nothing from him. That isn't a problem for me, but my daughter suffered in the process. *You* negotiated the deal."

"I was doing my job," he said, but by the way he grimaced as he said the words, he understood how lame they sounded.

"That's not much comfort to me now, Parker. If you want to know what stole the happiness from my life, look in the mirror." She turned to follow the girls so she didn't have to acknowledge the hurt that flashed in his eyes at her words.

# *Chapter Six*

"I shouldn't be here right now." Mara sighed as she took a seat in a booth across from her friends Kaitlin and Brynn the following night at Trophy Room, Starlight's popular downtown bar. Even at half past five on a weeknight, the bar was more than half full of happy customers. From what Mara had been told, Trophy Room was a Starlight institution. The interior was old-school with a modern flair. A row of cozy booths lined one wall with high bar tables situated around the open center and a ten-foot-long bar with a cherry top that spanned the other side of the space.

"You have at least an hour," Kaitlin said, pushing a margarita glass in her direction. "That's time enough for a quick drink."

"The good parents are watching the practice," Mara mumbled, earning a delicate snort from Brynn, who was seated next to Kaitlin.

"Hoping their kid will be crowned the kindergarten second coming of Messi, no doubt." Brynn took a small sip of her drink.

Mara frowned. "Who's Messi?"

"Lionel Messi. One of the greatest soccer players of all time," Brynn explained. "Plays for Barcelona."

"Why do you know that?" Kaitlin asked then held up a hand. "Never mind. You have a ten-year-old boy. Enough said."

"I have no such aspirations." Mara licked a bit of salt off the rim of her glass. "I'll be happy if Evie doesn't puke or get knocked over. I'm already feeling guilty for encouraging her to sign up for soccer. It seemed like a fine idea, but there's a decent chance she'll be miserable all season. I'm the worst."

"You're not the worst," Brynn assured her, her tone deadpan. "It's the mom's job to make our kids try things that push their limits. What would they have to talk about in therapy down the road otherwise?"

Mara laughed. It amazed her that Brynn could still find anything to joke about after what she'd been through. Yes, Mara had left the courtroom feeling like she'd had her skin filleted off her body, but it was nothing compared to what Brynn had endured. Paul might be a heartless, lying cheater, but she hadn't learned all of that while also dealing with his death.

"I'm afraid Evie will have plenty of fodder for the therapist's couch," Mara said, taking a small sip of margarita. The tang of lime burned her throat, but she relaxed for the first time all day.

Brynn held up her glass in mock salute. "Maybe she and Tyler can get a group discount."

"You two are freaking me out," Kaitlin told them, taking a piece of celery from the plate in the center of the table and loading it with spinach dip. "I'm not even married and already I'm worried about how Finn and I are going to mess up our kids."

"You'll be great." Brynn patted Kaitlin's shoulder. "Finn loves you, and he's a stand-up guy. You're going to get married and have gorgeous kids with crazy good hair."

Both Mara and Kaitlin laughed again.

"Priorities," Kaitlin said.

Mara leaned in like she was divulging a state secret. "Paul has a receding hairline."

All three women dissolved into another fit of laughter.

"Now I feel worse." Mara dabbed at the corners of her eyes. "Evie is stuck at practice, and I'm here drinking and having fun. I shouldn't be enjoying myself if there's a chance she's miserable."

Brynn picked up a pita triangle and pointed it toward Mara. "She's in great hands with Josh, so there's nothing to worry about. He'll make sure she's okay."

"Speaking of great hands…" Kaitlin wiggled her eyebrows. "Tell us about spending time with Parker."

"I was stuck with him," Mara said, dropping her gaze to the scratched tabletop. She traced one fingertip along a particularly deep gash, "because he had to watch Anna yesterday afternoon."

Kaitlin rolled her eyes. "I can name a half-dozen women off the top of my head who would like to be stuck with Parker."

"Stuck *on* Parker," Brynn added with a snort.

Mara pointed at her. "You're cut off."

"I haven't even finished one."

"One too many," Mara countered.

"Stop trying to distract us from discussing you and Parker." Kaitlin's smile was devious. "I heard he filled out the Starlight Elementary T-shirt pretty darn well." She nudged Brynn. "There's a fund-raising idea for you. Auction off single men in school merchandise. You'll raise thousands."

"Mara can bid on Parker," Brynn said, rubbing her palms together as if she was warming up to the idea.

Mara threw up her hands. "I'm not bidding on anyone. Definitely not Parker."

"Don't deny it. You two have chemistry."

Mara opened her mouth to protest but couldn't quite force her mouth to form the words. She thought about the way her body had responded to that brief kiss.

"You're blushing," Kaitlin told her.

"I want a reason to blush," Brynn mumbled.

Both Mara and Kaitlin turned to their friend. "Really?" Mara asked. "You do?"

Brynn ran a finger along the salt rim of her margarita glass. "I lost my husband, but I'm not dead."

"Oh."

Mara glanced toward Kaitlin, who looked as shocked as she felt.

"We could help find you a date," Kaitlin said.

"No one in Starlight wants to go out with me." Brynn sniffed. "The poor, grieving widow."

"Or me," Mara added, hoping to make Brynn see she wasn't alone. "The bitter divorcée."

"You have Parker," Brynn said.

"I do not."

"You need an online dating profile, Brynn." Kaitlin reached for another celery stick. "But first we need to figure out whether it's good to swipe left or right. We can set up profiles for you both. We'll go on triple dates."

"I'm not interested in online dating," Mara said.

"Because of Parker." Brynn grinned cheekily when Mara glared at her. It was funny now that Mara had believed Brynn was as quiet and reserved as she'd seemed when they were first introduced. All her outward propriety masked a wicked sense of humor and a potentially hidden penchant for adventure.

"No," Mara insisted and hoped the bar's dim lighting hid the blush she could feel rising to her cheeks. "But enough of your delusions about Parker and me. Let's talk about finding a man for the grieving widow. I like the sound of that—it's like a romance novel setup."

Kaitlin picked up her phone from the table and tapped at the screen. "We should start with a checklist."

"I don't have time to date," Brynn said. "Not right now. I just got my substitute-teaching certification and I'm heading up the fund-raising efforts for the school's gym."

"Requirements for a booty call then," Kaitlin amended.

Brynn inclined her head as a slow smile spread across her face. "I hadn't considered that, but it's not a bad idea." She leaned forward as if revealing a secret. "Daniel was the only man I've ever been with and I got pregnant the first time we…you know."

A throat cleared suddenly and all three women glanced up to see that Jordan Schaeffer, the bar's owner, had approached the table.

"I hope I'm not…um…interrupting." The beefy former football player tugged at the ends of his wavy hair, looking like he wished he hadn't overheard any part of their conversation. "I stopped by to see if there was anything I could do for you ladies. I guess… I think…you seem to have things under control."

Mara choked on her laughter at the idea of his offer being related to a booty call for Brynn.

"Do you want to host the Founder's Day Craft Fair at the bar?" Brynn asked, ignoring their previous topic of conversation. "It was supposed to be in the school gym, but that's not an option at this point." She wasn't the least bit embarrassed as far as Mara could tell. It only made Mara like the single mom even more.

Jordan didn't look any more comfortable, his golden-brown eyes going wide. "Is that a joke?"

"Kind of," she admitted. "But I've got a big mess on my hands for the event, so if you have any ideas let me know. Otherwise, I think we're taken care of here."

"Great," he said as he backed away, clearly grateful for the chance to escape.

"Awkward," Brynn said around another bite of pita and spinach dip. "This is why I can't think about dating in Starlight. I'll need to open up the geographic pool, but not until I get through the craft fair. I don't want some new man to think I'm a lunatic before he gets to know me."

"Good point," Mara agreed.

"Right now," Brynn said with a sigh, "I need a venue."

"What about switching the location to the high school?" Kaitlin asked.

Brynn shook her head. "They have a volleyball tournament on the schedule for the third weekend in October. We've already got vendors booked that weekend, so I don't want to change the date."

"The mill," Mara murmured, her mind suddenly racing.

"The lumber mill?" Brynn's tone was dubious.

"Yes." Mara pushed the drink out of the way and scooted forward. "I'll need to talk to Josh, but it would be the perfect grand opening celebration. If we can get things up and running at the coffee shop and a couple of the flagship merchants moved in, you can use the space that was supposed to be the restaurant."

"Maybe," Brynn agreed slowly. "Our booths don't need a ton of space."

"We'll be creative," Mara said. "If the weather's still nice, some of the vendors can set up in the courtyard. I'll arrange for a few food trucks to be there. Isn't there a dance involved with Founder's Day?"

"I've got the band booked already. We're going to turn the whole thing into a fund-raiser for the gym roof."

"The mill would be perfect." Mara felt an unfamiliar thrum of excitement skitter across her belly. It was the same thing she always felt at the start of a new project when she'd figured out the vision she wanted to create. This was no different. It would be impossible to get a full restaurant up and running in the time Josh had, especially with his limited budget. But maybe they didn't need that. Maybe they only had to think out of the box about the space and how to use it.

"It might work." Brynn drew in a shuddery breath. "I could kiss you right now."

"Swipe right," Kaitlin advised with a wink.

"I'll still need buy-in from Josh," Mara added. "I think the plan might work for you both."

"You'll be involved, too?" Brynn asked. "I can coordinate everyone from the craft fair, but my time is limited now that I'm going to start subbing. Sally Kay, the second-grade teacher, is going out on maternity leave next week and I'm supposed to be covering for her part-time."

"Mara's already committed to helping," Kaitlin answered before Mara had a chance to.

When she didn't chime in her agreement immediately, Kaitlin lifted a brow. "Right?"

"I'm helping with the coffee shop because Aunt Nanci asked. As far as the rest…"

"I thought you were going to retool the design of the space so Josh could open on time."

"Yes, but I've kind of changed my mind." She shrugged. "It's been hard to—"

"Be so close to Parker without jumping his bones?" Brynn asked conversationally.

"No one says *jumping his bones* anymore," Kaitlin told the other woman. "We need to update your sexy-times talk before you start swiping."

Mara laughed, trying to ignore the anxiety pooling in her belly at the thought of working with Parker. He was exactly the reason she'd considered minimizing her involvement, but the Founder's Day idea appealed to her on a number of levels. Besides, she truly wanted to help Brynn. "I'll run it all by Josh. If he goes for the idea and wants me a part of it, then I'm in."

"Of course he'll want you," Kaitlin said.

Brynn wiggled her eyebrows. "Not like Parker wants you."

"Oh, my gosh. You have to stop."

"I've been a good girl my whole life," Brynn said, clearly unrepentant. "I'm thinking of unleashing my inner bad girl."

"Do you have one of those?" Kaitlin asked.

"There's no doubt she does." Mara scooted her chair away from the table. "I've got to get to soccer practice before it's over. I want to watch for a bit."

"I hope Evie does great," Brynn said. "Let me know what Josh says about the fair. I'll have to make some changes to the promotional information that's already gone out and need to get started right away."

"Say hi to Parker," Kaitlin added.

"He won't be there, thank heavens."

Kaitlin only shrugged. "The next time you see him, then. It's bound to be sooner than later."

"Not if I have anything to say about it. See you, ladies. Thanks for the drink and the laughs."

She walked out of the bar, silently lecturing her libido to calm itself. At the idea of seeing Parker again, certain parts of her body had done a little happy dance, despite how much she wished she could curb her reaction to him.

She'd have to find a way to control her attraction, especially since she had no doubt Josh would welcome as much time as she was willing to put into the mill project.

That meant she'd be close to Parker, and she had no doubt that meant trouble.

"I can't believe you do this sober," Parker muttered as he jogged to the middle of the field where his brother stood.

Josh glanced over his shoulder at the parents watching from the sidelines. "You can't say that out loud. I don't want anyone thinking I'm drinking at soccer practice."

"If they're here watching, I doubt they'd blame you. This is like herding kittens who've downed a case of energy drinks."

Josh laughed at the joke, and Parker felt a momentary sense of accomplishment. His brother had always been the serious sort, but he'd sensed an additional layer of gravity shrouding him since Parker returned to Starlight. He understood it, of course. Between Anna's cancer, Jenn leaving and now the stress of the mill project, he couldn't imagine how Josh was managing all of his emotions.

He also couldn't understand why his brother had agreed to coach this motley group of rug rats. He glanced over at the kids shooting on the oversize goal at the end of the field. They were supposed to be practicing ball handling but it looked more like a pinball machine gone crazy with balls rolling in every direction.

"They're getting better," Josh said before blowing his whistle and dividing the kids into two lines for a passing drill.

"Then they must have really sucked at the start," Parker muttered.

"Mommy says *sucked* is a bad word."

Parker whirled to find Evie standing directly behind him. She used a grubby finger to push her glasses up on her nose, her big eyes solemn behind the lenses.

"Nice job," Josh said with another laugh. "You doing okay, Evie?"

"Yep," the girl answered and although Parker didn't believe her for a minute, Josh seemed to accept the answer. He patted her dark head before heading over to the rest of the team.

"Did you puke?" Parker asked when the two of them were alone.

She kicked one cleated toe at the grassy field. "Nope."

"Did you almost puke?"

Her shoulders slumped an inch. The small, defeated movement made his heart pinch. "Almost."

"What happened?"

"I dunno. Caroline pushed me out of the way, and Anna called her a poopy-head and she said I was the poopy-head because I miss the ball when I kick. Anna was mad, and Caro was mad and I felt pukey."

Wow. That was a big download of information. Parker scrubbed a hand over his jaw, trying to figure out the best way to respond. He would have liked to pull Caroline out of the drill and drag her over to her poopy-head mom for a lecture on bullying.

But he didn't know which one Caroline was and more important, understood making a scene wasn't going to help Evie get through the soccer season.

"I agree with Anna," he said, even though he knew that was probably inappropriate, as well. He didn't care. He was the assistant coach and not a parent, which gave him a bit of a pass. "How did Coach Josh and I not see that?"

"I dunno," Evie repeated. "But I miss the ball a lot." She clenched her fist in the fabric of her unicorn T-shirt. "Will you ask Coach Josh if I can sit on the bench on Saturday? I'll be a good cheerleader. I promise."

Parker blew out a breath. This kid killed him.

"Everyone plays," he said gently. "That's how Coach Josh runs the team."

"Yeah, I know," Evie agreed. She glanced around him toward the rest of the team. "I gotta go practice."

"Hey, Evie?" Parker put a hand on her shoulder when she started to move past him.

She looked up, her milk-chocolate-colored eyes wide. In some ways, Mara's daughter reminded him of Josh as a kid—small and unsure and a perfect target for demon kids like Caroline. Parker had never experienced that sort of uncertainty. He'd been confident, athletic and a pint-size master at hiding the emotional trauma in his life. Josh had struggled while Parker instinctively understood what had to be done to survive and flourish.

He was back in Starlight to help his brother, but that didn't mean he couldn't spread the wealth a bit while he was here.

"What, Coach?"

The word *coach* hit Parker like a swift uppercut to the jaw. It was a role he'd never expected to play, especially for a dozen chattering kindergarten girls, but he found he liked the idea of it. The teams he'd been on through recreation leagues and in high school had meant the world to him, giving him an outlet for his aggression and the feeling of belonging he'd never had at home.

Maybe he could be the person who offered that to Evie.

Maybe it could make up for what he'd helped do to Mara during the divorce proceedings.

"How would you like some private soccer lessons before the game?"

She tilted her head, reminding him of an unsure puppy trying to figure out whether he was offering a treat or a correction. "Would Anna come too?" she asked, shifting her gaze to the field beyond him once again.

"If you want her to then—"

"No," she admitted, sounding almost embarrassed about leaving out her friend. "Just me. Will you not tell her or her daddy?" She shrugged. "I just wanna be not bad anymore and she's already so good."

How the hell could Paul Reed cut this adorable, gentle girl out of his life? The man might be a genius at running a hotel conglomerate, but he was an absolute fool in his personal life to give up something so precious.

"No one will know but us..." He paused then added, "And your mom. We'll have to get her permission." His gaze zeroed in on Mara, who stood on the sidelines several feet away from the rest of the parents, staring at him and Evie. She hadn't been there the whole time. He would have noticed. His body immediately tightened, a visceral reaction he couldn't control even if he tried.

She wore a pair of dark tapered jeans and a cream-colored sweater. The weather in Starlight had turned consistently a few degrees cooler over the past couple of days as autumn took firm hold of the valley.

Parker didn't mind the change. It remained sunny and comfortable during the day, temperatures dropping only as the sun set.

He liked how cozy Mara looked, even though he could almost feel the agitation radiating from her. Her hair was pulled back into a high ponytail and he could see the hint of gold dangling from her ears.

"Wave to your mom," he told Evie now, "So she doesn't think I'm trying to corrupt you over here."

"Mommy worries," the girl said, raising a hand in Mara's direction. Mara's features softened as she waved back. Parker couldn't help but notice she didn't make eye contact with him.

"It means she loves you." He wished his own mom had worried more when he and Josh were kids. Or that Lillian had taken more action to protect them.

Josh called Evie's name, and the girl froze for a moment. She was terrified of soccer, and Parker hated it.

"Will you talk to Mommy after practice?"

"You bet," he promised. "Head over with the team. You're almost finished."

The girl nodded and walked away, looking about

as enthusiastic as if she were heading toward a firing squad. He could have sworn she muttered, "Thank God," under her breath as she moved toward the other girls.

Evie Reed was five going on forty-five, and her old-soul personality absolutely charmed him.

He followed her to where Josh stood with the rest of the team. His brother gave a recap of practice and a pep talk to get the girls excited for their first game. Parker watched the girls' faces as he listened. Their expressions ranged from determination in Anna to subtle panic in Evie's big eyes. A couple of the girls held hands and danced as Josh spoke. Another girl, a redhead with long braids, stood on her head.

To his credit, Josh didn't get distracted or seem frustrated with the team, most of whom had the attention span of a gerbil. He kept the speech short and sweet then instructed the girls to help gather the orange cones and random balls littered around the field.

They did so with the same squealing energy they seemed to bring to every aspect of practice.

"Nice work." Parker grabbed the mesh ball bag. "Do you remember Coach Jamison?"

"Your high school football coach?" Josh asked, one brow raised. "I remember him being a loud-mouthed jerk."

"He was definitely intense," Parker agreed. "It

worked for football players. He had a tendency to spit in your face while he was screaming at you."

"Nasty."

"Yeah, well." Parker patted his brother's shoulder. "Even he wouldn't have been able to keep those girls in line. He would have given up and headed to the bar an hour ago. You're good with them. I'm impressed."

"Thanks." Josh shrugged but couldn't hide his smile. "Anna wanted to be on a soccer team, and they needed a coach."

"They're lucky it's you."

Josh picked up a ball and tossed it to Parker. "You make a decent assistant. Who knew my big brother would be able to handle not being in charge for once?"

Parker thought he detected a slight edge to the words, but before he could ask Josh what he meant, the girls returned with the balls and cones.

A few of the moms waved to Josh and gave Parker a not-so-subtle once-over as they walked toward Parker's SUV and Josh's truck, which were parked next to each other in the lot.

"Don't sleep with any of the moms from the team," Josh said quietly.

"That's offensive," Parker countered.

"Be offended." Josh hefted the equipment bag into the truck bed. "Just don't sleep with them."

"I wouldn't—"

"Are you tired, Uncle Parker?" Anna asked,

bouncing past him to climb into the truck. "Daddy said you're going to sleep."

"Um…" He paused at a snort of laughter from behind him, and turned to find Mara standing there.

"Are you and your daughter spies or something?" She frowned.

"You're both experts at sneaking up on people and listening to private conversations."

"Maybe you were too busy checking out the soccer-mom brigade to notice me approach."

*I'm only checking out you*, he wanted to answer but held his tongue. "Jealous?" he asked instead, earning a louder burst of laughter.

"Don't flatter yourself." Her chin hitched. "Why were you talking to Evie?"

"Hey, Mara." Josh came around the side of his truck. "Evie did great tonight."

"Uh-huh." She smiled but not with any confidence. "The game on Saturday should be fun."

"You're a terrible liar," Parker said as Josh waved to another parent across the parking lot.

"Unlike you," she shot back then took a step away as his brother turned, glancing between the two of them. "I was talking to Brynn tonight," she told Josh. "She's in charge of the Founder's Day Craft Fair this year and needs a new venue because of the damage to the gym."

Josh shook his head. "Bummer. It's going to take months to repair. I'm going to submit a bid for some of the work if the timing is right with opening the mill."

"That's what I wanted to talk to you about—"

"You've changed your mind and want to be my new designer?"

Emotion flashed in Mara's eyes but disappeared too quickly for Parker to name it. "Actually—"

"Daddy!" Anna's voice rang out from the open window of the truck's backseat. "I'm hungry."

"Almost ready, sweetheart," Josh called. "Okay if I give you a call after dinner?"

Mara nodded. "Sure."

Josh headed around the truck again, and Parker turned back to Mara, only to find her heading to her car.

He caught up with her in several long strides. "We need to talk."

Her gaze remained straight ahead. "No, we don't."

"It's about Evie."

This time there was no question of the emotion in her eyes when she turned to him. Pure rage.

"What do you want with my daughter?" she asked through clenched teeth. Parker had read stories about people coming between grizzly-bear mamas and their cubs. He imagined it felt something like this. He had no idea what prompted the reaction from Mara, but she was definitely in full mama-bear mode. He needed to diffuse it quickly.

He held up his hands. "It's not bad. I promise.

She's nervous about Saturday's game, so I offered to do some private coaching with her."

Mara's eyes widened and her mouth dropped open.

"I told her I'd have to talk to you first, get your permission. That's all."

She stared at him a beat more then gave a small nod. "I'm sorry I overreacted." She crossed her arms over her chest like she wanted to shield herself from him. "Your words and the way you said them…" She shook her head. "I need to commit to helping Josh with the mill's design, but I can't make myself do it. The reasons aren't important. I appreciate you offering to help, but it would probably be better if I asked Josh to—"

"Evie didn't want Anna involved," he interrupted, not wanting to examine his feelings about Mara turning to his brother instead of him. Of course she would. She and Josh were friends, and despite the way she'd responded to Parker's kiss, she didn't seem to like him very much.

"Really?" Mara glanced toward her SUV. The back door was open and he could see a book propped on Evie's knees in her booster seat.

"I'm sure you can handle it if you don't want me involved." She already had enough reasons to dislike him, no sense giving her one more. Even if he wanted to spend more time with Mara, she was Josh's friend. The whole point of Parker being in Starlight was to support his brother. Chasing away someone important to him and Anna couldn't be part of the plan.

She flashed the barest hint of a smile. "I can't play soccer."

"It's not complicated at this point. If you can kick a ball, you're golden."

"I hate to admit it, but that might be an overestimation of my skill. I tried taking Evie out in the backyard to pass the other night, and she quit after five minutes because she had to do too much running after my stray kicks."

"You seem preternaturally capable at everything, Mara. I like knowing there's something you can't do."

"The list of my failures is legendary," she said with an eye roll. "You can call my mother for the unabridged version."

"I doubt that's true," he said, hoping she could hear the sincerity in his voice. He'd known her only a short time, but already Mara challenged so many aspects of his ordered world. Over the past week, details of her divorce case had come back to him. She was different than how her ex-husband had portrayed her, and what Parker had believed to be true. If he started looking at the spouses of his clients as sympathetic, where would that leave him in the courtroom?

A big part of his success was built on his tenacious drive and ability to stay emotionally unattached. After the way he'd grown up, he'd learned to see things as black and white. He didn't want to operate in the shadowy world of shades of gray.

"Mommy?" Evie called, and Mara immediately trotted over to the Toyota. She leaned into the vehicle for a minute then straightened and shut the door. Color tinged her cheeks when she returned to stand in front of Parker.

"Would you be available to stop by tomorrow around five?" she asked, glancing at a spot just over his left shoulder. "Evie would love to have your help."

He could tell how much it took for her to invite him into her world, and he did his best to ignore all the ways the idea of being a part of it appealed to him. "Sure," he answered simply, pulling his phone from his back pocket. "Where do you live?"

She rattled off an address in the historic neighborhood a few blocks from downtown. "We're staying with my aunt," she said, sounding embarrassed at the admission.

"I'm sure she's glad to have you there."

Her gaze flicked to his, a frown marring her delicate features. "It's weird when you're nice. I can't get used to it."

He gave a gasp of mock horror. "I'm a nice guy."

She opened her mouth like she wanted to argue then gave a little shake of her head. A strand of wispy hair escaped the ponytail, falling against her cheek. He wished he could be the man to tuck it behind her ear. He wished a lot of things when it came to this woman.

"Whatever you say," she told him. "We'll see you tomorrow night."

Parker watched her walk to her car and remained rooted in place as she pulled away. Evie waved from the backseat, and he returned the wave. His heart suddenly felt too big for his chest, like it wanted to grow but didn't have the room within his body.

This was what Starlight did to him. The town made him forget himself and the man he'd become. At the moment, he couldn't tell if that was good or bad, but he knew these weeks had the potential to change things in ways he couldn't imagine.

## Chapter Seven

By the time five o'clock the next evening rolled around, Mara was an exhausted bundle of nerves. She hadn't slept well the night before so had climbed out of bed at four in the morning to start a double batch of her favorite blueberry scones.

She'd delivered the pastries to the coffee shop then dropped Evie at her school, which had reopened that morning, the gymnasium portion of the building indefinitely barricaded.

Then she'd returned to Perk to submit the weekly order from Nanci's wholesale coffee supplier out of Seattle. Her heart had seemed to skip a beat when a couple of regular customers popped into the office to say how much they missed having Mara behind the counter.

Blown away at the thought of being missed, she'd actually put on her red apron and joined the staff for a few minutes. The familiar routine of pouring coffee and creating art in the foam relaxed her. At first she'd tried to exchange casual banter with the people in line, but even to her ears it came off awkward and stiff so instead she'd concentrated on making each drink perfect.

Mara had never mastered the ability for easy small talk, but she could bust out a complicated latte order with no problem. Her mother would have been horrified to see her in this kind of job. She'd been angry and critical when Mara had explained her plan for moving to Starlight from Southern California. "We wanted more for you," her mother had said when Mara returned from her cousin's wedding excited for a new start.

She understood at a bone-deep level what a disappointment she was to her parents. Her older brother Harry had graduated from medical school and was currently finishing a prestigious surgery fellowship in Utah. Mara's decision to study interior design had seemed frivolous to her mom and dad. They hadn't understood her love of transforming space and the creativity that went into it.

She'd somewhat redeemed herself when she'd been hired by Paul's company. Working for a prestigious hotel chain had satisfied her mother to an extent. Marrying the owner had been even better. Her parents spent minimal time with Paul during her marriage to him, but he checked off the boxes for the things they found important. The things Mara had thought were important to her, as well.

Until Evie came along and changed everything.

She drew in a deep breath when the doorbell rang. If spending time playing nice with Parker would make her daughter more confident on the soccer field, Mara supposed it was a small price to pay.

And also a practice run for the inevitability of seeing him at the mill. Josh had been thrilled she wanted to be involved and loved the idea of coordinating the grand opening with the Founder's Day celebration and craft fair. They'd talked for a while after the girls were in bed last night and worked out a few details. Josh wanted to give Mara a desk on-site, but she'd insisted it would be easier for her to do most of the initial work at home.

She felt a kinship to Little Red Riding Hood trying to dodge the Big Bad Wolf with her need to avoid Parker. But somehow she'd managed to invite the wolf into her home and hated to admit how excited she felt to spend time with him.

"Evie?" she called as she headed to the front door, but her daughter didn't appear.

She was reluctant to greet Parker without Evie as

a buffer yet couldn't very well leave him standing on the front porch.

"Hey," he said when she opened it. He stood there, gorgeous as ever in jeans and a gray Henley, and she cursed her body's reaction to him. It was as if energy zipped through her, a chemical reaction to being near him.

What was it about this man that turned her into a pile of sexually charged goo every time he smiled?

"Thanks again for offering to do this," she said, starting to fold her arms over her chest then dropping them to her sides. She had to find a way to make her peace with Parker, at least for the time he was in Starlight. He wasn't her enemy. Not anymore. Maybe he'd been during the divorce, but if it hadn't been him dragging her name through the mud, Paul would have found another attorney just as cold-blooded.

If she decided Parker was no longer the bad guy, did that mean she *could* be attracted to him without hating herself? Could she kiss him again with no guilt?

Her stomach swooped and pitched at the possibilities racing through her mind like it was the last lap of the Indy 500. Possibilities like his naked body pressed against hers and—

"You okay?"

She blinked when Parker snapped his fingers in front of her face.

"Oh." She blinked again. "I was just… I got lost in thought."

His lips quirked. "I'd pay way more than a penny for those thoughts," he said, his voice pitched low. "If your blush is any indication of where your mind was wandering, I'm all in."

*All in.*

Mara's mouth went suddenly dry. "Come in," she blurted, tripping over her own feet as she stepped back. "Into the house," she clarified. "The backyard or…" She glanced up the stairs and called for her daughter again. "I need to find Evie. Right now."

"I'm here, Mommy."

Her sweet girl appeared from the kitchen, wearing a shirt that said "You make my heart smile," neon pink athletic shorts and rainbow-colored socks pulled up to her knees and over her shin guards.

"You look ready for action," Parker said, hefting up the bag of balls in his hand. "I've got these and a portable goal in the back of my car. We'll be all set up in minutes."

"I'll take your balls," Mara said then choked on the words. "The balls." She cleared her throat. "The soccer balls."

She reached for the mesh bag, her hand stilling when Parker's larger one covered it. Forcing a smile, she glanced up at him.

"I know what balls you meant," he told her with

a wink, his smile stealing the breath from her lungs once again.

She sure as heck hoped he couldn't read her thoughts the way he implied. That would lead to certain disaster for both of them.

"I'll carry the bag out to the yard," she said, keeping her words measured. "You can get the goal and meet us around back."

"You bet."

She closed the door behind him then pressed her forehead against it, the smooth wood cool on her heated skin.

"Are you okay, Mommy?"

Not at all, she thought.

"Fine," she whispered. "Just fine."

"She shoots and scores," Parker called, pumping his fist in the air when Evie's kick sent the ball slowly rolling into the goal.

The girl bounced up and down then turned and grinned at him. Her wide, guileless smile sent his emotions into overdrive. As happy as he was to have spent the past hour with her, it should be her father doing the coaching, not some virtual stranger. Especially not one who'd essentially helped her dad both gain a pass to shirk his duties and get off with no financial ramifications.

No matter how many times Parker told himself he'd just been doing his job, he couldn't shake the feeling he held some responsibility for the current state of Mara's and Evie's lives. The girl had been a toddler at the time of the divorce, and he didn't remember ever meeting her. Paul hadn't been interested in custody, other than using the threat of coparenting as a way to force Mara to relinquish any request for support.

He had half a mind to call his client and rip him a new one for that extreme display of selfishness. But what right did he have? Maybe Evie was better off in the long run. Hell, Parker would have been thrilled to have his father out of the picture when he was young, even if it had meant financial struggle for the rest of them.

The sound of the back door opening drew him out of his moody musings. Evie's smile brightened even more as Mara walked toward her.

"Mommy, I kicked a goal."

"I saw, sweetie." She opened her arms wide and Evie ran forward for a hug. "I've been watching from the window. You're really improving." She smoothed a hand along Evie's long braid. "You'll do great in the game tomorrow."

The hope in the girl's eyes as she turned to him made Parker's chest ache. "Your mommy's right," he confirmed. "You've made a lot of progress. Remember what we worked on, okay?"

She nodded. "Thank you, Coach."

Parker cleared his throat. "Sure thing."

"Go wash up before dinner," Mara said, patting Evie's head.

"Can Coach stay for dinner?"

"We're only having spaghetti," Mara said with a grimace. "I'm sure *Coach* has more exciting plans for a Friday night."

"As a matter of fact, no." Parker moved forward. "If you have extra, I'd love to stay."

Mara gave him a look over Evie's head, but he only smiled in return. "Is it okay?" he asked.

"It's okay," Evie told him without waiting for Mara's answer. "Right, Mommy?"

"Um…sure. Wash your hands and take your shin guards and cleats off. I'll help Coach finish gathering his…" She shook her head. "The soccer equipment."

Parker smothered a chuckle at how Mara stumbled upon sexual innuendos while discussing soccer.

Evie didn't seem to notice that her mother had turned beet red again, but Parker found it charming.

As the girl ran toward the house, he grabbed the mesh bag from the grass and grinned at Mara. "You can talk about balls without worrying I assume you're talking about my—"

"Enough." She held up a hand. "No more soccer talk."

"If you insist. I don't have to stay for dinner if it makes you uncomfortable."

"It's what Evie wants," she said instead of answering.

"But not you?" He couldn't help but push a little. He knew the attraction wasn't one-sided, and for some reason it mattered that she admitted it.

"I wouldn't normally serve a guest sauce from a jar and frozen meatballs."

"Frozen balls?" His grin spread when Mara scrunched up her nose. "At least we've gotten off the topic of soccer."

"Don't ruin my appetite," she told him with a laugh.

God, he liked making her smile. How could something so inconsequential make him feel so good?

"I wouldn't dream of it."

"You're incorrigible," she muttered.

"You kind of like me that way," he countered.

She only rolled her eyes in response. "Let's go before your ego gets too big to fit through the door."

He hefted the soccer goal onto one shoulder. "Lead the way."

Mara took a sip of wine as she watched her daughter laugh at another one of Parker's booger jokes. At the start of dinner, she'd grabbed a bottle from the rack above the hutch in her Aunt Nanci's dining room. It should feel strange to entertain at a house that didn't belong to her, especially when the dinner guest was part of the reason she no longer owned her own home.

But Parker had diffused the potentially awkward

situation with his humor and charm. Mara could tell Evie was smitten, and unfortunately, the girl wasn't the only one.

Mara must be more desperate than she'd realized when watching a man help set the table got her all hot and bothered. Pretty much everything about Parker affected her in some way. She should have been working during the hour he spent with Evie in the yard but instead had spent much of the time staring out the kitchen window, telling herself she was a concerned mom and not a pathetically lonesome stalker.

Although Paul had been less than thrilled when Mara shared the news of her pregnancy with him, she'd expected him to warm to the prospect of being a father once Evie was born. He had no children from either of his previous marriages, which Mara hadn't questioned until he'd pulled away during the months leading up to Evie's birth. He hadn't given his lack of desire to be a father as a reason for being twice divorced, but she knew at least one of his ex-wives had remarried and started a family.

Only with her marriage crumbling around her did Mara understand the price she'd pay for becoming a mother. And Evie was worth it every day. Mara did her best to give the girl everything, to be enough that her precious daughter wouldn't notice the lack of a father in her life.

Which was ridiculous. Of course Evie understood

what she didn't have. Mara's father had been distant and uninterested, and the pain of his tacit rejection had haunted her for years.

"Mommy, did you hear that one?" Evie asked.

Mara placed her glass on the table and smiled. "I missed it, honey, but I know the joke was a funny one based on your smile."

"Tell it again, Parker," Evie urged.

He flashed an apologetic grin at Mara. "How do you make a tissue dance?"

She shook her head. "I don't know."

"Put a little boogie in it," Evie shouted, dissolving into a fit of giggles. "Anna's gonna laugh so hard."

"I can imagine. Where do you come up with all of these winners?" she asked Parker.

"I used to tell them to Josh when we were kids," he answered with a shrug. "They made him laugh when there wasn't enough laughter in our house."

Something that looked suspiciously like sorrow flashed in his eyes for the briefest second, and her heart skipped a beat.

"Can I have dessert now?" Evie asked.

"Sure." She tapped a finger on the edge of Evie's plate. "Bring your dish to the sink. I brought brownies home from Perk today. They're in the pantry. We should have enough for everyone."

Evie climbed off her chair at the dining room table and headed into the kitchen.

"Josh doesn't talk about your dad. I've heard more

from other people around town and what you've explained about him."

"If you're listening to people in town, I can guarantee you don't know who he really was." The words were spoken casually, but she could see the maelstrom of emotions they evoked.

Before she had a chance to respond, Evie returned with the glass storage container that held the brownies. "Mommy makes the best brownies, too," she told Parker. She had a smear of chocolate on her cheek that gave away the fact she'd had hers before offering to share the rest.

"No pressure to like them," Mara said quickly. "Honey, Parker might not want dessert yet. He just finished dinner."

"Oh." Evie switched her gaze to Parker, looking at once hopeful and cautious.

"You bet I want dessert." He gave an exaggerated eyebrow wiggle. "Sometimes I eat dessert before dinner."

Evie sucked a bit of dried chocolate off the middle of her palm then grabbed a brownie from the container and held it out toward Parker.

Mara grimaced "Use a napkin to pick up the—"

"Looks delicious," he said as he took it, not batting an eye. He made a sound of approval as he bit into it, and Mara felt satisfaction burst within her like summer fireworks.

"This is amazing," he told Mara. "Aren't you going to have one?"

"Mommy doesn't like sweets," Evie informed him before turning to Mara. "Can I watch a show?"

"Sure," Mara answered before realizing she'd be left alone in the quiet dining room with Parker.

"Seriously," he said when they were alone, "where did you learn to bake?"

"I'm self-taught." She stood up and began clearing the table. Was this why they said the way to a man's heart is through his stomach? "It's just a hobby."

"But you bake for the coffee shop, too?"

"When I have time."

He followed her into the kitchen with his plate and the pasta bowl.

"Other than soccer, is there anything you can't do?"

"Keep my marriage together," she blurted. She placed her dishes in the sink with a clatter, hating how that failure hung over her like a dark cloud. "I didn't mean that to come out. We don't need to keep talking about my failed marriage."

"If you want to talk, I'm willing to listen." Parker opened the dishwasher and began loading the plates she handed to him.

Mara blew out a breath. "I wish you'd worn one of your expensive suits tonight. It makes it easier for me to remember why I don't like you when you're dressed all fancy."

"I didn't realize you were starting to forget."

She was way past starting, and the deep timbre of his voice so close to her sent ripples of awareness cascading along her spine. "How are things going out at the mill? From everything Josh told me, you've been making a lot of progress the past few days."

"What a subtle subject change," he said with a chuckle. "The project is moving along. It helps that I can manage things on-site while he coordinates materials and subcontractors without spending all his time there. It works well for both of us."

"It's strange that he bought a property where he doesn't like to go."

"He thinks the renovation will change his feelings about it and prove that he's moved past everything that happened when we were younger. Dad had a lot of problems originating with the mill, and he took out his frustration on his family. I guess it's like people who have an aversion to hospitals because they had a parent who was sick when they were younger."

"I wonder how many of them become doctors or nurses?"

"Good point."

She handed him the last utensil then rinsed out the sink.

"Do you think he'll sell it?"

"I don't know. He could really make something of the mill if everything goes according to plan. I hope this project eliminates his aversion to it."

"You don't have that stigma, though?" she couldn't help but ask as she retrieved the dishwasher detergent from the cabinet.

He took the bottle from her like it was the most normal thing in the world to be cleaning up after dinner together. "I left Starlight after high school, and literally never came back. It's different for me. This is still Josh's home."

She watched him pour liquid into the dispenser then hit a few buttons to start the cycle. He replaced the container in the cabinet, shut the door and then straightened. "You're frowning. Did I do something wrong?"

"No. I'm just impressed."

"I started a dishwasher. Not exactly splitting the atom."

"You did dishes."

He looked confused. "So did you, after working all day and making dinner. You might…" He leaned in closer, his breath tickling the hair that fell across her ear. "Think about setting your standards higher for what you expect from a man."

She should probably be offended by the comment, but it sounded so ridiculous coming from Parker's mouth that she burst out laughing. In fact, once she started laughing, she didn't stop until she was wiping away tears.

"I tell awesome booger jokes and now I've made you laugh until you cried." He hitched a hip onto the counter. "You'll probably need to invite me back, even if I don't understand what was so funny."

"You represented my ex-husband in our divorce, and you're giving me advice on my standards for men." She pointed at him. "You have to admit, it's funny."

"I'm sorry for my part in hurting you."

He spoke the words quietly, but they ricocheted through Mara like a cannon. The thing was, she believed him. As much as she wanted Parker to remain in the enemy category, he no longer fit there. He wasn't a two-dimensional caricature of a coldhearted lawyer. He was the guy who'd put his life on hold to help his younger brother, had volunteered to coach her shy daughter and now had happily worked next to her cleaning up the kitchen.

Some women might want roses and diamonds, but Mara was a single mom. To her, loading the dishwasher was sexy as hell.

So sexy that she put aside all the smart reasons she had for keeping her distance from Parker. She stepped forward and pressed her mouth to his.

She'd meant the kiss as a thank-you, or perhaps a peace offering, but immediately it turned hot and heady. Parker shifted then placed his hands on her hips, moving her closer until her breasts grazed the fabric of his Henley.

She wound her arms around his neck and drew

her tongue across the seam of his lips, heat building inside her at the sound of his low groan.

It made her feel powerful to know she affected him. His fingers trailed up and under her thin sweater, sending shockwaves through her when they grazed the skin above the waistband of her jeans.

A moment later the tremors turned to ash as the sound of something crashing infiltrated her fuzzy brain.

She broke away from Parker, spinning on her heel only to breathe out a curse when she realized the source of the noise.

"Mr. Paws," she muttered, striding forward to pick up the backpack that her aunt's overfed orange tabby cat had pushed off the kitchen table. Evie's art supplies, which included markers in every color of the rainbow and several notebooks, spilled out onto the hardwood floor.

"Saved by the cat," Parker said behind her, humor lacing his tone.

"This cat hates me." Mara went to pet Mr. Paws, only to have him bat at her hand, claws out. "Ouch. See what I mean?"

"Cats don't hate. Some of them are just particular about how they want to be loved." She watched in fascination as Parker made the same move she had moments earlier. Instead of striking, the cat tipped his head and pressed it against Parker's palm, clearly enjoying the attention.

"Jerk," she muttered then held up a hand when Parker made a sound of protest. "The cat, not you."

"I appreciate that."

She knelt on the floor and began to gather Evie's things. "Is he purring?"

"Sounds like it."

"Figures." Mr. Paws might be a jerk, but she couldn't exactly blame him for succumbing to Parker's charms. Hadn't she just done the same thing?

Butterflies skittered across her stomach as he joined her in picking up the art supplies. "You don't have to help," she told him.

He placed his hand over hers. "You kissed me."

She stared at where their fingers overlapped. His were long and tanned, covering hers completely. It made her feel small, but not in a bad way. He made her feel protected and cared for, which showed how low her standards had actually dropped.

This man wasn't her knight in shining armor. He wasn't anything except her friend's brother and a darn good kisser. She imagined he was darn good at other things, as well.

"I won't do it again," she promised.

"Even if I ask nicely?"

She forced her gaze to his. "You and I aren't a match, even if I was interested in a relationship." She pulled her hand from under his, curling it into her belly. "Which I'm not."

"Do you mean kissing and stuff can only be part of something more serious for you?"

"And stuff?" She gathered the last of the markers. "Is that a technical term?"

"I can use technical terms if you'd prefer." He handed her a notebook with a unicorn on the cover. "I can go into great detail with what I mean by *stuff* where you're concerned."

She shook her head, trying to hide her smile. "I understand the gist, and I'm not looking for anything serious. Or anything at all." She arched a brow. "Not even *stuff.*"

"You'd like the stuff I had in mind."

She stood, placing the supplies on the table. "If I didn't already know you were a lawyer, I'd guess it. You enjoy arguing too much to be anything else."

"I prefer the term banter."

"You also like to have the last word."

"Not always."

She gave his arm a playful nudge. "See what I mean?"

"There you go pushing me around again."

Mara giggled then clasped a hand over her mouth. She wasn't a giggler. She didn't do banter. Or flirt. Hell, she'd barely done any of that at the start of her relationship with Paul. He'd simply chosen her and she'd acquiesced without argument. He cut to the chase, and she'd convinced herself she preferred that. He'd been her first serious boyfriend and then her husband, and she was just coming to realize she'd never stopped to consider why they always did things his way, even in the bedroom.

Parker tapped a finger on the tip of her nose, breaking into her thoughts. "You're thinking about stuff."

"Not your stuff," she shot back.

"Oh, I know." His grin was wicked and full of promise. "You'd look more blissed out if you were thinking about my stuff."

"Do you ever give up?"

He shrugged. "Do you want me to?"

"No," she answered after a long pause.

His grin widened and he leaned in and brushed his lips across hers. "I'll see you at the game," he said against her mouth.

Mara blinked. "I tell you not to give up, and now you're walking away."

"Not walking away," he said, backing up a step. "Saying good night for now." He winked. "I want you to have a chance to miss me, and that can't happen if I don't leave."

"It's going to be less than twenty-four hours until I see you again. I won't miss you."

"Sweet dreams, Mara," he told her then headed down the hall with a wave.

"They won't be about you," she called, and he laughed because they both recognized her words as a big fat lie.

## Chapter Eight

Parker arrived at the soccer field the next afternoon, nerves flitting through his stomach the same way they did when he went into court for a big case. Excitement and anticipation shot through him. Bizarre when a soccer game between two teams of kindergarten girls shouldn't mean anything to him.

The stakes couldn't get much lower, and still he didn't know how to turn off his emotions. The idea made his skin itch. He'd never had an issue with feeling too much—with feeling anything really—before returning to Starlight. This place was doing a number on him, and he had to find a way to get it under control.

But right now he had a team to support.

He jogged over to where Josh stood with his team in a huddle. One of the moms had made matching pink bows for the girls, since they'd voted on Pink Ponies as their team name. Instead of athletic jerseys, they had T-shirts with a drawing of a pony wearing shin guards on the front. Josh wore an XL version, and Parker tried to ignore how ridiculous his brother looked since Parker was sporting an identical shirt.

"Do you have it?" Josh asked, shading his eyes from the noonday sun. They'd lucked out with another day of gorgeous fall weather, although the forecast called for rain to start later.

Parker nodded and pulled a stuffed animal out of the plastic bag he carried. "Girls," he said, keeping his voice serious. "This is our mascot, Penelope the Pony."

"Hi, Penelope," the girls said in unison, as if they were greeting a living creature instead of a toy.

"What's a math cot?" one of the girls asked.

"Penelope will bring us good luck." Parker gave the stuffed horse a small shake. "I'm going to put her on the goal so you all know where to shoot."

He and Josh had realized at practice yesterday that the girls had a tendency to head for whatever goal they noticed first after a ball came to them. No one played the position of goalie at this age, but if they scored for the other team, it would count against them.

"Yay, Penelope," Anna shouted, and her teammates cheered.

Josh clapped a hand against the clipboard he held. "The most important thing we're going to do today is have fun," he told them. "You go out there and try your hardest, remember you're all on the same team, and have fun." He glanced toward the referee, who motioned the team forward. "Let's go play."

The girls filed after him onto the field as their fans clapped from the sidelines. Parker fell in step next to Evie. "You doing okay?"

She gave a tight nod.

"How's the stomach?"

"It's not pukey."

Her voice trembled slightly, but a nonpukey stomach was a decent start.

"Remember what we talked about yesterday as far as dribbling and defending. You've got this, kiddo."

They lined up across from the opposing team, girls from a neighboring town who wore uniforms of pale blue with their numbers outlined in gold glitter. The referee, an older man with a shock of white hair and an easy smile, went over the rules for conduct and asked the girls to repeat the code of sportsmanship.

A month ago, Parker would have laughed at the absurdity of his current situation. Usually he slept late on Saturdays if he didn't have plans. Maybe he'd go for a run or to the gym. One of the guys he knew from another firm had a boat, so sometimes they'd head out fishing or he'd meet up with friends for a game of pickup basketball.

Countless times, he'd driven past community fields around various Seattle neighborhoods and had never given an ounce of thought to the kids playing on recreational teams. Hell, he'd never even realized he liked kids. Now he couldn't imagine a better way to use his time and it still baffled him how the slower pace of life in Starlight fit him.

Because of the age of the girls, one coach from each team was allowed on the field to offer encouragement during the game. The starting lineup took their positions with Josh near the midfield, while Parker and the subs watched from their makeshift bench, which consisted of a row of camp chairs they'd pulled out of Josh's garage.

Parker's chest tightened as he watched his brother interact with the girls, cheering them on when they had the ball and keeping things positive at the times when the other team had possession.

It quickly became apparent that Anna and Caroline were the stars of the team. Parker didn't think much of the girl who'd tormented Evie, even if she did have some impressive ball-handling skills for a kindergartner. But he loved watching his niece play; her enthusiasm and fearless attitude blew him away. No one who didn't know her history would ever have guessed what she'd been through.

How could his former sister-in-law have walked away from this?

Yes, cancer was huge and scary, especially in a child. But Anna was doing great now and he couldn't imagine any mother willing to miss out on these moments.

The game was adorable. A few girls remained focused on the ball while others played patty-cake-type games or rolled around in the grass. He did what he could to keep the team sharp, subbing in girls at regular intervals so everyone got a turn.

"You're up next," he told Evie near the end of the first half.

She shook her head. "Not yet."

He glanced down, alarmed at the girl's pallor. "Pukey stomach?"

"A little, but I don't want to go in yet."

"Evie, you did well yesterday. You'll be great out there."

She grabbed his hand, squeezing his fingers like she was adrift in the ocean and he was her only lifeline. "Not yet."

"Okay. It's fine." He caught Josh's gaze and subtly shook his head. His brother nodded, and the game continued.

Evie didn't let go of his hand, and he gently rubbed his thumb back and forth against her soft skin, hoping to reassure her. At halftime, the girls who'd been playing came off the field. The whole team gathered at the sidelines, one of the moms coming over to distribute bags of orange slices.

With Evie occupied in the team huddle, Parker separated himself from the group and got Mara's attention.

"Evie looks petrified," she said when she'd walked over to him.

"A little freaked out," he agreed. "But she's managed not to toss her cookies."

"Is she going to play?" Mara wrung her hands together, a frown line forming between her eyes.

"I hope so, but I don't want to force her."

"This is horrible."

"She's fine."

"She's going to be traumatized."

"I won't let that happen."

He heard her sharp intake of breath and quickly amended, "*We* won't let that happen."

Mara nodded. "Thanks for helping her. I trust she's safe with you."

If she'd handed him the Nobel Prize, he couldn't have been prouder.

"I need to get back to the team."

"Sure." She reached out and placed a hand on his arm. "Thanks again, Parker."

The second half went much as the first had, with girls alternating between concentrating on the game and picking the proverbial daisies. With two minutes left on the clock, he crouched next to Evie. "Are you ready?"

She bit her lower lip and swallowed hard then nodded.

He patted her shoulder. "I'm going to put you in for Caroline on offense."

The color left her face in an instant. "No."

"It's going to be great. You're ready, girl."

"Not Caroline," Evie pleaded. "If I mess up her position, she'll be so mad."

That was part of the reason Parker wanted to make the substitution. He believed in this sweet, insecure girl and knew succeeding as a sub for one of the team's power players would turn the tables in her self-confidence.

But he also understood the damage it could cause if things didn't go well.

"How about defense?"

Evie nodded eagerly.

Parker made the substitution and watched with the barest hint of trepidation as Evie ran onto the field. This was safe, he figured. So far Caroline and Anna had kept the ball on the opposite side of the field, giving the goal watched over by Penelope quite the workout. At this age, there was no official score but Parker was keeping count in his head, and they were up four to three.

The game continued until the final minute, when a player from the Thunder Bolts dribbled the ball around Caroline then passed it to one of her team-mates. The girl who should have intercepted the pass was twirling in circles so the ball sailed right past her.

The Thunder Bolts' player seemed shocked when the ball rolled to a stop at her feet but immediately turned and headed toward the goal.

"Oh, no." Parker glanced toward the sidelines where Mara looked about as pukey as Evie had felt earlier.

When he turned back, Evie's eyes had gone wide as the other player barreled toward her. Despite her obvious fear, the girl remembered their lesson from the night before.

She bent her knees and assumed a defensive stance. The offensive player gave the ball a huge kick, and it sailed into the air right toward Evie.

Parker half expected the girl to duck or dive out of the way, but she shifted slightly to her left to guard the goal more fully. The ball knocked into her stom-ach with enough force to send her back a step but then bounced off and rolled out of bounds just as the referee blew the whistle to end the game.

The fans erupted into cheers and applause as he and Josh shared a relieved smile. Only then did he realize Evie hadn't moved. She stood stock-still for another few seconds then fell straight back onto the grass.

Mara's terrified shout registered in his ears, but

he was already running onto the field. He and Josh reached Evie at the same time.

The girl was gasping for air, tears running down her cheeks. "Get everyone back," Parker said to Josh, dropping to his knees. "She got the wind knocked out of her. That's all. She needs space."

He murmured reassurances to Evie as Josh ushered the rest of the team away. Mara was on the girl's other side a moment later.

"Can't breathe," Evie managed to say.

"It's okay, sweetheart," he told her. "Close your eyes and breathe in and out. Steady now."

"Mommy's here." Mara leaned in close, running a gentle hand over Evie's face. "You're going to be fine."

Even though he knew Evie wasn't truly hurt, Parker hated the worry lacing Mara's tone. She'd trusted him to keep her daughter safe and the girl had been injured.

Talk about traumatic.

He might enjoy helping to coach the girls, but clearly he was ill equipped to make the right decisions. Why hadn't he just let Evie sit out this first game?

"Let's sit up," Mara said gently. "Keep breathing." She wiped the tears from Evie's cheeks as they helped the girl to her feet.

Parker waved to Josh and gave him a thumbs-up.

"You all right there, munchkin?" the referee asked, rubbing a hand across his belly.

She nodded and the ref chuckled. "You made one heck of a block," he said before heading back across the field.

Evie stilled then looked from Parker to Mara. "I blocked the ball?"

Parker felt his mouth drop open then shut it again. "You sure did," he told her. "It was a really hard kick, too."

"I know," Evie agreed. "I lost my breath."

"It's okay, baby girl." Mara hugged Evie to her side. "You don't ever have to play soccer again. I know I said it would be good for you but—"

Evie pulled away. "I can't quit." She pressed a hand to her stomach. "I blocked the ball. Right, Coach?"

"Yes," Parker agreed slowly. "We have some work to do on technique, but I'm proud of you, kiddo."

She grinned. "I need to be with the team. Coach Josh is talking to them."

Mara made a soft snort of disbelief as the girl skipped over toward the rest of the Pink Ponies.

"What just happened there?" she asked after a moment.

"Your kid discovered her inner athlete," he suggested.

"I didn't think she had one of those."

"I knew it all along."

"Thank you," Mara said softly. "For everything you did for her."

He shrugged, suddenly uncomfortable with the emotion lacing her words. He liked Mara more than was smart for either of them. He wasn't a long-term bet for a single mom who'd been burned by a nasty divorce. A divorce he'd had a large part in facilitating. This role of coach and family man was playacting, even if it felt right.

"No biggie," he lied. "Tell Josh I'll see him tomorrow, okay?"

"Tomorrow?" She frowned. "You aren't going to the ice-cream celebration with the team?"

It scared the hell out of Parker how much he wanted to join them, which made his decision easier than he would have thought.

"I've had my fill of white-picket-fence life for a while. I'm heading back to Seattle for the night." He forced a laugh, dropping just the right amount of derision into his tone. "I need to have some real fun... trade in the ice-cream parlor for a bar. Starlight's small-town sweetness is making my teeth ache."

With every word he spoke, the storm clouds in Mara's gaze darkened. He was torn between being the man she wanted him to be and reverting back to the coldhearted jerk so familiar to him. Parker had a good reason for his cold heart. At least that's what he'd convinced himself through all these years. A few mind-blowing kisses weren't going to change anything.

"Real fun," she repeated, as if she were turning the words over in her hands to examine them.

"You know what I mean."

She folded her arms across her chest. "I do."

The tiny section of his heart that had opened to this woman wanted her to argue. To push him to do the right thing.

But she was too proud for that, and he admired her all the more because of it.

"Enjoy your fun," she said, making her displeasure in his choice clear.

He could think of nothing he wanted to do less than get in his car and drive away. He turned and walked toward it anyway.

Mara got out of her car and handed a cup of coffee to both Josh and Brynn the next morning.

"Tell me you brought muffins, too?" Josh rubbed at his eyes.

"Almond poppy seed," Mara confirmed, reaching into the backseat for the bag.

Josh gave her a quick hug. "You're the best."

Brynn chuckled. "Late night?"

"Sort of." He shrugged and pulled a muffin out of the brown bag. "Anna has night terrors sometimes. They started after Jenn left. The doctor says she's still processing the loss."

"I'm sorry," Brynn said. "Tyler has been sleeping with me since Daniel died. I know I should make him stay in his own bed, but I can't bring myself to do it."

Mara sighed. "I wish Evie wanted to cuddle or had bad dreams or something I could fix." She shook her head. "Never mind. Forget I said that. I'm a horrible mother. Of course I don't wish for her to have nightmares. She's stoic, and I don't know how to help her. We haven't even been through half as much as either of you, yet I feel like I'm the most out of control."

Josh and Brynn stared at her for several long moments, and then both of them burst into laughter. "If you think I'm in control," Brynn said, wiping at her cheeks. "You need to peek a little closer."

"Look around to see how not in control I am at the moment." Josh held out his arms. "I'm a pathetic grown-ass man who's relying on my brother to help bail me out of my mess."

"I'm a pathetic divorcée who lives with my aunt," Mara muttered.

Brynn leaned in like she was sharing a secret. "My kid is ten years old, and I'm still wearing nursing bras because I haven't had a reason to buy new ones."

Josh paused with the muffin halfway to his mouth. "That's too much information."

"But you win in the game pitiful one-upmanship." Mara put her arm around the other woman's shoul-

der. "Also, we're going to set up a date to go lingerie shopping."

"Can I come with you?" Josh asked with an exaggerated eyebrow wiggle. "You'll probably want a
man's opinion."

Brynn laughed. "That's a strong no."

"Gross," Mara added. "It would be like modeling
for my brother."

"Speaking of brothers," Brynn said, looking at
Josh. "Where's yours? I thought he might be here
for the planning."

"He'll be back tomorrow," Josh said around a bite
of muffin. Funny, he didn't seem bothered by Parker's absence the way Mara was.

"He had to go back to the big city." Mara hated the
feeling of rejection she couldn't quite shake. "There
wasn't enough to keep him entertained in Starlight."

Brynn gave her a questioning look, but Josh didn't
seem to pick up on her irritation. "He's doing me
a huge solid with his help. I don't know what the
hell I was thinking buying this property in the first
place. As if I didn't have enough reminders of my
dad around town…"

"It was a big deal when the mill left and the town
council couldn't find another business to take over
the property."

"The one glaring failure of his years as mayor that
he always thought would ruin his legacy." Josh balled
up the muffin wrapper and tossed it into a nearby

trash can. "He couldn't ever let it go, and now I'm stuck in the same position."

"But you're turning it into something new," Mara reminded him. "You're going to be a success here, Josh."

"And then what?" he asked. "I'm a contractor, not a property manager. Once this place is up and running, I want to move on to the next project, but a retail space like this is going to take daily oversight."

"Hire me," Brynn blurted.

Mara turned to her friend. "I thought you were a teacher?"

Brynn kicked at the dirt with the toe of one boot. "I'm not anything. I don't even have a college degree, but I want to go back to school. The district normally hires subs with more education, but they know me so they're making an exception." She looked from Mara to Josh. "I want a career, not just to be someone's substitute. I could do this, Josh. I know it."

He ran a hand through his already messy hair. She had no doubt Josh would do the right thing and he didn't disappoint her. "I need income from the retail spaces to make it work. Mara's given me a new design that will make things run more smoothly, but we still need to fill the space."

"You've got the coffee shop," Mara said.

Brynn glanced toward the main building. "What about a space for local artists? A cooperative of sorts, filled with gifts and crafts."

"I like it," Josh admitted.

"I can talk to Betsy at the community center gift shop." Brynn clapped her hands together. "She knows everyone in the area. We'll find tenants, and I'll keep them happy. I'll work so hard. I promise I won't let you down if you give me a chance."

"Let me put together some numbers and see what it would take for me to pay you a decent salary."

"I'll work for free," Brynn offered.

"You need to be able to support Tyler," Josh reminded her. "No mother should ever be in a position where she can't make the right decisions for her family."

"I wish your brother had half your character," Mara told him.

He frowned. "He's the one who told me. There was a time when our mom wanted to leave, but she had no support system and no money of her own. She was stuck married to my dad, and we all paid the price."

Mara felt like she'd just been slapped across the face. How was it possible Parker could say those words yet still do what he'd done to her in court?

"Then maybe someone should needlepoint that sentence and frame it for him so he doesn't forget when he's destroying someone's character in court." She forced a laugh, as if she were making a joke.

"He isn't perfect," Josh admitted. "The way we were raised took all the 'fun' out of dysfunction.

We were in survival mode more often than not, and it was only exacerbated by the fact that most of the town thought our dad was the second coming. It was tough, but he's trying to do better."

Unbidden, a vision of Parker with Evie popped into Mara's brain. He'd certainly tried hard enough with her daughter.

"I always thought he took the easy way out," Josh continued. "He left Starlight and never looked back. But he also never dealt with his issues. I hope working on this project will be as cathartic for him as I need it to be for myself."

"You're doing the right thing," Brynn said, placing a gentle hand on his arm.

"Most days it doesn't feel that way, but I appreciate the thought nonetheless. Now let's take a look at what progress we made this week. I think we're at a place where you'll be able to see the vision."

As they followed Josh into the mill, Mara tried not to think about Parker and what he'd survived from his childhood. It made it too difficult to stay angry with him, and she understood her anger was the only thing saving her from wanting more.

## Chapter Nine

Parker drove into Starlight as the sky above the town turned from shades of pink and purple to gray. Night settled on the valley like a blanket. His breath caught at the beauty of the mountains outlined like a charcoal sketch against the waning light.

He could appreciate the peace of the hour now, but as a kid he'd dreaded this time of day. It meant his father was coming home and whatever normalcy they'd managed to cobble together could be wrecked the instant Mac walked through the door.

Of course, there were stretches of time when his father's temper lay dormant. Days, weeks, and on rare occasion a span of months when his father would be normal, like other dads. He'd kiss his wife when he walked through the door, smile and ask about their days in a quiet, steadfast way, and the brothers would begin to believe that maybe things had finally changed.

Until something triggered him, sending them all back into the tailspin of anger. One of the worst stretches was during Parker's sophomore year of high school. Josh was a freshman and their dad up for re-election. For the first time since he'd become mayor eight years earlier, one of the members of city council had brought up the idea of term limits. Mac had been open to it in public, assuring the civic leaders that he was interested in what was best for Starlight, not continuing his own political dictatorship.

Behind closed doors, he railed and raged, always looking for an outlet for his frustration. More often than not, he'd found it in Josh, who didn't have Parker's innate survival instincts. Parker had done his best to protect his brother, but Josh didn't make it easy.

At the same time, the Dennison Mill shut down, leaving dozens of locals with no jobs. Mac had made it his mission, and a large part of his campaign platform, to sell the property and find an even better tenant. One that would revitalize the local economy.

He'd won the election and there had been no more talk of term limits. But he'd never managed to revive the mill or repurpose the property, and that failure had come to represent everything to him.

His father was gone and the mill finally getting a second life. Despite the struggles that had come with it, Parker was so damn proud of his brother for taking on this project. He had to admit being a part of it helped heal some of the long-buried scars of his past, as well.

He drove through town, hushed and peaceful at this time. The glow of light from the windows of houses he passed seemed to mean more than it did in the city. Here he could feel the warmth emanating from the homes and imagined families or couples gathered around tables for dinner or to watch a football game on television.

Assumptions were dangerous. Parker knew that better than most. People had assumed things about his family growing up that were nowhere near the truth.

Pulling into his brother's driveway, he blew out a breath. It amazed him that although he thought he'd left his past behind, it was so much a part of who he was—as if it were sewn into the very fabric of his being.

He let himself into the house, careful to be quiet since it was past Anna's bedtime.

Josh sat in the family room, the TV tuned to football but with the volume muted. Parker had texted to say he was returning tonight and noticed a bottle of single-malt scotch and a two glasses on the coffee table.

"Hot date?" he asked, shrugging out of his jacket as he entered the room.

"I thought the plan was to come back tomorrow morning?" Josh sat forward and poured three fingers of liquor into each glass.

"I didn't want to fight Monday rush-hour traffic."

Josh gave him a look that silently called Parker out on the lie.

"You're still my little brother," Parker said, taking the glass then lowering into one of the club chairs flanking the sofa. "Don't make me come over there and prove it."

"You missed us. Admit it." Josh grinned. "You're not the island of emotionless solitude you want everyone to believe."

"I have a great life in Seattle. I have friends—"

"Acquaintances," Josh countered. "Who you don't really care about."

"I care," Parker lied.

Josh didn't look convinced.

"Don't discount a successful career."

"It brings you no joy."

"I'm not Santa Claus." Parker resisted the urge to grit his teeth. "Joy isn't on my priority list."

"Maybe it should be."

"Where's your joy?" Parker demanded.

"Anna." Josh smiled. "Ice cream with the Pink

Ponies." He took a slow sip then set down his glass again. "The girls missed you after the game."

"That's the biggest lie you've told tonight."

"You should have seen Evie's face when the girls were retelling the story of her block. She became a hero in that moment. You would have thought she'd taken a bullet to the stomach instead of a soccer ball."

A dull ache started in the region of Parker's heart. There was no way he'd admit how much he would have liked to see her grin. "This is your life," he said instead. "Not mine. I'm here to help but I'm not going to suddenly become part of this community. We both know I'm only passing through."

Josh lifted one shoulder, let it fall again. "You still have feelings."

"I don't have feelings," Parker mumbled, aware of how ridiculous he sounded.

"Right," Josh said with a laugh. "Tell me about your nonfeelings for Mara."

Parker threw back the rest of the whiskey in his glass, welcoming the way his throat burned.

"I thought so." Josh leaned forward. "She's special, Parker."

"Okay."

"And she's been hurt. You had some responsibility in that."

"I was doing my job," Parker insisted without much conviction.

"Let's talk about your job. I remember when

you said you were going to become a divorce attorney." Josh held out a hand and Parker passed him the empty glass. "Although back then you called it family law."

Parker sucked in a breath. "I know what I said."

But his brother wasn't finished. "You wanted to help families navigate the tough times so no one would end up feeling as helpless as Mom did in her marriage."

"I don't need you to tell me about my career goals."

Josh poured more whiskey into the glass and pushed it across the table "Are you sure? Because unless Mara has wildly exaggerated the bitterness of her divorce and her husband's propensity to be a world-class jerk, you helped put a wonderful woman and dedicated mother into the same predicament as Mom."

"Mara's ex wasn't abusive," Parker said through gritted teeth.

"Maybe not physically," Josh conceded. "But you've spent enough time with her to understand the number he did on her self-confidence."

"She's better off without him."

"Yes, but it's been a monumental struggle for her when it shouldn't have been. Not with the money that man has."

"She didn't fight hard enough."

"Would you say the same thing about Mom?"

Acid scorched Parker's gut. "It's not the same and we both know it." He stood up and stalked to the fireplace, tapping a hand against the brick and wondering how much damage he'd do to his knuckles if he slammed his fist into it. "What's with the knight in shining armor act?" he asked, turning on his heel. "Are you looking to swoop in and rescue Mara?"

"She doesn't need me to be her hero," Josh answered, leaning back against the sofa cushions. The more distressed Parker became, the calmer his brother appeared. It was a strange role reversal for the two of them, and it didn't sit well. No part of this conversation felt comfortable for him. Why the hell hadn't he stayed in Seattle? His life might be empty there, but at least it didn't make his whole body feel like it was on pins and needles.

"Then she certainly doesn't need me to be anything."

"She likes you."

Parker released a breath. "That would be stupid for both of us."

"No doubt," Josh agreed easily, "but I can tell."

"How?" Parker asked, unable to stop himself.

"She blushes every time your name is mentioned and then looks angry because she can't stop it."

Parker felt his mouth curve into a smile despite his best effort to keep a straight face. He could see Mara clearly in his mind, her shiny hair and luminous skin flushed an adorable pink. He liked it best when she realized how she was reacting. Her eyes would grow dark and it was difficult to tell whether she was more frustrated with herself or him. Either way, he loved garnering a reaction from her.

"You're just as bad," Josh added. "Look at you with the moony eyes."

"I'm seriously going to kick your butt if you make one more mention of that." Parker dropped his gaze to the hardwood floor. "I don't moon at anyone."

"You have a chance here."

He stilled then forced himself to meet his brother's gentle gaze. "A chance at what?"

"Redemption," Josh said without hesitation.

"I don't need to be redeemed." The acid churned again, but this time it felt more powerful. A wave cresting, ready to obliterate everything he'd worked to build in his life. All the walls and the self-control.

"Dad would have said the same thing."

"Are you comparing me to our father?"

"No. You're nothing like him."

The words felt like a balm to Parker's tattered soul, if only he could believe them. "And yet…"

Josh was at his side in an instant. "You aren't him," his brother said, gripping Parker's arms.

"You're the one who pointed out how I'd helped ruin Mara's life. I might have never laid a hand on a woman, but my actions—"

"You're a good man." Josh gave Parker's arms a not-so-gentle squeeze then stepped back. "I couldn't have made up this much time on the mill renovations without your help. Anna adores you. Mara has every reason in the world to hate your guts, but she can't because she sees who you are on the inside. We all do, Parker. I only wish you would, too."

They stood in silence for several seconds. There was so much Parker wanted to say, but he didn't know how to get the words out without breaking down, and he'd never allow himself to show that kind of weakness. He wanted to believe his brother but didn't know how to move past all the flaws he saw in himself to become something different. Someone more.

In the end, he shook his head and turned away. "I can't." Did he sound as miserable as he felt? He stood staring at a chipped square of brick above the fireplace mantel until he heard Josh leave the room.

When he knew he was alone, he grabbed the bottle of scotch from the table then dropped to the sofa. Closing his eyes, he tipped the bottle to his mouth. He didn't know how to make himself better, but he could sure as hell find a way to stop feeling so damn much.

"You look like hell," Mara said, whistling under her breath then grinning as Parker held up a hand.

"Are you trying to call all the dogs in the state to you with that piercing noise?"

He sat at the desk in the office he shared with

Josh, staring absently at the plans in front of him. He didn't glance up, and Mara wasn't sure whether to feel sorry for his obvious distress or gloat that he'd chosen Seattle over her and now seemed worse for the wear because of it.

She chose gloating.

"Fun weekend?" She pulled out the chair from the smaller drafting desk, making sure to drag it across the concrete floor so it made a loud scraping sound.

Parker moaned and pressed his fingers to either temple.

"How was traffic coming out of the city this morning?"

"I came back last night," he said tightly.

"You're in recovery mode from Saturday night still? That must have been quite a party." Mara's sunny mood from the morning plummeted. She didn't know why his weekend activities bothered her so much, but they did.

It was better, she'd tried to tell herself. She needed a bit of physical distance to help break the invisible thread of connection that linked them together. His life remained in the city, and she would never go back even if the opportunity presented itself. With time and distance she'd realized the person she'd become in her old life wasn't who she wanted to be.

She'd tried to save her marriage after Evie's birth had driven a wedge between her and Paul. It had felt strange to keep her devotion to her baby hidden, but she'd done her best to maintain two separate existences. The first was Mara the mom, her heart so full of love for her daughter it felt constantly on the verge of bursting.

The other role became increasingly more difficult. Paul had expected her to go back to work, putting in hours and remaining at his side for events and parties, just as she had before their daughter had come into the world.

Mara had hired a nanny, and ignored the pang in her chest each time she had to say goodbye to her baby. Lots of mothers worked. She could manage it. But it became more. Paul had become increasingly disinterested in her and Evie.

They'd never spoken about it, but Mara had quietly tried to manage what she assumed was the manifestation of his disenchantment with fatherhood.

Now she had feelings for another man who lived a different life than the one she wanted for herself and her daughter. Despite his kindness toward Evie, there was no doubt in Mara's mind that she couldn't be what he wanted in a woman, not for the long term anyway.

"I did laundry," he muttered then reached into the desk and pulled out a bottle of aspirin. She watched as he shook two of the pills into his hand and swallowed without bothering with water to wash them down.

"You've got a two-day laundry hangover?" She snorted. "I was born at night, Parker. Not last night."

"Josh and I had a drink when I got back last night."

"I saw him outside working on the siding when I came in. He's fine."

Parker shrugged. "He stopped. I kept going."

She stood, stepped closer to the desk. "So you stayed home to do laundry then came back here and got drunk alone in your brother's house?"

"About sums it up."

"Why?"

He stared at the desk in front of him for so long, she though he might not answer. When he finally looked at her, the intensity of his gaze made her heart feel like it might skip a beat. "You."

"Me?" The word came out a croak, and Mara cleared her throat. "What do I have to do with anything?"

"I drank to distract myself from thinking about you." He pushed away from the desk and stood. "I got so damn drunk that I couldn't possibly drive. That was the only way I could be sure I wouldn't show up at your house and admit what an idiot I'd been to walk away from you on Saturday."

"You're an idiot?"

"Don't pretend the news comes as a shock." Parker walked slowly toward her, and every instinct for self-preservation she had told her to walk away. Or run. That would be smarter.

She didn't move.

"I'm no good for you," he said when he was in front of her. "We both know it. I can never be the kind of man you deserve." He reached out, his thumb grazing her cheek. "Somehow that doesn't stop me from wanting you."

Mara's pulse hummed. "Welcome to the club." Although his mouth didn't move, it felt like he smiled at her words.

"I want you," he repeated. "Nothing I do seems to stop it. We're here together on this project. I gave my word to my brother. It might be easier for both of us if I could leave Starlight and not come back, but that isn't an option yet."

*Yet.* One word reminded her how temporary Parker's presence in her life would ultimately be. Her mind raced. Because temporary meant an end date, and an end date meant she could stop herself from truly falling for him.

"What's option B?" she asked, hoping she already knew the answer.

He lowered his mouth to hers, and her body purred to life in response.

"This would be temporary," she forced herself to say when he finally pulled back. "No strings."

He nodded, his blue eyes filled with the same level of passion she knew must be reflected in hers.

Her body liked the idea of it immediately, but a little voice inside her head warned her it wouldn't be as easy to cut ties with Parker as she wanted to believe.

Mara ignored that voice.

"It's a deal." She held out her hand, and Parker grinned as he took it.

"Did we just make some kind of sex pact?" he asked with a chuckle.

"I prefer to think of it," she told him, "as a mutually beneficial temporary arrangement."

"That's a lot of words."

"You're an attorney," she reminded both of them. "You like words."

"I like you." The rough timbre of his voice sent shivers rippling down her spine.

She leaned up on her toes and kissed him again. It felt exciting and new to be able to give in to the temptation of Parker. He cupped her cheeks in his hands, as if her mouth on his was a precious gift, one to be cherished. She couldn't remember the last time she'd felt cherished.

"You're the best hangover cure I've ever experienced," he said against her lips.

"You should try a milkshake and a hamburger at the diner in town. It's a surefire remedy."

"Great. I'll take you to lunch."

Her head snapped up, the lustful haze she'd been in suddenly doused with icy water. "I can't go to lunch with you."

"Why?"

"People will talk."

"Let them talk."

"Spoken like someone who doesn't live in a small town anymore. You don't know how it is around here."

"I know exactly how it is," he countered. "We work together, so if you need a reason we'd be out to lunch, there you go. I can do temporary, but that doesn't mean I'll be relegated to some dirty little secret. I want to spend time with you. Both you and Evie."

Her stomach did a series of flips worthy of an Olympic tumbler. "I don't want Evie to get attached to you," she said quietly, not bothering to mention she was as worried about her own possible attachment as she was about her daughter's.

"I'm her coach," he argued. "And her best friend's uncle. It won't seem strange for me to be around."

True, and she'd been fine when Parker wanted to help coach her daughter. Was this really any different? Just because they'd decided to act on their attraction to each other?

She could handle it, and maybe it would be good for both of them. Mara had no intention of getting serious with a man any time soon. She had little interest in dating even if she had the energy for it.

"Fine." She took a step back, folding her arms across her chest. "But don't think you're going to be Mr. Charm-School and sweep either of us off our feet."

"I wouldn't dare." He winked. "Although you're

only human, so I'm not sure you have a fighting chance with regard to my charm. It's like a force of nature. I can't control it."

She threw her head back and laughed, mood restored.

Josh walked in at that moment, darting a questioning gaze at each of them. "What's so funny?"

Mara turned toward him. "I'm going to date your brother."

He gave a grunt of disbelief. "Oh, yeah. That's hilarious."

"It's true, though." She patted his shoulder. "Just temporarily while he's in Starlight. Don't worry. It's nothing serious. Two consenting adults who—"

"I can't go there." Josh held up a hand. "That is the worst idea in the history of ideas."

Parker shook his head. "Maybe we could have eased him into it?"

"The direct method is better. I stopped playing guessing games when I got divorced. It will be fine."

"I bet someone uttered those words after the Titanic hit the iceberg," Josh muttered.

Mara only smiled, refusing to be deterred. Only by bulldozing her way through this could she keep things under control and in perspective.

Temporary. No strings attached.

They all turned toward the window as a large truck pulling a flatbed trailer loaded with lumber trundled into the parking area.

"That's the wood for the trim." Parker ran a hand through his hair as he took a step toward the door. "I'll tell them where to unload and get the sawhorses ready."

"Coward," Mara said under her breath as he moved past.

"Yep," he agreed readily. "See you for lunch."

"We're not on the Titanic," she said to Josh when they were alone.

He raised a brow. "The Hindenburg?"

"We're keeping it simple. You already know there's something between your brother and me. What better way to get rid of an itch than to scratch it?"

"That's also a great way to make it spread."

She blew out a breath. "We're not talking about poison ivy."

"I'm aware, Mara." He walked to the desk and took the seat Parker had vacated minutes earlier. "You're both adults. I'm not going to make a big deal of this, but I will tell you to be careful."

"I've got it under control."

"You're not as tough as you want people to believe." He pointed a finger at her. "For that matter, neither is Parker. He's trying, but I'd guess this is unchartered water for him."

"Dating?" Mara sniffed. "I doubt it."

"Dating a woman where he doesn't call all the shots. My brother and I grew up in the same house.

We've dealt with the ramifications in different ways. I tend to commit too quickly. I want to save people the way I wished someone would save me. It's not healthy. Maybe if I didn't take everything on as a crusade, my own marriage wouldn't have fallen apart."

"Don't you dare blame yourself." Mara placed her palms flat on the desk and leaned forward. "Your daughter had cancer. Of course you're going to be a crusader. Any parent would. Your ex-wife's actions aren't your responsibility. She left, Josh. It's horrible but that's on her. Even if for whatever reason she didn't want to be in the marriage anymore, there's no excuse for walking away from Anna."

"Thank you. Sometimes I go down the rabbit hole and…"

"I know." She sat down across the desk from him. "I'm the same way. Maybe if I'd been better at balancing things. Maybe if I'd kept Paul happy, my daughter would still have a father." She held up a hand when he would have argued with her. "I understand what I'm doing with your brother, and the reason I mentioned it in front of you is because we're friends. I'm due for some fun, Josh. You and I are both due."

He groaned. "Don't make me think about you and my brother together."

"Agreed," she said with a laugh. "Just know our friendship won't change."

"I can't call you my casual sex sister-in-law?" he asked with a smirk.

"Well, you can." She plastered on her brightest smile. "But only if you're looking to get your butt whupped."

"Just take care of your heart," he said, suddenly serious.

"I will," she promised, a lump forming in her throat. She had friends in Starlight. It was home, and as much fun as she knew she'd have scratching all the itches with Parker, she'd never jeopardize the life she'd built for herself and Evie.

## Chapter Ten

"I've changed my mind." Mara spoke more to herself than Parker. She pressed her back against the brick building. A cold wind whipped up from the alley across the street, and she drew her cable-knit cardigan closed tight with one hand.

It was forecasted to turn warm again by the weekend, but the early part of the week called for cooler, rainy weather. It was just the kind of day Parker would have liked to spend under the covers, preferably naked with Mara. Although that seemed like a long shot given the change in her mood from earlier.

"You don't want a burger?" Parker frowned, unsure what to make of this nervous, jittery woman.

He'd gotten so used to the confidence Mara projected. Even when he knew it was a facade, it still impressed him. He couldn't understand what had happened from the time they'd left the mill to when he'd parked his truck around the corner from Over Easy Kitchen, which had always served Starlight's best burgers.

"I have lunch meat and a loaf of bread at the house." She gave him a panicked smile. "Let's eat there."

That plan actually worked for Parker, but it didn't explain her sudden burst of nerves. "Why?" he asked slowly.

"People will talk." She repeated her argument from earlier, darting a glance to either side.

"About what?" he coaxed, feigning ignorance at her concern.

"Us."

"Mara." He reached out a finger and tipped up her chin until she met his gaze. "As much as the idea appeals, I'm not exactly planning to ravish you in the middle of the restaurant. So unless you can't resist throwing me down on one of the Formica tables, I don't think we're going to give them much to talk about."

"It's a small town. They don't need much."

"People have seen us together before today. I'm sure most everyone knows why I'm in town and that you're helping with the design for the mill."

She pointed a finger at him. "Is this a date?"

Wrapping his fingers around hers, he brought her hand to his lips, brushing a kiss across her knuckles. "Will it freak you out if I say yes?"

She scrunched up her nose. "Probably."

He leaned in until he could feel her sweet breath against his cheek. "Yes."

Her eyes drifted closed and her chest rose and fell in several shallow breaths. "Okay." She swallowed and met his gaze. "I'm starving so it's time to be done freaking out. Let's eat."

"That's good to know," he said as they started down the sidewalk again.

"What?"

"You don't like arguing as much when you're hungry."

"But I'm happier after I've eaten," she told him. Her cheeks were tinged pink from the cool air and her eyes bright, making her look even more beautiful than normal.

He smiled, something he did a lot around her and not enough in his regular life he realized. They entered Over Easy. There were several new restaurants in Starlight, trendier establishments that served microgreens and locally sourced everything. He liked that Mara hadn't balked when he suggested this place. It was easy enough to do trendy in Seattle. In Starlight he wanted a guarantee of a great meal.

She bypassed several open tables in front of the

window and headed to a quiet two-top near the back. Parker waved to a few people he recognized but didn't stop to talk because he wanted to stay with Mara. She slid into the chair, grabbed a laminated menu from the stack behind the napkin dispenser and held it up in front of her face.

After taking the seat across from her, he plucked the menu out of her fingers.

"I wasn't finished looking," she protested. "Get your own."

A waitress wearing a black T-shirt and denim skirt, an improvement over the polyester uniforms Parker remembered from his childhood, approached the table. It made him the tiniest bit nostalgic for those celebratory family dinners they'd had at these tables. For once, he thought about his father without bitterness. Mac had always been on his best behavior when they were out in public. There were plenty of moments when Parker had felt like he was being paraded in front of the town to prove that Mac was the benevolent family man of his public image. But sometimes Parker still appreciated the feeling of being a normal family.

Over Easy had done that for him. Now he wanted it for Mara.

He ordered an iced tea and Mara did the same. The young waitress explained the special burger of the week then went to get their drink orders.

"Did you see how she was looking at us?" Mara asked, eyes narrowed, when they were alone.

"You did request extra lemon," he said, keeping his features serious. "That's kind of high-maintenance."

"She knows." Mara darted a glance over her shoulder as if they were being watched.

"Knows what?"

"That I'm considering whether to throw you onto the table and have my wicked way with you."

Parker felt his mouth drop open then snapped it shut when Mara burst into a fit of giggles.

"I can't believe I thought you were really nervous," he said, shaking his head. "I felt bad for you. Turns out you might be the world's best actress."

She gave him a proud smile. "I was nervous, but you made me feel better. Thank you."

"Tell me more about your wicked ways."

"I intend to after lunch."

Parker immediately called the waitress over to take their orders, earning another round of laughter from Mara.

He couldn't remember a time when he'd felt so happy. He was used to expensive meals and swanky restaurants but sharing a burger and fries with Mara beat out anything else. They talked about the renovations and her plans for the design, the vendors who'd already committed to leasing retail space and Mara's idea for a local artisan co-op.

He asked about Evie, surprised at how much he already cared for the young girl. It still shocked him how easily Paul Reed had been able to allow his family to walk away. The fact that Parker had played such an active role in allowing the man to avoid paying child support irritated like a burr under his skin.

"I'm rethinking how I manage my clients," he blurted after taking his last bite of burger.

"Okay," Mara said, clearly confused by his outburst.

"Not that it matters," he clarified. "But I wanted you to know. I put together some guidelines for the new associate I hired and for my assistant as far as how we're going to handle our clients and their spouses. We have resources and training available to help stabilize people and get them back to functioning normally without boatloads of emotional trauma. That's how I want to operate my practice. I wouldn't call it a mission statement...more of a—"

"A manifesto perhaps?" she asked tightly. "Are you having a Jerry Maguire moment, Parker?"

He almost welcomed her sarcasm. Mara wasn't going to let him off easy and he respected her because of it. "What happened to you during the divorce negotiations was wrong, and I'm embarrassed about my part in it."

"You were doing your job." The fact that she repeated his words didn't lessen the sting.

"No." He shook his head, pushing his plate to the

edge of the table. "As Josh reminded me, the reason I became a divorce attorney is to help people find solutions. I wanted my clients to have the options that weren't available to my mom. But somehow things changed so now it's all about winning. You reminded me there's more than one side to every dispute."

She studied him as the waitress came to clear their plates. Parker handed the woman his credit card, unsure of why he'd revealed so much to Mara unprompted.

"Are you saying I did the people of Seattle with marriage problems a huge service?"

"Just by being you," he confirmed. "In between loads of laundry, I went through my current case files. I'm actually driving into the city later this week to meet with the new guy. We're going to brainstorm some ideas for alternative dispute resolution."

As they walked out, Parker stopped to speak with the restaurant's longtime owner. Mara stood at his side but seemed uncomfortable when he tried to include her in the conversation.

"Why are you so guarded?" he asked as they headed back toward his SUV.

"Do I need to reference our previous conversation about what the divorce did to my self-esteem?"

He shook his head. "I get that part, but you've lived in Starlight a year now. You've made it your home."

"Yeah. What's your point?"

"I watched you at the soccer game. You didn't stand with the other parents."

"I was there to support my kid," she said with a sniff. "Not to make friends."

"My point exactly. You're smart, interesting and wicked funny. Why don't you want friends?"

They stopped on the sidewalk next to the Audi. Mara bunched the soft fabric of her sweater between her fingers and gathered it close, which Parker guessed had more to do with her nerves than the cool air. "Remind me to ask for your help if I ever put together an online dating profile."

He didn't react because he knew she was joking, but the thought of Mara dating did uncomfortable things to his insides.

She blew out a breath. "I have friends. Your brother, for one. Kaitlin, who happens to be dating your buddy Finn. Brynn is a friend of mine, too. We're getting pretty close."

"You've been working at your aunt's coffee shop. You must meet half the town coming through there."

"She pays me to make coffee, not to chitchat."

"Mara."

"It's not easy for me," she said after a moment, looking out toward the street like she couldn't stand to make eye contact with him. "You're on sabbatical from your life in Seattle. I left mine behind, and at the time I thought it was a perfect fit for me." She gave a harsh laugh. "I was important. People respected me, or at least that's how it felt. I had a great wardrobe, got expensive haircuts and my nails done." She held out her hands for his inspection. "Look at what a mess they are now."

"You have beautiful hands." Her fingers were slender and while her nails weren't painted, they were delicately almond shaped.

"I'm not fishing for a compliment, Parker. It might seem shallow, but it's what I knew. I thought it made me who I was. I could be proud of my accomplishments. But it was an illusion Paul shattered when he left. I'm here in Starlight to make a better life for Evie because I failed at the one I had. If I don't make many friends, it's because I'm not going to open myself up for people to judge me. I don't like to let people in because if I do, it gives them the power to hurt me."

"You don't know that's going to happen."

"I can imagine."

"This town isn't like that."

She pointed a finger at him. "How would you know? You left this place in your rearview mirror years ago."

"Don't be like me." Her gaze slammed into his, but he forced himself to continue. "I've closed myself off from personal relationships because it's easier. But you're different, Mara. You have a lot to give."

"And you don't?"

"You didn't argue when I told you my heart was quite possibly two sizes too small."

"I was still angry."

"You were right."

She stepped toward him and lifted her hand, then cupped his cheek. He leaned into her softness, the faint scent of lavender enveloping him. Her skin was warm, and he let the heat of her melt the chill that seeped through his bones. "You're a better man than you believe yourself to be."

He covered her hand with his. "I wish that were true."

"We're quite a pair," she said with a quiet laugh. "Both of us doing the lone-wolf thing because we don't want to be hurt." She trailed her thumb across his bottom lip. "What do you think about an extended lunch hour today?"

His breath hitched in his chest. "Do you mean…"

"Come home with me."

"Yes," he agreed and the smile she gave him was worth any risk to his heart.

Butterflies danced across Mara's belly as she led Parker through the iron gate at the back of the house ten minutes later.

They hadn't spoken much on the ride over, and she'd worked to keep her nerves at bay. What kind of conversation was appropriate for a moment like this?

*I hope you're as amazing in bed as I imagine.*

*I hope I don't disappoint you.*

*I hope this doesn't end with my heart broken.*

Nope. Better to keep it simple.

She fumbled with the keys, embarrassed at the slight tremble of her fingers.

"Hey." Parker gently turned her so she faced him.

"Ignore me," she said, rolling her eyes.

"Never," he answered. "We don't have to go any further. If you want to turn around and—"

"I want this," she interrupted. "I mean, if you do."

"More than you can know." He leaned in to kiss her, his solid body pressed closer to hers, turning her knees to melted butter.

She sighed and he made a sound of pleasure as if he couldn't imagine anything better than breathing in her breath.

It's worth it, she thought. No matter what happened after today, she wouldn't let herself regret this moment.

As soon as they were in the house, Parker claimed her mouth again. His kisses ignited a fire in her that burned away all her doubts. And when he lifted her into his arms, she reveled in the hard strength of him. The house was quiet, which added to her desire. How long had it been since she'd done something for herself with no thought toward the consequences of her actions? Her body hummed with a desperate need. This wanting was like a secret gift, one to unwrap and treasure. Mara planned to make the most of it.

"Bedroom?" he asked, his voice hoarse.

"Upstairs," she answered, twining her arms around his neck. "Second door on the left."

Mara pressed kisses to his strong jawline as he maneuvered them up the staircase. Moments later they entered the guest bedroom that was hers since she'd moved in with her aunt.

The room had simple furnishings—a pine dresser and shaker-style headboard on a queen-size bed with a colorful quilt Mara knew had been made by her grandmother.

Parker lowered her to the floor but didn't let go. It was as if he couldn't bear to release her, and his big hands made her feel cherished and safe in a way she wouldn't have expected to matter.

They tore at each other's clothes, stripping off layers in between deep kisses. As much as she wanted to savor this time with him, she couldn't force herself to slow down.

"So beautiful." He gazed down at her when she stood in front of him wearing only her bra and panties. She said a silent prayer of thanks that she'd retained a fondness for the expensive lingerie she used to favor, knowing the pale pink bra and matching panties enhanced her body.

But as Parker's gaze met hers, she had the distinct impression he wasn't talking about the flimsy bits of lace she wore. Maybe it was wishful thinking, but he seemed more attracted to who she was on the inside than anything else.

"You're not too bad yourself," she said with a throaty laugh as she made a show of letting her gaze trail over Parker's lean frame. She had to play off the emotions cascading through her, for both of their sakes. They'd agreed on a fling, the scratching of a mutual itch. No sense making it into something more than it was meant to be.

It was also no chore to admire his body. Muscles stretched across his chest, not the crazy kind that flexed like he'd spent too much time in the gym. Parker's body spoke of muscles earned by hard work, which couldn't be right given his penchant for expensive suits and time behind a desk. But her body responded nonetheless, and she felt her own limbs grow heavy with need. Then he stepped closer, cupping her breasts in his big hands. She gasped as his thumbs grazed over her lace-covered nipples.

The sound from the back of her throat should have embarrassed her, but she was way beyond caring what anyone thought. This moment was hers to own, and she'd earned the pleasure.

She took a step toward the bed, leaning down to pull the sheets and quilt back.

He followed her down, his body covering hers in a way that made her want to stay like this forever.

Glancing at the nightstand, she suddenly froze.

"What's wrong?" he asked immediately, propping himself up on his elbows.

"This is the part where I'm supposed to pull a condom from the drawer," she said. "Only I don't have any." She shook her head. "I haven't done this…any of this…since the divorce. Now I live with my aunt." All those lusty thoughts from moments earlier disappeared in an instant. "I'm like some kind of Victorian cliché, only it's worse than spinsterhood. I'm a maiden divorcée."

His gaze softened as he flashed an amused half smile. "You have a daughter, Mara. I think that eliminates you from the category of maiden."

"I'm a born-again virgin."

"First, I don't think that's a thing." He smoothed the hair away from her face, his touch gentle and reassuring. "Second, this isn't a problem."

After dropping a quick kiss on her mouth, he reached for his jeans, pulled his wallet from the back pocket and took out a condom packet.

"Okay." She drew in a deep breath. "You've got it covered."

"For now," he said with a wink. "If this goes the way I think it's going to, I'm going to need to restock in the near future."

"What if it doesn't?" she couldn't help but ask as he lowered himself to the bed again.

"It will," he promised and kissed her. "Stop overthinking."

She laughed softly. "Good luck with that."

"I guess I'll have to do a better job of distracting you." Resting his weight on his elbows, he tugged her bra straps off her shoulders and down her arms. The cool air had no sooner touched the tips of her breasts when he drew one nipple into his mouth. His tongue worked its magic, circling the sensitive peak as he drew his other hand along her body to the waistband of her panties.

Instinctively she opened for him as he dipped one finger into her center. She could have shouted an alleluia when he stripped the lace from her hips then returned his hand to its ministrations. Her back arched as he found a particularly sensitive spot, and this time he caught her cry in his mouth. The tension she'd held for so long unwound even as pressure built inside her. She moaned then cried out his name but his fingers continued to work in a sensual dance until finally she couldn't hold on any longer. Her body shattered into a million shards of golden light, the pleasure swallowing her whole.

Parker raised his head, grinning at her like the cat that just ate the canary. "What are you thinking now?" he said, kissing the base of her throat.

"No thoughts," she answered, her breath still ragged. "My brain disintegrated."

He chuckled. "Then I guess my work here is done?"

"Oh, no." She grabbed the condom packet from

the nightstand and handed it to him. "You've only just begun."

"I was hoping you'd say that," he told her before ripping open the packet with his teeth.

Mara watched as he sheathed himself then settled between her legs. She reached up and wrapped a hand around his neck, pulling him closer for a long, slow kiss.

At the same time, he entered her and she groaned into his mouth at how perfectly he seemed to fit with her.

They set a rhythm that suited them both, and Mara once again gave in to the pulsing need. Slowly, the pressure built again, only this time it was as much concentrated in her heart as her body. While she'd never been a fan of casual sex, the act also hadn't seemed to hold the sentimental meaning she'd read about in books and seen in movies. Apparently, it took the right man to elevate it to that level.

For better or worse, Parker was that man for her.

As he moved inside her, he whispered sweet words against her ear and while she tried to remember this was only physical, her heart refused to believe. Tears sprang to her eyes and she blinked them away as the release surged through her, washing away anything but the humming electricity of her desire. A moment later, Parker called out her name and she felt his body shudder as she held him.

And her entire world shifted. She might go back to acting like nothing had changed, but deep inside Mara knew she'd never be the same.

## Chapter Eleven

"We need to have a serious conversation."

Parker tried not to react to Finn's words as he took a seat at the high-top table in an almost quiet corner of the Trophy Room. The bar was crowded and several people had greeted him by name as he entered. He liked the easy familiarity more than he'd expected. In Seattle he found it simple to remain fairly anonymous, even at the restaurants and bars he frequented. He was just another man in a nice suit who tipped better than average. In Starlight, he had a history that he couldn't escape, but the past didn't hurt the way it once had.

Nick and Finn had ordered him a beer, and he took

a long drink, trying to look unconcerned by their stern expressions. It had been a week since he and Mara had first been together. Was it possible their secret relationship was already public knowledge?

They'd been careful to keep things on the down low in public. Josh knew, but even at the job site Parker made sure to show no outward affection toward her. His brother had given him an arch look when they'd returned from that first lunch, but when Mara started to explain their long absence, Josh had simply held up a hand.

*We're working off a "don't ask, don't tell" policy as far as I'm concerned*, he'd said.

Which was fine with Parker.

Sort of.

He wasn't the type of guy who wanted to discuss his feelings for a woman. In fact, if that type of guy existed, Parker had yet to meet him. But he also didn't like the feeling of being Mara's secret. When he'd seen her at soccer practice, she'd ignored him almost completely. Although he had been happy to see her talking to a few of the moms without appearing that she wanted the ground to swallow her whole.

He'd wanted to put his arms around her, to swing Evie onto his shoulders after practice and take them both to dinner or pick up carryout and listen to how their days had gone.

Instead, Mara left with a brisk wave and hadn't

texted him until several hours later, asking if he wanted to stop by since Evie had gone to bed.

Of course he had, but being relegated to an after-hours booty call cut him in a way he didn't care to examine. He was a master at casual so couldn't figure out what had changed.

He'd convinced her to let him come over for dinner the following evening and he'd loved the normalcy of petting Mr. Paws, playing Go Fish with Evie then listening from the hallway as Mara read her favorite bedtime story.

Maybe he'd given away his feelings before he even admitted them to himself.

"What's the deal?" he asked, placing his glass back on the table.

"Rudy Marshall is getting ready to retire," Nick said, his voice pitched low.

Finn nodded in agreement. "He hasn't announced it, but my dad confirmed the news. They've been friends for years."

Parker shrugged. "Are you throwing him a party and need a venue? Because that's an idea we've been considering for one of the outbuildings at the mill. Converting it into a private party room. As far as I know, there isn't—"

"The town's attorney is retiring," Nick interrupted. "What does that mean to you?"

"Very little," Parker answered. "I barely know the guy other than he was one of the few people who didn't seem to think my dad walked on water back in the day." He grabbed a handful of pretzels from the dish in the center of the table. "He can't be the only attorney in town anymore. Someone will take on his clients."

Finn tapped a finger on the scuffed wood tabletop. "Someone like you."

"Me?" Parker laughed, ignoring the unexpected zing down his spine. "I specialize in divorce."

"People in Starlight get divorced." Finn took a long pull from his beer.

"Not many," Nick added. "I think we're actually quite a bit lower than the national average."

Finn tipped his bottle in the other man's direction. "I like those odds."

Nick nodded. "You and Kaitlin are strong. No worries there."

"Exactly." Finn popped a pretzel in his mouth. "Because I wouldn't be fool enough to mess it up again. I'm damn lucky she gave me a second chance."

"She loves you," Nick said.

"Damn lucky," Finn repeated.

"Hey." Parker slapped his hand on the table several times to get their attention. Both men turned to stare at him. "You two are the most easily distracted guys I've ever known. How the hell have I put up with you for so many years?"

"Absence makes the heart grow fonder." Nick

flashed a cheeky grin. "You need to get back here more often."

"He needs a reason," Finn said. "Like a woman."

"Name one woman in Starlight who'd give our boy the time of day."

"I could name several," Finn said with a laugh. "But none worth the trouble."

Parker's gut tightened at the thought they might be lumping Mara into that category.

"You've been working pretty closely with Mara Reed." It felt as if Nick were reading his mind.

"No way," Finn said immediately. "She's friends with Kaitlin and I can guarantee she wouldn't give Parker the time of day. Hell, he represented her ex-husband in the divorce."

"I'm joking." Nick held up his hands. "Mara makes the best dirty chai I've ever had. She's way too good for Parker."

Parker choked on a pretzel. "Excuse me?"

"No offense, man." Nick waved a hand in the air. "It's all conjecture anyway. Mara isn't even your type."

"What's my type?" Parker asked, almost afraid to hear the answer.

"Not so brainy and broke, typically," Finn offered. "You don't exactly love an intellectual challenge."

"That's not true."

"Not in your dating life anyway." Nick signaled

the waitress for another round of drinks. "Your career is another story."

"Which is why Rudy getting ready to retire is such great news."

"Are we finally back to the topic at hand?" Parker shook his head, far too frustrated by their easy dismissal of the possibility that he'd date Mara. Granted, this was just what they'd agreed upon—a secret relationship no one else would know about. But still... somehow this judgment from his friends burned a sour hole in his gut.

"It's worth setting up a meeting to discuss the potential," Finn suggested.

"No," Parker countered, "It's not. My life is in Seattle." He looked at Finn. "Up until Daniel's death, yours was, too."

"Things changed," Finn explained as if Parker didn't know the story. "I had a chance with the girl of my dreams and I took it. Look at how awesome my life's become because I was willing to put my heart on the line."

"My life is already awesome." Parker narrowed his eyes when both of his friends laughed.

"You need to risk something." Nick smiled at the pretty waitress who approached the table with a tray of three beers. "Thanks, Juls."

The willowy brunette arched a brow. "I had fun last week," she told Nick. "Any chance you're free again this Friday? I have the night off."

There was a slight stiffening in Nick's shoulders, and Parker knew what was coming next. He'd seen this routine since high school.

"I'd love to." Nick held up his hands, palms up. "But I'm on duty all weekend. I'll text you and we'll figure out another time."

"Sure," Juls said, disappointment clear in her tone. "Anything else for you guys?"

"All good," Finn replied, keeping his gaze trained forward.

Parker did the same, afraid of what the woman might read in his expression otherwise. "Nothing for me. Thanks."

"We'll talk soon," Nick said, picking up his beer.

She nodded and walked away.

"You're a tool," Finn muttered when they were alone again.

As alone as they could be in a semicrowded bar. Despite the groups of people joking and laughing at the tables around them, their trio was left alone. Parker liked it that way given the direction the conversation continued to head.

"What?" Nick feigned innocence. "I have to work."

"You're not on duty *all* weekend, Chief." Parker shook his head. "The poor woman doesn't even realize you're blowing her off."

"It's not like that," Nick insisted.

"I can't believe you're getting on my case for taking risks. When was the last time you were in a serious relationship?"

"Not my thing." Nick's mouth thinned.

"What about Brynn?" Finn asked quietly.

For a moment, Parker thought Starlight's police chief might get up and walk out on them.

"We've been through this already," Nick answered finally. "Brynn and I are friends. She's still grieving her husband, who happened to be a buddy of mine. Even if I wanted something to change, it isn't the right time."

"She and Mara were talking about some kind of online dating profile yesterday when Brynn stopped by the mill."

Nick choked on his swallow of beer.

"Kaitlin asked if I knew of any nice bankers Brynn could date." Finn patted Nick on the back until the other man knocked away his arm. "Looks like the time might be right for her," he added.

Nick opened his mouth as if to argue then gave a harsh shake of his head. "Not going there with either of you right now. If she wants to date, more power to her."

"You could lose her a second time around."

"I've already told you, I can't lose something that was never mine to start."

They sat in silence for several long moments. Parker could see the frustration etched on his friend's face at the thought of Brynn dating again. Nick and

Brynn had been close in high school, although never romantically involved. Everyone had known about her crush on Nick, who was too busy dating cheerleaders and bad girls to pay much attention to the quiet, studious girl next door.

When Nick finally realized that what he'd wanted had been in front of him the whole time, it had been too late. Brynn was pregnant with Daniel's baby and the wedding was already planned.

"So, Parker…" Finn lifted his beer in salute. "It's clear why we want you to move back to Starlight, right? You must miss these crazy nights on the town."

Parker and Nick laughed at the ridiculousness of the statement. Although, he did miss the easy camaraderie of his two friends. He'd spent years building a life in Seattle but still hadn't cultivated the kind of close-knit friendships Starlight offered.

"I swore when I left I'd never come back."

"That was a long time ago," Nick reminded him. "Things change. Finn's a great example."

"Community banker at your service," Finn said with an exaggerated bow.

"Do you ever think you'll get bored?" Parker couldn't help but ask. Before returning to Starlight, Finn had been on the fast track to a vice president position at a multinational bank.

"I'm helping people that I care about at First Trust," Finn answered. "My life used to be about margins, growth percentages and the bottom line. Now it's about making a difference in someone's life. It might not be glamorous, but it's a million times more fulfilling than the world of corporate banking."

"I'm happy for you." Parker shrugged. "But it's not for me."

Finn nodded. "If you change your mind, give Rudy a call. I'm sure he'd be glad to talk to you. He's worried about his legacy and who will step in to take care of his clients."

"His wife's been on him to retire for a couple of years now," Nick added. "He's told me he feels like he's deserting the people who need him."

Parker thought about how easy it had been to walk away from his clients in Seattle. Of course, he'd left them in good hands with his new associate and he was still putting in a couple of hours a day via email or with phone calls along with driving to the city once a week.

But no one, not even his circle of friends, seemed to really notice that he'd left. He didn't care to examine what that said about the quality of his relationships.

"I've got to go," he said, checking his watch. He'd promised Evie he'd bring over supplies to make s'mores in the firepit on their back patio.

"Hot date?" Nick asked with a chuckle.

"Something like that," Parker answered, earning a fresh round of ribbing from both his friends.

"You're holding out on us," Finn said as Parker rose from the table.

But Parker had no intention of sharing anything about Mara at this point. "See you boys later." He lifted a hand and waved even as he turned to walk away.

Mara tried to keep her expression neutral as Parker patiently helped Evie turn her marshmallow over the fire.

He'd arrived thirty minutes earlier with a grocery bag of s'mores supplies. Evie had been thrilled at the prospect of roasting her own dessert, and Mara had felt a pang of guilt that she hadn't introduced her daughter to s'mores before now. Add it to her list of small but meaningful mom failures.

She shook her head and flashed a reassuring smile when Parker gave her a questioning look across the firepit.

One thing she was trying to master was the art of giving herself a break. Did any mother in the world really have that skill down? It made her want to reach out to her own mother just to ask the question. Nina Dyar had always seemed so self-assured, never doubting her skill as a mom.

Maybe Mara's lack of confidence originated in the fact that she was so different from her mom. She hadn't been one of those women who knew instinctively how to soothe a baby or what to do when

Evie's diaper rash got severe. The best she could say about herself was that she tried. Could it be enough?

"Mommy, you're on fire," Evie shouted.

With a start, Mara pulled the charred confection out of the fire and blew out the flame that had consumed her marshmallow.

"Another one bites the dust," Parker told her, one thick eyebrow arched. It was the third marshmallow in a row she'd burned. "Luckily, we have an extra."

Mara sighed and scraped the gooey mess off the end of the roasting stick. "My hero," she mumbled, sparks zinging along her skin as his glacier-hued gaze crashed into hers.

"Hardly." He gave a strangled laugh. "But I can manage a golden marshmallow."

Evie clapped as he pulled the stick from the flames. "It's perfect."

Everything about this night was perfect, and Mara had to remind herself not only that Parker wasn't her hero, but also that she didn't need him to be. In the past couple of weeks, handling things while Aunt Nanci was in Texas with Renee, Mara had discovered a kind of courage she hadn't realized she possessed. Too bad her new boss-lady persona didn't include managing to conduct an affair while keeping her heart out of the mix.

She placed a piece of chocolate on a graham cracker square and held it out toward Parker. He lowered the stick until the marshmallow rested on the chocolate, and she closed the other graham cracker square over it and squeezed it shut. It really was a perfect s'more.

Evie's brown eyes widened as Mara blew on the sandwich then handed it to her. The girl bit into it, chewing even as she grinned.

"Next," Parker said, and Mara repeated the process.

"I'll share with you," she told him, taking a bite then handing the s'more to him. Instead of taking it, he leaned forward and bit down on the graham cracker, winking at Mara as he did.

She drew in a sharp breath, realizing she had it bad if watching Parker take a bite of a s'more was sexy as hell.

"How's it going, sweet girl?" she asked her daughter, needing to remind her brain it was in control of this moment, not her body or her heart.

"Mommy, can Parker come with us to go apple picking?" Evie licked a bit of marshmallow off the back of her hand. "He can reach the high branches, and then you can teach him how to make apple pie since he taught us how to make s'mores."

"He might already know how to make apple pie." Mara realized she was grasping at straws.

"Do you?" Evie asked him, taking her last bite.

"Not yet," he said, "But I'd love to learn."

"Okay." Evie nodded. "Mommy will teach you.

She's good at baking, just not marshmallow roasting. I'm gonna wash my hands. I don't like sticky."

Mara watched her daughter skip toward the house, then turned to Parker.

"How do you do that?"

"What?"

"Bond with her." She bit down into the chewy, chocolaty goodness of the s'more before handing the last bite to him. "My shy kid forgets she's an introvert when you're around."

"I'm glad."

She flipped the switch to cut the propane to the firepit, and the flame disappeared with a soft whoosh. It cast the corner of the patio into shadow. She zipped up her fleece pullover as a shiver passed through her. Silly, she told herself. The firepit hadn't given off enough heat to actually warm her. "You don't want to learn how to make apple pie."

"Sure I do," he countered, stepping closer and cupping her cheeks in his palms. "I'm having visions of you in an apron."

Her eyes drifted closed as he kissed her, lips soft and cool from the night air. He tasted like chocolate, and she sighed into him, immediately caught up in the moment and the way her body reacted.

"Aprons aren't sexy," she said against his mouth.

"They are if that's all you're wearing."

She broke the embrace with a laugh, gathering the

supplies she'd placed on the seat of one of the Adirondack chairs that encircled the fire pit.

"I'm not that kind of baker."

"Teach me anyway," he said. "I'd like to join you and Evie."

"Josh and Anna are coming too," she said as they walked toward the house. "And a few other of the girls' friends with their parents." She nudged his arm. "I invited people."

He nudged her back. "Yeah?"

"It's the new friendly leaf I'm turning over."

"See what a great influence I can be."

Mara bit down on her lip because she didn't trust herself to answer. She couldn't remember a time when she'd been so happy. Even though they'd agreed to keep things both casual and secret, Mara wanted more. The Dennison Lumber Mill would open in a couple of weeks, on schedule and to great acclaim if the plans came together the way she hoped they would. After that, Parker was returning to Seattle for real. Their time together would end, and she knew nothing could stop her heart from breaking.

Nothing but the thought that maybe he wanted more, in the same way she did. Perhaps he was falling in love in the same way she was.

Her heart fluttered in her chest as the understanding of her feelings for Parker spread through her body. Love. Was it possible after only being together a week? It didn't seem like it. Yet her heart refused to be denied.

"If you're not comfortable with me being there," Parker told her as they entered the house, "I get it."

She blinked, trying to get a handle on her tumbling emotions. "It's fine. I'm sure Anna will want you there, just like Evie."

"What about you?" he asked, placing a hand low on her back.

"Sure," she said, the word coming out in a squeak. "We'll all have fun together."

He gave her a funny look. "We'll all have fun," he repeated.

"Mommy?" Evie entered the kitchen wearing her butterfly pajamas.

Mara took a quick step away from Parker. "You're ready for bed," she said, moving toward her daughter. "What a big girl."

"Can Parker read to me?" Evie asked softly, dropping her gaze to the floor.

Lungs squeezing almost painfully, Mara glanced at Parker, who nodded. "Sure, sweetie. That's nice of you to ask."

"It sure is." Parker came forward. "Do I get to use different voices?"

"What kind of voices?" Evie asked, sounding intrigued.

"Well," he said, deepening his tone. "Are there

any grizzly bears in your stories? This is exactly how a bear sounds in my mind."

The girl laughed as Mara tried to calm the panic gripping her chest. No one besides Mara or Aunt Nanci had ever read Evie a bedtime story. "You and Parker pick out a book in your room. I'll be up after I finish cleaning down here."

Evie grabbed his hand, then led him up the stairs as she chattered about her favorite books and one in particular that included a bear.

Apparently Mara wasn't the only one who'd fallen for the man. She pressed her palms to the counter and leaned forward, drawing in a few calming breaths.

Yes, they'd had an agreement about the parameters of their relationship, but he seemed as interested in a deeper connection as she was. Sometimes life gave a person what they didn't even realize they needed.

Mara needed Parker.

It was different than anything she'd ever felt. She'd fallen in love with him, but not once did she worry about losing herself or the person she wanted to become. As strange as it was, Parker brought out the best in her. With his quiet support, she'd discovered a strength she hadn't known she possessed.

He *had* to feel it, too.

She'd give it time. Seattle wasn't far, but the city felt like a different world compared to Starlight. She had no intention of letting go of her life in the small town, so they could take it slow.

Words like *I love you* would have to wait. Better to hold back and see how things unfolded after the Founder's Day weekend events.

She straightened the kitchen and wiped down the counters before heading upstairs.

Parker's voice could be clearly heard as he gave an enthusiastic reading of one of Evie's favorite picture books. Mara had never anticipated she'd be willing to let someone in her life again so soon, but Parker made it easy. She tamped down the thread of worry that this was all *too* easy and joined the two of them in Evie's bedroom.

"He does funny voices, Mommy," Evie announced as Parker closed the book, her eyes dancing with joy.

"So I hear." Mara pulled down the covers on the bed and her daughter climbed in, grabbing her favorite stuffed teddy bear as she did.

"Good night, Evie," Parker said as he smiled down at her. "Sweet dreams."

"'Night," the girl said.

Parker left the room and Mara finished their bedtime routine, saying prayers and cuddling for a few minutes while Mara gently tickled her daughter's arm.

"Is Daddy ever going to visit?" Evie asked as Mara turned off the lamp on the nightstand.

"I don't know, sweetie," Mara said honestly and

then added, "Your daddy is always busy with work but I bet he misses you a ton." The lie made her throat raw, but what else could she tell her daughter? No child deserved to hear that their father didn't care a bit about their existence.

Evie seemed to accept the answer, and Mara tucked her in with a kiss. She made her way downstairs slowly, trailing a hand over the wood bannister.

"You've got a great kid," Parker said when she walked into the family room. He sat on the edge of the sofa, elbows propped on his knees. Somehow seeing him there made all the emotions she'd kept a tight rein on for the past two years bubble up and threaten to burst like a fissure in a dam under pressure for too long.

She swiped at her cheeks and forced a smile. "She's the best."

"What's wrong?" Parker was on his feet in an instant, but when he would have gathered her close, she held out her hands. She couldn't let herself depend on him that way, not until she felt more certain about their status.

"It's nothing."

"You're crying."

"Only a little," she said with a laugh. "Evie asked about her dad. I think it's because you've been so great with her. Paul wasn't an involved father before we split up, and I don't think Evie remembers the specifics. It was all she knew. Now she wants more."

"But she's seen how Josh is with Anna." Parker ran a hand through his hair, the idea that he'd caused upset for Evie clearly not sitting well with him. "She has other friends with great dads. It's not as if she has no example."

"You're different," Mara explained. "You care about *her*, not her friends."

"Of course I do. She's an amazing kid."

"Unfortunately, that fact doesn't seem to matter to her own father."

"I'm sorry."

Mara couldn't help but wrap her arms around his waist. "You didn't do anything wrong. I'm glad she's bonded with you. It's important for her to have men she can trust in her life."

Parker seemed more distressed than she was, and it only made her heart melt even more. He pulled her against him, resting his chin on the top of her head. "But this is also why we set limits for being together, so no one, especially Evie, gets hurt in the end."

This was her chance, Mara thought. A perfect opening to mention the idea of their time together continuing. She swallowed, heart hammering in her chest at the risk she was about to take. *No risk, no reward*, her father used to say. Of course, he'd been referring to meeting the high expectations he set for his family, but the adage fit this situation, as well.

"I've got to go into the city for a couple of days,"

he said before she mustered her courage to speak. "I'll be back by the weekend."

"Oh." She tamped down her disappointment. She knew his life remained in Seattle, so why did it feel like a betrayal for him to return to it?

His arms tightened around her. "I'm taking off first thing tomorrow morning. What do you think about me spending the night? I don't want to let you go quite yet."

"Yes." Mara couldn't resist the opportunity to spend the night in his arms. This would be the first time he'd stayed the entire night with her. Before now, they had stolen moments or a few late nights together that had ended with him leaving in the wee hours. "But you'll need to be gone by the time Evie wakes up."

"Understood," he said and kissed her until she felt dizzy. "Let's watch a movie."

Mara felt her mouth drop open. "That seems a little…" She waved a hand in the air, not sure how to express what she was thinking.

"Boring?" he asked with a laugh.

"Normal," she corrected.

"Normal is underrated." He took her hand and led her to the couch. "Now that I know we've got all night, I just want to hang out with you. Netflix and chill or whatever the current term is."

"That means have sex." She dropped onto the sofa

next to him, snuggling in when he draped an arm over her shoulder.

"We'll get there," Parker said with a gentle kiss to the side of her head. He grabbed the remote from the armrest and flipped on the television. "Offensive humor or action adventure?"

"My vote is for superhero," she said with a grin.

"A woman after my own heart." He called up the latest movie in a popular comic book franchise, and they settled in to watch.

Mara tilted her head to study him as the opening credits rolled.

"What?" he asked.

"You're a cuddler," she said, not bothering to hide her shock.

He scoffed even as one side of his mouth kicked up. "Maybe."

"What have you done with the real Parker Johnson?"

"He's tied up in the basement. I'm like a mastermind villain with my own nefarious agenda."

"I like agenda."

After kissing her again, he gave her a playful push back against the couch cushions. "Pay attention, sweetheart. You'll miss the important details of the story."

Mara turned her attention to the movie, but she couldn't help her mind from wandering to the enigma that was Parker and how happy he made her.

And when he clicked off the television as the end scene played and turned to pull her across his lap, that happiness morphed into pure joy. They feasted on each other for long minutes and then moved upstairs to her bedroom.

Their lovemaking was tender and quiet, both due to Evie sleeping across the hall and because Mara knew that like her, Parker understood something more was happening between them. Something precious and special that she had to believe neither of them would take for granted.

## Chapter Twelve

Mara walked into Main Street Perk the next afternoon, still on the high from spending the previous night wrapped in Parker's arms. He'd been gone when she awoke, but he'd left a freshly brewed pot of coffee waiting for her in the kitchen. If a man who made coffee wasn't a keeper...

Nope.

Mara shook her head. She'd told herself she wasn't going to get too far down the road of imagining a future with him, at least not until after Founder's Day and the mill grand opening.

One of her aunt's close friends was babysitting Evie after school so Mara didn't have to bring her into the shop. Normally Evie liked spending time in the coffee shop's cozy kitchen or coloring at one of the café tables. But between her work on the logistics for the craft fair and managing Perk, it felt to Mara like she'd been dragging her daughter all over town recently.

She mentally flicked away the guilt that tried to claw its way into her consciousness. Evie was happy right now. Mara was happy being this busy. She'd forgotten how she thrived on productivity and a packed schedule.

After checking in with the staff behind the counter, she headed for her aunt's office. Nanci had called yesterday to report that everything was going well with Renee and the pregnancy. They were due to induce her cousin in the next few days, and Nanci planned to spend another three weeks in Texas once the baby was born.

She missed her aunt's maternal presence in her life but had started looking for an apartment to rent after Nanci returned home. Mara could never repay her aunt for helping her make a new start, but it was time Mara and Evie had a place of their own. This was her life, and she needed to really claim it.

One of the regular customers, Grady Underwood, called out a greeting, saying he missed her mochas. She smiled and walked over to his table, then spent a few minutes making small talk about the food trucks she'd booked for Founder's Day. The conversation was a bit forced, but he didn't seem to mind.

In recent weeks, many of the walls Mara erected around herself had begun to fragment. It wasn't just with Parker. Taking a more active role in managing the coffee shop and being a part of the renovation of the mill made her feel like part of the community. It wasn't easy for her to let down her guard. For years, she'd been so driven in relentless pursuit of the perfect life that she'd actually forgotten how it felt to simply live. Now she was learning to embrace the messiness and everything that went with it.

A few other people said hello or asked about Nanci and Renee. Mara had just opened a spreadsheet in the shop's accounting software when someone knocked on the partly open door.

She glanced up to find a woman who looked vaguely familiar staring at her. The tall blonde appeared to be around Mara's age but with a sleek bob and precise makeup that made Mara feel frumpy and old beyond her years.

"Hi," the woman said, waving nervously. "Do you remember me?"

Mara frowned. "I feel like we've met before, but I apologize I can't exactly remember where."

"In Seattle," the woman answered. "I'm Aimee Reed."

The breath whooshed out of Mara's lungs. "Paul's new wife," she murmured.

Aimee nodded. "Our first anniversary is coming up at Christmas, so we won't be official newlyweds anymore."

Mara couldn't do anything but stare at the other woman. Her former husband's wife was here in Starlight. She knew Paul had married his mistress, but she hadn't seen either of them since the divorce was finalized.

In fact, she'd only laid eyes on Aimee once. The day she'd left court, newly divorced and reeling from shame and guilt, she'd walked out into a typically misty day in Seattle to see her ex-husband embracing this woman. She and Aimee had locked eyes for the briefest of moments before Mara turned and walked away.

"What do you want?" Mara asked, gripping the edge of the desk.

Aimee stepped into the office, her perfume overpowering in the small space. "Do you have a few minutes to talk?"

Mara wanted to say no. She should say no, but something in the other woman's eyes stopped her.

"Does Paul know you're here?"

Aimee shook her head. "I'm pregnant," she blurted then burst into tears.

Mara tried to process the words as she jumped up from the chair. She pulled Aimee into the office, then closed the door behind her. The way the gossip mill worked in a small town, news of a stranger crying in Perk would be all over the place in hours if Mara didn't get Paul's wife to settle.

She ushered Aimee to the small side chair pushed into one corner and handed her a box of tissues from the bookshelf. It took a few minutes for the woman to calm down enough that the tears ebbed, leaving her red faced and clearly miserable as she stared at Mara.

"I'm sorry," Aimee mumbled. "I didn't know who else to talk to."

"If you're looking for someone to host a baby shower, I'm probably not your best bet."

"Of course not. I mean, I'd invite you if you wanted to come but—"

"It was a joke."

"Oh, sure. Sorry," Aimee repeated, looking both contrite and embarrassed.

As much as she wanted to, Mara couldn't muster any animosity for this woman. It would be like hating a kitten.

She pressed two fingers to the side of her head. "Why are you here, Aimee?"

"I'm afraid to tell Paul."

"It's going to be a difficult secret to keep."

Aimee hiccupped and grabbed another handful of tissues. "I don't want it to be a secret. I want him to be happy about it. I love him."

Mara's stomach gave a lumbering roll as she thought about the first few weeks when she'd known about her pregnancy but before she told her husband.

She'd also had visions of his joyous reaction but had been sorely disappointed at the lackluster reception her news received.

"Maybe he will be," she said, unable to offer much else.

When Aimee's face crumpled again, Mara realized there was more she could give the other woman. The whole truth, which she hadn't even admitted to herself up until now.

"Things were rough between Paul and me before I got pregnant. He wanted me to be a certain way, or I thought that's what he wanted." She shook her head. "It wasn't working for either of us."

"Did you think a baby would help?" Aimee asked after blowing her nose into the wad of tissues.

"It wasn't like that. My pregnancy was a surprise, but it made me happy. It also seemed to shine a spotlight on all the ways our marriage was already failing. If you and Paul are strong, this will be good news for both of you." She said the words with as much enthusiasm as she could muster, trying to ignore the stab of doubt in her gut.

She expected to feel more—anger, bitterness— but there was nothing except sympathy for this woman and her plight. Mara still hated that her ex wanted nothing to do with Evie, but she'd found a different kind of happiness, a bone-deep knowing she'd made the right choice.

"I think we're strong," Aimee said, not sounding

the least bit certain. "I want us to be strong. Paul had a horrible childhood, and I know that's why he's afraid of being a father. But if we can get past that…"

Mara managed a smile. "I'm still not sure what this has to do with me."

"I saw an email last night," Aimee explained. "He's got an appointment today with his divorce attorney. I'm afraid he's not going to give us a chance."

Mara's stomach pitched. "You must be mistaken. He can't be meeting with Parker."

Aimee nodded. "Parker Johnson," she confirmed. "I met him once during your divorce proceedings. He was nice to me then, but from what Paul told me, he really went after you in court."

"Paul was the one who was out to get me." She swallowed, her throat so dry she could barely get the words out. "Parker was just doing his job."

"It's a dirty job."

Mara didn't respond. If she thought about it too hard, it was still difficult to reconcile the man she'd come to know these past couple weeks with her previous opinion of him.

"Why are you telling me all of this?" Mara's stomach felt sick and she just wanted Aimee to leave so she could have some time to process the shock. "Do you want me to talk to Parker?"

Aimee scrunched up her nose. "The lawyer?" She shook her head. "No, of course not. Why would you talk to him?" Before Mara could answer, the other woman continued, "I was hoping you could call Paul."

"My ex-husband? Your current husband?"

"I think it would make a huge impact on him," Aimee said, nodding.

"So would a sledgehammer to the side of his head."

"He feels terrible about his relationship with your daughter."

"Who is also *his* daughter," Mara felt compelled to point out.

"I think he's consumed with the mistakes he made." Aimee pressed a hand to her flat stomach. "He can't be happy because he's so worried about messing up again. It kills him to have no contact with Evie."

"He made that choice." Mara didn't bother to hide her bitterness now. "He knows where I am. The judge granted him visitation rights. All he has to do is arrange it."

"But he knows you don't want him to be a part of her life. You told him he'd end up hurting her like he hurt you. That final day in court. Those were your words, and he took them to heart. He thinks he's doing the right thing by staying away."

Mara suddenly felt like she'd been the one to take the blow to her head. She closed her eyes and thought back to the nightmare of the divorce proceedings. She'd been so angry. Although she didn't remember telling Paul to stay away, a vague sense of familiarity settled on her. She couldn't possibly be the reason Evie had no father in her life.

"Why would he listen to me?" she asked, more to herself than Aimee. "She's his daughter. If he wanted to see her…"

"You know how messed up his childhood was," Aimee said gently. Paul had grown up in various foster homes, an unwanted kid who'd turned his circumstances around all on his own. "He didn't have much faith in himself in the first place."

It was too much. Mara needed to get away. She needed to think about what to do next. Aimee looked so sweet and gentle sitting there. And soon Evie would have a baby sister or brother. The idea of sharing her daughter with another family almost broke her in two.

Oh, no. Was it possible she'd pushed Paul away so she wouldn't have to share? She'd always resented how her parents had favored her brother and made her feel like she never measured up to their expectations. Now it felt like she'd done something even worse to her own child.

"I'll think about it," she agreed, unable to give any other answer.

"Think fast if you can." Aimee stood and took a step toward the door. "I'm worried about him meeting with the attorney but I don't want to ask because…" She gave a small laugh and dabbed at the corners of her eyes. "At this point, innocence is bliss, especially with my raging hormones."

"Ice cream helps," Mara said. "At least it did when I was pregnant."

"Ice cream regulates hormones?" Aimee looked intrigued.

"No, but it makes you forget about them for a while."

"I hope you and Paul can work things out." Aimee reached out and placed a hand on Mara's arm. Her fingers were delicate with perfectly manicured nails in a bright shade of crimson. The kind of nails Mara used to have when she had the time and money to make them a priority. "Both because I think it would help me and I'd like my baby to know her big sister."

Mara stood in the middle of the tiny office for several minutes after Aimee left. She kept her knees locked, afraid to move because they might give way. If she crumbled now, it felt like she would never get up again.

Just when she thought her life was on track, the past few minutes threw everything into chaos again. Parker had spent the night holding her, but he'd left for the city to meet with her ex-husband. It didn't make sense. He knew what the divorce and Paul's actions had done to her. She wanted an explanation but could she trust that he'd tell her the truth and not just what she wanted to hear?

She'd let down her guard only to feel betrayed

again. There was a reason she'd sworn off love. If only she'd been smart enough to remember it.

"Look at you, all grown up."

Parker straightened from the chair where he'd been sitting in the outdated lobby of Rudy Marshall's downtown office and shook the older attorney's outstretched hand.

"It's been a while, Mr. Marshall."

The man made a face. "Good lord, call me Rudy. You go around Mr. Marshall-ing me and I'm going to feel older than I already do."

"You look the same as I remember from high school."

Rudy gave a loud belly laugh. "For an attorney, you're a terrible liar."

Something about Rudy's friendly demeanor made Parker relax. He had no idea why he'd been so nervous at the prospect of meeting with Rudy. He had no intention of returning to Starlight for good or taking over a small-town law practice, even one that had thrived for decades.

But out of respect for Rudy and for Nick and Finn, Parker had decided he should decline any potential offer in person. At least that's what he'd told himself after he made the call from Seattle.

He ignored his two lonely, restless nights in the city. How could a few weeks back in his hometown change everything?

Mara had changed everything.

He hadn't seen her since he'd left her sleeping in bed three days prior. It was going to be difficult to keep from her the fact that he'd met with her ex-husband while in Seattle. He didn't want to lie in any case, but how could he make her understand?

Paul Reed wasn't the type of client to be shuffled off to a junior associate. The man had stalked into the office, ranting about his fourth wife and the supposed troubles in his marriage. But something about his complaints had felt false to Parker. Maybe because he'd heard a similar story when it came to Mara, but now he understood what an amazing woman she was.

At first, it had been more than awkward when he'd pushed back with Paul. But Parker believed the man loved his wife, and as it turned out, Paul's blustering was hiding a deep fear of fatherhood. He had suspicions Aimee was pregnant, and much like it had with Mara, the news triggered all kinds of fear in Paul.

When Parker probed deeper, Paul had broken down and admitted he regretted not having a relationship with Evie or treating Mara with the respect she deserved. He was terrified of losing his new wife, who he claimed to love with his whole heart.

Parker thought he'd talked him off the edge, encouraging him to share how he felt with his wife. It was more difficult to offer unbiased advice when

Paul mentioned that he wanted to reconnect with Mara and be a true father to Evie.

Every caveman instinct in Parker had roared to life. And while his brain understood how powerful and positive it could be for Evie to have a relationship with her father, Parker realized he wanted a chance to fill that role for the girl.

Maybe two daddies wasn't such a bad idea. Of course, he hadn't mentioned to Paul that he'd connected with Mara in Starlight. That news was none of the other man's business.

The question plaguing Parker after their meeting had more to do with how he was going to make it work long term with her.

He blew out a breath as Rudy led him into the inner office. Who was he kidding acting like he had no interest in small-town law? He'd entertain anything that would put him closer to Mara. He only hoped she felt the same.

"I was surprised to get your call," Rudy told him, taking a seat behind the enormous cherry desk.

Parker frowned. "Nick and Finn told me you wanted to talk to me."

"Oh, I did. I do." Rudy scratched two fingers against his meaty cheek. "But I'm still surprised."

"Me, too," Parker admitted before thinking about what he was saying.

Rudy let out another laugh. "You hightailed it out of here so fast, I thought you'd never return."

"Josh needed me."

"He's always needed you," Rudy said quietly. "I imagine it goes both ways."

Parker bristled at the notion he needed anyone but the older man didn't seem to notice.

"Your dad did a real number on both his boys."

"I'm fine," Parker said through gritted teeth. "I never let him get to me."

Rudy held up a hand, as if waving away the denial. "No boy—or girl for that matter—has the kind of father you did and gets out of it unscathed."

"What do you know about the kind of man Mac Johnson was?"

"More than you think."

"Everyone in this town loved him." Parker sat forward. "He was a favorite son."

"Not to me." Rudy shook his head. "I *knew* your father."

Parker's heart started a swift flutter in his chest. "Why you and no one else?"

"He was a good actor, and your mother helped him maintain the mask. I've heard she's doing well now."

"She's happy."

"She deserves that. You all do." Rudy shuffled a stack of files then pulled out a single piece of paper. "My wife says I have to retire."

"You need to listen to her. From what I've been told, a happy wife equals a happy life." Parker reached up and adjusted the knot of his tie. He'd gotten too accustomed to not wearing a suit in his hometown. "You're not the only attorney practicing in town anymore. Why not let someone who's established take over your clients?"

Rudy chuckled. "Because none of them are good enough."

"How do you know I am?"

"I've followed your career. You're a great attorney, but I have a feeling you need something more." He pushed the piece of paper across the desk. "I also know this is your home."

"I wasn't planning on moving back here."

"Yet you called."

Parker blew out a breath. "I did." He picked up the paper and read through the generous-to-Parker buyout plan. "I'm not promising you anything at this point. It's a big decision, and there are a lot of factors that will go into making it."

"Like Mara Reed?"

"What do you know about Mara and me? No one knows about the two of us."

"Your brother does."

"Did Josh tell you?"

"Not exactly," Rudy admitted with a Cheshire-cat smile. "But he dropped a few hints you might be willing to consider a change based on the state of your personal life. You belong here, Parker. This isn't your father's town anymore. You can make it your own."

"I've got a good life in Seattle." Parker wasn't sure who he was trying to convince with the words.

"You'll have a better one in Starlight."

Parker folded the paper and stood. "Give me a couple of days." He had no idea if he could truly handle the move to Starlight and part of him still held out hope he could convince Mara to come to Seattle.

He and Rudy shook hands, and he left the office more confused than ever. He wanted to go straight to Mara and talk to her about how he was feeling but instead walked the streets of his hometown.

A lot had changed over the years for him, but the quaint neighborhood surrounding downtown remained same as he remembered. Large oak trees canopied the street, the leaves a kaleidoscope of autumn colors that contrasted with the still-green lawns. He turned down Silver Oak Circle, a street he'd avoided since his return. There at the end of the cul-de-sac was the house he'd grown up in.

His father had kept the lawn and landscape meticulous, believing the outer appearance of their home would hide what was going on behind closed doors.

For the most part, it had. The house, with its two-story red brick facade, was stately and classic, not offering a clue to the past Parker wanted to forget. But he'd never been able to appreciate the simple beauty of it. It had felt like a prison to him, and he'd escaped as soon as he could. Someone had hung a wooden swing from one of the branches of the tree out front. A few low rosebushes had been planted along the porch and a neat row of ornamental grasses lined the front walk.

As he stood there, a gate slammed shut and moments later two boys came around the side of the house. "He's right behind us," one of them shouted as they ran across the grass.

Parker took an instinctive step forward. He'd learned running from his father only made things worse in the long term. Both boys crouched down on the far edge of the house, out of sight from where they'd come.

He was about to call out when another boy appeared, carrying an oversized Nerf gun. "Come out, you scaredy-cat poop heads," he called. "Maybe I'll show some mercy on you." The kid looked up and met Parker's gaze, his eyes going wide with alarm.

"Brendan, Joey," he yelled, his tone suddenly concerned. "Come on. Mom wants us to help her in the garden." He continued to watch Parker, his expression wary. "She's right around back. She can hear me if I yell."

Parker gave what he hoped was a reassuring wave to the boy and turned back the way he'd come. Freaking out young children wasn't his intention but he seemed to have managed it anyway. Although the boy in the yard couldn't have been half as overwrought as Parker. He didn't realize how erratic his breathing had become until he was around the corner from the old house.

He mopped his sweaty brown with the sleeve of his shirt. It was stupid to react back there, ridiculous to believe that the family who lived in the home now could ever be as dysfunctional as his.

Understanding his panic was irrational and stopping it from happening were two different things.

Maybe Rudy Marshall had the right idea. Parker's dislike of Starlight had nothing to do with the town itself and everything to do with his childhood memories. It was time to make new ones, and he hoped with all his heart that those would involve Mara.

## Chapter Thirteen

"I can't believe I was that much of a fool," Mara said as she and Brynn worked together at the mill later that afternoon.

She'd decided on a color scheme of pale gray and robin's-egg blue for the common space and had been able to secure donations from a couple of local stores of rugs and artwork to make the main room look cozier. She'd also spent several evenings folding origami cranes that would hang from the ceiling, greeting patrons as they entered.

"He does have to honor attorney-client privilege," Brynn said, crouching down to straighten a wool rug.

"What if our whole relationship has been a ploy to gather information on me to give to Paul?"

"Why would he do that?" Brynn frowned. "And what do you mean by relationship? I thought this was just a fling."

"Well, yes. That's how it started."

"I think the bird is dead," Brynn said stepping forward. "Why don't you hand it over?"

Mara looked down and gasped at the mutilated paper crane crumpled in her fist. "I'm so sorry."

"We'll give it a proper burial." Brynn winked. "Maybe you should let me hang the rest of them. I don't want an entire flock of cranes to be massacred."

"I'd never do that." Mara squeezed shut her eyes and blurted, "I'm in love with Parker."

"You don't say?" Brynn asked gently. "What a shock. Here I was so confident you'd be able to resist Parker's devastating looks and charm."

"You're making fun of me."

"Never."

"I'm a fool," Mara repeated.

"Give yourself a break."

"I can't afford to. Not with a daughter to raise on my own. What kind of role model am I for her?"

"You're a woman who carved a new life out of your wreck of an old one. You put your daughter first and you're making things work, not matter what." Brynn placed her hand over Mara's, the touch surprisingly comforting. Mara wasn't used to wanting or needing support, but she somehow knew Brynn wouldn't judge her.

"It's hard being a single mom."

"Preaching to the choir." Brynn laughed softly. "But it's okay to want your own happiness along with hers. If Parker gives that to you—"

"He can't be on my side and still represent my ex-husband or men who want to shirk their responsibilities. I thought he understood."

"Are you sure that's what your ex is trying to do?"

Mara bit down on her lip, the conversation with Aimee replaying in her mind. "His current wife told me he's stayed away from Evie because it's what I wanted."

"Is it?"

"No," Mara answered immediately then shook her head. "I don't know. It makes me feel like a horrible person, but the truth is it's simpler for me without Paul being involved. It's selfish and I have to reach out to him, but I'm so worried he's going to take Evie. He has so much more to offer her."

"What could he have that's more powerful than unconditional love?"

Mara rolled her eyes and then started up the ladder she was using to reach the origami installations. "A beautiful house and a boat to take out on the weekends. Lots of money and a membership to a country club with an Olympic-size indoor pool. Endless shopping trips and vacations to sunny beaches." She threw up her hands. "Disney World."

"Tyler has always wanted to go to Disney World,"

Brynn said with a nod. "Daniel told me it was too much and we'd spoil him."

"Paul will spoil Evie."

"You don't know that."

"She'll want to live with him and not me." Mara clapped a hand over her mouth when the last word came out on a strangled sob. "What if she chooses him over me?"

"She won't. Evie loves you. You're her mother."

Mara gave a shaky nod. "I have to call him. No matter how much it scares me, if he wants to be a part of her life, I need to facilitate it."

"Are you going to talk to your ex about his current marriage?" Brynn scrunched up her nose. "That's a lot to ask."

"I know," Mara agreed. "Despite everything, I liked Aimee, and she really loves Paul."

"So much that she entered into a relationship with him while he was still married to you."

"It's difficult to explain, but I don't blame her." Mara climbed off the ladder. "I can see now that I married Paul for the wrong reasons. He was secure and successful, and I thought I needed that because I didn't believe in myself. I tried to fit into a life that was wrong for me. We were wrong for each other. If it hadn't been Aimee, it would have been someone else. Someone who would be a stepmother to my daughter whether I like it or not."

"So she's potentially the best of the worst?" Brynn chuckled. "What a ringing endorsement."

"You know what I mean."

"What are you going to do about Parker?" Brynn asked, glancing toward the open door at the far end of the building as the sound of a truck pulling into the parking lot drifted toward them.

"I didn't expect to feel this way," Mara admitted.

"But you do."

Mara nodded. "Aimee seemed to think Parker was the one encouraging Paul to give up on their marriage."

"He's a divorce attorney." Brynn shrugged. "Happy marriages aren't exactly good for his business."

"I know, but this is different. It's personal. I thought he understood what the divorce did to me. He knows Paul lied and I can't believe he'd support him in hurting another woman the way he hurt me. I won't have someone like that in my life. Never again."

Brynn came over and gave her a quick hug. It felt strange because Mara wasn't used to that kind of easy affection with friends. But she thought she'd like to become accustomed to it.

"Enough about me," she said when Brynn pulled away. "How's the dating app situation?" She and Kaitlin had finally convinced Brynn to put up an online profile. They'd spent an evening laughing as they reviewed dating websites to find the one they believed would be the right fit for the sweet and sassy single mom.

Brynn lifted her shoulders then let them drop again. "I haven't had the nerve to log on," she admitted. "In fact, I'm probably going to delete my information. I have no business dating with a son who needs my full attention."

"Then you think I shouldn't date because of Evie?"

"It's not the same thing. You got divorced. My husband died, and the trauma of that is too much."

"At least Tyler knows his father loved him. Evie has to deal with the fact that her dad lives an hour away but chooses not to see her." She sighed. "Here we go again, comparing crappy situations. I need to call Paul and figure out how to fix this for her."

"But first you need to talk to Parker."

Mara forced herself to nod. "Adulting is hard."

"Which is why we have chocolate," Brynn told her.

"And friends." She gave Brynn another hug. "Friends and chocolate will see us through."

Mara opened the door to her aunt's house the following evening, her heart screaming in protest at the sexy half smile Parker flashed.

"I missed you," he said without preamble.

"You have a funny way of showing it." She shifted so she filled the doorway, not ready to invite him back into her home. Her brain hadn't found a way to reconcile the knowledge of his meeting with her ex-husband. She'd spent the past three nights tossing and turning as she scrutinized their time together from the lens of what she could only consider a betrayal on his part.

It would be easier if she'd found a way to dull her reaction to him in the few short days he'd been gone. Tonight he wore a faded blue-checked flannel shirt, jeans and rugged boots. His hair looked windblown and a dusting of stubble covered his strong jaw. He leaned in as if to kiss her and she caught the subtle scent of sandalwood mixed with laundry soap. She gave a slight shake of her head even as her body wanted to plaster itself against him.

He frowned and straightened. "Did I miss something?" The words were spoken softly but his deep tone made her skin tingle.

Stupid skin.

"Not one call or text," she answered.

"I didn't think… I was only gone for a few days." He ran a hand through his hair. "I'm sorry. Things were crazy in Seattle and then at the mill when I got back. Finishing touches before next week."

"I'm aware of what's going on with the mill."

"Parker?"

Mara turned to find Evie making her way down the steps, the favorite stuffed bear tucked under one arm.

"Hey, girl," he said. "How was practice earlier?"

"You missed it," Evie told him. Mara took a step toward her daughter.

"Honey, I thought you were asleep."

"I wokie up." Evie rubbed at her eyes. "Then I heard you talking."

"Parker just stopped by for a second, but now he's leaving."

"Not quite yet," he said from directly behind her.

She gritted her teeth as he closed the front door.

"I dribbled real good," Evie reported shyly. "All the way down the field. Past Caroline even."

"'Atta girl." He reached out and smoothed a strand of damp hair away from Evie's face. The girl must have been out cold. His presence felt far too right in the quiet foyer. Mara thought she might break a molar with how tightly her jaw was clenched.

"Little girls need sleep." Mara pressed a kiss to her daughter's forehead. "I'll take you back upstairs."

"And Parker?" Evie asked with a yawn. She stretched out her arms, and he immediately lifted her into his before Mara could protest.

She tamped down a swell of emotion as she led the way to Evie's bedroom. She tried not to think of the last time Parker had followed her up these stairs. Her raw throat was why she shouldn't have gotten involved with Parker in the first place. Not to mention the dull ache in her heart.

He was counseling her ex-husband on another divorce. Although Mara had no reason to offer sympathy to the woman who'd been her husband's mistress before she became his wife. But something told Mara that Paul was the love of Aimee's life in a way he'd never been for Mara.

Because he wasn't Parker.

Would she ever learn to stop being such a fool for love?

Evie's eyes drifted closed as soon as Mara tucked the covers around her.

"She's precious," Parker said, so close she felt his breath on her ear.

Without responding, Mara turned and headed back downstairs.

"It's late," she said as her feet touched the colorful rug that covered the entry floor. "We can do this tomorrow."

"What is it we're doing, Mara?" Parker placed a hand on her arm and spun her until she faced him. "I'm really sorry I messed up on the communication thing. My schedule was packed in Seattle and there were some things I had to work out. But now—"

"Did you meet with Paul?" she asked, proud her voice didn't waiver.

Parker's expression didn't change but by the pale pink tinging his cheeks, she knew he understood the gravity of her question.

"Paul is my client," he said as an answer. "That isn't new information."

Her thoughts tumbled around upon themselves as

if they were a piece of fluff being blown by a strong wind. "Aimee Reed came to see me. She's afraid he's going to divorce her."

His eyes darkened. "You know I can't discuss this with you. If I'd known…"

"Don't lie to me," she said through clenched teeth. "At least have a little respect."

"I respect you. That was never a question."

"It was to me," she told him, swiping at her cheeks. Darn it. She didn't want to cry. "I shared so much." The vulnerability she'd shown him swelled inside her, but instead of the sweet sense of security she'd had before, now it was all sour and pathetic. Once again, Mara felt pathetic. "I told you everything, and now you can use my weakness against a woman who truly loves him."

His mouth tightened into a thin line. "Do you believe I'd do that?"

She wanted to deny it but the sliver of doubt that had niggled at the back of her mind since the conversation with Aimee suddenly consumed her. "This was never meant to last," she answered instead, needing to believe if she cut ties before he had a chance to that she'd recover more easily from the heartbreak.

"Mara."

"We both know it." She drew in a shuddery breath. "My life is here." She turned toward the small table that sat to one side of the foyer and picked up a stack of papers. "I'm looking for apartments to rent. It's time for Evie and me to make our own way. Starlight is our home and I need to put her first. What I might want and what she needs are two different things."

He gave a hard laugh. "Meaning me?"

"I don't want you," she said without hesitation. "I couldn't want a man who would..." Despite her certainty that this was the right path, she couldn't force her mouth to speak out loud what duplicity had cost her. "I had an itch." She shrugged. "You scratched it and I appreciate that. We had our bit of fun, Parker. It's over. I don't know what you told Paul about me, and it doesn't matter anyway."

They stared at each other for several long moments. She wanted him to argue. Expected him to refute the accusation. The stupid, in-love part of her hoped he'd tell her this had all been a misunderstanding—like waking from a bad dream—and things could go back to normal.

But until a few weeks ago, alone had been her normal. Of course she'd return there.

She searched his eyes for some sign he felt the same pain she did. Misery loved company and all that. It felt as though she was looking at a stranger. His blue gaze gave away nothing. He looked at her as if she were nothing.

"Say something," she demanded when she could take the gaping silence no longer.

"You've said enough for both us," he answered.

"I'm the bad guy. This is how it was always meant to be."

His breath hitched and for one brief second, the raw pain so reflected in his eyes stole her breath. Was it possible she'd made a terrible mistake? Could she have succumbed to her own doubts and fears on impulse without knowing his side of the story? Because there were always two sides. She knew that.

"Parker?" She breathed his name on a tentative burst of air.

He waved her away. "You did me a favor," he said, his voice like polished marble. "Saved me the trouble of letting you down easy."

"This isn't easy."

"It is for me," he countered. "Goodbye, Mara."

And without another word, he walked out of the house, the door softly shutting behind him.

"You can't leave now."

Parker didn't bother to look up at his brother as he zipped the duffel bag in the guest room of Josh's house.

"You'll be fine, Josh," he said, opening the nightstand drawer to make sure he hadn't forgotten anything. His heart stuttered as he noticed a crayon drawing Evie had given him. It showed the two of them on a grassy field with a soccer ball between them.

He started to push closed the drawer again but

then grabbed the picture and stuffed it into his bag. He'd throw it away back in Seattle.

"We're in this together," Josh argued, taking a step closer.

Parker finally met his brother's frustrated gaze and shook his head. "I've done my part. Construction is almost finished. You have retailers moving in next week, and with the additional revenue from the craft fair, there will be no problem making your loan payment this month."

"That's not the point."

"It was always the point." Parker forced a smile. "You knew this was a temporary arrangement."

"I also know you've been happier in Starlight than at any time I've seen you in the past. This is your home."

"Nope." He looped the duffel bag strap over his shoulder. The rest of his luggage had already been loaded in the Audi. "I'm happy I was able to help." He swallowed. "I'm glad I got to spend time with you and Anna."

"What about Mara?" Josh's eyes narrowed. "You have feelings for her."

"I have feelings about sleeping with her." Parker made sure to put just the right amount of "entitled jerk" into his tone. "But like everything else around here, she's a little too small-town for my taste. I mean, you're welcome to her if you don't mind sloppy—"

Josh shoved him hard. "Are you looking for a fight, Parker? Will that make you feel better? You want to work off some of your temper the same way Dad used to?"

"Don't ever compare me to him." Parker's fists clenched at his sides. He'd certainly likened himself to his father enough through the years, but hearing it from Josh cut him to the core.

"I'm sorry," Josh offered immediately. "I didn't mean it. You know that."

"Yeah. I know."

"Anna's going to miss you. The whole soccer team will miss you."

Parker couldn't help his smile. "You can handle cat-herding duty without me. But I want to see you and Anna more often. Come into the city or I'll meet you."

"But not in Starlight?"

Mara's face flashed across Parker's mind and he rubbed a hand against his chest, trying to relieve the corresponding ache. "I need a break from Starlight."

Josh studied him then nodded. They walked to the front door in silence.

"Are you sure you won't come back for the opening?" Josh asked when Parker had stepped onto the front porch. "The success of Dennison Lumber is as much yours as it is mine."

"I don't need any credit." Parker did his best to flash a smile. "It really was good to be involved.

As crazy as it sounds, I think Dad would have been proud."

Josh muttered a curse. "What does it say about me that he's been gone over a decade and I'm still chasing his approval?"

"It says you're human." Parker thought about Paul Reed and the demons that plagued him. He hoped his former client would man up and take an active role in his daughter's life. Evie deserved the best. Mara did too and he felt like the biggest fool on the planet for thinking he was worthy of a future with her. He should have known it was too good to be true. He'd done too much damage to be able to repair it.

Of course she didn't understand the truth of his meeting with Paul, but she believed the worst of him. Sooner or later he'd prove her right. He might not have his father's penchant for violence, but Parker wasn't going to take a chance on hurting a woman he loved.

He'd rather absorb the pain on his own.

He said goodbye to Josh with a promise to meet for dinner so he could hear how things went at the Founder's Day celebration.

As his headlights illuminated the two-lane highway leading out of town, Parker ignored the emptiness that lingered on the edges of the dark road. He had to keep his eyes straight ahead. Moving forward was his only choice.

## Chapter Fourteen

Saturday morning brought gray skies and the threat of rain. Mara secretly hoped the weather might warrant canceling Evie's soccer game. She'd spent yesterday camouflaging her emotions, first at Main Street Perk and then at the mill. She'd fooled everyone at the coffee shop easily enough. A benefit of not being great at small talk on a good day was that the bad days didn't look much different.

Josh, on the other hand, had taken one look at her and pulled her in for a big bear hug. "Go home," he'd told her. "Watch TV and eat ice cream out of the carton or whatever it is women do when they look as awful as you."

"You need to work on your words of comfort," she said with a sad laugh. But the fact that he'd been able to make her smile meant the world. She'd convinced him that staying busy was better than wallowing in her heartbreak, and he'd actually put her to work staining the reclaimed wood that covered one wall of the building's renovated bathroom.

Most of her contributions had been in the area of design or decor, so she'd actually enjoyed the opportunity to pitch in that way. The entire site was taking shape the way she planned, and she felt gratified at how well her vision worked for the project.

A day immersing herself in work had been just what she'd needed, and she'd fallen asleep in Evie's bed, waking only when the first light of dawn slipped between the gaps in the curtains covering the windows.

Which meant she'd been awake for hours with nothing to do but think. Even baking a batch of chocolate-chip cookies for the team hadn't taken her mind off Parker. The quiet kitchen only intensified the voices in her head, the ones that accused her of giving up on him without a fight.

Mara had fought for her doomed marriage, but she'd still been left alone in the end. She had to believe she'd done the right thing in breaking up with Parker. The thought of him counseling her ex-husband made her stomach churn with both anger and disbelief.

She wished the anger could stifle the stabbing ache in her heart but knew only time would heal that wound.

She hoped.

"Now I remember why I never liked soccer," Brynn said with a sigh.

Mara gave her a gentle nudge. "What's wrong with soccer?"

"The weather," Brynn answered, resting her head against Mara's shoulder. "Outdoor sports should be allowed only in the loveliest weather."

"Good luck with that in Washington."

"Exactly," Brynn agreed with a shiver. "How are you doing?"

"Fine."

"Liar."

"Evie misses Coach Parker." Mara pointed toward her daughter, who stood on the far side of the field, arms folded tightly across her chest. The girl looked miserable.

"Is she cold?" Brynn asked.

Mara shook her head then shifted to glance at the parents huddled a few feet away. "There's another dad helping coach since Parker returned to Seattle. Kind of intense. He yelled at Evie."

Brynn let out a strangled snort. "Oh, no, he didn't."

"It's okay, Mama Bear." Mara patted the top of Brynn's head. "Evie might be shy, but she's also discovered quite the mulish streak. The assistant dad also yelled at the girl who's always bullied Evie, and my kid stuck up for both of them."

"Good for her."

"Yeah. Josh missed the whole interaction, and he put Evie in on defense. So far, she's let three balls roll by without moving."

"A peaceful protest. She's a nonconformist at age five. I love it."

"I doubt the other parents feel the same. She might get kicked off the team."

"Josh won't let that happen," Brynn promised. "He's a stand-up guy."

"Unlike his brother?"

"I'm sorry you're hurting," Brynn said with another shoulder squeeze. "But I can't believe Parker used you. I don't want to sound naive. It's simply not the guy I know."

"Me neither." Mara sighed. "I'm worried I didn't *really* know him. What if I was too distracted by the chemistry and easing the loneliness of single parenting?"

"It's so darn lonely." Brynn's voice sounded wistful.

"Evie's hurting, and it's my fault. I essentially cut her father from her life and now I've let her get close to a man I knew wasn't in it for the long haul."

Brynn stepped away then turned to face Mara. "Did you actually know that?"

Mara shook her head. "I'm too confused to know anything at this point. Other than I have to do what's right for my daughter."

"Okay." Brynn nodded, almost more to herself than Mara. "First things first. You need to talk to your ex."

"I called his office and made an appointment to meet with him next week. If he wants to be a real dad to Evie, I'm going to help him."

"You also need to figure out what's going on with him and his new wife." Brynn leaned in. "And with Parker. Attorney-client privilege only goes one way. Your ex can tell you what happened at that meeting."

"I'm not sure I want to know."

"Ask anyway."

Mara sniffed. "Are you this brave in your own life?"

"Heck, no." Brynn flashed a cheeky grin. "But I did respond to one of my online matches last night. We're meeting for coffee next week."

"Nice. I want to hear…" Mara gasped, her lungs constricting, as Evie suddenly ran at a girl from the other team with high pigtails dribbling the ball toward the goal. She'd never seen her daughter move so quickly, and definitely not on the soccer field.

Looking not at all like herself, Evie stole the ball and began to run down the field. The pink tip of her tongue poked out from between her lips as she concentrated on her ball handling. Maybe Parker had missed his calling as a youth soccer coach because Mara barely recognized her daughter.

She could hear the players and parents cheering through the ringing in her ears, but all her attention remained on Evie. When she got close to the opposing goal, the girl planted her feet for an instant then ran at the ball, sending it sailing into the air. It hit one of the goalposts and Mara cringed, her heart in her throat. But instead of bouncing away, the ball dropped into the goal.

Evie had scored.

Brynn shouted and hugged Mara. "She *is* the second coming of Messi."

As Evie's teammates surrounded her, Mara met Josh's gaze across the field. Grinning, he held up his hands as if to ask how that goal had just happened.

She shook her head as she returned his smile.

A few of the parents congratulated her. Despite the still-intense pain over losing Parker and her fears with regard to talking to Paul, Mara's heart felt full.

At the end of the game, she hugged her daughter, crouching down so she and Evie were at eye level. "That was an amazing goal."

Evie nodded, glancing over her shoulder. "I'm going to hang out with my friends," she said, pointing to where the rest of the team stood together, enjoying cake pops one of the parents had brought for an end-of-game celebration.

"Sure," Mara said, chest squeezing. "I'll be here with the other mommies and daddies."

"Can we call Parker later?" Evie asked, wiping a hand across her forehead. "I want to tell him 'bout scoring."

Mara's lungs felt like they'd been flattened by a semi. "We'll see." She smiled and ruffled Evie's hair. "Go get your cake pop, girl."

"'Kay. Love you, Mommy."

"Love you, too, Evie-Stevie."

Mara curled her hands into fists, welcoming the pain of her nails digging into her palms. Her daughter wanted to call Parker. How were either of them going to let him go?

Parker sat behind his desk the following Tuesday, frustrated beyond belief at how much trouble he was having reacclimatizing to his regular routine.

It was as if he'd been on some stellar once-in-a-lifetime vacation for the past few weeks instead of scrambling to renovate an old lumber mill in a town he'd left in his rearview mirror a decade earlier.

But he couldn't seem to shake the feeling that his normal life no longer fit the man he was…or more important, the man he wanted to be. Sunshine and blue skies had met him in Seattle, a few more weeks of fall before the winter gray permeated everything. For Parker, the landscape paled in comparison to Starlight, although he understood that had more to

do with the depth of his emotional ties than anything else.

He glanced up when someone knocked on his
door. Josh stepped into the office.

Parker immediately strode forward and wrapped
his brother in a huge hug. "Man, this is a surprise.
Good to see you. How are things? How's Anna? Does
she miss me?"

Josh's eyes widened with shock as Parker pulled
away. "Um…you know it's been less than a week
since you left?"

"Yeah." Heat flooded Parker's cheeks. He was
acting like an idiot, greeting his brother as if they'd
been separated for years. It felt like a lifetime ago
that he'd driven out of his hometown. Since returning to Seattle, he hadn't slept more than a few hours
a night and he had trouble focusing on anything.

"She misses you," Josh said gently.

Parker cleared his throat. "Bring her into the city.
We can show her the pier and go to the aquarium.
I've heard it's—"

"I was talking about Mara."

"Don't go there," Parker said. "You know there's
no chance for us."

"Never say never." Josh smiled but it didn't reach
his eyes. "Lucky for you, I have my own woman
trouble to deal with at the moment. You're off the
hook for now."

"Are you dating someone?" As far as Parker knew,

his brother hadn't been with a woman, even casually, since the divorce.

"Jenn called yesterday. She wants to see Anna."

Parker cursed under his breath.

"My thoughts exactly."

"Sit down." Parker walked behind his desk again and slid into the chair. Damn. He could feel the tension radiating from his brother. He'd been so happy to see Josh, he'd missed it at first. He'd missed so much.

"Of course I want Anna to see her mom." Josh grabbed at his head with both hands, leaving his hair standing on end like Parker remembered from when they'd been boys. "Everything happened so fast when she left. I was dealing with the cancer treatments and then the bills, so I didn't exactly process any feelings around my marriage. There wasn't time. I had to keep moving..."

"Moving forward," Parker murmured, as he'd told himself on the drive out of Starlight.

"Yes," Josh breathed.

"Do you still love her?" Parker felt compelled to ask. Once again, he realized he'd failed his brother. Almost a month living under the same roof, and they hadn't talked about the details of Jenn leaving or how Josh felt about it now. Divorce was business for Parker, but if Mara had taught him one thing, it was that the emotional toll of ending a marriage left way worse scars than any financial ramifications.

Much like it had been with their father.

"Not in the way a husband loves a wife," Josh admitted. "Although I'm not angry, either. I'm..." He shook his head. "Empty." The word sounded wrong coming from Josh. His brother had the biggest capacity for love Parker had ever seen.

"You're not empty. I've seen you with Anna. Hell, with the soccer team. You connect with every subcontractor that works at the mill. You aren't empty." Parker took a breath. "If you're empty, I must be a cavernous void of emotion."

Josh laughed. "Only a little."

"What do you want to see happen with Jenn?" Parker asked after a moment.

"In the divorce we agreed—"

"I don't care what came before. Tell me what you want, and I'll make it happen. No offense to my former sister-in-law, but I'll cut her off at the knees if that's what it takes to protect you."

"Stop."

"I'm serious."

Josh sighed. "I know, and I appreciate it. Remember what we talked about before you left? You don't have to be some merciless tyrant. That's not why you became a family law attorney."

"Divorce attorney," Parker corrected.

"Don't pretend like you weren't changed by your time in Starlight. By Mara."

"I'm not discussing her." Just hearing her name

made Parker's pulse quicken. "If you want help with your ex-wife…in any capacity… I'm here for you. But nothing about my life is going to change."

"I do want help with Jenn." Josh laughed without humor. "Not cutting her off at the knees, but I have a tendency to roll over when faced with conflict. I never learned how to manage it with Dad, but now I can't stop myself."

A tight ball of regret formed in Parker's throat. "If you need me to be strong for you…"

"I need you to teach me to be strong for myself and for Anna."

"We can manage that," Parker promised.

Josh's shoulders sagged and when he smiled, it finally reached his eyes. "You help me and I'll teach you how to be vulnerable."

Parker barked out a laugh. "No thanks. Full up on vulnerable over here."

"You haven't even scratched the surface."

"Which is just how I like it."

"You don't like being alone," Josh said quietly. "You don't like living without Mara."

Parker should have argued but why bother? He wasn't going to fool his brother.

"Let's figure you out first," he answered instead. "Then we'll worry about me."

## Chapter Fifteen

The next morning, Mara pressed her fingers to the picture window in the lobby of her ex-husband's company headquarters. From this vantage point, she had an unobstructed view of the Space Needle, Elliott Bay and the Cascade Mountains to the east. Little did she realize when this had been her workplace that one day she'd leave it behind and make her home in the picturesque valley.

She remembered the first time she'd walked into the expansive space on the thirty-fifth floor of the tallest high-rise building in downtown Seattle. She'd been both overwhelmed and slightly awestruck, willing to do anything to prove she could make it in the real world.

Now she could laugh at her younger self. If that girl had known how real things would get…

"Mara."

Paul looked the same as she remembered. Her ex-husband was just shy of six feet tall with a lean build he highlighted by favoring expensively tailored suits. His hair remained dark brown with a few slashes of gray near his temples, giving him an air of maturity that wasn't always reflected in his behavior.

To her surprise, she had no immediate physical reaction to seeing him. The anger, hurt and bitterness that had been her bosom companions for so long didn't make an inkling of an appearance. Instead, a sense of peace seeped into the very fiber of her being. This man had no power over her, and the pain he'd caused was part of her past.

She was smarter now, stronger too. Maybe not all the time or in every situation—Parker's face drifted into her mind and she forced it away. For Evie and for herself, Mara would stay in control.

"Thanks for agreeing to meet with me," she said, offering a small smile.

Paul blinked, as if surprised by her amicable tone. "I'm glad you called."

The young assistant who stood a few paces behind him, a woman Mara didn't recognize, cleared her throat. "Do you need anything, Mr. Reed?"

Paul kept his gaze on Mara. "Coffee?" he asked. "You used to take it with too much sugar."

She wanted to laugh at the censure inherent in his comment. During their marriage, that kind of veiled criticism would have sent her into a tailspin of self-incrimination.

"Sugar doesn't do it for me anymore," she said then met the beleaguered gaze of his assistant. "Nothing for me. Thank you."

The woman nodded and scurried away.

"Let's talk in my office," Paul said.

Mara followed him down the hall, aware of the stares she received. She kept her eyes trained on her ex-husband, not wanting to reconnect with anyone from her former life. She might be making peace with her past, but she was still aware the coworkers she'd thought were her friends had turned their backs on her during the divorce.

They entered the large corner office and Paul immediately went to stand behind his antique cherry desk, the one Mara had found online and had shipped from Chicago when she'd redone his office.

"You didn't change anything," she murmured, turning in a circle to survey the room.

"I like my office," he answered simply.

"Me, too," she agreed. She'd spent months working on the design and choosing the decor. It had been one of her first big assignments within the company and marked the beginning of her romantic involvement with Paul. In hindsight, she realized he hadn't needed his office space redecorated but had used it as a reason to spend time with her. His intention hadn't mattered, though, because she'd loved what she created.

"I'm assuming the purpose of this meeting isn't to reminisce about your undeniable talent for design?"

"No," she answered, taking a slow step toward the desk. "Although I'm intrigued by your description of me. That's quite a change from what I remember in the courtroom."

"We were at war." Paul lowered himself into the chair. "Now we aren't."

Could it truly be that uncomplicated? He'd gone after her because it was what people did in a divorce, and now time and perspective had softened him.

Paul was not a man who could normally be described as soft. From the hard angles of his tanned face to his unwavering need for success in business, his focus was laser sharp and legendary. He'd focused on destroying her and had nearly succeeded. But now...there was something in his features, a gentling she wouldn't have noticed if she didn't know him so well.

"You really love her." Mara dropped into the chair across from the desk, her knees weak.

"Evie? Of course I do, Mara. She's my daughter. I may not have been—"

"Aimee," she clarified. "Your wife. You love your wife."

A muscle ticked in his jaw. "I'm not discussing my marriage with you."

"She came to see me."

"Why?" he breathed.

Mara wasn't sure how much to reveal. Aimee had asked her to intervene, but the other woman's pregnancy seemed too private to mention if Paul didn't already know. "She loves you, too. Very much." Mara flashed a sad smile. "She's afraid you're going to do to her what you did to me."

Silence stretched between them, punctuated by the rhythmic tapping of his gold pen on the desk pad.

"It's different," he said finally. "I'm different."

Maybe Mara should have been hurt by the words. It would have been easier to process if he were to treat his current wife with the same callousness he'd shown Mara. But she didn't want that for Aimee or for Paul. If Evie were to have a relationship with her father, Mara wanted him to be happy. She wanted anything that would benefit her daughter.

"Have you told her?" Mara leaned forward. "She knows you met with your divorce attorney."

"Parker?" Paul sniffed. "So what? My business meetings have nothing to do with—"

"You love her," Mara interrupted, in no mood to entertain Paul's blustering. "I didn't ask for Aimee to come to me, but she did. Talking to the man who facilitated the failure of your previous marriages doesn't give a wife a ton of confidence in your commitment to her."

"Those failures were on me, not Parker." His gaze dropped to the desk. "I failed you most of all. I failed our daughter."

"It's not too late."

He jerked up his head. "For you and Evie," she quickly clarified, swallowing back a burst of hysterical laughter. "I'm not looking to reconcile. Despite your best efforts to ruin it, I believe your marriage to Aimee is strong. I'm glad she makes you happy, Paul."

"Are you happy?"

Mara's chest tightened. "I'm working on it. Evie makes me happy. She's amazing."

"I'm sorry for what I've done to her. I did talk to Parker, and he wasn't as compassionate as you in telling me that I'm acting like an insufferable tool."

Mara felt her mouth drop open. Parker had said that to Paul? It didn't make sense. When she'd accused him of supporting her ex's bad behavior, he hadn't denied it. He hadn't put up any sort of fight. She schooled her features, not wanting Paul to see how much this affected her. "Another surprising description, especially coming from a man you pay."

"He's spent some time away from the office, and it seems to have given him a new perspective." Paul paused, his eyes narrowing. "You're living in Starlight now?"

Mara nodded.

"That's where he's from, too. It's a small town. Surely your paths have crossed."

"Evie's best friend is Parker's niece," she said, going with the simplest explanation.

Paul seemed to accept it without question so maybe Mara was a better actor than she thought.

"I imagine you hate him as much as you do me."

"I don't hate you." Her mind reeled. She'd been so hurt by Parker's perceived betrayal but now realized she was to blame for destroying what had been growing between them. Mistrust and fear had made her react without thinking, and she could only imagine how her accusations cut him to the quick. Maybe she'd misunderstood what Paul had told her. "But just to be clear..." She cleared her throat. "Your divorce attorney was the one to counsel you not to walk away from your marriage?"

"I had the same reaction," Paul said with a chuckle. "Especially given how Parker had handled my other situations."

"Situations," Mara muttered. She was a situation.

"I guess the best divorce attorneys," he continued as if she hadn't spoken, "know when to advocate for successful marriages, as well. My crappy childhood and the fears I have around being a father don't excuse how I treated you and Evie. I can choose to be better. I see that now. Parker really helped talk me off the ledge."

"He did?"

Paul nodded, warming to the topic. If nothing else, her ex-husband had always enjoyed hearing himself speak. "He had a rough childhood, too. I didn't realize until he shared some of the details." He waved a hand. "Not that you care about him, but turns out he had a lot of wisdom to share with me. He didn't mention meeting Evie, but he talked about his niece. Anna, right?"

"Yeah." Parker hadn't told Paul anything about Evie. Or her. He'd been loyal and she'd been…awful.

"I appreciate you coming here," Paul said, his voice gentling. "I'm glad Aimee came to you so you can see how wonderful she is. She'd treat Evie like her own daughter."

Mara stared until finally he registered her mounting shock, because he held up his hands. "Not that I'm looking to replace you. You're Evie's mom and…" He cursed under his breath. "I'm messing this all up and I wanted to make it right. Please, Mara. Give me a chance to make things right."

"Okay."

His mouth dropped open as if he couldn't believe what she'd just said. That made two of them.

"Do you mean it?"

"Yes." She took a deep breath, let it out along with as much fear and resentment as she could manage. "We both made our share of mistakes, but we're going to do better. For Evie. I'm not saying that it will be perfect—or that I'll be perfect. But I want to try to get along. Our daughter needs both her parents."

"He was right." Paul huffed out a laugh, leaning back in his chair and scrubbing his hands over his face.

"What do you mean?"

"Parker said you'd agree. I told him he was crazy. That after how I'd handled the divorce, you'd never willingly allow me time with Evie. Somehow he knew you'd want the best for her."

"He believed in me."

"He's a way better man than I gave him credit for." Paul laughed again. "Especially for an attorney."

Mara's heart squeezed like someone had it in a vise. She'd messed up everything with Parker, and she had no idea how to fix it. If she could fix it. Part of her wanted to give up. She had enough going on in her life. Surely her heart would eventually mend.

But the part that Parker had helped heal fought against any thought of raising the white flag on their love story. She'd learned she had more strength than she knew, and now was the time to use it.

It took another hour to work out an initial visitation schedule for Paul and Evie. As scared as Mara had been to invite her ex-husband back into their lives, now it felt normal and right. Right for her daughter, which was all that counted.

As soon as the elevator doors swished open on the ground floor of the office building, she pulled out her phone.

"Josh?" she said when her friend answered. "I've messed up badly, and I need your help to make it right."

"This day marks a new beginning, both for me and for the Dennison Lumber Mill."

At the enthusiastic applause that met the end of his brother's speech, emotions welled in Parker. He hadn't planned to come back to Starlight for the opening, but Josh and Anna had called and begged him.

It was fighting dirty to enlist a six-year-old in his plea, Parker had told Josh, but his brother remained unapologetic. "We did this together," Josh had reminded him. "I need you to help me see it through."

So Parker had made the drive early Saturday morning, grateful when the fog that enshrouded Seattle lifted as he came through the mountain pass leading to Starlight.

He hadn't seen Mara yet, although Evie and Anna had run up to him when he'd first arrived to tell him all about Evie's goal at the soccer game the previous weekend. He was so damn proud of Mara's daughter and his heart ached thinking he wouldn't be a part of those special moments in her life.

At this point, he could look back at their argument

and think of a dozen ways he could have handled the situation differently. Yes, she'd made assumptions about him but could he really blame her? He'd played a supporting role in the destruction of her life. Her experience hadn't given her much reason to trust men, and definitely not him. Maybe if he'd been honest about his feelings or fought for her.

Instead, he'd walked away, allowed his belief that he couldn't be the man she deserved to turn him into just that.

Mara needed someone who wouldn't give up on her and Evie.

This week without them had been awful, but it had also afforded Parker the space he needed to realize he wanted a second chance if she'd give him one.

He had every intention of making his case and he understood his future depended on him not messing it up. He'd get through the Founder's Day celebration first. Mara had worked too hard for him to come in and hijack this day and make it about him. He wanted to honor her, and a big piece of that was respecting her efforts.

It still killed him to make small talk with people as he snuck surreptitious glances around the mill to try to find her. As he did, he couldn't help but be impressed by the turnout and the success of their undertaking. Pride washed through him knowing he'd helped make his brother's dream a reality.

His mom had even agreed to drive over later and

check out the craft fair and the changes to the mill. He hoped it would be as cathartic for her as it felt to him. The interior of the main lumber-company building was lined with booths of varying crafters and artisans. From paintings to pottery to hand-knitted sweaters, the kaleidoscope of color amazed him. Although most of the construction had been finished before he left, the design details Mara had coordinated at the last minute added to the festive mood. There were origami cranes fluttering overhead and strands of twinkling lights strung along the perimeter of the space.

A line of patrons waited to order at Dennison Perk, which was the name they'd given to the new coffee-shop location. Disappointment lanced through him at not finding Mara behind the counter. Of course, she was on-site somewhere, and he craved just the simple pleasure of being able to see her. He'd missed her so damn much.

Finn approached from the coffee shop's counter, munching on what looked like a chocolate-chip scone. "The brothers Johnson pulled it off," he said, wiping a hand across his mouth. "This place is better than I'd even imagined."

"Me, too." Parker blew out a breath. "I still can't believe we got so much accomplished. Thanks for your help with the financials. It would have been difficult to finish without the loan extension."

Finn grinned. "I told you small-town life is exciting. How would I have the chance to make this kind of difference for people pushing paper at a big bank?"

"The chamber of commerce should put you on retainer. You're relentless."

"Starlight is your home," Finn said.

"I know," Parker agreed quietly. "I've got a few details to work out but—"

"Do those details have anything to do with a certain hazel-eyed single mom who bakes awesome pastries?"

"Yeah." Parker glanced around again but there was still no sign of Mara.

"Walk outside with me," Finn suggested, popping the last bite into his mouth. "I want to check out some of the food trucks."

"You just inhaled a scone."

"Why do lawyers have to argue about everything?" Finn nudged Parker's shoulders. "Just come with me."

Parker wanted to refuse so he could continue to search for Mara. Then he reminded himself he didn't need to rush. He had the rest of their lives to spend proving his worth to her. If she'd let him, anyway.

"You're not going to raise any money if you refuse to kiss the customers." Sam Sheehan's voice was loud enough that several people turned to stare at Mara.

She gripped her stomach as another wave of panic surged through her. "I can't do this."

"Go away, Sam," Brynn said, giving the older man a not-so-gentle nudge. "We've already explained this is a private kissing booth."

"Then what is it doing in the middle of the Founder's Day Craft Fair?" Sam demanded.

Hysterical laughter threatened to escape from Mara. "He has a point," she muttered.

She still wasn't sure how she'd let Kaitlin and Brynn convince her a kissing booth was a good idea. All she'd known was that she wanted to do something huge to show Parker how sorry she was for doubting him. Now she realized she had a decent chance of being humiliated in front of most of the town. What if she'd hurt him so badly he wasn't willing to give her another chance?

Kaitlin and Brynn had put together a makeshift booth for her next to the pop-up chocolate shop in the mill's open courtyard. The plan had been to keep the kissing-booth sign covered until they spotted Parker, but a breeze had whipped up about ten minutes earlier, blowing away the strip of paper concealing it.

They'd quickly taped up another cover but not before a line of potential kissers had formed in front of her. Her friends had shooed away all but the most determined of the men—namely Sam the insurance man. Still, several clusters of locals hovered nearby, curiosity clearly swelling as to what kind of craziness was in store for the day. A small-town community loved a good weekend festival, but they loved the potential for juicy gossip even more.

"I should talk to him in private," Mara said to her friends, biting down on the inside of her cheek.

"You wanted a grand gesture," Brynn reminded her.

"I'm an idiot."

Kaitlin patted her shoulder. "A fool for love sounds more romantic."

"What if he's left already?" Mara asked, hating the catch in her voice. "Josh said he had to put Anna on the phone to finally convince him to come today."

"Then we'll think of something—" Brynn broke off with a squeak. "He's here. He's coming this way. He's—"

"Let's go." Kaitlin pushed Brynn toward the back of the booth. She grabbed the paper covering the sign and followed the other woman. "You've got this, sweetie," she called over her shoulder.

Mara recognized the exact moment Parker spotted her. His eyes widened a fraction as Finn clapped him on the back.

The crowd in front of her seemed to instinctually part when he moved toward her. One side of his mouth curved as he glanced up to the sign above her.

"It's a fund-raiser for the gym roof," she blurted then felt hot color flood her cheeks. She *sounded* like an idiot.

"You're taking this business of becoming part of the community pretty seriously, huh?"

She almost laughed. "It's nice that you came back for the opening," she said quietly, suddenly embarrassed by her plan for a grand gesture. What did she care about what anyone else thought of her attempt to make things right with Parker? He was all that mattered. "It means a lot to Josh."

"Sure," he agreed readily, studying her face. She couldn't read his expression but at least he didn't seem angry with her at the moment.

A small victory but it gave her a glimmer of hope.

He eyed the empty donation jar sitting on the red-and-white-checked tablecloth draped over the booth's narrow front counter. "Business is slow?"

"She won't let anyone kiss her," Sam shouted from behind Parker. Mara was vaguely aware of Brynn shouting for the man to shut his trap but her focus remained on Parker.

"I was waiting for you," she told him.

"Because I'm the rich, big-city attorney so you can charge extra?"

She laughed then blurted, "Because I love you."

His thick brows drew together as if her words didn't quite compute. "Love kissing me or love—"

"You." She reached up and pulled down the cardboard sign. "I do love kissing you," she said, "but this was mainly to get your attention."

"Sweetheart," he said with a soft chuckle, "You always have my full attention."

That glimmer of hope blossomed into a sparkling shower of light. "I'm sorry," she said before he had a chance to speak. "I know now you didn't betray me and I'm so sorry I didn't trust you more. I came close to broken and I'm still working to put the pieces back together again. Sometimes it feels like they don't all fit in the right way."

"You fit with me," he told her.

"I do?"

"Always," he promised then reached out and dashed away the tears that fell down her cheeks. "Don't cry. I never want to make you cry, Mara."

"Happy tears," she explained. "Not happy-ish. Bone-deep, love you with all of my heart *happy*."

He leaned in to brush a gentle kiss across her mouth. "I love you. I love you broken or totally together, happy or sad. I love you through it all, Mara. There's nothing I don't want to experience with you. I should never have walked away because my whole heart belongs to you."

She twined her arms around his neck and he deepened the kiss, her senses swirling and her heart filled with love.

They finally broke apart at the resounding cheers from the crowd. It felt as though half the town was a part of this moment, and Mara wouldn't have it any other way.

Evie ran forward and Parker swung her into his arms. "Kissing is gross," her daughter informed them, pointing to the discarded sign.

"Not when you love someone the way I love your mommy," Parker told the girl.

Evie considered that for a moment. "You can love her," she relented finally, "but it's still kinda gross."

Mara ducked under the booth's counter to wrap her arms around her daughter and Parker, knowing whatever came next, she'd found the future she always wanted with this man.

He was her forever future.

*Epilogue*

Two weeks later, Parker stood in the center of his brother's backyard, smiling as he glanced toward the giant unicorn bounce house situated in the corner. Maybe it wasn't traditional entertainment for a wedding reception, but Evie maintained that Parker and Mara's love story had started at Anna's birthday party so it was only right that they have a bounce house as part of their wedding day.

*His* wedding day.

He glanced behind him at the arbor he and Josh had built, which Mara and her friends had decorated with wildflowers earlier this morning. They'd only invited their closest friends and family to the celebration. It meant more than he could say to have his brother at his side with Finn and Nick smiling at him from the front row.

In addition to the bounce house, Evie had asked for a sundae bar along with a strawberry-flavored wedding cake. Mara's only request had been a honeymoon in Hawaii, and he'd happily booked the three of them on a first-class flight leaving tomorrow morning. Parker would have said yes to a horse-drawn carriage, a mariachi band or even a postceremony round of beer pong. He was simply so damn happy to be marrying the woman of his dreams.

There had been no question in his mind that he didn't want to wait to make Mara and Evie his official family. He'd even called Paul to explain the situation. His client—former client at this point—hadn't been thrilled with the news but he'd finally wished Parker well and given him a strangely paternalsounding warning about taking care of Mara.

It was an easy vow for Parker to make.

He'd put in motion plans to sell his practice in Seattle and was already working with Rudy Marshall to transition the older attorney's clients to Parker. Several of his colleagues in the city had expressed disbelief that Parker had so quickly changed his tune on marriage, but Parker knew he was making the right choice.

Mara meant everything to him. Who better to be a good husband than a man who appreciated the value of love and family because he understood the depth of pain on the other side?

He'd never purposely cause Mara an instant of pain and felt a soul-deep commitment to loving and supporting her no matter what came their way.

The string quartet they'd hired from the local high school went silent for several seconds and then began a hushed version of "Pachelbel's Canon in D."

Evie and Anna appeared first, arms linked as they skipped down the makeshift aisle, grinning and giggling along the way.

Parker had explained to Mara's ex-husband that he had no plans to usurp Paul's role in his daughter's life but would love Evie with his entire heart. After so many years of keeping his emotions walled off, it felt good to allow himself to love unconditionally. He'd been missing out on so damn much in life, but thanks to Mara his future was brighter than he could have imagined.

His breath caught in his throat as her gaze locked with his. She wore a cream-colored dress made of lace and satin. It had a scoop neck and long sleeves and was fitted to her curves until flaring out just below her waist. Her hair was pulled back into a low knot, a few dark tendrils curling against her neck.

Parker blinked as tears sprang to the backs of his eyes, which didn't make any sense because Parker Johnson didn't cry. But the happiness bursting through him wouldn't be contained.

He swiped at his cheeks and tried not to lose it completely.

"It's okay," Josh whispered at his side, and Parker realized it was more than okay. The profound sense that he was doing the exact right thing filled him with more joy than he'd ever experienced.

Rudy Marshall, who was officiating the ceremony, shoved a tissue into his hand.

As Mara drew closer, Parker reached out and laced his fingers with Mara's then tried to give her the tissue with his other hand.

Her smile gentled. "Um… I think that's for you." She took it from him and dabbed at his cheeks, and that's when Parker realized he was all but bawling in front of their friends and family. He could have cared less.

"I love you," he told her and pressed his lips to hers.

Rudy cleared his throat, and Mara pulled away with a laugh.

"Perhaps we could make it through the vows before any more kissing?" the older attorney asked, one heavy brow raised.

Parker nodded, worried that if he tried to say more he might totally lose his composure. His emotion seemed to set off a chain reaction. By the time he and Mara made it through the vows, which they'd written for each other, there wasn't a dry eye in the backyard other than Evie and Anna, who couldn't quite figure out why all the adults were crying.

But Parker knew that everything was okay because all the mistakes he'd made in his life—and there had been plenty—led him to this woman and this moment. And it was perfect.

"For the rest of my life," Mara said to Brynn and Kaitlin as she held up her champagne glass for another toast an hour later, "I'm going to look at my wedding photos and everyone is going to have puffy eyes and tear-stained cheeks."

"All you'll remember is the happiness," Brynn said gently, and Mara couldn't help but wrap her new friend in a tight hug.

"I'm sorry if this is hard for you."

Brynn immediately pulled back, shaking her head. "I'm so happy for you and Parker. You deserve the love you've found with each other."

"You deserve love, too," Kaitlin said, draining her glass. "I'm not going to speak ill of the dead, but your late husband was a royal ass."

Brynn stifled a giggle, and Mara shook her head. "Honey, I think you just did speak ill of him."

"Not half as bad as what I was thinking," Kaitlin countered.

"I have Tyler," Brynn told them, glancing over to where her son danced with Evie and Anna. "Being a mom is enough for me. I can live vicariously through you two in the romance department."

Mara shook her head. "We're definitely finding you a boyfriend. As soon as I return from my honeymoon it's the top priority."

"Who's on top?" Parker came up behind Mara, bending forward to place a quick kiss on her cheek. "Because I'm not picky."

"TMI." Brynn made a show of covering her ears with her palms. "For real."

Finn and Nick joined their table, and Mara couldn't help but notice that Brynn's shoulders stiffened slightly as Nick sat down next to her. All three men wore black tuxes. Although the wedding was small, Parker had insisted they go formal on the attire. Mara knew that part of that was the pleasure he took from making his friends put on the "monkey suits" as they called them, but she didn't care about the reason. Parker looked so handsome in his black tux with the crisp white shirt it almost took her breath away.

"We're going to find a boyfriend for Brynn," Kaitlin told the three friends. "We've been talking about it since the summer, but now it's happening."

"After the honeymoon," Mara told Parker when he let out a small groan. "*You* are my priority for the next ten days."

"I've given up on love," Brynn said softly. "No dating apps necessary. Some of us aren't meant for it."

"Amen, sister. Love is for suckers." Nick held up his hand for a high five but instead of giving him one, Brynn pushed back from the table.

"I'm going to dance with the kids," she said then walked away.

"Damn," Parker murmured. "She left you hanging hard, Nicky."

"Which you deserve," Finn added. "Since you just called us suckers."

"I was trying to help." Nick ran a hand through his hair and grabbed Brynn's half-full champagne glass, then drained it in one gulp.

Despite the fact that he'd shoved his own foot into his mouth, Mara felt a sharp pang of sympathy for the police chief. It was obvious he cared about Brynn, but between their past and her grief and anger over Daniel's death, Nick obviously didn't know how to bridge the distance between them.

"She should have another chance at happiness," Finn told him. "If anyone deserves—"

"I know what Brynn deserves," Nick interrupted and the naked longing in his eyes when he glanced toward the dance floor shocked Mara. She'd been so wrapped up in her own life that she hadn't looked closely enough at the police chief's feelings for his old friend. "I can tell you there isn't one man around here who's good enough for her."

Mara reached out and squeezed his hand. "There must be someone."

He met her gaze and quickly shuttered the vulnerability from his own. "Can I get anyone a drink?" he asked, straightening.

"Nothing for me," Parker said as he tugged Mara up from her chair. "But I would like a dance with my beautiful wife."

Mara followed him into the backyard, where the rental company had set up a temporary dance floor. As if on cue, the up-tempo song ended and a sweet country ballad began. The kids shouted protests at the slower music and ran toward the bounce house while Kaitlin and Finn joined them on the dance floor.

"Nick likes Brynn," Mara said as Parker wrapped his arms around her and they began to sway.

"We all love Brynn," he answered, a small frown pulling at the corners of his mouth. "She was like a sister to Nick back in high school. By the time he realized he felt more for her, it was too late."

"But it's not too late."

"You aren't going to set up Brynn and Nick." He kissed the tip of her nose. "I'm feeling as hopeful about love as a guy can get and even I know that ship has sailed."

"What if the ship came back to port?" She scrunched up her nose. "Ships do that, you know."

"I don't want to talk about our friends at the moment." His hands slid along her back, drawing her closer until the lace of her gown brushed against his tux.

"Shall we talk about how I have the most handsome husband in all the world?" She smiled when his cheeks flushed with color. "And how much I love that he cries and blushes?"

Parker let out a soft chuckle. "It's like you ripped the man card right out of my hands."

"You're the best man I know," she assured him. "I love you, Parker Johnson."

"I love you, Mara Johnson."

With a contented sigh, she rested her cheek against his cheek, knowing with her whole heart that the love between them would last the rest of their lives.

\* \* \* \* \*

# COMING SOON!

We really hope you enjoyed reading this book.
If you're looking for more romance, be sure to
head to the shops when new books are
available on

# Thursday 3rd
# September

To see which titles are coming soon, please visit

## millsandboon.co.uk/nextmonth

# MILLS & BOON

## Coming next month

### CHRISTMAS REUNION IN PARIS
Liz Fielding

She straightened from her task, took one last glance
around. The man was staring out at Paris, already ablaze
with lights for the Christmas season, but she didn't see
the view, only the face mirrored in the glass.

Chloe gasped his name.

'James…'

It was no more than a whispered breath, but his gaze
flickered from the lights of the city to her own image
mirrored alongside him.

For a moment, as they looked into the reflection of
each other's eyes, her heart stood still. Would he recog-
nise her? Remember her?

The thought had barely formed before he spun around
so fast that, as if he had disturbed the earth's rotation,
the room rocked.

She flung out a hand as her world tilted, throwing
her off balance but there was only air to grasp until
strong fingers clasped hers, his body steadying her world
as he stepped into her, supporting her, holding her, saying
her name.

Not a ghost, but the living man with whom, a lifetime
ago, she had shared an intense, passionate teenage love.

A doomed romance that had brought disaster down
on both their heads but, in his arms, she had forgotten

reality, naively blanked from her mind the future planned for her by ambitious parents.

For a few short months, lying spooned against his body, feeling the slow, steady thud of his heart beating against her ribs, the softness of his sleeping breath against her neck, anything had seemed possible.

Now, unbelievably, he was here, grown into the promise of the youth whose every kiss, every touch had stolen her senses, his fingers entwined in her own, a hand at her back, holding her safe against the breadth of wide shoulders, their bodies touching close. Looking at her as if he could not believe what he was seeing.

His eyes were still that thrilling swirl of grey and green that, for years, had haunted her dreams. To look at his wide, sensuous mouth was to feel his lips angled against hers, feel the heat of his need echoed in the desire pounding through her veins and for a moment, weakly, she leaned into him.

'Chloe…'

*Continue reading*
**CHRISTMAS REUNION IN PARIS**
Liz Fielding

*Available next month*
www.millsandboon.co.uk

# LET'S TALK

# Romance

For exclusive extracts, competitions
and special offers, find us online:

f facebook.com/millsandboon

🐦 @MillsandBoon

⬡ @MillsandBoonUK

**Get in touch on 01413 063232**

# MILLS & BOON

## THE HEART OF ROMANCE

## A ROMANCE FOR EVERY KIND OF READER

**MODERN**

Prepare to be swept off your feet by sophisticated, sexy and seductive heroes, in some of the world's most glamourous and romantic locations, where power and passion collide.
**8 stories per month.**

**HISTORICAL**

Escape with historical heroes from time gone by. Whether your passion is for wicked Regency Rakes, muscled Vikings or rugged Highlanders, awaken the romance of the past.
**6 stories per month.**

**MEDICAL**

Set your pulse racing with dedicated, delectable doctors in the high-pressure world of medicine, where emotions run high and passion, comfort and love are the best medicine.
**6 stories per month.**

*True Love*

Celebrate true love with tender stories of heartfelt romance, from the rush of falling in love to the joy a new baby can bring, and a focus on the emotional heart of a relationship.
**8 stories per month.**

*Desire*

Indulge in secrets and scandal, intense drama and plenty of sizzling hot action with powerful and passionate heroes who have it all: wealth, status, good looks…everything but the right woman.
**6 stories per month.**

**HEROES**

Experience all the excitement of a gripping thriller, with an intense romance at its heart. Resourceful, true-to-life women and strong, fearless men face danger and desire - a killer combination!
**8 stories per month.**

**DARE**

Sensual love stories featuring smart, sassy heroines you'd want as a best friend, and compelling intense heroes who are worthy of them.
**4 stories per month.**

To see which titles are coming soon, please visit

**millsandboon.co.uk/nextmonth**

# JOIN US ON SOCIAL MEDIA!

Stay up to date with our latest releases, author
news and gossip, special offers and discounts, and
all the behind-the-scenes action
from Mills & Boon...

 millsandboon

 millsandboonuk

 millsandboon

*It might just be true love...*

# MILLS & BOON

## HISTORICAL

Awaken the romance of the past

Escape with historical heroes from time gone by. Whether your passion is for wicked Regency Rakes, muscled Viking warriors or rugged Highlanders, indulge your fantasies and awaken the romance of the past.